THE QUEEN'S GAMBIT

DEBORAH CHESTER

ACE BOOKS, NEW YORK

This is a work of fiction. Names, characters, places, and incidents either are the product of the author's imagination or are used fictitiously, and any resemblance to actual persons, living or dead, business establishments, events, or locales is entirely coincidental.

THE QUEEN'S GAMBIT

An Ace Book / published by arrangement with the author

PRINTING HISTORY
Ace mass-market edition / December 2002

Copyright © 2002 by Deborah Chester.
Cover art by Jean Pierre Targete.
Cover design by Judy Murello.
Text design by Julie Rogers.

Visit our website at
www.penguinputnam.com
Check out the ACE Science Fiction & Fantasy newsletter!

ISBN: 0-441-00997-2

ACE®
Ace Books are published by The Berkley Publishing Group, a division of Penguin Putnam Inc., 375 Hudson Street, New York, New York 10014.
ACE and the "A" design are trademarks belonging to Penguin Putnam Inc.

PRINTED IN THE UNITED STATES OF AMERICA

10 9 8 7 6 5 4 3 2 1

PART I

Chapter One

Pheresa du Lindier was kneeling on a tiny embroidered prayer cushion, searching her soul yet again for answers, when a tremendous jolt threw her to one side. She landed on her hip with bruising force, her full skirts tangled about her. Overhead, the lamps swayed violently on their chains, casting wild shadows about the stuffy cabin. Her jewel-studded Circle flew from her fingers to roll across the floor. Pheresa tried to grab it, and failed.

"After it, Oola!" she ordered in vexation.

One of her attendants scooped it up from where it had slid beneath the tiny, bolted-down table, then hurried over to assist Pheresa to her feet.

She was already upright, brushing dust from her skirts with angry slaps of her hands. It embarrassed her to be rendered so clumsy. Oola handed her the Circle and began to smooth her gown for her.

"Is my lady hurt?" she asked with an anxiety that only increased Pheresa's feeling of irritation.

She was so tired of being fussed over, of being watched for

the least sign of discomfort or illness. She was never left alone for a moment, and the constant scrutiny and lack of privacy had her nerves in shreds. Yet she knew if she gave way and allowed her temper to escape the iron control she'd clamped over it, the news would be delivered immediately to the king as certain proof that she remained unwell and unfit. Her enemies were waiting for any excuse to pounce.

"My lady?" Oola asked, peering at her through the uneven light cast by the dim lanterns. "Are you hurt?"

"Nay! I'm well," Pheresa said, and shifted her gaze to her other attendant lest her anger show. "Verine, look outside and see if we've docked."

Verine peered out the tiny round window of the cabin. "Yes, I see the palace walls!" she called out excitedly. "We are here at last! Oh, my lady, think of it. Home!"

Pheresa shut her eyes a moment to savor the notion. Now she could hear a series of muffled thuds and shouts as the crew ran about their duties. The barge shuddered, forcing her to brace her feet to keep from being thrown off balance again. Oola clung to her, but Pheresa pulled away and stood gripping the polished bulwark that arched over her bed.

"My cloak and outdoor slippers, quickly," she ordered. "Verine, finish putting my writing things away and extinguish these lamps. Let us be ready to disembark."

The tortured squeal of wood rubbing against something it shouldn't made her wince. The barge jolted again, and they came to a complete halt. Pheresa, still unused to the peculiar rocking sway of the barge after the past three weeks of riding it down the Charva River's slow-moving current, found the sudden steadiness of the craft reassuring. Her heart filled with the knowledge that they were finally home. The ordeal that had begun last autumn was nearly over.

Tears sprang to her eyes, and for a moment she felt overwhelmed with exhaustion. So much had happened, most of it too dreadful to think about. And now, there was only the state funeral of Prince Gavril to endure before it was finished. She would rest for days afterwards, she promised herself. She would lie abed, or walk in the warm, tranquil gardens of

Savroix. She would renew her spirit and find peace of mind once more. She would move past her tears and confusion and find a way to heal her heart.

A thunderous knock on her door made her jump.

Verine hurried to open it, and Sir Brillon stood framed in the narrow doorway. The church knight was a tall, rawboned man, with a scarred face and zealous black eyes. Clad in chain mail and a distinctive white and black surcoat, the slashed marks of his order marking one shoulder, he stood with his spurred feet braced apart. One gloved hand gripped his sword hilt; the other fist rested on his hip. He and a small squadron of men had been assigned to oversee Pheresa's protection during the long journey southward from Nether. Pheresa had learned to consider him more a jailer than a protector, for he was forever watching her, forever making notes of what she did or said. She had caught him intercepting her letters, but her furious confrontation with him had come to nothing. Sir Brillon merely said he was obeying orders, his cool audacity leaving her red-faced and sputtering.

She glared at him now, resenting him for having forbidden her permission to walk the deck and take fresh air this past week. He claimed the weather was too inclement for her. She knew that this final stretch of the Charva was bordered with towns and trade centers. She'd heard the people cheering the king as the royal barges swept by. Sir Brillon had orders to keep her out of the populace's sight. Whether he answered to the king or to one of the cardinals, she had not yet learned. She suspected the latter.

"Sir Brillon," she said in a strong, forthright voice, concealing her resentment of him as best she could, " 'tis indeed wonderful to see Savroix at last. I thank you now for your service during this sad journey, and bid you good-bye."

His black gaze flickered down during this speech, then flashed back to meet hers. "The king is disembarking now, my lady."

She forgot her antagonism instantly, and gestured for Oola to place her cloak across her shoulders. "Then I must hurry and join his majesty."

Sir Brillon held out his hand. "Nay, my lady. There's no hurry. You're not requested to join the royal presence."

"According to whom? You?"

"Nay, my lady. I merely follow orders."

She tightened her lips to hold back a sarcastic retort. "Of course."

"The gangway is narrow, my lady, and the rain makes it slippery. We must disembark in seemly order. His majesty first. Then the coffin. Then the other passengers in order of their importance."

Pheresa's head snapped up, and the small cabin suddenly fell silent. Verine and Oola exchanged looks and busied themselves tidying and packing. Her lungs felt compressed by an iron weight, and her temples were throbbing. This was as open an insult as he'd ever given her.

She drew on her gloves with quick, angry tugs of the supple leather. "I am betrothed to the Prince of the Realm," she said with quiet steeliness. "My place is with the king."

Sir Brillon bowed. "Of course, my lady. You are to precede the passengers, but follow the coffin. Or such were the orders given to me. I but relay them."

"Then let us go."

He stepped back from the doorway, and she emerged into the cramped passageway that smelled of pine tar, damp, and musty tapestries. Small lamps hanging from chains illuminated the way dimly. She walked briskly to the steps leading up to the deck. Fresh air, moist with rain, gusted down into her face, and she filled her lungs gratefully.

Sir Brillon followed on her heels as she ascended the narrow steps, his spurs jingling quietly.

Topside, she emerged beneath a small awning that sheltered the steps from the weather. A curtain of rain swept the deck in a sudden downpour, making the crew swear and scurry. The deck, normally staid and quiet, with a protected seating area for watching the scenery at one end, was now a scene of chaos. Courtiers stood in the way of the crew placing the gangway across the narrow span of water between the barge and the palace.

Savroix's walls towered overhead, and when she glanced up, Pheresa could see the faces of guardsmen peering down at them from the battlements. This was the oldest section of the palace, and the most fortified. Right now, the massive gates stood open, and officials in rain-soaked finery hovered just inside them.

A fanfare of trumpets announced the king's presence. Pheresa saw him striding across the deck toward the gangplank. Verence's handsome looks had worn considerably on this journey. His shoulder-length hair was heavily streaked with gray. His remarkable green-and-blue eyes, normally so keen and lively, looked dull and weary today. He glanced at her as he strode by, but did not smile.

Pheresa hastened to lower herself in a curtsy, her heart pounding in sudden anticipation. He had noticed her, had looked her way. She had not spoken to him in many days. Would he now beckon for her to join him? Would this be at last the moment when she gained his favor?

The king nodded to her, and walked on with his officers and entourage close about him. Pheresa's heart sank to her slippers, yet at the same time a corner of her mind berated her for indulging in such foolish hopes. Now was not the time for his majesty to announce his next heir. She must be patient. She was the best candidate to succeed Gavril as next in line for the throne. Whom else could Verence choose? Yet his son must first be buried properly, with the full honors of state. When that was done, the new Heir to the Realm would be chosen and announced. She must give Verence time to finish his grieving.

The blaring trumpets faded before a solemn drumroll. Gavril's coffin, swathed in cloths of dark blue and silver, was hoisted from the bowels of the barge and placed across the shoulders of six church knights. Careful of their burden, they walked the rain-slick deck toward the gangway.

Conscious of many eyes watching her, Pheresa curtsied to the coffin as it was carried past her. The stink of Gavril's corruption polluted the air, and Pheresa involuntarily reached for the small purse of salt swinging from her girdle. Although

Gavril's remains had been salted and frozen in preparation for the journey southward, it had been a long journey indeed, a slow journey, delayed by winter weather and other difficulties. He was frozen no longer, and the rot of him was nearly unbearable no matter how much incense was burned to conceal the smell in the barge hold.

Shuddering, she knew she would never forget the horrors she'd survived in Nether. She could not inhale that terrible stench without thinking of Nonkind. The images of the soultaker destroying Gavril were burned into her memory. His screams still rang at times in her ears.

Fighting away such memories, she clutched her salt purse even tighter and forced herself out from beneath the awning to follow the coffin.

Sir Brillon hurried beside her, crowding her much too close.

She glared at him. "Keep your distance, sir!"

Another downpour drenched her in seconds. He moved even closer and held up a fold of his cloak to protect her. The rain thundered down with stinging force, and Pheresa faltered a moment, half-tempted to turn back to whatever shelter she could find.

Instead, she moved forward. Sir Brillon shouted something in her ear, but she could not make out what he said. She crossed the gangway, her feet sliding a little in the water that bounced on its surface. Lightning flashed overhead, making her squint, and thunder boomed, echoing between the river and the palace walls.

Then she was across, breathing hard, her clothing soaked and heavy, her slippers ruined and leaking water. She hurried through the tall gates into the spacious courtyard beyond. Everything was confusion, with courtiers running to duck out of the rain. Pheresa paid no attention to who disembarked after her. Instead, she glanced around, saw the coffin bearers carrying their burden through a different door than where the king had gone. She drew up the hood of her cloak and attempted to follow Verence, only to find Sir Brillon's arm pointing to her right.

"That's closer, my lady. Hurry!"

She saw a canopy stretched above a doorway and headed for it, hurrying now, almost running. More thunder boomed overhead, and the day was nearly black.

Moments later, she found herself beneath the canopy, gasping for breath and wiping water from her face with relief. "Thod above," she said, shaking out her sodden skirts. "What a—"

"Inside, my lady," Sir Brillon interrupted. He gestured at the doorway, where a priest was beckoning. "We must get you dry and warm at once."

"Yes." She glanced behind him in hopes of seeing where her attendants had gone, but Oola and Verine were not in sight. More people were spilling into the courtyard, along with knights and the servants in charge of unloading supplies and luggage. Pheresa hurried through the doorway, unfastening the ties of her cloak as she went. "Any passage will lead to the Grand Corridor from here. I shall want—"

She broke off in order to respond to the priest's respectful greeting.

"A fire for her ladyship," Sir Brillon ordered.

A page in bright livery appeared and bowed to Pheresa. "This way, my lady."

With a smile for the child, she followed willingly. All she could think about was getting to her state apartments and changing out of her wet garments. It was so chilly indoors she could see her breath. Gloom filled the passageway, for many of the sconce lamps were not yet lit. She smelled the faint scents of beeswax, wool, and incense. Far in the distance she could hear the muffled intonations of chantsong, pure in its adoration, beautiful.

She sighed happily and smoothed back her dripping hair. How good it was to be home. Only another day or two of dreary duties and then—

"In here, my lady."

As the page spoke, he pushed open a heavily carved door leading into a sumptuous apartment lined with crimson silk. A fire burned briskly on the hearth, and a bowl of apples on the table gave off a delicious fragrance.

It was so beautiful, civilized, and comfortable that she wanted to clap her hands in delight. Instead, she shook her head at the page. "Thank you, but please conduct me to my private apartments. I wish to rest."

"Come inside, Lady Pheresa," said a dry, thin voice that sent a prickle of unease running up her spine. "I have prayed much for your safe return. Now that you have finally arrived, please honor me by accepting my hospitality for a few moments."

She did not recognize the voice, but she knew its owner meant her little good. Alarmed, she would have retreated, but Sir Brillon stood behind her and did not move aside.

"Let me by," she said to him. "I do not wish to—"

"The cardinal wants a word, my lady," Sir Brillon said, gripping her arm with fingers like steel. "Do him the courtesy of a little interview."

Pheresa glared at Sir Brillon, but his black eyes met hers implacably. She realized, feeling suddenly chilled, that she'd entered a neatly laid trap. Thanks to the disorganization of the disembarkation and the distraction of the weather, she'd allowed herself to be ushered through a door no one else was using. She had been neatly cut off from the rest of the royal party, and although she could come to no true harm here within the walls of Savroix, she disliked such coercive tactics. They reminded her too much of her hostage days in Grov.

"Please do come in, my lady," the dry voice said.

Seething, she stood rooted in place, her brown eyes afire as she glared at Sir Brillon. "Your hand offends me, sir," she said in a low, very sharp voice. "Remove it at once."

He released her with a slight bow, the twitch of his lips mocking her. Drawing herself very erect, Pheresa walked forward.

The cardinal rose from a chair and advanced to meet her. Attired in long white robes with a yellow sash of office and a diamond-studded Circle glittering on his chest, he was a short, very thin man, sporting a tidy gray goatee in the fashion favored by the clergy. His green eyes were large and remarkable in his narrow face. They watched her with the coldness of a falcon marking its prey.

She recognized him now as Theloi, considered very conservative in his dogma, far more so than Noncire, whom he had apparently replaced. A few months ago, Pheresa would have found herself shy and nervous in this powerful man's presence. Now, although she did not like the way he studied her, she reminded herself that she had survived encounters with much more dangerous men.

"Please sit close to the fire," he said. "Would you care for wine?"

"Nay, lord cardinal. I wish to retire to my apartments and change into dry clothing. Surely there is a better time for this meeting."

"Of course, of course." He glanced at Sir Brillon, who was prowling about the edges of the room like something caged, then returned his gaze to her. "You dislike my eagerness, but then I could not wait longer to see this Lady of the Miracle. This Lady of the Chalice."

Pheresa concealed her grimace. She disliked being called either. 'Twas how the knights in Verence's army referred to her now. She hoped the practice was not going to be spread about the court.

"Please," she said in protest. "I received the gift of restored life and health from the Chalice, but that is all. To call me by such phrases is to imply that I possess some magical powers or can pass along the wondrous blessing of the Chalice. I cannot."

"So, I understand, you have claimed far and wide," Theloi said.

She drew in a sharp breath and glanced involuntarily at Sir Brillon. "You are well informed, lord cardinal."

"Come, come, my lady. Let us not parry words but instead speak plainly. The church is most interested in what has happened. It is, you understand, our business to investigate the matter thoroughly."

"There is nothing to discover," she said uneasily. "I was ill.

I would have died. The Netherans had me drink from the Chalice, and I was restored. That is all."

Theloi smiled at her. "You are far too modest, Lady Pheresa. That can hardly be all. You understand that our most learned scholars wish to discuss the event in all its particulars."

"Perhaps one day—"

"No, my lady. Now."

She frowned. "Certainly not now. I have endured a long, difficult, most tedious journey. I wish to retire to my apartments. Later, the church scholars may petition me for an interview, but not until—"

"My lady, you misunderstand," Cardinal Theloi said firmly. "Your personal effects have been transferred from the royal barge to a wagon. You will leave directly from this room for the nuncery at Batoine. There, you will live comfortably but retired, while the details of this miracle are explored and a full—"

"Never!"

"Lady Pheresa, you have no choice."

Her heart began to pound. She darted a swift glance around the room and noticed that Sir Brillon stood between her and the door. Fear pierced her before she battled it down. She must not panic, she told herself. Theloi could not do what he threatened without her cooperation. No matter what he said, he did not rule Savroix, and he did not rule her.

She stared at him through narrowed eyes. "I do not believe I heard you correctly, lord cardinal. You mentioned a choice?"

"I said you have no choice, my lady."

"You are mistaken," she said sharply. "The king will not permit this abduction."

"The king does not interfere in matters of the soul."

"My soul is intact, thank you."

"Ah," Theloi said quietly, "but Prince Gavril's is not."

She caught her breath, but said nothing. Suddenly she felt cornered indeed, frightened, and unsure of her ground.

Theloi's green eyes watched her with chilling confidence. "I think you begin to understand."

Her mouth felt dry, so dry she could not swallow. She made no effort to speak.

Theloi said, "His highness was Nonkind at the time of his death, was he not?"

"You know he was."

"Such a pity. He was a young man of tremendous beauty and promise. 'Tis said the king grieves hard."

She felt a renewed surge of pity for Verence. He went about so melancholy and bleak, his joy in life obviously gone. Nightly he ordered prayer vigils for the soul of his doomed son, but no amount of prayer could restore what Gavril had lost.

"His majesty mourns Gavril deeply," she admitted.

"But to no avail," Theloi said without mercy. "Unless the church decides to intervene and help Gavril's soul reach Beyond."

"Decides?" she echoed with scorn. "Do you churchmen have no pity? Where is love and understanding? Where is the desire to help all that you can, without regard for politics or gain?"

Theloi's green eyes flashed. "I serve Tomias!" he said. "Serve his teachings. To respect and serve those teachings is to obey what has been set forth in Writ: *And let the condemned stand before Thod in judgment, knowing the full pain and torment of wrongdoing. Let no mercy be written beside the sinner's name, to cancel his transgression. Let all tremble before Thod, and bow. For only a few shall not perish.*"

The holy words thundered at her as Theloi's voice gathered power and projection. She held herself rigid to keep from flinching, and finished the quote, *"Yet even the worst may know hope of forgiveness after a time of punishment, if enough prayer is said on his behalf. Let all hearts join in petition, and Thod will hear their pleas."*

"You dare to quote Writ!" Sir Brillon said in outrage from behind her.

She ignored him, but Theloi glanced his way with a frown, and Sir Brillon fell silent.

Theloi folded his hands inside his sleeves and regarded her

without expression. "You have remembered your pious studies well."

She started to say that she had been educated at a nuncery school, but held her tongue. Theloi obviously knew that.

"There is a slim chance that eventually Gavril will receive the mercy of Thod," he said. "But no guarantee. Certainly there is no chance without the devoted prayers of all clergy across the realm."

"Why would you withhold such assistance?" she asked.

Theloi turned away from her and stood by the fire, gazing down into its orange flames with a brooding expression. The light flickered along his cheekbones, casting patterns of light and shadow across his face. "The Chalice has been missing for a generation, hidden and lost to all. Now it is found. This is a time for rejoicing, a time of many wonders to follow. You, my lady, are one of them. You must be protected."

She tossed her head proudly. "I have other plans."

He looked at her. "Your ambition is known to me."

"Had I married Gavril before his death, succession would be mine."

"But you did not."

Pheresa frowned. She did not need something so obvious pointed out to her. That was the crux of her current problem. Yet if she was not named Verence's heir, who would be? And when was the king going to decide? She sighed, wishing that he had already made his choice. Had he named her heir before they left Grov, or even during the journey homeward, she would have been met today with a respectful reception. There would be no secret meetings of intrigue with cardinals, no veiled threats, no talk of being shut away for the rest of her life in a nuncery while church scholars debated over whether she should be named a saint or not.

"No one can come into such close contact with the holy Chalice and not be touched forever by it," the cardinal said.

Pheresa held out her hands in frustration. "I have gained no special powers. I am whatever I was before."

"Impossible."

"You will not put me away or imprison me," she declared. "My destiny lies elsewhere."

"To be named a saint is the supreme honor. To serve in the footsteps of Tomias is the greatest calling."

"But I am not called from within," she protested. "I will not lie and say that I am."

"Thod has called *you*. And to his service you will go." Theloi smiled at her while she stood silent with rage and frustration. "Already we have begun negotiations with Nether for the Chalice to be brought here."

"They'll never surrender it."

He frowned. "The Netherans are backward barbarians, unfit for the privilege of guarding the Chalice from harm. The fact that it has been lost for nearly twenty years is proof of their ineptitude."

"It was not lost, only hidden," she said tartly. "The king of Nether kept it safe—"

"Nonsense. That lie has been told to cover their bumbling, but the truth is known."

"You forget, lord cardinal, that I have just returned from Nether and know the truth of these events," she said. "As does King Verence."

Theloi studied her a moment and raised his thin brows. "So you would dare threaten a cardinal, dare threaten the church. You have changed a great deal this past winter, my lady, or else Noncire was wrong when he said you were a spineless little creature, pretty, but of no benefit to the throne or the realm."

The words hurt deeply, as they were meant to. Once, Pheresa's eyes would have filled with tears. Now she stared dry-eyed and stiff at this cruel little man, her face hot from his insult.

"Cardinal Noncire," she said in a quiet, cold voice, "died in Gant, tortured by Nonkind evil. His judgment was less than sound in many areas. I do not think you should depend too much on the accuracy of his perceptions."

"Well said," Theloi acknowledged with a gesture. "Perhaps you are not spineless after all. But you should not be queen, and you won't be."

Pheresa lifted her chin. "That decision is not yours to make."

"Ah, but there is the matter of Prince Gavril's lost soul—"

"That is cruel and beastly! The king will not bow to such extortion."

"Take care, my lady," Theloi said in a voice that made her fall silent. "You can go too far. I think I need not warn you that you do not want me for an enemy."

She wanted to reply in kind, but prudence held her tongue. She was alone here, and Sir Brillon could carry her off bodily into the twilight to Batoine. Who would stop him, or realize what he was about? At that moment she wished with all her heart for a protector, someone she could trust. Realizing she had only her wits to save her, she told herself she'd better start using them.

"I—I agree that we grow too heated in our argument, lord cardinal," she said at last, stammering a little as she fought to control herself. "Let us consider the situation more clearly."

"The situation is very clear," Theloi replied impatiently. "You are to go to Batoine at once and await examination by church counsel. Although Sir Brillon has done his best these past few weeks to see you unsullied by excessive contact with common folk, it is imperative that you now be isolated and kept in purity for—"

"You forget, lord cardinal," she broke in hastily, "that I am not free to journey elsewhere. There is the funeral."

Theloi waved this aside. "A mere detail. Your absence can be put down to illness."

"My responsibility is to be present," she said firmly. "Gavril was my betrothed, and I must attend him in this final ceremony."

Theloi frowned. "Do not pretend grief you do not feel, my lady. It has been noted that you avoided the prayer vigils on the journey and would not go near the wagon bearing his highness's coffin."

Her hands clenched tight at her sides. Desperately she

stared at Theloi and let the hot, bitter tears swell in her eyes. They rolled down her cheeks, and her throat worked against a surge of feelings.

"You understand nothing," she said, her voice raw with all that she had kept under tight control since leaving Nether. "Nothing! I loved him and then—and then—" She choked and pressed her hands to her lips to hold back the rest. Oh, yes, she thought bitterly. She had loved Gavril until the day he came to visit her as she lay ill and dying in her encasement, when for the first time he dropped his charming mask and ceased to pretend he cared. That day she gazed up into his dark blue eyes, ablaze with his resentment of her, and saw the truth. He wanted her to die and release him from the obligation of trying to rescue her. He prayed for her death, so that he could abandon his quest and go home.

She'd pledged herself to a man who'd never cared for her. And in doing so, she'd turned her back on another who was honest, true, and noble of heart. Faldain had saved her life, not Gavril. Faldain had offered her his heart and hand with simple honesty at the Harvest Ball, and she'd rejected him because she wanted to be queen. She hadn't known then that she could have been queen of Nether instead.

And now, Gavril was dead. She'd sought a second chance with Faldain, offering herself freely to him with all her gratitude and newfound hope. She'd gone to him with all Mandria momentarily in her hands as dowry, and he hadn't wanted her.

What was wrong with her, she wondered bitterly, that no man would love her? Lifting her tear-streaked face, she met Cardinal Theloi's gaze through her blurred one.

"A woman's tears," he said coldly, "are her most effective weapon."

"The king will not understand if I am absent," she whispered. And all the while she was thinking that during the funeral she would have a chance to speak to the king and beg him to keep her at court. He had refused to see her of late, but he had refused to see anyone. At the funeral she would be at his side and she would make her plea then. "Lord cardinal," she said now, "I was bound to Gavril. I must perform this last public duty for him, even if you truly mean to cloister me thereafter."

"Ah, yes, your remarkable sense of duty," Theloi said thoughtfully. "You have become renowned for it. Despite your tears, I think you love duty more than you ever loved your prince."

Stung, she opened her mouth to protest, but he gestured for silence.

"Very well," he said, "attend the funeral. The populace will not be allowed to get close to you. Sir Brillon will stay at your side to ensure you are not soiled by too much proximity with lesser beings."

She did not like the idea of Sir Brillon's zealous escort, yet even he could not prevent her from conversing with the king during the ceremony. Filled with relief, she barely kept herself from smiling. "Thank you."

"The funeral will be held tomorrow. It is only a short delay," Theloi said. "As soon as your duty ends, you will leave for Batoine. That, I promise you."

Determined never to set foot within the nuncery's walls, Pheresa gave him the slightest possible inclination of her head. "May I now withdraw, lord cardinal? I grow chilled in these damp clothes, and I wish to rest before the rigors of tomorrow."

Theloi held out his hand to her, but Pheresa could not force herself to kiss his ring as she should have. Annoyance flashed in his eyes as he lowered his hand to his side. At once she knew she had erred in offending him, but she did not care. He had offended her more, she reminded herself, and turned and hurried out with Sir Brillon on her heels.

The young page was still waiting outside in the passageway. Pheresa gave him a stern look, unwilling to forgive his part in Theloi's little trap. *I must be more careful,* she reminded herself. *I must take care not to get separated from others. I must watch my back. I must be vigilant for my own safety, for no one else is.*

"My lady?" Sir Brillon said, reaching out to take her arm. She drew away from him in distaste, angered once again by his familiarity. "Keep your distance, sir!" she said sharply. "You are no courtier. You will walk behind me, as is fitting for your place."

Sir Brillon's mouth compressed in a hard line. The scar across his face turned pink, but after a moment he bowed to her and stepped back.

Another enemy made, Pheresa thought to herself. She did not care. If she did not succeed in obtaining the king's intervention tomorrow, she was doomed anyway.

Chapter Two

The state funeral of Prince Gavril of Mandria began at mid-morning beneath dark, gloomy skies. No rain fell, but a damp, chilly wind blew as though it meant to bring back winter instead of spring. Crowds lined the streets of Savroix-en-Charva, the men holding their caps, the women wearing black ribbons.

Solemn drumbeats thudded in slow unison, keeping cadence with the funeral march of the palace guards. At the head of the procession walked the banner bearers, carrying the flags of the king, Prince Gavril, and the church. Gavril's pennon was bundled and tied to its pole, while the others flew free. A groom in black livery led a magnificent horse brushed to a glossy sheen, its long mane woven with black ribbons that bounced and streamed out with every proud toss of the animal's head. The stirrups of Gavril's silver-adorned saddle were crossed over the seat, indicating death. Behind the horse, a coffin draped in blue-and-silver cloth was borne on the stalwart shoulders of six church knights.

Pheresa, still betrothed officially to the dead Heir to the

Realm until the close of the ceremonies, walked directly behind the coffin. As custom demanded, she walked barefoot and wore a plain black gown of sackcloth, very itchy and coarse woven. No jewels adorned her. She wore her golden hair uncovered, its glory tamed in a thick plait that hung down her back. She was permitted no cloak, and the unpleasant wind cut through her thin clothing. The stone pavement chilled her feet, which were already bruised from the long walk from the palace into the center of town.

Nothing, this day, was going as planned. She had intended to ride in the king's carriage, swathed in warm, somber furs, her hair confined in a snood, her face veiled from the curious. During the night, she had practiced what she intended to say to his majesty, knowing she must make her plea succinctly, couched in terms of condolence and respect. She knew better than to criticize the church for its plans for her; Verence obviously was in no mood to offend priestly officials while he sought mercy for Gavril's soul. But she wanted the king to understand how close he was to losing her as well as his son.

As yet, she'd had no opportunity to approach his majesty. The ancient service was being used, which meant this lengthy procession, a full mass, and the necessity of Pheresa walking behind the coffin as one symbolically tied to the dead.

In her ungloved hands she carried a naked broadsword by its blade. Its cold metal numbed her fingers, and she had to take great care not to cut herself for it was freshly honed to a sharp edge. It was old-fashioned and heavy, its weight making her arms tremble. She did not know how she could manage to carry it the whole distance, yet she must. Grimly she forced herself to walk erectly, with her usual poise, not stumbling or wincing when pebbles bruised her feet, not letting the heavy sword dip toward the ground. Gavril had never carried this weapon that King Verence gave him when he was invested into knighthood. Gavril had been ungrateful for the traditional gift, wanting a new weapon, not a venerable one.

Pheresa felt grateful she did not have to carry that evil, tainted weapon Gavril had acquired for himself. Tanengard had driven him mad and consigned him to darkness. Good riddance to it, she thought.

As the procession wound into the city's heart, the crowd grew thicker. Although subdued this day, the noise was constant, with many folk wailing or sobbing at the sight of Gavril's coffin. It had been said that Gavril was unpopular with the common people, but there was no evidence of that now.

And many murmured about Pheresa as she passed them:

"She drank from the Chalice."

"Never did."

"Aye! Heard it told from me wife's brother, who went to fight them heathens."

"Oh, sweet Tomias be praised! Look at her face, her hands. Do you see holy light?"

"She's beautiful."

"Step forward, Junie, you and your brother both, and look at the good lady with her heart all broke."

"He died for her. That's the one he died for."

"They say she found the Chalice herself and tried to redeem the prince with it, but he would not be saved."

"That's her! Look! Look! The Lady of the Miracle."

"Ooh! She's clothed ever so plain. Where are her jewels and the fine clothes a princess should wear?"

"Why'd Thod put a miracle on her and not his highness? 'Tain't right."

"Hush! She'll throw a curse on you. She's the Lady of the Miracle, and you give her respect."

"My lady! Bless my child that his leg may heal!"

A woman thrust her young boy to the forefront of the crowd and tried to run up to Pheresa, but Sir Brillon was suddenly there, his dagger in his hand as he pushed them back. Others surged toward her, calling out supplications, but the guards dealt with them swiftly.

The procession went on, and Pheresa walked with it, refusing to look back at the sobbing woman, who still called out pleas for mercy.

Tears of pity stung Pheresa's eyes. She wanted to tell that

woman, and all of them, that she was no saint with special powers. It was cruel and impious of the church to spread rumors about her that raised such false hopes in these simple folk. Yet there would be time enough later, she assured herself, when she was safely Verence's heir and beyond the church's reach, to dispel the rumors. Besides, if she failed today to save herself, the rumors about her would not matter.

The procession turned to follow a bend in the street. Ahead, she could see the cathedral spires rising tall to a leaden sky. Behind her rolled the king's carriage. She was not supposed to look back, but she'd seen Verence riding bleak and stone-faced beneath his crown. Listening to the grinding noise of the wheels on the pavement behind her, she told herself there might be a chance to speak to him when he alighted from his conveyance at the cathedral steps.

"My lady," Sir Brillon said softly, coming up beside her so quietly she did not hear him until he spoke. "Take heart. 'Tis almost over. You'll be gone from here soon."

She considered his words a threat, not comfort. Feeling the net closing ever tighter about her, she frowned in intense frustration and was tempted to run immediately to the king's side.

That impulse faded in a rush of common sense. No matter how tempting, so foolish an action would only fail. She swallowed hard, concentrating on holding the heavy sword properly, and ignored Sir Brillon.

He said nothing more, much to her relief, and dropped back to her heels. She kept walking, her lips tightening in anger. How she hated him and wished him far away.

She had hated Gavril, too, before it was all over. Hated him for his madness, his arrogant stupidity, and resentment of her. He'd blamed their betrayal by the Netherans, their imprisonment as hostages, and the execution of their armed escort all on her. Conceited and spoiled, Gavril had been unwilling to accept responsibility for his own foolhardy mistakes. Had her fate been left up to him, she'd be damned now, as he was, her soul lost forever and her body a rotting vessel vulnerable to Gantese command.

The horror of it all swept over her anew, driving chills

through her body. She stumbled and nearly sank to her knees. A sigh went up from the crowd. Somehow she righted herself and continued on.

"My lady," Sir Brillon said anxiously, "allow me the honor of taking the sword."

"Nay," she said, striving to keep her fatigue from her voice.

"'Tis too heavy for you, and gladly will I carry it in your stead."

"I will fulfill my duty, sir."

"Your duty now is to be preserved in chaste sanctity—"

She glared at him. "Get back from me, sir. Gavril's sword is for me to carry, not you."

Sir Brillon's black eyes bored into her. His gloved hand reached out as though to take the sword despite her command, but Pheresa stepped away from him and walked on. She kept her head high, but her heart was hammering. He had only to seize her and say she was swooning, and the officials would probably let him carry her away without protest.

With all her willpower, she ignored her weary, trembling arms and forced herself to keep going. The procession was entering the square now. She had only a short distance to go.

Sir Brillon kept pace with her. "My lady, I think only of your welfare. The cardinal knew this would be too great a strain—"

She felt as though she were being boiled. He had the manners of a lout and deserved to be treated as one. "You offend me, sir," she said in a low, furious voice. "You interrupt my prayers. You defile these final moments with my betrothed. Leave me be."

Sir Brillon's face turned crimson, then white. He said nothing more, to her relief, and fell back a pace. She felt a twinge of guilt for her lie, but only a twinge. If she must play a hypocrite's part in order to get rid of him, then so be it. She did not mourn Gavril. Had he lived, she would never have married him. But today, the dead Gavril served her better than the live one ever had.

The avenue widened into a spacious square that served the

cathedral. Ringed on three sides by stone buildings carved in both plain and ornate architectural styles, the square featured a statue of King Verence's grandfather on horseback, holding an upraised sword. As the funeral procession entered, a flock of plump white padegins rose from the paving stones with a loud flapping of wings and wheeled about in the air. Their soft, cooing cries sounded mournful against the solemn drumbeats.

The bearers of flags and coffin halted at the steps of the great cathedral. The groom leading the beautiful black horse vanished with the animal, his part in the ceremony done. Wishing she, too, could slip away, Pheresa stood where she was supposed to. Her sore feet ached with cold. Her hands felt stiff and cramped from holding the heavy sword so carefully for so long. A splatter or two of rain fell on her head and shoulders. She glanced up, but although the skies had darkened ominously, the rain still held off. The wind felt sharp and cruel, and she shivered in her sackcloth gown. It was as though Gavril's spirit haunted the day, his anger and petulance reaching forth from Beyond.

She shook off such depressing thoughts and watched crimson carpet being swiftly unrolled down the cathedral steps. Church officials in gold-embroidered robes and mitres appeared in the doorway, and a priest with a yellow sash and a harried expression approached Pheresa.

"The ceremony inside has been explained to you, my lady?" he asked her.

"Yes."

Sir Brillon stepped forward. "I request she be relieved of it. She is overwearied and much disheartened by the strain of the day. Let another perform the ritual for her inside."

"No!" Pheresa said. "I wish to continue as I have been instructed."

"Very good, my lady," the priest said sternly.

"I think only of the lady's welfare," Sir Brillon persisted. "She will not think of it for herself."

"Are you her protector, sir?"

"Yes."

"No, he is not!" Pheresa said. "And I am quite well."

The priest frowned. Behind them, the king had arrived, and the carriages bringing the courtiers were now pulling up inside the square. Knights, country barons, and chevards on horseback began to dismount in some disorder. The prominent citizens of Savroix-en-Charva filed in behind them on foot. Squires and heralds moved discreetly about, trying to marshal everyone into correct order.

"Let us remember that this is a solemn occasion, sir knight," the priest said to Sir Brillon. "Not a place for courtly niceties and flirtations."

Sir Brillon turned scarlet at the rebuke. He belonged to the Order of Saint Qanselm, a sect of particularly fierce fighters who took vows of celibacy and poverty. They were known to be zealots in whatever cause they embraced, and Sir Brillon was no exception.

His black eyes narrowed with fury as he gripped the hilt of his sword. "How dare you—"

"Good sir," Pheresa said sharply, swift to take advantage of his blunder, "you have disturbed my prayers, and now you seek quarrel with one of the priesthood. Have you lost your senses?"

She stared at him in severe disapproval, much aware of the king's presence nearby. Others were turning to observe the disturbance, and Sir Brillon reluctantly inclined his head. "If my lady will grant me pardon. My intentions have been misunderstood."

No, they have not, she thought grimly to herself but said nothing while the priest shooed Sir Brillon a short distance away. Although she had won this small battle, Pheresa knew she did not yet have a complete victory.

Another priest came forth, this one flanked by yellow-robed acolytes with shaved heads. He offered each of the coffin bearers a sip from a plain wooden goblet, then came to Pheresa.

"The cup of bitterness and grief?" he asked.

Pheresa eyed the goblet with distaste. It was black and stained with age. As the man held it up, a whiff of the contents caused her nostrils to flare. She wanted to refuse, but she was all too conscious of Sir Brillon watching her, of everyone—especially the king—watching her. She'd insisted on playing the role of the mourning bride. Now she had to go through with it all.

"My lady?" the priest said, sounding surprised. "The cup of bitterness and grief?"

He would not ask her a third time. She heard murmuring from the onlookers and nodded a quick acceptance of the offering.

The brew tasted worse than she expected. Concocted of a mixture containing gall, wormwood, and anceit, it burned her tongue. Somehow she swallowed her mouthful and afterwards felt clammy and sick.

Perhaps such punishment was just, she told herself weakly, holding down a shudder while the cup was taken to the king. She was lying to everyone today, and even worse, lying to herself. Every time she assured herself that she would never have married Gavril, she lied. Even mad and cruel, he'd been worth a throne. She still wanted to be queen with an angry, bitter determination that had only grown stronger during the journey back from Nether. It was all that was left to her. Without it, she would lose completely, and that she could not accept.

The king coughed hoarsely as though he, too, found the mourning cup foul. Pheresa drew herself erect. She was the niece of the king, and she wanted his throne. He could name any heir he chose, now that his son was dead, and she wanted him to choose her.

King Verence descended from his carriage. His tunic was a shade of dark burgundy that reminded Pheresa of dried blood, and over that he wore a cloak even darker. His shoulder-length hair hung loose, mostly gray now, and there were dark smudges beneath his eyes. He stared straight ahead at his son's coffin and neither waved nor spoke nor acknowledged the crowd.

Pheresa felt her heart break for him anew. King Verence had ridden away to war with his army, only to come home with a slain son, that handsome prince with so much spirit and promise, who had fallen to such a tragic end.

Only the king had truly loved his willful son, Pheresa thought with compassion. What a shame that Gavril had been so unworthy of his father's love. He had broken his father's good and generous heart. Gavril had died a madman, died in perhaps the most horrible way imaginable, died Nonkind and not human, and still Verence loved him despite his folly and transgressions.

Pheresa stared hard at the king, willing him to look at her now. He had been kind to her on the journey homeward, kind but increasingly remote. She believed he cared what befell her. Surely he understood that she loved Mandria as deeply as did he. She wanted to be a steward in his footsteps, guiding the realm and ruling it with a just and compassionate hand.

But now, standing here, with Sir Brillon waiting to take her away forever, she wondered if she'd misjudged the king's interest and favor.

An order rang out, and the drumbeats stopped. The palace guards strode forward in unison to line the steps on either side of the carpet.

The king's protector, grim-faced and vigilant, spoke quietly in his master's ear, and Verence visibly pulled himself together. His shoulders straightened. His head lifted. Something regal flashed in his eyes, and he stepped forward.

As he approached the steps, a line of youths emerged from the cathedral, swinging braziers of incense that filled the air with colored smoke and cloying fragrance. Pheresa disliked the smell of it, but it was better than the stink of Gavril's coffin.

As Verence passed Pheresa, he glanced at her but did not speak.

She curtsied to him. "Majesty," she said, but her voice was too soft.

He turned away, striding quickly up the steps and into the church. His protector followed close on his heels.

Another order rapped out. The coffin bearers started slowly up the steps, the incense smoke writhing around them.

Pheresa followed. The carpet felt warm and soft beneath her cold, numb feet, welcome indeed.

Inside the cathedral, however, the carpet ended and the stone floor proved to be icy cold. The gloomy interior was filled with shadows that made her stiffen instinctively. Wishing she could rid herself of her lingering fears and horrors, Pheresa reminded herself that there was nothing of Nonkind to harm her in this place.

A draft blew past her, and despite the incense she inhaled a whiff of corruption that seemed to mock her self-reassurances. She battled a surge of panic and managed to keep in step with the coffin bearers ahead of her. Gavril was Nonkind no longer, she told herself. He could not rise again under the control of a Believer. When he was laid in his tomb today, he could not shuffle forth tonight and strike her down. He had been burned with holy fire and salted. The Netherans had even immersed his remains in water until he was frozen in ice. Although the ice had long since melted in Mandria's warmer clime, he remained dead. She must remember that and believe it. She and Verence had not brought Nonkind to Savroix.

The air pressed damp and still against her face, smelling of incense, lamp oil, and antiquity. It was colder in here than outdoors, and she longed for her cloak and a pair of warm slippers.

Overhead, the vaulted ceiling soared as though to reach the very heavens. Pheresa walked the length of the nave, then waited while the coffin was slowly lowered onto a stone bier. The bearers turned about, saluted the coffin, then filed past her on both sides, each man nodding solemnly to her in turn.

She stood at the end of the coffin, her back to the people now filling the church. They took their places with quiet rustles and nervous coughs. She still held the sword, waiting for her part in the ceremony. Sir Brillon had seated himself on a nearby bench among liveried attendants, his eyes watchful. Pheresa surreptitiously glanced at the king's pew, where his majesty now knelt in prayer. She drew in a careful breath. When it came time for her to put down the sword, she was supposed to retreat, but instead she intended to join the king's side calmly yet boldly, where she would remain. Sir Brillon could not possibly interfere then.

Her plan was simple enough to succeed. She drew in another breath, feeling her heart pounding in anticipation.

On the other side of the church, she saw her parents sitting in state, her father—the Duc du Lindier and a marechal of Mandria—wearing furs and a heavy chain of gold, her mother—Princess Dianthelle—clad in sumptuous gray velvet and ermine, a tiny scroll of Writ clutched in her gloved fingers.

Last night there had been no chance for Pheresa to seek out her parents or speak to them. She had hoped for a message from her mother, but received none. Pheresa was never surprised by her mother's coldness and her father's indifference, but it hurt just the same.

Cardinal Theloi appeared among the high officials now filing into view. Pheresa met his green eyes without expression, but inside she was flooded with relief that he had not placed himself at the king's side. That had been her greatest worry. Now she felt confident that her plan would succeed.

The service began, and she let her mind go blank, refusing to listen until the moment came when someone gestured discreetly to her. She stepped forward, the momentary silence roaring in her ears, and laid the sword across Gavril's coffin. The act symbolized the cutting of their troth, and the relinquishment of her rights as Gavril's bride. A sense of freedom swelled through her. She let her hand linger a moment on the coffin before she stepped back.

Chantsong rose up in pure sweetness, the voices blending and echoing to the vaulted ceiling.

She turned around to face the crowd, her heart pounding and her face hot with anticipation. Now was the moment. She must not falter. Although a strange mist seemed to engulf her, she walked steadily toward the king. Everything faded around her but the sight of his majesty. Each step brought her closer to him, closer to safety.

She bumped into a hauberk with a surcoat of white and black over it. Sir Brillon stood in her path. An elderly priest was at his side. Smoothly they intercepted her and turned her away from the king's pew. Despair filled her. She wanted to cry out to Verence to help her, but it was impossible. Nothing came from her throat, not even a whispered protest.

"This way, my lady. This way," the elderly priest murmured, guiding her to a box pew containing several highborn ladies.

Sir Brillon, his black eyes gleaming with triumph, closed the door of the pew and stood there as though to guard it. Two of the ladies glanced at her in curiosity and moved apart to make room for her. Pheresa sank down on the seat. Wanting to cry, certain her face was scarlet, she wrapped her cold feet in the hem of her skirts and fought to maintain her composure. Inside she was drowning. She could not think, could not reason. Fear and despair held her fast.

What was she to do now? Nothing. There was nothing she could do, she told herself wearily.

Now that she'd been foiled by Sir Brillon, what other opportunity would she have of reaching the king's side? None. She knew how the rest of the ceremony would go. The king would enter the crypt to see his son interred, and he would leave by another exit. She would go straight to Batoine, never to be seen or heard from again.

She was shaking so hard one of the ladies next to her put a comforting arm around her shoulders. Pheresa barely noticed. If only Verence had beckoned to her, or even spoken to her outside on the steps.

When she'd been betrothed to Gavril, gaining access to the king was difficult. Now she had no chance at all. She might be the king's niece, but her position at court was once more what it had been . . . very small. She had no powerful allies on her side, no means of influence. Her mother could have helped her, but chose not to.

She forced herself to accept the bitter truth. Had Verence truly wished to put her in favor, he would have done so during their homeward journey. What a fool she'd been, living on false hopes, refusing to see the truth. Even if she'd reached the king's side today, would he have listened to her? Would he have cared? He could be a kind man, but he was so lost in grief that nothing seemed to matter to him now.

She grew aware of faint whispers beneath the sounds of the service. The ladies next to her murmured comments behind their hands, and several of them cast her swift looks of appraisal.

Pheresa no longer cared if they stared or talked about her. She was finished, her dreams in ruins. Forcing her mind away from thoughts of her imminent incarceration in the nuncery, she sent her thoughts in another, equally painful, direction.

"Make yourself Mandria's queen," Faldain had said the last time she saw him, and she'd fastened on that course of action, using it to hold off the numbing hurt of his rejection. Faldain had told her to be ruthless and strong. But she was neither of those things. She was gentle, composed, and dutiful, qualities, she supposed bitterly, ill suited for a monarch.

The sermon ended, and everyone rose. As the prayer began, and the responses were made by the mourners, the bearers carried the coffin down into the crypt. Looking haggard, Verence followed, vanishing with his attendants into the shadows.

Sir Brillon leaned over the short wall of the pew. "The carriage is waiting outside," he informed Pheresa softly. "Your cloak is in it, aye, and a heated brick to keep you warm. As soon as the king departs, we'll go."

She heard him through a faint roaring in her ears. Everything seemed unreal now. The unthinkable was indeed happening. The church was stronger than she. It would prevail in this matter, and she was helpless to stop it.

Something made her look up, and she saw Cardinal Theloi staring at her from where he stood near the altar. Their eyes met, and he gave her a tiny nod of satisfaction.

The mists around her cleared, and she felt renewed anger. With it came the determination to thwart him somehow.

Intending to run for it, she reached for the door of the pew. But there was a sudden flurry of activity as a small page came hurrying up the aisle.

Evading Sir Brillon's outstretched hand, the child bowed

to Pheresa and said, "His majesty wants you to come right away."

Her panic faded in a surge of relief. Stepping out of the pew, she went past Sir Brillon, and when he tried to accompany her, she frowned.

"No, good sir," she said in a clear voice. "The king sends for me alone. You are not bidden to follow."

Frustration blazed in his black eyes. Concealing her sense of triumph, Pheresa walked away, keeping her expression calm and quiet, while inside her heart thudded and she wanted to shout aloud.

Thod be praised, the king had not forgotten her after all. She was not to be left in the clutches of the churchmen.

With her spirits and strength restored, she descended the worn stone steps into the crypt. At the bottom, a priest waited with a flaming torch to guide her through the maze of eerie tombs and statues to where Verence waited impatiently.

One look at the king's grim face sobered her high spirits. She curtsied to him in silence.

"You should be here for this," he said, his voice echoing around the vault. "Together we shall finish it."

Plentiful torchlight illuminated the area, holding back the shadows. Gazing about, Pheresa gained a confused impression of damp-glistened stone and low ceiling beams. She had never been in the crypt before, the burial place of Mandrian kings. She found the immense weight of history and tradition oppressive.

Verence offered her his hand, and she rested her fingertips lightly on his knuckles as together they walked forward to where the priests and church knights in attendance waited.

The prince's tomb gaped open; the torchlight did not reach far into its black depths. She and Verence halted, but the king continued to grip her hand very hard.

Words were spoken. The sword she had placed atop the coffin was removed. Verence stepped forward and kissed the coffin.

For a terrible moment, Pheresa thought she was expected to do the same. But as she hesitated, Verence took off his cloak, putting it around her shoulders and holding her close against his side while the coffin was lowered into the tomb. The stone lid closed it with a thud that boomed through the vault.

She flinched, and Verence's grip tightened. His face revealed nothing, but she felt his strong body tremble. Tears shimmered in his eyes.

"Dear uncle," she said softly, "I am so sorry."

Verence stared at the stone effigy carved in Gavril's handsome likeness. A muscle worked briefly in his jaw as though he were fighting for control of his emotions. "A waste," he said gruffly. "A damned, stupid waste."

Before she could speak, he thrust her roughly away from him and strode toward a flight of narrow stairs leading outside. His protector hurried after him, and with a start Pheresa realized the king was leaving.

Gathering his heavy cloak around her, she cast aside her usual dignity and ran to catch up.

"Your majesty!" she called. "Please—"

The protector blocked her path as the king started up the steps. Someone opened the door at the top, and a shaft of gray daylight plunged into the gloomy crypt.

"Please, lord protector," Pheresa said urgently, all her fear in her voice. "Let me speak to him."

"Not now, my lady," Lord Odeil said. "He is leaving Savroix to hunt. He must have time alone."

"But the priests are going to cloister me!" she cried out desperately. "Your majesty, please! I don't want to go to Batoine. I don't want to live out my days in isolation or be interrogated for sainthood."

Verence paused on the top step and looked back at her with a frown. "What is this?"

She held up her hands to him imploringly. "Please let me stay at court. I want only to—"

"Of course you will stay at court."

Relief made her weep. "Thank you! And may I ask about the—"

"No more now," Verence said wearily, turning away from her. "I must get away."

"But, your majesty—"

Verence was gone.

She stood there at the foot of the steps, and felt raindrops splattering her upturned face. Lord Odeil hurried after Verence, and she thought in disbelief, *No one heard this exchange except the priests. Theloi will still do as he pleases.*

But then an equerry wearing a burgundy tunic appeared and came hurrying down the steps. "Quickly, my lady. It's starting to rain. I am to escort you back to the palace in all haste."

Feeling as though she'd been saved from the jaws of disaster, Pheresa put her hand in his and allowed him to assist her up the steps. Together they hurried through the rain around the corner and back into the square. Sir Brillon came running down the steps to intercept them, but the equerry bundled her into a fine carriage bearing the royal crest and shut the door.

Huddled beneath the king's warm cloak, Pheresa wiped the rain from her face and listened to Sir Brillon arguing with the equerry.

"The king said that I am to see Lady Pheresa safely back to Savroix," the equerry said firmly.

"But she is to leave for Batoine at once," Sir Brillon protested. "I have my orders."

"So do I, sir knight. Would you refuse the king's express command?"

Red-faced with frustration, Sir Brillon retreated. Peering at him through the window, Pheresa felt safe at last. If nothing else, she had gained herself a few days' respite. She knew Theloi would not abandon his plan to remove her from court, but now she had time to plan also. Watching Sir Brillon stride angrily away, she allowed herself a smile and turned around, to find herself face-to-face with her mother.

Princess Dianthelle, her legendary beauty undimmed by the years, sat there in gray velvet and ermine, diamonds glittering at her throat and on her slender fingers. She stared at Pheresa with acute displeasure.

"You fool," she said in a voice that cut. "Batoine was the perfect solution for you. Now you've botched everything."

Chapter Three

The northwest coast of Mandria could be bleak and damp in the spring. This morn, the skies looked black with the ominous promise of storms coming in from seaward, and the waves crashing onto the rocks below Durl Hold were rough and violent.

Sir Talmor, adjutant to the chevard of Durl, kicked his reluctant horse down the treacherous little trail snaking along the cliffs. The fortress of Durl Hold, ancient and still strong despite centuries of being blasted by sea and wind, stood at the top. Overlooking the ocean, the stout walls blended so perfectly with the stone they rose straight and sheer as part of the unassailable cliffs themselves. But despite its strength, the fortress was small and inconvenient. Its keep was tiny, and the accommodations primitive and cramped. The chevards of Durl had abandoned it long ago and built a larger, more modern hold at the base of the cliffs, snugged into a protected spot of high ground between beach and the hills rising eastward. With the fortress available for emergency protection against armed attack, less attention—and coinage—was spent on building stout walls to guard the new hold. Resembling a small palace, the rambling stone edifice was added onto by each succeeding chevard, so that parts of it remained in a state of perpetual construction. Low garden walls surrounded it, and its turrets were designed to capture the view rather than to serve as lookout points.

There had been a time, in the past, when the fortress had often been necessary. But Mandria's coast was secure. Sentries grew bored on duty in the fortress, watching prosperous merchant ships sailing by on the horizon. Only in the autumn was there any excitement, when raging storms swept in hapless ships to founder and break on the rocks. Salvaging the wreckage gave the village fishermen an extra bit of prosperity to tide them over during the bleak winter months when the sea was an icy monster full of tempests and treacherous currents.

But it was springtide now, with buds swelling the tips of the gnarled little trees that clung precariously to the hillside and cliffs. The sea hollies looked fresh in new green and displayed sprays of delicate white blossoms. Here and there, sundrops growing among the rock crevices poked up their tiny heads in glorious color.

The currents running past the headland had shifted, and the fishing boats had been venturing daily farther and farther into the taming sea. Come sunset, they returned with swollen nets, for in the spring the codni and brill migrated into these coastal waters. At night, laughter could be heard in the village. The folk went to and fro about their business with smiles and quick steps.

But no smiles or laughter today, Sir Talmor thought. No fishing boats out plying the nets today, with death waiting for any man who dared defy Lord Pace's order. Today, they mourned Prince Gavril, as did every hold across the land. The Heir to the Realm was being buried, and due respect must be given.

Talmor sighed. According to the orders in the dispatch brought by courier, the state funeral held in Savroix today was to be observed by every hold and village across the realm. At noontide precisely Prince Gavril would be laid to his final rest. At noontide precisely, Durl Hold must acknowledge the event. After much thought and stewing, Lord Pace had decided not to use his tiny—and very precious—horde of saltpeter to salute the prince.

"Damne! A waste of good supply," were his exact words. The saltpeter had been imported at exorbitant cost to blast away some of the granite cliffs so Lady Alda could expand the north wing. Lord Pace intended the stone to be used to finish building a seawall across the harbor. The saltpeter was not going to be blown to the winds in honor of a prince dead and of no use now to his erst subjects.

Instead, Lord Pace had elected to light bonfires on the cliff edge past the fortress. They would shine as a beacon to any merchant ships out to sea. They would look spectacular from the beach. They might even be visible to the shy hill folk, who so rarely ventured to Durl. If the fires weren't visible, Lord Pace asserted, the smoke certainly would be.

Accordingly, he had ordered three bonfires built to exacting specifications. At noontide, on his signal, they would be lit and a prayer spoken. Afterwards, a somber feast of salted fish and flat mourning cake would be eaten, followed by priestly exhortations to consider one's soul. Then all folk would disperse and go home.

There was to be no jousting or games, much to the disappointment of the hold knights. Word was that the village folk were grumbling about the loss of a day's catch, with naught reward to show for such abstinence, but Lord Pace knew what was proper and he had no intention of permitting any activity that resembled celebration.

"The king has watchers," he'd said, when his daughters moaned against his edicts. "Eyes and ears, alike, reporting to his majesty from everywhere. Aye! We'll do this proper, with the right show of respect. Somber garments. Somber eating. Let the priests have the day to preach us into sour stomachs, if they wish. On such occasions we should eat lightly. 'Tis a funeral, not a feast day."

A dreary day, Talmor thought, squinting at the sky. The

wind had died, and a fine mist was falling. He could see fog rolling in from Goose Point. The tiny island was already shrouded with gray, just the top of its lone pine visible above the fog. His mood darkened more. After all this fuss and bother about the bonfires, which could have been built on the beach with a great deal less trouble, the fog might well engulf everything. Then it wouldn't matter if the fires were lit or not, for who would be able to see them?

His horse stumbled on the trail, snorted, and took another reluctant step. Loose shale and pebbles shifted beneath Canae's iron-shod hooves, and Talmor pushed deeper into his stirrups, bracing himself and leaning back to keep his balance as the horse went downward.

Lord Pace no longer rode up to inspect the fortress, even in good weather. His joints hurt him on damp, cold days, especially his hips, although he wouldn't admit it. Today, he had sent his adjutant to see that all was prepared according to his orders.

Inspecting bonfires, Talmor thought with irritation, was a job for a squire, not a knight of good rank. Yet Lord Pace was known for ignoring tradition and convention. He thought nothing of ordering his sentry knights to redig the south ditch whenever the pikes on that side of the hold began to topple in the soft, sandy soil. Such a job was for peasants, and caused much resentment in the ranks. Yet Lord Pace did as he pleased, without a thought for morale. It had taken Talmor three years to work his way up to his current position of adjutant. Little had he known that his new status would mean that he was often barked at like a servant. Instead of advising the chevard on matters of strategy or evaluating the training of the men or collecting reports on the strength of the walls or inspecting the armory, he was sent to fetch scrolls or instruct the master of horse as to how the mounts were to be shod . . . or to inspect piles of firewood that were to be torched simultaneously in a matter of minutes.

Talmor tucked his chin lower and tried to quell his rising sense of dissatisfaction. On a day like this, it was hard to consider his blessings and not wish himself in one of the upland holds, where battle action was a frequent occurrence and there was something *useful* to do. Still, there was a job at hand to be finished, and he told himself to get on with it.

The fog to the south seemed no closer. Talmor hoped it would stay seaward until he reached safe ground. A steep, narrow trail such as this was best used by a goat, not a knight in full armor atop a charger.

As for his suit of mail, the hours spent polishing and oiling it were going to be wasted, for he was certain he would rust ere he reached the ceremony planned for hold and village. His new surcoat, orange and gold in Lord Pace's vivid colors, was splashed with mud and soaked through. Mud dripped from his spurs, and his charger—a big, nervous brute already ill-tempered from being washed and combed at dawn—pawed and balked on the trail yet again. Canae was a fine horse for battle or jousting, but useless as a courser up and down pig trails like this.

Talmor kicked him again, and the horse tossed his armored head, grumbling around the bit as he lumbered down the trail.

A cold, fine mist condensed on Sir Talmor's tanned face, and he shivered in acute dislike of such weather. His mixed, lowlander blood was too thin for this cold, and he felt the winters more keenly than most of the other men. They teased him, urging him to grow a thick beard to warm his jaws, and although he was not a man with a ready sense of humor, he endured the joking stoically. Better to be teased than stoned.

"All's ready, then, Sir Talmor?" called out a youthful voice.

Talmor glanced ahead at one of the beacon boys, standing tall on a large boulder, his flag held ready in eager hands. Four such boys were arrayed on the trail between hold and fortress, ready to pass the signal once it was given.

This particular boy was scrawny and growing like a weed so that his leggings were too short for him and his wrists dangled from his sleeves. His name was Lutel, and Talmor thought he showed promise.

Smiling, Talmor gave him a small salute that made the boy

stand taller, with his chest puffed out. "Keep ready now," Talmor said. "It's almost time. His lordship wants no mistakes."

"I'm watchin' below, sir, just like ye ordered. But this rain's about to come in, sure as sure."

"Fog," Talmor said.

"Nay, sir. Not in this wind. That be rain comin'. A hard one."

Talmor frowned seaward. The waters were running green beneath the dark skies, and where the fog—or rain—met sky the horizon was lost altogether. Goose Point was gone from sight now, the pine tree engulfed completely.

At that moment, a finger of unease slid up his spine. Talmor felt suddenly cold to the marrow, as though he'd been plunged in icy water. In that second he could not catch his breath, and in the next he was shaking as though with the ague.

No, he thought angrily, shoving such instincts aside. *Not again. I'm done with all that.*

"Sir?" Lutel asked uneasily. "Are ye ill? Ye look queer about the gills—"

"Never mind how I look," Talmor said gruffly. He was furious with himself for this slip. He'd come to Durl vowing never to use his magical ways again, no matter what the provocation. And now, long after he'd convinced himself that he'd finally driven away that part of his heritage, his powers caught him by surprise today, as strong as ever. "I'm not ill."

But he felt clammy and cold. A light sweat broke out across his brow, and he fought the impulse to wipe it away.

Something is wrong, he thought, then scowled and tried again to close off such thoughts.

"Sir?"

With an effort, Talmor forced his attention back to the boy, who was staring at him in concern. He believed the boy had been talking all this while, yet he could not recall a word of what Lutel had said.

"Did ye see somethin' out yon?" the boy asked.

Talmor's gaze swept the vista and saw nothing except the sky, the waves, the rain, and a flock of birds blown about in the wind. Yet his sense of unease stayed with him. *What is out there?* he asked himself. He felt cold, as though standing by his grave.

"Sir?"

"Never mind," Talmor said, as much to himself as to the boy. "There's nothing to watch for except the signal from below. Now, boy, see that you keep sharp watch for it."

"But the storm—"

"You leave the storm be. And watch for the signal. That's your job, not watching the weather."

"Aye, sir," Lutel said smartly. "No ganderin' off for me. Not today."

"Good. I depend on you to do a good job," Talmor said, and rode on.

"Sir!" Lutel called out.

Surprised, Talmor drew rein and glanced back. The boy was gazing seaward, contrary to his direct orders, his flag dipping dangerously close to the ground.

Irritation flashed through Talmor. He twisted in his saddle to glare at Lutel. "I just told you to—"

"Sir! Look yon!"

Talmor ignored where the boy was pointing. He was disappointed in the lad, and drew in breath to give him a sharp reprimand.

"Boats! Look yon! Who be comin' in?"

Talmor's anger at the boy shifted to the fishermen who had defied Lord Pace's orders. "They'll pay for this," he said darkly. "His lordship gave strict orders against fishing—"

"None of ours, sir," the boy said. "Those ain't boats I recognize."

That icy chill slid down Talmor's spine a second time. He turned in his saddle and saw a cluster of boats approaching fast in tight formation. No sails; these were rowed vessels, cut low to the sea, skimming its surface with every flash of the long oars. Talmor counted four such craft, blinked, and another formation of four boats appeared out of the storm. He swore softly to himself.

"No sails!" Lutel said in a moan. "They's rowin'! That means—"

A flash of horror swept through Talmor. Now he understood the danger he'd sensed only moments before. These boats held death to everyone at Durl and the village. "Vvord raiders," he said grimly.

"Skull folk," Lutel whispered. His eyes were wide, and his thin chest heaved with emotion. "Thod save us—"

"Hold your fear!" Talmor snapped. His initial sense of shock was fading, and he could think rapidly now. The village was wide-open to disaster. The repairs to the seawall were but half-finished, and it was doubtful any sentry was keeping proper watch today. All the village folk were out in their finery, vulnerable to attack. The hold itself stood wide-open for all to come and go as they pleased. By now most of the knights would be assembling on the jousting field out behind the hold, where the ground was at its most level. And above . . .

He squinted up at the fortress, where no alarm had as yet sounded. No one was keeping watch. Sir Inthiere, the fortress commander, had once served in the palace guard at Savroix. Today he was lachrymose, full of gloomy reminiscences of Prince Gavril as a "wee bit, just getting used to the gait of his pony." When Talmor had left him, only a few minutes ago, Sir Inthiere was heading to the cellars. No doubt he intended to spend the day ale-muddled, if not outright drunk.

Anger swept Talmor. He'd told Sir Inthiere to keep the sentries sharp. But why should he be listened to? There'd been no sea raiders for thirty years, perhaps longer. Only the old folks remembered past dangers, spinning terrible stories on gale nights to frighten children into good behavior. As for Talmor, since he'd come here he'd thought long and hard about why and where the fortress was built, as well as the dangers it had served to protect its inhabitants from. Now, as impossible as it seemed, that danger had returned.

"Lutel," he said sharply, "raise your flag."

"You mean give the signal now?"

"Wave your flag for danger!"

Visibly flustered, Lutel whipped up his flag, nearly dropped the pole, then moved it in the correct warning signal under Talmor's fierce eye.

"That'll do," Talmor said. "Repeat it until the fortress takes notice and sounds the trumpets."

"Aye, sir."

The fear quavering in Lutel's voice made Talmor pause. He took the time to give the boy a reassuring look. "Steady now. Keep your head. Stand your position as long as you can, but if they get past us, you run to the fortress. Clear?"

"Aye, sir, but I got to warn my family—"

"You have your orders! Stand your ground!"

"Aye, sir."

Talmor gave him a brusque nod. "I depend on you, Lutel. You're the only sentry worth having, this day."

The boy looked stronger for the praise.

Relenting, Talmor said, "Your family will be warned. I'll see to it."

Relief flashed across Lutel's thin face. "Oh, thank ye, sir."

Talmor spurred his horse forward. Snorting, the brute leaped down the trail, skidded on loose ground, nearly lost his footing, and somehow managed to keep from going over the edge of the cliff. Down they plunged, going faster than was sensible, and all the while no warning sounded from the fortress.

Glancing back, Talmor saw the orange flames of the first bonfire shoot up toward the darkening skies. Then the second one caught. Acute frustration filled him. What were the fools doing? The danger signal was unmistakable, yet they were apparently so focused on their part in the ceremony that they hadn't recognized it. Why didn't they sound the trumpets and give the folk below some warning?

He wanted to wheel his horse around and go galloping back to shout the men into proper order, but he kept Canae headed down the steep trail. His duty was to report directly to Lord Pace. The chevard gave the orders here, and Talmor knew he must obey the proper chain of command.

Inside, however, he felt an exhilarating tangle of anger,

fear, and rising anticipation. There had been an ominous warning or two from farther up the coastline during last autumn, warnings that Lord Pace had brushed off back even before Aelintide.

"Raiders from the Sea of Vvord? Bull dung!" he said in his gruff way. "Tales to frighten old women. There's been no trouble out of Vvord since my father's day. Why should they come now?"

Why indeed? Talmor thought grimly as he was nearly jolted from the saddle. *Because we've grown fat and lazy and prosperous. Because the king called half our fighting force to muster when he went forth to battle in Nether, and not all of them have returned. Because we used to keep warships here to guard the coast, and we no longer have them. Because we're ripe for the plucking.*

And still the trumpets did not sound.

He ground his teeth, but there was no help for it until he reached the upper beaches. He could feel time rushing past him, precious time that would give the hold and village just a few minutes' warning, a chance to run, to grab weapons, to get inside the walls. Would all the people living in hold and village be able to fit inside the small fortress? If a siege commenced—Thod help him, but he did not know if the raiders besieged their victims—but if a siege commenced, there weren't enough food supplies to last long. Who, in the panic soon to come, would think to haul food from the bountiful cellars of the hold? And water? Hadn't someone said recently that the old fortress cistern was cracked and leaking again?

Thod's mercy, Talmor thought to himself in momentary panic. They'd been caught like fools. They deserved disaster.

Then, from far above him, he heard the wavering notes of a trumpet blare against the freshening gusts of wind. Heartened, he spurred Canae into leaping off the trail and skipping the last small switchback. Skidding recklessly, the big horse thudded onto solid ground with a jolt that snapped Talmor's teeth together and went galloping toward the jousting field.

As he rode, Talmor was busy untying his cloak and flinging it off. He drew his sword from its scabbard and held it ready. From this angle, he could no longer see the boats on the other side of the headland. But once horse and rider rounded the headland and came to the mouth of the harbor, disaster would arrive swiftly.

The trumpet came again, sounding the call to arms. Talmor saw the assembled knights, lined up in two straight rows facing each other, ignoring the call. He wanted to shout at them, although he was too far away to be heard. Why didn't they heed the warning? What were they doing?

As he drew closer, he brandished his sword and shouted, and only then did they begin to break formation. Several stood in their stirrups to stare up at the fortress, where the bonfires were blazing. Others gawked at Talmor as though he'd gone mad.

Lord Pace, on foot, and wearing a long tunic and cloak rather than armor, was waving his arms and swearing at the top of his lungs.

"Thod's bones! They've ruined it, the stupid louts. Ruined the ceremony. Ruined the whole—"

"My lord!" Talmor called out, drawing rein before him with such force Canae reared up. "Sea raiders to the northwest, approaching by boat. At least twelve boats by my last count. Probably more by now."

Lord Pace swung around to glare up at Talmor. Stout and double-chinned, the old man looked fiercer than usual with his white hair blown into wild disarray by the wind. He was clutching the folds of his cloak to keep the garment from billowing off his shoulders.

"What?" he shouted. "Damne! What're you bleating about, sir? Is this some kind of merry prank?"

"Sea raiders," Talmor repeated urgently. "Vvordsmen. They'll be in the bay within minutes. The village will go first. We've got to get the people headed up the cliff to safety."

Consternation broke out among the knights. Sir Moule, craggy and weather-beaten, kicked his horse forward to Talmor's side. Others drew their weapons in readiness.

"Hold there! Hold!" Lord Pace shouted, while nearby his

portly wife and two daughters clutched their streaming veils and stared in visible disbelief.

"My lord, your orders?" Sir Moule asked urgently.

"Hold, I say!" Pace bellowed with a stamp of his foot. He turned his glare on Talmor. "How dare you speak such nonsense! How dare you issue orders! Do this and do that. Ahead of yourself, sir. Ahead of yourself."

A squire came running up, white-faced and breathless. "My lord! Compliments of Sir Pentigne, standing as watch commander, but there's a contingent of six-and-twenty rowed ships coming in around the headland. My lord, they've got skulls painted on the bowsprits."

Lady Alda screamed and tried to swoon. Her attendants held her up, calling out for assistance. Her daughters gathered up their skirts and ran for the hold.

Ignoring his family, Lord Pace stared at the squire as though he did not believe his ears. "What?" he sputtered. "What's that you say?"

His protector Sir Albie stepped forward with a ferocious scowl and drew his sword. "Skull folk," he said. "Hah! Time to drive them back from whence they came."

A cheer rose up from the mounted knights. Orders rang out from the master-at-arms.

Lord Pace stood where he was, glaring and blustering, confusion in his eyes. "They can't be here," he insisted. "We drove them off. My father taught them—"

"My lord," Talmor said, leaning down from the saddle impatiently. "There's no time. Get yourself and your good lady to safety. Never mind the hold. Head directly for the fortress and—"

"What? Run for my life?" Pace bellowed in outrage. "You!" he said with a gesture at a nearby servant. "See that the women are escorted to the cliffs. And where's my horse? My armor? Damne! Where's my squire when I want him?"

"Nay, my lord," Sir Albie said firmly. "No fighting for you."

"The women," Lord Pace said, not listening. "They'll go

for them first, the savage brutes. We've got to get all the women rounded up and hidden away."

"Be easy there, m'lord," said the squire who'd brought the message. "Sir Pentigne has already sent all females in the hold up fortress way with an armed escort. I am to bring your lordship to safety also."

"What?" Lord Pace looked insulted. "Damne, I'll not run like a baseborn coward. Where's my sword? Albie! My horse! My sword!"

The protector's experienced old eyes met Talmor's and an unspoken word passed between them.

"Get him to high ground if you can," Talmor said.

"He won't go," Albie replied.

"Go?" Lord Pace glanced around furiously. "Put off this blithering nonsense. We've fighting to do. Talmor, take charge of half the knights here. See that you hold the sea-wall."

Talmor's heart sank. Crumbling, half-fallen, propped up with timbers, and covered with scaffolding for repairs, the seawall had been intended to close the wide mouth of the harbor and make its opening defensible. It was impossible to defend in its current state of disrepair. He'd just been handed a suicidal task.

"Sir Talmor!" Lord Pace yelled. "Did you hear me?"

"Yes, my lord. At once."

He glanced around to choose his men, but Lord Pace was still talking.

"They'll come right over the gap, the murdering savages. Their boats have next to no draw, so they can do it. Hold them as long as you can, then fall back in order. That will give the rest of us time to make the hold defenses ready. Its walls will withstand them; that, I'll swear to."

"My lord," Talmor said, "they'll hit the easiest target first. The village is—"

"Damn the village! I'll waste no men on a cluster of huts."

"It's the fish they'll want—"

"They want women and my gold," Lord Pace said, as

though Talmor were a fool. "I'll give them neither. Now get to it!"

"My lord." Saluting the chevard, Talmor wheeled Canae around and shouted orders.

In moments, he had gathered his small contingent of five-and-thirty men and went galloping down the hill from the jousting field to the beach. The villagers, most of whom had been walking up to the field for the ceremony, had paused to stare up at the bonfires. Now they scattered before the galloping knights with cries of alarm.

"Get to the fortress!" Talmor shouted at them. "Don't go back to your houses." He saw Lutel's mother—a laundress—and her clutch of younger children. "Raiders are coming! Save yourselves and run to the fortress! Quickly!"

The villagers scattered like chickens, some screaming and heading for the cliffs, others turning back for loved ones or possessions despite his instructions. Many of the men headed for their boats, but already the raiders were filling the bay. They came through the gray sheets of rain, silent, deadly, and swift, and poured into the bay. As Lord Pace had predicted, some of them even came through the gap where part of the old seawall had crumbled and fallen, leaving only the foundation stones standing a few feet beneath the water's surface.

A corner of Talmor's mind observed the display of magnificent seamanship as they steered through the tricky currents that eddied through and around the gap, the rowmen managing the long oars perfectly. But Talmor had no time to waste admiring the skills of his enemy. He and his men were already too late to defend the wall.

He drew rein abruptly and wheeled around to face his men, his mind rapidly trying to come up with an alternative course of action.

Meanwhile, the raiders went first for the fishing boats bobbing at anchor in the harbor. Swarming the small, sturdy craft, they destroyed sails and nets, while others stove in the sides at the waterline. The sounds of muffled thuds and splintering wood echoed across the water.

Howls of anguish rose from villager throats. Men ran foolishly into the water, swimming out in a vain attempt to save their vessels. Laughing, the raiders clubbed them to watery deaths and continued their work. Already many of the vessels were sinking.

Along the small wharf, yesterday's catch glinted on the wooden racks where fish—gutted and skinned—hung in thin slivers to dry. Nets lay across the drying racks to protect the catch from marauding gulls, but nets would not hold against the skull folk.

Grimly, Talmor turned back to his men. Their faces were fierce with anger. They held their weapons in readiness.

"Your orders?" rasped out Sir Moule as he drew up his mail coif.

Talmor hastily pulled up his own, remembering that he'd almost left it off this morning. He longed now for his helmet and his shield, but with sword and dagger he must make do.

"They'll land on the beach in the next few minutes," Talmor said. "We're too late for the wall."

"Then we should retreat to the hold," Sir Feil said. "And man it as strongly as we can."

Talmor had already estimated the force coming against them. Durl's knights were outnumbered perhaps four to one. "When they land," he said grimly, "they'll be at their most vulnerable. We're on horseback. We have armor and all the advantage of our training. We shall hold the beach."

Sir Feil's eyes bugged out. "Look yon, sir! They're more numerous than fleas on a dog. I say we retreat to where we can do good."

His protest infuriated Talmor, for it undercut his authority with the others, but he held his temper. "We are the first line, and we shall hold it!" he said boldly. "We're knights of Durl, sirs."

They cheered at that.

Talmor lifted his sword. "We're worth a dozen such savages apiece. If any of you doubt that, you've no place with me."

They cheered again, and Talmor wheeled Canae around and sent the big horse galloping across the sand to meet the foe. The raiders were coming in fast now, their oars flashing faster as though to meet his challenge.

Five-and-thirty men against three hundred, possibly more, Talmor thought as he leaned low over Canae's whipping mane. And only forty additional warriors behind them to defend the hold and fortress. He felt his heart sink anew, then swiftly bolstered his courage. Trained knights could hold these barbarians.

It had been his intention to charge Canae into the water, knee deep if necessary, but as the boats came closer, he saw some of the raiders busy hauling forth large sacks of coarse wet cloth. They dumped the contents into the surf, and although he caught mere glimpses of bulbous heads and uncoiling tentacles, Talmor slowed his horse with a ruthless hand.

Twisting about in the saddle, he shouted, "All of you! Stay out of the water, no matter what you do!"

Not waiting for anyone to respond, he veered Canae at a slightly different angle, slowing the reluctant horse yet more. He did not want the raiders to land, did not want their feet to pollute the shores of Durl, but he could see the monsters bobbing to the surface with flashes of dark liquid eyes before they dived beneath the waves. The water was boiling white, churned by oars and the rapid clutch of tentacles that coiled about dead, floating bodies and yanked them abruptly from sight.

With wailing cries, the raiders landed, running their boats right up onto the shore and jumping off in droves. They moved incredibly fast, seemingly unhampered by either the shallow waves or the deep sand. Brandishing cutlasses, daggers, and clubs, they were pale, muscular men, giants in height and brawn. Shirtless, they wore wide leggings cut short at the ankle and boots with studded soles. They had no hair. Every man was shaven and beardless, with smooth chests and hairless arms. As they called out and shouted, their language was guttural and harsh, impossible to understand.

They came in a rush, running faster across the sand than

Talmor expected. He tightened his loins, and Canae sprang forward at full charge, his hooves throwing up sprays of sand.

Talmor's men followed the charge with war cries of their own. The raiders checked only slightly, their shouts rising into a shrill, earsplitting noise.

Then the rain reached the shore, and in the space of a heartbeat Talmor found himself engulfed in a heavy downpour. Canae snorted and stumbled beneath him, nearly pitching Talmor from the saddle. He steadied the horse and heard sounds of confusion and vicious oaths behind him.

The rain pelted down fiercely, mixed with hail. Flinching under it, Talmor saw the raiders running toward him, impervious to the elements. Their eyes glowed as though lit by fire. Red eyes, orange eyes, yellow . . . all the colors of flame.

Talmor stared at them in sick dread, for surely they were not men at all.

"Dear Thod, what are they?" Sir Moule called out.

At once Talmor realized he was dangerously close to losing his men. If their nerve broke, if they ran, then Durl Hold was finished.

He cast aside his own fear and tightened his grip on his sword. "They're our enemies, men!" he called out loudly. "And they're soon to die! For Durl!"

Kicking Canae into a startled gallop, he resumed his charge. Thudding hoofbeats behind him told him that his men followed.

Just before he reached the raiders, Talmor raised his sword and urged his horse faster. He was a fierce, bronze-faced man clad in full chain mail, his horse wearing armor like a great behemoth, unstoppable and fearless. Horse and rider crashed into the foremost Vvordsman. Canae knocked the raider down and trampled over the top of him, rearing up to strike down the next man with deadly forefeet as he'd been trained. Talmor swung his sword as the horse came down, and cut off the head of a third raider. Blood spurted across Talmor's hand and wrist, and he noted with relief that these giants weren't demons at all but mortal. And he'd taken three down in the first moment.

Satisfied, he roared ferociously and attacked his next opponent. Around him he heard the sounds of his men crashing into the midst of the battle. The raiders' cries became squeals of death as more went down. But others quickly filled their places, and within minutes they swarmed around Talmor on all sides, while Canae circled and kicked to keep him safe.

Hacking with his sword, Talmor had no time to marvel at the raiders' foolishness in not wearing armor or even carrying shields. Yet they didn't fall back. They kept on fighting as though as well equipped as he. A club thudded into his back with such force he nearly toppled off balance. Robbed of breath, Talmor twisted in the saddle to evade another blow and brought his sword up and over with a blow of retaliation that took off the man's arm. Screaming, the savage fell back, blood spurting from his wound, while another raider came swarming up into the saddle with Talmor.

Taken by surprise, Talmor felt the sting of a dagger driven through his chain mail into his ribs. He could not use his sword at such close quarters. The raider was right in his face, orange eyes glowing as he twisted the dagger and gibbered hatred at Talmor. Grimacing, Talmor smashed his sword forearm into the Vvordsman's nose, breaking it with a splatter of blood, then drew his dagger and stabbed the man through the heart.

He fell, but three others swarmed Talmor on all sides. He fought them off, taking the punishing blows of clubs although by now a wicked, piercing pain in his side warned him he might have ribs broken. His dagger wound felt numb, and he could not tell how much blood he was losing. Ignoring these problems, he fought on with gritted teeth.

Then Sir Banjermel appeared at his side, swearing loudly with every blow of his sword. "Talmor, fall back with me!" he called out over the din of weapons and war cries.

"Nay! We stand!" Talmor shouted back in refusal, but now he saw that the majority of the raiders had landed farther along the beach and divided their forces. Some hit the village, already looting and burning the modest houses of thatch and wood. The rest were streaming toward the hold, screaming fiercely.

Sir Banjermel yelled something else that Talmor couldn't hear. He understood, of course, that it was time to retreat. He'd accomplished the delay that Lord Pace had asked for. Shooting his companion knight a look of gratitude, Talmor waved his arm as a signal for the other knights still alive and fighting.

A swift glance gave him an imperfect count. He thought he still had twenty men. Who they were he couldn't tell at this moment.

"Fall back!" he shouted at the top of his lungs. "To the hold! The hold!"

They clustered together and began to retreat, still fighting every step. When they finally gained a tiny respite, Talmor sent his mount hopping over the bloody bodies of slain foes and spurred him toward the hold.

It rose before him on the hillside, a pretty palace that rambled past its defense walls. Lord Pace's banner flew bravely from the turret, but the raiders were already storming it. Fire blazed from an upper window, and in dismay Talmor urged his horse faster. He headed toward the weakest part of the wall, where the fighting looked heaviest, hoping to crush some of the attackers from behind and pin them against the knights defending the hold.

As Canae crested the ditch where the pikes were supposed to serve as a deterrent to invaders but could not hold because of the soft ground, he heard Sir Moule shout a gruff warning behind him.

Talmor was still turning his head when something hard and powerful hit him from his left side. He saw a black shape, the blur of something moving fast at his head.

The world exploded in a rainbow of colors and fire. He felt himself flying through the air, his horse and saddle left behind. Then the fire went black inside his skull, and he knew nothing else.

Chapter Four

In her mother's carriage, Pheresa curled her hands into fists beneath the concealment of King Verence's cloak. She was intensely angered by what the princess had just said, so furious that she could not find words to reply. She could not even bear to look at her mother, who was so different from her, so contrary, so *cold*. Not for the first time, Pheresa wondered how they could possibly be related to each other. Yet they were. She drew a deep breath, feeling as though she were on fire. Her ears were roaring, and Princess Dianthelle's face and form blurred for a moment.

"That's right," the princess said contemptuously. "Weep those pretty tears the way you always do. Why can you not discuss matters rationally whenever I give you my attention?"

Outside the carriage, the cathedral bell began to toll the death knell for Gavril, one stroke for every year of his life. *I survived what he did not,* Pheresa thought. *I am strong enough now to deal even with my mother.*

"I am not weeping," Pheresa said quietly. "And how can you call me a fool for not going to Batoine? I do not belong

there. I have no intention of ever being shut away in that
nuncery."

"It is the perfect place for you," the princess said with a
shrug. "What else do you intend to do with yourself? You cannot remain at court."

Pheresa stared at her. "Why not?"

But her mother's hard, brilliant eyes were frowning intently at her attire. "Whose cloak is that?"

"The king's."

"I suppose you think yourself clever in gaining his favor.
Or have you?"

Pheresa's feeling of satisfaction deepened. It was gratify-
ing to render her mother uncertain. But she knew she could
not deceive the princess for long. Dianthelle kept superb spies
at court, and she had little patience for games. Still, Pheresa
could not resist toying with her. "I have the king's cloak," she
replied.

"But not his favor. No. In that, at least, nothing is as yet
settled."

The relief in her mother's voice made Pheresa frown. She
wondered what her mother was up to. "I am surprised you
bother with me today, Mama. You hadn't ever bothered to
reply to my letters."

"Why should I?"

Hurt, Pheresa struggled to keep her voice even. "Because
I am your only daughter. Because I have been in grave danger. Because I thought you might be glad I survived it."

"Do you wish congratulations?" the princess asked coldly.
"You wrote me to say you were well again. That, I'd already
heard. You wrote to say you were returning to Savroix with
the king. That, of course, was obvious. Duty required you to
do so. But now your duty is over. And you should depart as
quickly as you can."

"Why?" Pheresa asked in puzzlement. "The king has bidden me to stay."

"Only because you have given him that calf-eyed look of
appeal you do so well. Really, Pheresa, by now you should
have more sense. Lingering at court will avail you nothing."

Pheresa's fists clenched harder. "I shall do as the king commands."

"And what is his pleasure?" the princess asked sharply. "What do you expect?"

Pheresa met her mother's brilliant eyes. They were eagle-keen, hostile, and entirely without sympathy. All her life, Pheresa had somehow come up short of her mother's expectations. She was never beautiful enough. She was never clever enough. She was never as popular or as skilled at intrigue as her mother wanted her to be. But now, Pheresa hoped to change her mother's opinion of her. Evasion was pointless. Dianthelle might as well know exactly what was at stake.

"Well?" the princess demanded.

"I expect the throne," Pheresa replied.

Her mother's eyes widened, and for a moment Pheresa had the pleasure of seeing her taken aback.

"What has Verence said?" Dianthelle asked sharply. "What has he promised? Has he named you his heir? When? I know you did not speak to him last night. Was it in the crypt? Who witnessed it?"

Pheresa tried to stem the barrage of questions. "Please. I did not say I'd been chosen. I said that's what I expect."

The tension in the princess's face dissipated. She slumped back against her seat as the carriage rolled forward at last. "You are a paltry creature, to trifle with me in this way."

"I do not trifle with you, Mama," Pheresa said. "I want to be named Heir to the Realm. Who else is better suited than I?"

"Any number of people." The princess uttered a sharp laugh. "How could I have brought such a fool into the world?"

"Thank you, Mama, for your support and encouragement," Pheresa said stiffly. "I am always so gratified to receive your good wishes."

Dianthelle slapped her. "Enough of your impertinence! How dare you speak to me in that mocking way?"

Pheresa's cheek stung fiercely, but she fought back tears of pain. Her anger was a tide of heat that made her want to lash out, to strike back, to jump out of the carriage and never see her mother again.

Curbing her fury with a will of iron, she glared at her mother, who glowered right back.

"You prattle of succession, but on what grounds?" Dianthelle asked. "What substantive promises have you from my brother?"

"None as yet—"

"You have none," the princess broke in harshly, "nor will you get any. If Verence hasn't named you his successor by now, then he never will. You live in a world of dreams and wishes, like a child."

"Why shouldn't I succeed him?" Pheresa demanded. "I am capable. I've been trained in—"

"Trained? Bah! What know you, except needlework and wounded looks? Despite all the advantages I've given you, you've accomplished nothing."

"Nothing?" Pheresa echoed, incensed. "I was betrothed to Gavril. I would have been queen!"

"The past is past. Gavril cannot make you queen now. And Verence will not."

Pheresa smoothed her hand across the cloak she wore. "His majesty is fond of me."

"What has that to do with anything? Do you think you will charm him? Successors are not chosen that way."

"I have been in his majesty's company these many weeks and he—"

"Yes, *many* weeks, and you have achieved nothing. Nor will you. In truth, girl, you lack the spine for the job. You would lose your throne in a month, were you given it. Verence is not such a fool. He knows he must have someone strong and popular, someone ruthless, someone with brains and wit enough to hold Mandria safe from its enemies."

"You have never believed in me," Pheresa said, frowning, feeling the old hurt she'd lived with all her life. "But I can do much more than you think. And although he has not yet chosen me, neither has he chosen anyone else."

"He will soon. He must! The people demand it."

"I am very popular with the people just now."

Some of the color drained from her mother's cheeks, and again Pheresa felt a small sense of satisfaction.

But almost at once, a look of calculation entered Dianthelle's eyes. "You have two courses open to you. Either you must be married, or you must be cloistered. The people would be happy if you were at Batoine."

"No!"

"Put your stubbornness aside and *think*! At this moment, the people still see you as Gavril's bride. They will like you less if you marry another. Seclude yourself and keep your popularity."

"What good is popularity if I do not partake of its benefits?" Pheresa replied. "Why should I shut myself away? I want to *live* now. I want—"

"No one cares very much what you want, Pheresa. It is better that you be put aside."

"Better for whom?" Pheresa asked suspiciously. "What rival of mine do you sponsor? And why can't you support me?"

"You have it in your head that I am your enemy, Pheresa, but I am not. You have no chance of getting the throne. It's time you stepped aside for a better candidate."

"You want the throne for yourself," Pheresa said suddenly.

Dianthelle lifted her chin regally, while a small, sleek smile played across her lips. She stared at Pheresa with all the arrogance and self-assurance she possessed, this beautiful, vibrant woman who was as bold as Pheresa was quiet. "I am the princess royal," Dianthelle said proudly. "To rule after my brother is my right."

"It is against law," Pheresa said.

A frown marred the princess's perfect brow. " 'Tis a stupid law! One that violates all common sense. I am the daughter of a king. Had I been firstborn, I would have inherited my father's throne. Why, then, should I not inherit my brother's?"

"It is against law."

"Oh, the law, the stupid law," the princess said impatiently. "You sit there, bound to it, as though it is holy."

"If we do not keep the law, we fall into chaos," Pheresa replied. "We might as well become barbarians."

"When a law is stupid, it should be set aside. The king can do that, if he but will. I am closest to Verence in blood. I am as strong-willed as he. Nay, stronger, for I lack his sentimentality. I can hold Mandria safe and put an end to this rebellion nonsense in the uplands."

For a moment Pheresa's old sense of inadequacy returned. She'd never been able to surpass her mother in anything. What chance did she stand now, if Dianthelle was to be her competitor?

But then her determination came back. Law, custom, and tradition were all against her mother, who had no right even to make a claim for the successorship. Dianthelle's advice, criticism, and contempt were simply weapons intended to knock Pheresa aside, to make her doubt herself. Sadness touched Pheresa's heart over the fact that she had no mother to love her, but at the same time she felt fierce and strong. She was not what her mother said about her. She valued integrity, duty, and honor, things her mother was inclined to sweep aside. Caprice and impulse were poor traits for a monarch, Pheresa believed, no matter what Dianthelle said.

Meeting her mother's gaze, Pheresa said softly, "The law is against your claim, Mama. You are too ruthless and strong, too intelligent to act so foolishly."

"Don't call *me* a fool, you—"

"I have intelligence that you've never given me credit for. And I—"

"You brought about Gavril's death, you little baggage! Thanks to you, we have no prince. Once that's circulated enough by the gossips, how long do you think your popularity will stand?"

Pheresa didn't flinch. "You forget something, Mama. Gavril didn't make me popular. He would have been a bad king, and most of the nobles know it, if not the whole realm."

"The people do not care about your logic, Pheresa. They—"

"They know I have drunk from the Chalice."

Dianthelle stared very hard at her daughter while her face

grew white and very pinched at the nostrils. She said nothing, and for the princess such silence was rare indeed.

The carriage stopped, and Pheresa glanced out at the main palace courtyard with relief. Now she could retreat to her apartments and lock herself in. She desperately needed to think. If she was to gain allies, she must devise a strategy and act quickly.

A servant came hurrying through the gloom and rain to open the door for them. Gathering the heavy folds of the king's cloak about her, Pheresa started to leave the carriage. Protocol dictated that she should let her mother alight first, but she was in no mood for courtesy.

The princess leaned forward and gripped her arm. "I make a poor enemy, Pheresa," she said in a low, harsh voice. "You cannot vanquish me with mere airs and boasts."

But Pheresa could tell that she was afraid of what Pheresa had said. Dianthelle was afraid of someone who'd both seen and touched the Chalice. They all were, whether they admitted it or not. Pheresa knew that was why the church wanted her cloistered. To keep her isolated lest she somehow produce powers no one could withstand.

There was no victory in being feared. Pheresa felt no satisfaction. "I do not want to be your enemy, Mama. I want your support. You could do much to advance my cause, if you would."

A sneer twisted Dianthelle's lips. "Why should I help you? Never have you done what I wanted you to do."

"You wanted me to prostitute myself to become popular at court," Pheresa said angrily. "You wanted me to lie, cheat, and scheme. You would have made me into your spy, and married me to some drab baron for a reward when I was no longer of use to you."

The princess uttered no denial. Her fingers dug even tighter into Pheresa's arm. "If you'd listened to me, you'd be married now and free to act as you please. You'd have money and jewels of your own, instead of living off the king's charity. You'd have influence and position, all the comforts of life. Instead, you have nothing. Your father has washed his hands of you. You're left without husband, status, or income. You nearly lost your life in that Thodforsaken country, and you caused Gavril's death. Even Nether's barbarian king didn't want you. He refused your hand in marriage, did he not?"

Pheresa gasped. "How did you—" Too late, she cut off her sentence.

Dianthelle smiled in triumph. "Ah, thank you for confirming that rumor. Well, my dear, I've always considered you a fool. For you see, were I on the throne, your succession as *my* heir would be certain. But as usual you have not thought things through. You're as selfish as you are stupid, and when Theloi succeeds in getting you cloistered, despite your little maneuvers today, I shall rejoice."

Before Pheresa could reply, her mother shoved her from the carriage. Catching her balance clumsily with the servant's startled assistance, Pheresa glanced back at the princess, but there was no point in saying anything else. The battle lines were drawn clearly now. Her mother, incredibly, was jealous of her. Bitter resentment was etched in every line of Dianthelle's face as she yanked the door shut in Pheresa's face. "Drive on!" she commanded, and the carriage rolled away.

Pheresa hurried inside through the pouring rain. She had no doubt that her mother would cause her as much trouble as possible.

Both ruthless and without scruple, Dianthelle was capable of doing anything, even falsifying an order from the king that would send Pheresa off to Batoine in the dead of night. Swallowing hard, Pheresa told herself that she must take every precaution to guard herself, until she learned whom in the palace she could trust.

Darkness . . . cold, icy darkness. Pheresa awakened with a start and sat up. Her heart pounded, and she held her breath to listen hard. No sound penetrated the quiet stillness of her bedchamber. Nothing stirred. The hangings had been closed by her servants when she went to bed, but now they hung open. She could see embers glowing faint red among the ashes of a dead fire. The room had grown chilly, nay, icy cold, as though winter had returned.

Pheresa felt as though an invisible hand clamped her in place, keeping her from moving. She could not tell what had awakened her. Surely no sound, no movement had disturbed her slumbers, yet what instinct stirred within her, urging her to get up, to get away?

She shivered, and that involuntary movement broke whatever spell held her frozen. Nothing appeared to be out of place, except that her bed-curtains were open. She knew they'd been shut when she went to sleep.

Who, then, had come in here and opened them? Why?

A tremor of something she could not name quivered across her heart. Was it Sir Brillon, come here by stealth to abduct her?

If so, where was he? At what moment would he come looming back?

A sound came from the antechamber outside her door . . . a soft, dragging step as though something shuffled her way. "Pheresa," a voice whispered. It was a ruined husk of a voice, foreign yet familiar. "Pheresa," it called again.

The sound of her name terrified her. She scooted to the edge of her bed, her heart pounding harder. "Gavril," she breathed aloud.

The dragging footsteps abruptly halted. Pheresa could not breathe. Her every sense strained to hear. She gripped the bed-clothes so hard her hands trembled. Thod's mercy, she had known it was a mistake to bring his tainted corpse home to Savroix. He had risen, and now Nonkind walked in lower Mandria.

"Pheresa . . . come forth to me."

A little sob escaped her. She whirled around and reached frantically beneath her pillow. What she was searching for had vanished, however. Fear swept her like fire. Flinging her pillows aside, she hunted her dagger and salt purse with increasing desperation. What had become of them? She never slept without both items close by. Who had taken them? *Who?*

Perhaps the same hand that had opened her bed-curtains.

The thought crossed her mind like something cold and stopped her frantic search.

Across the chamber, her door creaked open. Pheresa jerked her gaze in that direction, yet she could not bear to look at Gavril's ruined face. She shut her eyes, her breath rapid and ragged now.

"Get away from me," she tried to say, but her words tangled in her throat. She lacked sufficient breath to speak them aloud.

"Pheresa . . . long have I searched for you. Come forth to my hand."

It was a horrible, hollow voice. The words echoed in her mind. Worst of all, she wanted to obey, wanted to climb from her bed and go running to the creature that summoned her.

Against her will, she opened her eyes. She had to see him, had to know despite her fear.

Shadows concealed his ruined visage. It was as though evil itself stood in her room. The air grew even colder, making her shiver uncontrollably. He reached out his hand and beckoned to her.

She swayed forward obediently before she realized what she was doing.

"Pheresa . . ."

"Get away from me!" she shouted suddenly. Fear swept through her, giving her strength enough to fight off the spell being woven around her. "In the name of Thod, get away!"

The creature shuffled forward across the thick carpet. Pheresa rolled off her bed on the opposite side and landed awkwardly in a little huddle on the floor. As she got to her hands and knees, she found a small lumpy object in the darkness next to her. It was her salt purse, fallen onto the floor sometime in the night. She clutched it with a little gasp of relief, then felt about quickly and found her dagger.

As she swiftly unsheathed it, a thud shook the frame of her bed.

Startled, she jumped to her feet, and in the gloom saw the creature shoving against her bed in an effort to pin her to the wall.

Terrible memories flashed through her mind, memories of that day in Grov when Gavril had been consumed by the soul-taker, and afterwards . . . and afterwards he had been a mind-less, soulless thing, a puppet commanded by a will other than his own.

He came for her now in the same mindless way.

The bed was shoved again, harder, and she scrambled out into the open. She tried to scream for her servants and the guards, but once more her throat would not obey her. Trembling all over, she saw her assailant turn and come at her again.

Digging into her salt purse, she darted at him and threw the salt.

Fire flashed in all directions, making her stagger back. Her eyes were streaming with tears and half-dazzled by bursts of colors, but in that momentary illumination she saw her attacker's face clearly.

It was not Gavril.

Nor Sir Brillon.

She had never seen this man before. Dark-haired, with pallid, unhealthy skin, he cringed back from the salt she'd thrown, his mouth open in a silent scream. He fell against a table and passed through it as though he had no substance. Then he was gone, and the room lay shrouded in gloom and shadow once more.

The icy cold temperature vanished, leaving the room as warm and comfortable as it had been when she retired. Only the scent of something burned lingered in the air.

Pheresa stood there, unable to believe what she'd seen, unsure if any of it had even happened. *Surely I am dreaming another nightmare,* she thought.

Yet never had her dreams been like this.

Frowning, she hefted the salt purse in her hand. It felt real enough, as did her dagger. When she walked forward she bumped into a stool. That felt real. She pinched herself, and pain flared in her wrist.

It *had* been real. It *had* happened.

Her thoughts were spinning, and suddenly her knees gave

way. She clutched the bed for support and dragged herself back beneath the covers. There was no need now to call her servants. She wanted no questions, no lamps lit, no fuss or bother. It was pointless now to reprimand her attendants for having failed to protect her. What could anyone do against an invader of the second world? And if she tried to describe what had just happened, who would believe her?

The folk of lower Mandria did not believe in magic. They lived in complete assurance that nothing Nonkind could reach them south of the Charva. So it had always been; so it must be now.

But Pheresa no longer had such convictions. Not since her days as a hostage in Grov had she felt entirely safe. The fact that salt had driven this mysterious visitor away only confirmed its evil.

Shivering, she pulled her blankets close and clutched her salt purse tightly. After a long, long while she forced herself to lie down, but she could not close her eyes or relax. The intruder might come back, seizing her the moment her guard went down. He had nearly mesmerized her tonight, and had she not found her salt purse . . .

With a shudder, she closed off that thought hurriedly.

What was he? she wondered. Ghost, spirit, evil wraith from the second world? He had come to her, summoned her by name. Why?

She shivered again, weeping in fear. What did he want? Why had he sought her here tonight?

And, most frightening of all, *when* would he return?

Chapter Five

Icy cold water ran beneath Talmor, filling his mouth and nostrils. He jerked up his head, snorting and coughing, dragged himself forward a few inches, then sank down. More than that required too much effort. He wanted only to sleep. Water surged beneath him again, hoisting him a little higher on the beach. Revived a second time, he had better luck this time in keeping his face out of the water.

He did not know where he was, but as he rolled onto his back and gazed at the sky, he expected to see daylight. Instead, the stars were twinkling in an indigo sky. The surf roared in his ears. The usual scents of seaweed and fish filled the air, but when the wind shifted he smelled smoke and the stink of burning hair.

The sea ran under him again, unpleasantly cold, and this time he thought, *tide*. Rolling onto his side, he sat up with a groan. Every inch of his body hurt, his head and side most of all.

Sitting up seemed to make the pounding in his skull more violent. He moaned, lifting his hands to his face, and realized vaguely that he must have been moaning for quite some time. His throat was terribly dry, and there was sand in his mouth. He spat out the unpleasant, briny stuff and stared at the bay in muzzy confusion. There was something he needed to remember, but memory and coherent thought swirled dizzily through his mind. Just as things started to make sense, they were gone, too elusive to grasp. He did not try very hard.

A big wave splashed over him, knocking him flat. He emerged, spluttering, wobbled onto his hands and knees, and crawled farther up the beach to get above the incoming tide. The effort made him weak and breathless. His head was splitting, but he kept going doggedly until he reached dry sand.

He bumped against a shape, half-seen in the gathering darkness, and felt of it without much curiosity. Damp clothing, hauberk, bearded face.

With a blink, Talmor abruptly withdrew his hand from the dead man. He frowned, looking around, and this time noticed more motionless lumps lying scattered across the sand. Out in the bay, a fishing boat was sinking slowly, stern tipped up like a duck diving for fish. The other vessels were gone, and a great deal of flotsam littered the water. He frowned at that, certain there was something important he should remember, but his head ached too much.

The fitful wind brought back the smell of smoke and fire to his nostrils. Only then did he notice the village, burning merrily. A handful of people were silhouetted against the orange flames as they passed buckets from hand to hand and threw water on the flames.

Talmor stared, worried by the sight but not sure why. Surely the huts should not be burning like that. Even the wharf was on fire. There should have been fish racks on it, and nets spread out for mending. Instead, he saw only destruction and bodies. In the distance, someone wailed in grief.

Raiders, Talmor thought with a jab of anger. The memory crystallized in his head, and he clung to it, trying hard to remember more. They'd come out of the storm and attacked the boats. They'd . . .

A terrible, clammy sensation swept him. He leaned over

and was violently sick on the sand. The pounding in his head became agony. He faded gratefully back into the darkness.

"Sir Talmor." A hand gripped his surcoat and shook him roughly. "Sir Talmor!"

Angered at being roused back into the pain, Talmor groaned and made a feeble swipe at the hand. Instead, his fingers were gripped hard, and the voice rose in volume.

"Oh, Sir Talmor! I've found ye alive, bless ye."

Talmor tried to tell the voice to go away, but although his lips moved, he did not think he actually said anything.

"Over here!" the voice shouted. "I've found Sir Talmor alive!"

Talmor winced at the noise and tried to crawl back into the darkness, but now there came other hands, other voices. He felt himself lifted, and something hit his hurt shoulder, making him yelp. There was the sensation of being carried, along with the worrisome potential of being dropped.

Wanting to be left alone, he struggled a little, but found himself held helpless.

Raiders, he thought again, with a stab of fear, and reached for his dagger.

His fingers found no weapon. A hand squeezed them, and a deep, familiar voice spoke in his ear: "Easy now, Talmor lad. We've got ye. Just bide quiet now. All's well."

Believing the assurances, he relaxed back into unconsciousness, only to awaken later with a start. This time, he found himself indoors. The air was stuffy and hot. A fire blazed on the hearth, casting ruddy light that hurt Talmor's eyes. He was lying on a cot, hard and most uncomfortable, with a blanket thrown over him. Beneath it, he'd been stripped down to his leggings. His ribs were bound so tightly he could barely breathe. Another bandage swathed his head, hot and surprisingly heavy. He lifted his right hand to gingerly feel the wound through the layers of cloth, and someone pulled his hand away.

"Leave it be, Sir Talmor."

Talmor found himself peering up into the middle-aged face of Pears, his squire. The grooves on either side of Pears's wide mouth were cut deep tonight. Ruddy, weathered, and nut tough, Pears looked worried, but he managed a small, not very convincing, smile for Talmor's sake.

"Found ye, didn't I?" he whispered. His voice was rough with emotion. "Guess they left ye for dead, aye, lying there with that great gout of blood on yer noggin. Otherwise, they'd have dragged ye off with the others, aye, and made ye a slave, damn 'em."

Someone else in the room uttered a moan. Talmor tried to lift his head and look about, but with gentle firmness Pears held him down.

"Nay, sir. 'Tis only another wounded man. Nothing to fret about."

Bits of memory started to come back to Talmor. There'd been the ceremony preparations, the storm, the sudden arrival of the raiders, the attack. "Seawall," he mumbled. His mouth ached with dryness. His tongue felt like a piece of wood. "Must defend—"

"Didn't," Pears said tersely. "Couldn't. Here, have a sup of this."

A cup was pressed to Talmor's lips, and his head gently lifted so that he could gulp down a few swallows. The water was fresh and cool, and eased him greatly.

Sighing, he let Pears lower him and adjust the blanket, fussing quietly with gnarled hands that trembled. It was unlike Pears to be so shaken. Talmor reached out and weakly held on to his squire's hand.

"We fell back to the hold, I remember. But after that . . . nothing. Something hit me, I think. I heard—"

"Aye, you were hit with a piece of the wall, sir," Pears said grimly.

That made no sense. Fearing his wits were starting to wander, Talmor frowned.

"Them flaming arrows set the scaffolding on fire, over where the new part of the hold was being added on," Pears said. "Aye, and of course some fool had stored the saltpeter there. It went off like the world coming to an end. Killed ever so many knights, and Lord Pace, too, bless 'im. Ye were nearly sent to Beyond yerself."

There were too many pieces of news to hang on to at once. Talmor's frown deepened as he struggled to grasp it all. "Lord Pace."

"Aye. A grim day this is, sir. A very grim day."

"Killed by raiders—"

"Nay. Killed by his own demon powder. He would have it. None could tell him different, not with him so sure he knew best. Ye know all too well how he was, sir. Never listened to good advice, did he?"

Talmor felt suddenly too weary to speak. His eyes drifted closed and in that soft place of half awareness before sleep, he heard another come near his cot.

"Has he roused?" a quiet voice asked.

"Aye, sir," Pears replied. "This time he seemed to know who he was."

"Then his wits are coming back. What does he remember?"

"Not much."

"Just as well. Have you potioned him?"

"He'll sleep natural now, sir. No need to pour that nasty stuff down his gullet."

"The pain will rouse him. Best to keep him dosed and quiet."

"Nay, sir. He heals quick, Sir Talmor does. The less fussing with salves and potions, the better he mends. I know what to do for him, sir, bless 'im. Indeed I do."

"Well, see that he rests. We need him on his feet as quickly as possible."

"Aye, sir. I know."

Talmor opened his eyes and saw the man's back walking away from him into the shadows. "What—"

Pears's hand gripped his good shoulder. "Hush, sir," he breathed. "He's going out. There, he's gone. No need for you to talk to him now, for all his high-and-mighty impatience."

"Inthiere," Talmor said weakly.

"Aye, Sir Inthiere, damn 'im."

The fortress commander was unpopular among the men, and Talmor didn't bother to reprimand Pears. Recalling Inthiere's drunkenness this morning and how his sentries had first failed to keep watch, then botched the warning signal, Talmor felt like damning the man himself. But not now. He felt terribly tired and shaken.

It was the latter that worried him. Pulling his attention away from Inthiere's faults, for all the sorting out of blame and fault could wait until the morrow, Talmor felt sweat trickling down his throat and chest. "Must it be so hot in here?" he asked.

Pears stared at him without expression. "Must it?" he echoed, but with a careful voice.

Shame burned through Talmor then, with humiliation dragging in its wake. He thought he'd managed to leave the past behind, yet this morning he'd had that premonition of trouble before Lutel sighted the boats. And now . . . it seemed some problems could never be solved, or escaped.

Sighing, he clenched his fist and felt the heat coiling there inside his palm. He could feel the violence building, both anger and shock entwined and ready to strike out. The air felt hotter than ever, as though the room were on fire. It was oppressive heat, the kind that was painful to breathe. But he knew it could get much, much hotter.

When he glanced up at Pears, he saw a glimmer of fear in the older man's eyes, fear swiftly hidden. But he could read the thoughts inside Pears's mind as plainly as though they were written on a scroll. If he chose, he could read deeper . . . every wish, every fear, every emotion. Swiftly Talmor averted his eyes. It was wrong to soulgaze, *wrong*. He had sworn he would never do it again.

A shudder passed through him. Gritting his teeth against the forces he could no longer reliably control, he said, "Quick! Fetch some water."

Pears hurried to bring a wooden pail of water. He lifted the drinking dipper, but Talmor glared at him. "Get back!"

Dropping the dipper, Pears stumbled back just as Talmor felt the violence inside him escape. It spewed from him, a blazing heat that shot down his arm with such power he cried out. A ball of fire burst into flames in mid-air, the force of it pulling him nearly upright. With all the willpower he possessed, he threw the flames at the water pail.

The fireball extinguished with a sharp crack of sound, and the bucket rocked back and forth. Steam rose from the wood. As Pears crept forward cautiously to peer into the pail, Talmor already knew it was bone dry.

The air in the sick room cooled at once. The violence in him was gone, spent. Exhausted, he dropped down on his cot and flung his arm across his stinging eyes. He hadn't lost control like that in years, not since the day he lost his temper with his half brother Etyne and burned him. Although Etyne recovered from his injuries, Talmor's father had beaten him, starved him for a week, then told him he must leave forever. Ten years had passed since then, and although he kept the hurt buried deep, it remained sharp. Talmor sighed. Ten years of ironclad control, with never a slip while he followed Sanude's training faithfully, yet tonight had proven his hard work for naught. He might as well still be that awkward boy of sixteen—angry, tormented, and frustrated in trying to find a way to belong and earn his father's love. He did not want to imagine what either Sanude or his father would say were they here now.

A faint, rational voice in the back of his aching head reminded him that he hadn't forgotten his training. He'd been too weak to hold his curse in check. That was all.

Only it wasn't all. It would never be that simple.

All his confidence, his self-assurance that he would never again unleash fire or utilize his other powers vanished before this brutal reality. Until tonight, he'd believed that he'd conquered himself. He thought he'd driven his abilities so far away that they were no longer a part of him, and he was at last a true Mandrian.

So he'd thought.

Bitterness welled up inside Talmor's throat, and he swallowed hard.

It seemed now he'd only been deluding himself. It was a

miracle that Inthiere hadn't been standing in the room to witness Talmor's darkest secret. Sir Inthiere was no friend, and
would welcome a reason to turn against Talmor.

Had any of the wounded men seen what just happened?
Talmor felt the old fear creep up around him. He'd heard no
one in the room cry out, yet he lacked the courage to lift his
head and see if any of the others were staring at him.

Ruin took only a moment, he told himself. No matter how
carefully a life was built, day by day, little achievement after
little achievement, it could all topple in a heartbeat. The first
sixteen years of his life had been lived in the agony of mis-
steps, disasters, and secrets. Then had come exile, and the
chance to start over. For ten years he'd lived without persecution, achieving his goals little by little, and now . . . and
now . . .

"I've brought more water," Pears said quietly.

Startled, Talmor rubbed his wrist swiftly across his burning eyes. He had keen ears, but Pears had come back so
silently Talmor hadn't heard him at all.

He squinted up at his squire, and saw the apprehension in
Pears's eyes behind his stalwart expression. Fresh humiliation
plummeted through Talmor. Here at Durl, Pears alone knew
the truth. Pears, who had served him all his life. *"When a servant fears you, a poor master you are."* So had Talmor's father always said. Right now, Talmor would give anything to
wipe that look from Pears's face.

"I don't need it now," Talmor said, referring to the pail of
fresh water Pears was holding. "Let it be."

Some of the tightness around Pears's eyes relaxed.
"Thought ye might be wanting a drink."

Talmor let Pears bring the cup to his lips. He drank, barely
tasting the water this time. It was a peace offering between
them. No more could be said.

But as Pears gently eased him down, urging him to lie
quiet and go to sleep, Talmor could read his squire's feelings.
It had happened tonight. It could happen again . . . and would.
They both knew that now.

In the morning, Talmor arose stiffly, every joint creaking

and sore. His headache had dulled to a faint throb; his ribs made him move stiffly, but he felt no more discomfort than that.

"Aye, healing right up, just like always," Pears said in satisfaction. But he avoided Talmor's gaze as he said it, and went to fetch warm shaving water and breakfast.

Talmor understood the deep-seated Mandrian fear of being enspelled or soulgazed. He pretended he did not notice and shifted his thoughts to more important problems.

Yesterday's raid had been a disaster. The village was burned to the ground, the fishing fleet destroyed. Nearly all the women and children had been taken as captives, and would never be seen again. Much of the hold had been looted and burned. Lord Pace, his protector, Sir Albie, and three-fourths of the hold's fighting men lay dead. A handful of knights, some visibly wounded, had been taken captive. The few men who remained included Talmor, Sir Inthiere, Sir Banjermal, and Sir Pentigne, plus a scattering of sentry-rank knights. Two of the wounded had died before dawn, and another, needing his mangled leg taken off, would probably die within hours. The survivors had retreated up into the small fortress, locking themselves in with limited supplies of food and water, for fear that the raiders would return.

As soon as he'd eaten, and Pears had eased him into a loose-fitting tunic, Talmor sent for Sir Inthiere.

The reply came back swiftly. Sir Inthiere was engaged with important matters, and Sir Talmor was to report to *him.*

"Now, now," Pears said soothingly. "What does it matter if he's taken charge? Aye, and him the only officer fit and on his feet."

Talmor stood up on rubbery legs. "He's no business taking command."

"Yer not fit to go out. Better to rest and face him later."

There was wisdom in what Pears said, but Talmor was filled with a strong sense of urgency. The raiders would probably return, lured back to the hold to loot more of it. Were there no danger, Talmor would have played the game of outwaiting Inthiere, letting the fortress commander run into a situation he could not handle and then be forced to seek Talmor's aid, but there was no time for such foolishness.

He went to Inthiere, with gritted teeth and a strong sense of exasperation.

The fortress commander stank like an alehouse. Despite that and his bloodshot eyes, he acted reasonably sober on this sad morn. Talmor found him standing on the ramparts, squinting seaward. The sea looked as gray as the sky, and was running rough.

"More storms coming in," Sir Inthiere said without greeting. "No raiders on today's sea, Thod be praised."

"They rode yesterday's storm in," Talmor said. "We'd best secure what remains of the hold."

"We'll not go back down there!" Inthiere said fiercely. "'Tis unsafe, indefensible. We'll stay up here in the fortress and count our blessings that we're still alive."

"What about food and water? Have we enough for—"

Inthiere turned a bloodshot eye on him, and said, "I've taken command, sir. I'm the only ranking officer who's fit for duty. Leave the details to me."

Anger swept Talmor. "Had you been fit for duty yesterday, had you even done your duty, the warning would have been sounded in time."

Inthiere stiffened. "You blame me for this? How dare—"

"I dare much. As Lord Pace's adjutant, I rank above you. Command is mine, until the king sends us his orders."

"You're nothing but a fetch-and-carry boy!" Inthiere said. "Had you held the seawall as his lordship bade you, none of this would have happened."

"I saw the boats coming in," Talmor said between his teeth. "I gave you the warning signal. Had you been watching, had your sentries bothered to look seaward at all, instead of sharing ale with you—"

"Ah, and now you accuse me of being drunk, of—"

"I do," Talmor snapped. "You're drunk now. Or close to it."

"That's a lie!"

"How many were killed because you and your men did not

keep watch? How many taken captive? The seawall could not be defended, but there was time to get everyone into the fortress had you sounded the warning when you should have."

"There isn't room enough up here for everyone from both hold and village."

Talmor stiffened, and silence fell over them both. It was a damning admission, and the fortress commander slowly turned red.

Talmor's head began to throb. He was furious, but beneath that emotion ran sorrow. "And so," he said very quietly, "you thought you'd make room by letting the villagers perish. The village is always expendable first, before the hold."

Inthiere grew redder than ever. His eyes dropped from Talmor's steady gaze. "'Twas his lordship's standing order. You *know* that."

"I know that we could have crowded in here and been spared for the few hours necessary. This was needless carnage, sir, and well you know it!"

"Easy for you to throw accusations," Inthiere said viciously. "Where were you when such decisions had to be made? Nowhere. Why did you and your men not hold the road between hold and fortress? You could have sent some of your knights this way, had you bothered to think of us. The brutes came howling halfway up to our gates before they turned back."

Talmor stared at him, appalled at the man's stupidity. "You were safe here. What need was there to waste men defending your gates?"

"Oh, yes, a waste. And I with the responsibility for the safety of Lady Alda and her daughters. Don't look at me with that superior air, sir! I know what you think of me, you the baseborn son of some southern lord, and no better than you should be. I have no highborn blood, but I'm an honest man. I've worked hard to get where I am, and you will not accuse or insult me this way. I did my duty, and you failed in yours. That's all there is to it."

Rigid, Talmor took a step back. "That is your report. Very well."

He turned to go, but Inthiere gripped him by the arm and spun him around so roughly he nearly cried out with pain. "You are not dismissed, sir."

"I do not acknowledge your right to command," Talmor said sharply.

"You will do so!" Inthiere shouted. "I am the ranking officer—"

"You are a drunkard and a fool. You have no business taking charge."

"I order you to retract that! On pain of—"

Talmor stepped up into the man's face and gripped his surcoat at the throat. "Do you challenge me, Sir Inthiere?" he asked in a voice like silk.

The fortress commander drew in his breath sharply. He tried to pull back, but Talmor held him fast.

Inthiere was blinking rapidly, and the choleric color drained from his face. "I—I will not fight a wounded man."

Disgust made Talmor shove him away. "Oh, easily said, sir. And how convenient for you."

"Take care, Sir Talmor. You were free enough to sneer and criticize when you were Lord Pace's favorite officer. You have no such position now. While you've been lying abed, I've had the thankless job of trying to cope with everything. You've no idea—"

"I have a very precise idea," Talmor broke in coldly. "Until the king sends his orders and a new chevard, we had better—"

"A new chevard!" Inthiere said. "But nay! Lady Alda and I are in league—I—I mean to say, we are determined to keep Durl Hold as it is."

"You mean ruined? Destroyed?"

"Don't be a fool. I am to command, and she will hold the title. All can go on as it has. What need has the king to know?"

Stunned, Talmor stared at him. He understood perfectly now. Small wonder Inthiere was feeling so sure of himself.

"Well, sir?" the commander said. "I ask you, what need has the king to know? He never comes to us up here. Why should Durl revert to the crown, just because Lord Pace left no male heir?"

Daughters could inherit some titles, Talmor knew, but females could not be chevards. Responsible for maintaining key defense points along the edges of the realm, chevards had to be warriors first and foremost. They worked hard, faced dangers, and did not lounge about at court in the king's exalted company. And when a chevard died without male issue, his lands were forfeited to the crown, to be redistributed and awarded elsewhere according to the king's pleasure. Lady Alda was committing treason by concealing her husband's death from his majesty just to preserve her title and home. She could not succeed with this mad plan, for the king had agents everywhere and would soon discover the plot.

Talmor frowned. Either the woman was as stupid as Sir Inthiere, he thought, or she had some other scheme in mind. Well, it was not a matter for him to untangle. He knew he must take himself far from here at once and avoid being implicated in such wrongdoing. He hated going, but to remain would be the greatest folly.

"I know you intended to so ingratiate yourself with Lord Pace that he would someday adopt you," Inthiere said now, "but your scheme has come to naught. I command here now, not you, and best you accept it. If you feel up to resuming your duties, go down to the hold and take charge of the detail gathering food and supplies."

Talmor let nothing cross his face. Coldly, he looked at Inthiere, and revealed his contempt only in his tone of voice. "His lordship is not yet buried and already you warm his bed, and his lady. Congratulations, sir. It seems you can strike at an opportunity when you see it."

Red surged anew into Inthiere's face. He drew back his hand to hit Talmor, but Talmor gripped his wrist hard and held him so that he could not deliver the blow.

Inthiere strained to break free, but although the effort made his head throb with pain, Talmor held him fast with superior strength.

"You go too far, sir!" Inthiere said furiously. "Damne, but you go too far!"

"My liege vows were broken when Lord Pace died," Talmor told him. "You may inform Lady Alda of my immediate departure from Durl Hold."

Releasing Inthiere so suddenly the knight staggered back to keep his balance, Talmor turned on his heel and started down the steps leading from the ramparts. Inthiere hurried after him.

"Wait! Lord Pace's flag has not been struck. You must keep your oath and remain in his service."

"I swore allegiance to him, not his banner."

Inthiere glared at him. "Officially, Lord Pace lies wounded. Durl has need of every knight. Continue to serve, and you'll be amply rewarded."

"What—"

"Desert," Inthiere said fiercely, "and I'll see that you become known throughout the realm for breaking your lance."

Fury boiled through Talmor. Was that all the threat Inthiere could muster? Yet as he glared at the commander, Talmor saw villainy in Inthiere's heart. The man was as vicious as he was weak of character, and he hated Talmor with a sick, jealous intensity.

Talmor frowned, knowing he could break the commander in twain if they fought, yet just as he was about to issue challenge, a wave of clammy weakness passed through him. His knees nearly buckled, and little black spots danced before his eyes. Fighting off the swoon, Talmor realized he must take care. He was in no condition actually to fight Inthiere, and he'd said more than was prudent in the circumstances.

"I—I see," he said.

Surprise widened Inthiere's bloodshot eyes as though he'd not expected so mild an answer. He puffed out his chest. "Then you'll stay on, and there'll be no more of your nonsense?"

"I'll cause you no further trouble this day," Talmor replied through gritted teeth.

"You'll submit to my command? Follow my orders without insubordination?"

Talmor bowed his head.

Smiling, Inthiere bounced on his toes. "Well, well. Your temper has cooled, I see."

"You mentioned a reward."

"Aye, we'll talk of that tonight at supper. You realize that you're too quick to find fault. Too hasty to judge. I must command respect if discipline is to be maintained."

"I understand," Talmor said.

Inthiere's eyes narrowed suspiciously. "Then you'll retract your insulting remarks?"

"Of course."

"Good. You look very pale, sir. Perhaps you'd better return to your sick room."

"Thank you, but I'll do better to work."

Inthiere gestured arrogantly. "Then you have your orders. Dismissed."

Talmor went down the steps as rapidly as his wobbly knees would carry him. It was all he could do to keep his hand off his dagger hilt, all he could do to hold his tongue.

His heart was thudding, and he felt hot with fever, but his mind was cold and clear. He knew exactly what he had to do.

At the bottom of the steps, he crossed the cramped courtyard for the stables. Just before he entered, he paused at the threshold and leaned a moment against the wall.

"Sir Talmor?"

It was Lutel, the village boy who yesterday had been the first to see the incoming raiders. Smeared with soot and grime, his bony wrists dangling from his sleeves, the boy looked dazed with grief and misery.

Pity touched Talmor's heart. "Yes, boy?"

"I'm glad ye be hale an' whole." Lutel's gaze darted to the bandages around Talmor's head. "Most everybody's been killed, seems like."

"I did warn your mother, as I promised," Talmor said gently.

Tears welled up in Lutel's eyes. "Aw, that be good of ye, sir. Ye saw her? And my sisters?"

"Aye."

"They ain't been killed, sir. I looked an' looked through all the dead, an' they ain't there." He swallowed hard. "I reckon they be slaves now, taken away—"

Talmor reached out and gripped his bony shoulder. "I'm sorry."

Lutel nodded with a great sniff and wiped his face with his sleeve. "Thanks for bein' kind, sir. If that's all, I got to go muck out the stalls."

Talmor frowned. "I want you to take a message to my squire."

"Aye, sir."

"Can I trust you?"

Lutel's eyes grew round and fierce. "Ye know it!"

"Will you enter my service and—"

"Aye! That I will! Oh, sir!"

"Hush," Talmor said, glancing around to make sure no one noticed his excitement. "Your family is gone, but perhaps you wish to remain here. They might return."

"How?" Lutel asked bleakly. "They got no way to do it. Old Othen says they don't never come back. He was a wee tot when the last raid came, an' he says folk talked of it for years, afeared to stray far from sight of the hold. He said he lost a sister an' a brother both to 'em, sir. An' years later he heard his brother was seen fightin' as one of the skull folk. Turned, he'd been. Turned to their evil." Lutel sniffed. "Elsa and De-nine be too little to remember us long. They won't come back. And my mother . . ." He buried his face in the crook of his arm, trembling.

"I need you," Talmor said quietly.

Lutel looked up, tears streaking his grimy face. "Then I be yers to the rattle, sir."

The boy's swift loyalty warmed Talmor's heart, but he kept his face without expression. This first service would test the boy's ability to do as he was told, and show if he could keep his wits about him.

"Tell my squire that he is to gather my possessions and stash them on the beach by midday. Tell him to make sure he's unnoticed."

"Be ye—I mean—be we leavin', sir?"

"Aye. And quietly, mind. Say nothing to anyone but Pears. Is that clear?"

Lutel nodded.

"Saddle Canae for me. I've been assigned to duty today at the hold."

"But, sir, yer not well enough. Ye—"

A look from Talmor silenced the boy.

Gulping, he made an awkward little bow. "Aye, sir. Yer horse. Anything else?"

"Get on with your work until midday. Then join Pears in the dunes to the southeast. Make sure you're not seen."

"But—aye, sir. I'll do it sharp, just as ye say."

Talmor meant to say more, but Sir Banjermel hailed him.

Giving the man a smiling nod in answer, Talmor glanced at Lutel. "See to it, then."

"Aye, sir." Lutel ran to do as he'd been told.

Sir Banjermel frowned after him. "That boy's a fool, always in the way."

"He lost his family in the raid."

Banjermel grunted without interest. "Thought we'd lost you."

"I'm hard to kill," Talmor said grimly.

Laughing, Banjermel clapped him on the shoulder. "So you are! Well, it's a mess, right enough, but I hear Lord Pace will recover. Word went round last night that he was done for, but today all's well."

"Is it? The hold's in ruins, and most of the knights are dead."

"Well, aye. There's that, of course. Damned savages caught us unawares, but they won't do that again."

Talmor said nothing.

"And the treasury chamber's intact. They didn't get his lordship's gold. More knights can be hired. In the meantime, well, we've had some battle action, eh? Good for the sword arm, and next time we'll have the devils where we want them."

Talmor started to warn Banjermel that if they stayed here under these conditions, they could be charged with treason, too, but with a laugh Banjermel strolled on. The gold, Talmor thought with a little nod to himself. 'Twas that Lady Alda was after, with Inthiere her willing accomplice. Well, they were fools to steal from the king. And they would not even give Lord Pace the respect of a decent burial or the rites to ease his soul's passage to Beyond. Disgust swept Talmor, but he reminded himself to hide what he felt today, or he might find himself under close watch, confined to quarters. As it stood now, with order slack and the men scattered, he had the perfect opportunity to slip away unchallenged.

After all, Talmor thought bitterly, *I was the perfect officer, always reliable and efficient.* Clearly it hadn't crossed Inthiere's mind that Talmor might fail, this time, to follow orders.

A small shiver passed through Talmor, but he wiped his brow of its fever sweat and when Canae, saddled and restless, was brought to him, he mounted up, swayed a moment in the saddle, and rode slowly out of the fortress that he would never see again.

Chapter Six

Pheresa, attired in a new gown of mushroom-hued silk, its long sleeves quilted with pearl studs in the newest fashion, walked rapidly down a long gallery of the palace past gossiping merchants and ambassadors waiting for audiences with various ministers. Her hair was beautifully dressed and plaited in coils about her shapely head. Anxiety had given her face a becoming flush. She walked with only two female attendants in her wake, and all eyes turned to look at her as she passed, for she quite outshone everyone else in the gallery and was completely out of place there.

Merchants Walk, it was called, this endless gallery with its paintings of ships, foreign dignitaries, and exotic cities far from Mandria. A dozen different languages at least were being spoken around her. Many conversations died as she made her way along the central ribbon of carpet, only to start up again with laughter and renewed animation as she passed.

Her face was burning, but she kept her chin high and her shoulders erect. She did her best to look calm and refused to permit herself the luxury of gawking around her.

Once, she would have died rather than come to this part of the palace where foreign visitors and dignitaries were housed. The courtiers in favor with the king never ventured to this wing. It was considered quite low, and rumors and stories circulated about the goings-on that took place for evening entertainment.

Well, Pheresa was no longer as gullible as she'd once been. Nor as timid. She doubted that foreign banquets and dancing were more lascivious than the orgies that went on in other parts of the palace. Indeed, although she was stared at, no one she'd encountered here was rude or discourteous to her. Several men bowed to her most gravely, and she rewarded these courtesies with a slight inclination of her head as she walked by.

She'd come here because the stakes were too high now to be weak or fearful. Although she had foiled the church's efforts to remove her from court, she knew her success was only temporary. Sir Brillon still dogged her unless she managed, as she had today, to elude him. Worse, her mother was circulating rumors against her. Pheresa needed help, and she'd come here to get it.

At the end of Merchants Walk, she reached a set of tall doors, heavily carved and imposing behind armed guards. An official hovered there, and he moved quickly to intercept her.

"May I be of service, my lady?" he asked in a thin, rather nervous voice. "Is your ladyship lost or—"

"I am not lost," she said in a quiet, clear voice, permitting none of her inner doubt and turmoil to enter her tone. "I have come to see Lord Meaclan. Will you announce me? I am Lady Pheresa du Lindier."

The official's eyes grew very round. He bowed with a jerk and seemed taken aback at her request. "My lady, I—I'm not sure—"

"Is Lord Meaclan here?"

"Yes, my lady."

"I am informed that he usually meets with the other ministers in council chambers on this day of the week, and that the meeting is usually finished by this hour. Am I correct?"

"Yes, my lady."

"Is Lord Meaclan finished today with his meeting?"

"Yes, my lady, but he has other appointments awaiting his—"

"I, too, have an appointment," she said boldly, and held the man's flustered gaze until he looked away. "Will you conduct me to his lordship?"

"Indeed, yes, my lady. But—but would it not be more seemly were his lordship to come to you? I believe—"

"I am not interested in what you believe," she said coldly. "Please do as I have requested."

Frowning, the official wrung his hands but obeyed, ushering her through the doors despite a protest from a foreign dignitary who evidently had been waiting these past two hours for some of Lord Meaclan's time. Pheresa regretted the necessity for rudeness in cutting past him, but her business could not wait. Pheresa had just learned that her mother had written to Verence, requesting permission to take Pheresa home.

Home, Pheresa thought with scorn. *Yes, and then Mama will hand me to the church for cloistering.*

Her home was Savroix, and she intended to stay.

She was shown into a rather plain antechamber, fitted with two hard benches and a small window that permitted scant illumination. The official vanished, and Pheresa's attendants began to giggle and whisper behind her until she quelled them with a swift glance. She seated herself with more pretense of patience than she actually felt, and knew that within minutes the news of her presence here would fly through the court.

Worry fluttered inside her heart, and she swallowed hard. *I must make this work,* she thought to herself. She was here only because no one suspected she would attempt so bold a move. She would not be allowed another such opportunity.

Her wait seemed endless, but lasted perhaps half an hour before the door opened and a servant in dark livery permitted her to enter the office beyond.

It was a room designed for work, not ostentation. Two large tables of stout oak filled most of the available space. A bench ran along one wall beneath windows overlooking the stableyard. Papers and scrolls were stacked everywhere, and a shelf held map cases and inkpots.

For a moment Pheresa had the feeling she'd made a mistake, but then Lord Meaclan rose from his chair behind the largest table and bowed to her. He was a middle-aged man of small stature and lean girth. His graying hair curled about his cheekbones, and he sported a narrow, neatly trimmed beard. His clothing was impeccable, richly patterned and fashionable without being too much the dandy. His dark, astute eyes swept over her with a blink of admiration, and she knew then that her instincts had been correct after all. Whether she could afford it or not, she must look the part she wanted, if ever she was to have it.

"Lady Pheresa," he said, his voice deep and cultured. He bowed to her and directed his servant to offer her a chair equal in comfort to his own. When she was seated, her magnificent skirts spread out around her, the servant was dismissed, and her own ladies were left, giggling and craning their necks, in the antechamber. The door closed firmly, and she and Lord Meaclan were alone.

He came around his desk to bow over her hand. "You surprise me by this unexpected visit. Indeed, this office is hardly the proper setting for such a resplendent lady of high rank and fashion. Have you not received my reply to your letter of inquiry?"

"Yes, my lord," she replied. Her mouth was quite dry, but she managed to keep her voice clear and even. She knew how important it was to hide her nerves. "It was most kind of you to grant me an interview in the public rooms ten days from now. Unfortunately, I lack the leisure to keep such an appointment."

His expression remained bland and courteous, but she saw the flicker of impatience in his dark eyes. "I am a busy man, my lady, and you—"

"In ten days I am likely to be ousted from my place at court and gone forever," she said swiftly, deciding to lay everything before him.

"You surprise me."

"I doubt that I do. You are minister of finance. You know everything that goes on at court. You know what's at stake now."

Lord Meaclan went back to his desk and sat down. He said nothing.

She sent him a tiny smile. "I have come to you for help."

Impatience flickered again in his eyes. This time, he did not attempt to hide it. "You wish a loan, my lady?"

Her hands curled into fists, which she kept in her lap. "My lord, let us not waste time with foolery. I seek to be named Heir to the Realm. I believe I can attain the king's favorable decision in time, but I need—"

"My lady, I am not in his majesty's confidence regarding these matters."

She met his eyes with some anger. She did not like his patronizing air or his habit of interrupting her. "I guessed as much," she said tartly. "That is why I am informing you of the particulars."

Lord Meaclan frowned. "My area is finance, not—"

"I have enemies, my lord, people who do not wish me to succeed my uncle."

"Ah."

She drew a deep breath and forced herself to make her request although by now she believed it would be futile. "I need allies, my lord. Strong ones, or I shall not survive court intrigue."

He said nothing, merely steepling his fingers together and studying her over the top of them. She endured the evaluation with outward composure, but inside she hated such scrutiny. *Someday,* she promised herself, *people will not look at me with such doubt.*

"I have gambled in coming to you," she continued, "for you may have already chosen to support a different candidate, as Lord Fillem has."

"Lord Fillem is old-fashioned. He believes a man should sit on the throne. There's a remote cousin from the southeast, I believe."

"Yes," she said. "Lervan. I have never met him, but I am more closely related to the king than he."

"Not as closely as your mother."

Pheresa frowned. "Her claim is illegal. I do not think the king will alter the law in her favor."

"It seems improbable."

"I would like your support," she said again. "You know we can help each other if I am successful."

Lord Meaclan allowed himself a very small smile. "And your ladyship thinks I am powerful enough to ensure your success?"

"I know you to have his majesty's ear. I also know that you have tremendous influence within the court. Your position ensures that, of course, since you control the royal purse strings—"

"Manage, my lady. I manage them. I do not control them."

She inclined her head. "Very well. You have that advantage, and your influence extends beyond Mandria's borders." She drew in a deep breath. "If you support me, others will follow your lead. I have the love of the people. I require alliance with at least some of my uncle's ministers."

"Well, that is plain enough. Let us consider a few other points, my lady."

"Yes?"

"The church should favor your candidacy, yet it does not. I wonder why?"

She met his gaze without evasion. "If you say the church should favor me because I am a woman, and therefore weak or easily influenced or controlled, 'tis not the case. I think certain officials fear I would be too popular to be controlled. My miraculous cure and my contact with the Chalice are matters of unnecessary ecclesiastical concern."

"Have you acquired magical powers, my lady?"

"No."

"A pity. You could then sweep your detractors aside."

She frowned. "I did not come here for your derision, my lord!"

"I spoke quite in earnest, my lady."

Believing he was toying with her, she was tempted to depart. Instead, she tried to control her temper and stayed put. "I, too, am in earnest, my lord," she said. "What is necessary to convince you?"

"Last year you arrived at court a wide-eyed innocent, if I may say so, my lady. To be blunt, you did not take. A timid mouse, I believe some called you. Many laughed at your attempts to catch the prince's eye."

Pheresa's anger raged, but she held it with an iron hand. "I was laughed at," she agreed evenly, "but in the end I was betrothed to Prince Gavril. I did not flirt or compromise myself in the wilder excesses of my uncle's court, because I believe in morals whether they are fashionable or not. I was poisoned, yet I lived. I was held hostage in Nether and nearly murdered, yet I have returned. It is a mistake, my lord, to underestimate me. In all that truly matters, I am not lacking."

He pursed his lips and tapped his fingertips together. "And what would you offer me, my lady, in exchange for this alliance?"

Her heart leaped in hope although she tried to check it since he could still refuse. Her first thought was to ask him what he wanted, yet with sudden insight she knew that would be a fatal mistake.

"I offer you the continued favor of the monarch," she began.

He frowned with a dismissive gesture. "My lady, that's hardly—"

"Allow me to finish, Lord Meaclan," she interrupted sharply.

"If I may speak bluntly, your ladyship has taken up a great deal of my time, only to state the obvious. I wish I had the leisure to counsel you in statecraft, but, alas, more pressing matters call me. Perhaps you might reconsider your bargaining position before you approach me again."

She nearly strangled with fury. Her hands clenched knuckle white in her lap. She could have argued or refuted his insulting remarks. Instead, she continued what she had come to say: "There have been occasional murmurs about your past, my lord. Not even rumors, mind, just murmurs. A whisper or two, seldom uttered, nearly forgotten, of how a young man, the youngest son of an impoverished noble, with no personal fortune, no land of his own, came so quickly to the notice of the king. There are the lingering questions of how your lordship came to own so fine a house, such large estates, in less than two decades of service to his majesty."

His face went wooden. His dark eyes were suddenly cold and wary.

"That shipping investment you made before the trade agreement with the Saelutian Isles," she went on, well aware that at last she had his full attention. "A bold financial move on your part, was it not? And so many noblemen lost money in the scheme, while you prospered. It seemed remarkable at the time.

"Your fine house and estates, purchased cheaply from a baron accused of treason. Who laid the accusations against him? Who found the proof of his misdeeds and profited from them?"

He didn't protest. He didn't shout or try to evade. He didn't deny. With his eyes burning like coals in his set face, he whispered, "It's easy to twist the truth into false rumor. Envious, less talented, and mediocre men will always cry foul when someone prospers more than they. Your rumors, my lady, are twenty years old. Buried, forgotten. How come you by them?"

She shrugged and did not answer.

"Old slanders," he said angrily. "The king was satisfied that I—"

"Oh, I do not accuse you," she said guilelessly, opening her brown eyes wide. "Indeed, my lord. If the king and my father both believe you were innocent of any wrongdoing, then I do not dispute their judgment."

"You would bring it all back, would you? You would try!"

"No," she said sharply, leaning forward. "But when the king dies—and please Thod that shall be many years hence—your enemies will revive the rumor. Let us speculate about the future monarch. If it is someone new to court, someone who does not recognize your invaluable service to the crown, then how simple a matter for your enemies to poison the royal ear against you. You could be ousted from office. Or worse might happen."

He lifted his chin. "I am not unprepared for contingencies."

"No doubt. But your prudence and preparation will only be seen as further proof of lining your pockets while in office."

"It's a lie!"

"Yes, my lord," she said calmly, pleased to see him on the defensive. Had he remained sleek and unperturbed, she would have had no chance. "You are efficient, trustworthy, and capable. Thanks to you, my uncle's treasury is fat and well managed. But we both know there exist people who are threatened by efficiency and honesty. There are malicious, inept, dishonest fools who would rather tear down what is decent and good than change what is wrong in themselves."

She looked right at him. "Were I someday queen, my lord, I would have no other than you as minister of finance. Can you say that about anyone else who might ascend the throne?"

He said nothing. His face was pale, his eyes ablaze, and he was clenching the arms of his chair. Watching him, Pheresa felt her spirits sink. He had misunderstood her. That had been the main risk she faced today. If he thought she was trying to coerce him or blackmail him, then he would resent her and turn on her like a cornered animal. She held back additional assurances, knowing that to say more would only cause harm. If he could not work out what she meant for himself, then he was not the man she believed him to be.

Finally, he loosed a great sigh and said in a cold, brittle voice, "It seems your ladyship is correct in saying people underestimate you. I have done so myself, and for that I beg your pardon."

She inclined her head graciously, her heart jerking, her mouth dry. Outwardly, she remained composed and still.

"Your ladyship asks me to trust you. I trust no one."

Somehow she managed to find her voice. "I understand, my lord."

"I never have."

"Of course."

"Your ladyship is seeking tremendous power. Until a few minutes ago, I would have said you have no idea of what that means. Now I must reevaluate."

"I am trying to prove myself," she told him. "Were I the fool—the timid mouse—that some people believe me to be, I would be dead and buried in Nether."

He nodded.

"I want to be queen," she said. "You want to remain minister of finance. Surely we can find common ground in these desires?"

"Even I cannot withstand the church's power if it becomes your enemy."

"Cardinal Theloi is my enemy, for he favors another. He is not the entire church."

Meaclan gave her an abrupt little nod. "Very well, my lady. It seems we need each other and must work together toward a common end."

She smiled and rose to her feet to mask her sense of overwhelming relief. "Thank you, my lord."

He stood also and bowed to her. "Your ladyship has given me much to think about."

"My first priority is to remain at court. If I am removed, on any pretext, I shall never return," she said urgently.

Meaclan raised his brows. "Really, my lady, I do not keep an army of protectors. I can support your claim to the throne, but I cannot prevent your abduction."

She heard the faint tone of derision returning to his voice, and frowned. "You disbelieve the danger I face."

"I do not dispute that your ladyship is worried. Perhaps I can persuade certain individuals that it is in the court's best interests for you to remain at Savroix. Let that be enough for now."

Bitterness surged through her. He was offering his help, but only under coercion and less than willingly. Was grudging support as damning as no endorsement at all? She walked reluctantly to the door and glanced at him one final time in appeal. Yet she could not find anything to say that would not sound like begging or repetition. She supposed, she thought with a sigh, that she should be grateful that she had managed to gain as much as she had.

"We shall talk again, in future," Meaclan said as he ushered her to the door. "Now I must excuse myself for another appointment, which cannot be delayed longer."

"Thank you for your courteous attention," she said. "I appreciate all your efforts on my behalf."

"Matters of state cannot be rushed." Lord Meaclan bowed, his face still noncommittal. "Good day, my lady."

The door opened, and Pheresa walked out into the antechamber. Sir Brillon stood there, cloaked and spurred as though ready for a journey. Her heart plunged to her slippers, and she stopped in her tracks. Her tiny dagger hung from a pretty chain and was concealed among the voluminous folds of her wide skirts; she gripped it now, as wary and tense as a forest animal who'd been cornered.

"Ah, there you are, m'lady," Sir Brillon said. His black eyes stared at her with ill-concealed anger. "I've been sore pressed to find you, but—"

"Why are you here?" she asked coldly. "What do you want?"

He bowed. "I'm to take you riding in the park. The exercise will keep your health at its—"

"No," she said, and added no courtesy to the refusal. She grew aware of Lord Meaclan standing at her shoulder, silently observing, and cast him a look of appeal. Perhaps now, she thought desperately, he would believe that she was truly in danger.

Sir Brillon stepped closer to her. "Come away, m'lady. This is no place for you. That dainty mare you particularly favor is saddled and ready."

She gave the knight as haughty a glare as she could muster. "No, Sir Brillon. I do not go riding at this time of day. There is no mare that I favor. I keep no horses at court."

"But—"

"You are mistaken," she said sharply. "I did not summon

you. I have no need of your services, however kindly offered or intended. Good day, sir."

Lord Meaclan said nothing.

Sir Brillon's eyes remained overbright and determined, but he managed a smile as he bowed. "As you wish, m'lady. I'll escort you back to the public rooms now. This is no place for your ladyship."

Inwardly Pheresa fumed. She knew the best thing to do was to accept his escort back through Merchants Walk, but it felt as though the shackles had been placed on her wrists. His very presence was abhorrent to her. She hated the way he stared at her and watched her with an unwholesome intensity. She did not believe a Qanselmite knight should look at any woman the way Sir Brillon stared at her. Inside her clothing, her skin felt as though insects were crawling over it.

She shivered involuntarily and caught a flicker of satisfaction in his eyes. That angered her even more. He *wanted* to frighten her, she thought, and despised him.

"Very well, Sir Brillon," she said after a long silence. Her attendants watched her, wide-eyed with curiosity. "You may escort me to the public rooms. There are new madrigals to be sung this afternoon, written in honor of Lady Lalieux's golden—"

Sir Brillon stiffened. "The king's mistress is no fit company for your ladyship."

One of Pheresa's ladies gasped, and Pheresa herself grew very cold and still. She stared at Sir Brillon without immediately replying, and when he met her gaze his face flamed scarlet.

"Do you presume to tell me whom I may or may not see?" Pheresa asked very quietly.

His mouth was clamped in a tight line. Disapproval radiated from him, yet he seemed conscious of having erred. He backed away and gave her a jerky bow. "Nay," he said stiffly. "But 'tis unseemly to—"

"If you are to escort me anywhere this day, Sir Brillon," Pheresa said in a voice like iron, "you will escort me to the side of Countess Lalieux. Otherwise, stand aside and let me pass."

Sir Brillon scowled, but as he opened his mouth, Lord Meaclan spoke:

"Lady Pheresa, I hope I have not kept you too long," he said smoothly. "'Twould be a pity to make you offend the countess with your tardiness. Her favor is an excellent advantage, and I would hate to see your ladyship lose it."

Pheresa turned to him in relief, which she swiftly masked under Sir Brillon's baleful eye. "How kind you are, my lord," she said with a radiant smile, and gave him her hand for a moment. "Good day."

"Keep to your musical pursuits," he said lightly, his dark eyes conveying a warning she understood most clearly. "And tomorrow, with your permission, I shall call on you for further discussion."

She curtsied. "I shall be pleased to await you, my lord."

With her hand still clutching her hidden dagger, she lifted her chin high and swept out, her attendants and Sir Brillon following. Down the ribbon of carpet leading along the gallery she went, a faint smile pinned to her lips, her thoughts spinning furiously inside her mind.

She had gained Meaclan's support, but as he had warned her, nothing could be accomplished quickly. In the meantime, she must do what she could to avoid the traps Sir Brillon kept setting for her. Go riding with him indeed, she thought with a spurt of renewed anger. Did he honestly think her such a fool? How easy to urge her to gallop to the king's wood, where she could be abducted easily out of sight of the palace. What would he try tomorrow, or the day after that? She quickened her pace, her heart thudding, and wished with all her might to be free of him. Yet he walked behind her like a shadow at her heels, ever watchful, ever vigilant, like a serpent coiled to strike at its prey.

Chapter Seven

Along the winding road from Aiesliun to Savroix lay countless leagues of fertile farmland, newly planted and starting to
green. Well-kept hedges bordered the fields, and small but
tidy villages were snugged in the gentle valleys where streams
meandered beneath pale green willows. It was a sleepy, pleasant region, and made for pleasant traveling. Riding along at
the lead of a small company of travelers, Lervan de Waite
shifted lazily in his saddle and squinted up at the angle of sun
overhead. About time for a rest, he thought.

"Jervis!" he called out. "Play us a tune."

"Aye, my lord."

The gentle strains of lute music filled the air. Smiling and
humming along with the melody, Lervan rode onward.

He was lightly cloaked and fashionably garbed. His saddle, bridle, sword, and trappings were new. At four-and-
twenty, he was long-shanked and beefy through the arms and
shoulders. His light brown hair blew back from his face in the
gentle breeze. He wore a bright green cap that sported a magnificent jadecock's feather, and beneath his mustache his red

lips were curved in a perpetual smile. On this fine spring day, life was as sweet as the skin of sun-warmed wine tied to his saddle. He was on his way to court, with every confidence that the whole world was about to be handed to him, and he intended to enjoy each moment to the fullest.

Father Fornel, a rather dour priest who'd been assigned the duty of schooling Lervan in all the things he needed to know before arriving at court, urged his donkey up alongside Lervan's bay courser. "A fine afternoon, my lord."

"Aye. I wonder if there's any good hunting in these parts. Know you what game is to be found here?"

"No, my lord," Fornel said austerely over the lute music. "I thought perhaps we might use this time to discuss the hierarchy of—"

"Not now." Lervan shot him a winning smile. "It's almost midafternoon, and I think we need to stop soon to water the horses and stretch our legs."

"There's little time now before we reach Savroix," Fornel replied. "You need to know so many—"

"I'll pick it up soon enough," Lervan said with confidence.

"I fear—"

The sound of girlish laughter from up ahead caught Lervan's attention. He straightened in the saddle and flung up his hand to silence the priest.

"Hear that?"

Fornel scowled. "Pay no heed, my lord. They're no concern of ours."

But Lervan quickened his horse to a slow trot and rode ahead of the priest. He'd seen plenty of pretty girls on the journey thus far, and he was always eager to see more.

The road curved and wound in this valley, no doubt to avoid a meandering stream bordered by well-grown connols and willows, but ahead Lervan saw a crossing. On his left stood a wooden footbridge, while the road itself forded the stream, which ran quick and shallow.

Flagstones had been laid across the ford to keep the footing solid for carts and wagons. Eyeing the mossy stones, Lervan deemed them too slippery for his horse and moved aside to choose his own crossing. As his mount splashed into the shallow water, he heard more giggles, accompanied by a flash of scarlet and blue in the bushes on the opposite bank. Various garments lay strewn about on flat stones near the support pillars of the footbridge. Lervan smiled to himself. No doubt the village maidens of the area had been doing their laundry.

Ever ready to seize an opportunity, Lervan reined up and stared hard at the thick bushes, where much rustling and giggling were going on.

"Come out, fair maids!" he called with a broad smile. "Come out and greet a weary traveler!"

Fornel drew rein beside him and frowned. "My lord, we should press on."

"Oh, be at peace, Father," Lervan said with a shrug. "Sir Maltric, do you find anything amiss here?"

"Nay," his protector replied, glancing about alertly. "We'll water horse and man alike."

"Good." Lervan grinned at the feminine faces peeping out at him now from the bushes. He gestured broadly. "Come forth and be hospitable!"

Giggling, three maidens emerged and picked their way back across the stream, with their skirts gathered high. The generous display of leg and thigh made Lervan pleasantly warm. Well interested, he ignored Fornel's frown and dismounted swiftly. His protector followed suit, while the others stayed on horseback.

One of the girls was homely beyond all hope, the second passable, and the third quite comely in face and form. Lervan smiled at her with all his considerable charm.

"Well, now," he said, "what a merry welcome you three wenches give a man. What say we rest a bit—you from your labors and I from my travels—while we all share the wine that I carry?"

The girls giggled, but the pretty one answered him boldly enough: "Nay, good lord and sir, but we are bound to finish our work and return home soon."

Lervan made a gesture, and his squire hurried to untie the wineskin and hand it to him. In turn he offered it to the girls.

"What say we quench our thirst at least? What harm is there in that?"

"Our mistress will know if we go home drunken," the maid answered him.

He raised his brows innocently. "And what is your name, my dear?"

The girl hesitated only a moment. Her eyes were dark, a little slanted at the tips. His open admiration seemed to please her vanity. "I am Vea, good lord."

"Well, Vea, it's not a drunken feast I crave, but merely a moment's rest. I have ridden a long way, and have much farther yet to go. I would like to walk a little and stretch my legs. Will you keep me company, Vea, for a few minutes? I would learn about the land hereabouts, and its people, and its customs." His smile widened suggestively. "Especially its customs."

"Vea, no!" whispered the ugly one in warning, but Vea's dark eyes remained on Lervan.

He went on smiling, studying the curve of her lovely cheekbones and the promising arch of her throat. She smiled back, ignoring her companion, and gave him a little nod.

"Of course I will walk with you, good lord and sir."

Well pleased, he took her hand.

"My lord!" Fornel said in annoyance from behind him. "Remember that you are bound for Savroix, with no time for such—"

Lervan cast him a lazy look, but warning lay in his eyes, and Sir Maltric gripped the priest's shoulder. Fornel fell silent abruptly.

"There is ample time," Lervan said, and returned his gaze to Vea. "Come, my dear."

"Have care, sister!" called the ugly one. "Remember your Toman."

Vea tossed her head without replying, and together they strolled away into the cool shade beneath the trees. Just out of sight of the others, she laughed, low and richly, and skipped ahead before she whirled about and faced him.

There was a laughing challenge in her face. "Are you really going to Savroix?" she asked, her eyes shining with excitement.

"Oh, yes. The king has sent for me."

Her mouth opened in awe. "Then truly you are an important lord."

"Truly, I might be." He smoothed back a lock of hair from her face and cupped his hand beneath the curve of her skull. "Come closer, little maid."

She leaned against him, her breasts soft against his chest, but just as his lips tasted hers, she laughed and pulled away. He laughed, too, catching her easily and pinning her against a tree this time. She smiled up at him, her ripe lips curved and merry. This time she let him kiss her, and her mouth was like honey, soft and rich, before she pulled away again.

He caught her chin in his hand and held her. "You tease me, my dear. 'Tis not fair behavior when I seek to claim you."

She shivered in his hold. "You move quickly, m'lord. You are but a stranger here, and I am promised to Toman."

He was fingering the curve of her bottom lip, studying it, reveling in the scent and proximity of her. She smelled of soil, grass, and soap. Her hands were work-reddened, and her wrists too thick and strong from hard work. In a few years she would coarsen and lose her teeth, but today she was lovely and his for the taking.

"When do you wed?" he murmured, nuzzling her temple while his hand wandered down her throat to her breast. He heard her jerk in a breath.

"After harvest. We were just 'trothed at Springfest. We—"

She broke off with a low moan as his caresses grew bolder. Lervan laughed, pressing her more insistently, but then she gasped and struggled against him.

"Don't, my dear," he murmured against her lips. "You know what I'm about, and your Toman will welcome a bride who's no longer shy."

"Hush, m'lord," she said in a fierce whisper. "There's someone joined your friends on the road. I hear them talking."

Lervan heard nothing but the pounding in his own blood. "Let them talk. I want—"

"Nay! We're too close. This way."

She gave him a swift kiss and tugged at his hand, drawing him deeper into the woods. They splashed across the stream, her legs white and firm, then she dropped her skirts and they scrambled up the bank, she giggling breathlessly and he grabbing at her from behind. Just before they reached the top, he pulled her down and rolled with her beneath the soft fronds of a fragrant bush. There, surrounded by a curtain of green dappled with sunlight, they sported with merry abandon until both were spent and breathless.

He lay there, the world still reeling, momentarily lost to sense and reason. Bees hummed lazily above his head, drunk on the flowers as he was drunk, and all was sweet and perfect.

She stirred after a moment, but he stroked his hand up her lovely thigh and held her, content to pillow his head in the scent and softness of her. She fingered his hair and murmured something, the words too soft for him to catch.

"Again?" he said drowsily. "Give me a moment, my dear."

She went on murmuring as though he had not spoken, and he smiled to himself. *When I am king,* he thought, *I shall make Vea my queen.*

He envisioned her standing in the palace in a gown of rich velvet, jewels sprinkled in her hair and dangling from her ears. A strange lassitude stole over his limbs as though he were bound. He could barely move. His breathing grew slow and heavy. He did not sleep, but neither did he feel alert. Her voice grew louder and more rhythmic now. The words she spoke seemed to be a chant, but they made no sense to him. She would be lovely, he thought. Her beauty would charm the court, and every night she would be his alone to claim. He imagined her lying sprawled in the vast bed, spent and pliant. Her dark eyes would be clouded and soft. A tiny pulse would race in her throat, and he would kiss her there . . .

A bird called from the treetops, breaking his vision. He blinked and thought of Vea in her ragged dress and long tangled hair, dirt smudged on her cheek as it was now. The absurdity of pretending this peasant girl could be a queen made him snort with laughter.

Her fingers curled in his hair, and her chanting grew louder, almost angry.

He let his own fingers wander, so that now and then her chanting faltered as she jerked in her breath. He wished she would hush her nonsense, but it seemed too much trouble to speak or even to kiss her into silence.

Even in this day and age, he told himself lazily, there seemed to remain a few pockets of backwardness, deeply rural parts of Mandria where the old ways still prevailed. Silly old superstitions, older even than the ways before Reform. Perhaps she thought this spell or prayer she uttered would keep her belly from quickening with child. He did not care. Shifting his head, which felt as heavy as a stone, he nuzzled her breasts where her bodice gaped open.

She pushed his head away, uttering her strange words with more insistence.

"Lervan!" a voice called from far away. "My lord!"

That was Sir Maltric's voice. Lervan blinked, and some of his lassitude broke. Frowning, he lifted his head and seemed to come to himself. Shifting his gaze to hers, he saw how intense, almost violent, she looked. She kept chanting the words, hurling them at him now as though to force him in some way to her will.

He sat up, although she tried to hold him, and put his hand over her mouth. She wriggled furiously, but his strong arms held her easily.

"What are you about, pretty Vea?" he asked in puzzlement. "Seeking to put a spell over me? Why? Am I not enspelled enough for you?"

She struggled again, but with a laugh he tightened his hold. After a moment she stopped, and he dropped his hand from her mouth.

"Take me to Savroix with you," she said in a strange, husky voice. "Take me there! Take me!"

"I shall take you nowhere but here," he said with a laugh, pushing her down again. He kissed her hard and long, pleasuring himself despite her struggles, and closed his mind to everything save what he wanted.

When he was finished, he gave her a last caress in farewell and straightened his clothes. As he picked up his cap, however, she sat up, flushed and thoroughly disarranged.

"I am yours," she said in that same fierce, husky voice. "I am to go with you."

"No, my dear," he said calmly. "You have been delightful, but now I must go."

"I go with you!"

"No."

She gripped his arm, and he loosed a little sigh as he pried her fingers from his sleeve. "Do not be tiresome, Vea. You know your place, and it is here."

"Then you will stay with me until I make you unable to leave me. You will stay." She tried to kiss him although he turned his head away. "Stay!"

He laughed. "Would you command me like a dog, Vea? Have done. Our sport is over."

"I do command you, good lord and sir. I command your heart. I command your loins. You must take me with you."

The desperation in her voice struck him as odd. He stood up abruptly and paused to glance down at her. In that quick moment her face looked different . . . not as pretty, the cheekbones flatter, the lips thin and pale, the dark eyes fierce and somehow dangerous. She opened her mouth, revealing small pointed teeth and . . . fangs.

Shocked, he stared at her, unable to believe what he was seeing. She hissed at him in fury, and he jumped back, his heart suddenly thudding.

She sprang at him, muttering something in a language he did not know, and caught him by his legs. He could not keep his balance and fell, arms flailing. The moment he hit the ground, she swarmed atop him, fangs bared and eyes wild. Her teeth snapped at his throat.

He knocked her aside with a sweep of his arm, sending her tumbling nearly into the stream. By the time he scrambled to his feet, she was coming on all fours like an animal, panting harshly in her throat.

"What are you?" he demanded, evading her grab.

She came at him again. "If I do not please you, Lord Lervan, take another of us," she said. "We each have training to capture you. Try—"

"I'll have none of you. Get back!"

"You are to rule Mandria. It has been foretold."

"Thank you for the prophecy," he said, backing away. "But my future has naught to do with you."

"So you think, good lord and sir. So you think."

She sprang at him again, and this time he lost his footing in his attempt to evade her. He fell awkwardly on his side, the wind knocked from him so that he could not call out to Sir Maltric. He lay there, half-stunned and furious, wondering what in Thod's name had spawned this madwoman.

Throwing herself across him, Vea gripped his jaw, her nails digging in painfully while she bit him where his neck joined his shoulder.

"You will take the spell. You will serve," she said grimly, trying to force open his mouth. "In the name of Ashnod, I command you—"

Fear burst through his heart. Shoving her off, he reached for his dagger. As she struggled to keep him pinned, he thrust his weapon through her side in a quick, fatal blow.

All the fury and madness left her face. She sagged against him, her eyes dull with shock. He pulled out his dagger and shifted away from her as she crumpled to the ground. Breathing hard, he cleaned his weapon quickly on the grass.

He felt shaken and sick. She was Gantese, and this had been a trap. How had they known? He'd had no inkling of the fabulous future perhaps awaiting him until a week ago, when Father Fornel arrived bearing a letter from Cardinal Theloi. The letter informed him that he had a strong chance of being named Heir to the Realm, but there had been no mention of any danger attached to this honor.

Quickly Lervan sheathed his dagger and stared down at Vea. She opened her eyes and stared right through him. Blood stained her side, and her breathing came quick and harsh. He backed away, appalled that he'd struck down a woman. Or was she a woman at all? Her beauty, apparently some magical illusion, was gone. She looked strange, peculiar, hideous.

"I'll be no puppet of Gant," he declared. "You should have been content to sport with me, my dear."

Anger blazed in her eyes. "My curse is on you, Lervan de Waite." A gout of blood gushed from her mouth, and she groaned. "You are marked now for those who will come after me. You *will* serve. 'Tis foretold. May blood and disaster cloud your reign. May all you touch wither and fail."

The air smelled suddenly of fire, and something unseen hurtled past him. He ducked, and fire exploded in the bush where only minutes ago they'd lain happily. Fear gripped his entrails, but Lervan clung to his bravado.

"Your curse has missed me, Vea," he said. "The only disaster this day has befallen you, not me."

She stared up at him through eyes that grew steadily dimmer. "So you think," she whispered, and died.

He stood there a long moment, staring at her while the bush burned and smoked behind him. Reaching inside his tunic, he gripped his Circle very hard while his pity for her faded swiftly. "So I know, witch," he said softly, and strode away.

After he crossed the stream, he ran, clutching his fine cap in his hand to protect it from being snagged by low-hanging branches. He did not look back. He wanted to be gone from that place forever, and he worried suddenly about the fate of his friends. Were the other girls Gantese witches as well? Had they enspelled his companions in his absence?

When he burst from the trees, it was to find them all standing about looking bored. They seemed startled by his precipitous arrival, and Sir Maltric stepped forward in immediate concern.

"Is aught amiss, my lord?" he asked.

Lervan found himself breathless and unsure of how to answer. A swift glance around told him the other maidens had gone, taking their laundry with them.

"A farmer came by, my lord, and rounded them up," Jervis said.

Still unsettled, Lervan brushed off the dirt and leaf bits from his clothing while Fornel scowled even harder. Some of the armed men were sending Lervan sly grins and nudging each other. He smiled at them in return, feeling less sick at heart than he had a few minutes ago. *If they only knew the truth of it,* he thought wryly, and kept silent about his adventure.

He did not know why. Perhaps he didn't want Sir Maltric to worry and fuss. Perhaps he didn't want to face Fornel's questions or endure some kind of cleansing ritual the priest would no doubt insist on performing. He'd killed the witch, and no harm had been done. The trap had failed, and that was an end to it.

"Let's be gone from here," Lervan said.

Soon the little crossing was behind them, and as Vea did not reappear as a walking ghost, shouting or hurling more spells, and nothing else came forth to hinder them, the tension in Lervan's shoulders slowly dissipated. He began to whistle again, filling his mind with memories of the sweetly willing milkmaid he'd left behind at home. Alica was the perfect companion, always pleased by his advances, always laughing, never one to whine or demand things she couldn't have. There was no need to think further of today's unpleasantness, he told himself, and swiftly forgot how close he'd come to disaster.

Two days later, he rode into Savroix, his ears ringing with Father Fornel's advice on palace protocol and how to conduct himself. He ignored most of it, his eyes filled with the immensity of the palace, the towering stone walls, the spires, the flying pennons, the pageantry, and the endless pomp. The palace held so many people—palace guards, servants, officials, and courtiers in addition to the visitors, ambassadors, emissaries, and countless others—that it seemed to be a town of its own. Yet there was Savroix-en-Charva, a bustling port city of such prosperity and promise he could not wait to explore it. At almost every corner, he saw well-favored maidens. And inside the palace, almost every face was comely. What finery they wore, these ladies in their jewels and silk gowns. Cosmetics and fragrance made them even more alluring. He felt quite giddy from the sheer abundance of milky skin, sweet lips, and sparkling eyes.

But there were duties to be performed before he could enjoy himself. He was given a set of splendid rooms, with windows overlooking one of the many gardens. He washed, clothed himself in his best tunic, quite a handsome bit of tailoring in vivid blue, and was already aware that he was completely behind the fashion. That would have to be corrected as soon as he began to receive an allowance.

And the allowance could not begin until he'd seen first Cardinal Theloi, his sponsor at court, then the king. He did not worry about the possibility that his suit would fail. Lervan believed completely in himself, his many abilities, and his charm. Furthermore, he loved to hunt as much as the king, if not more so. How could the monarch fail to approve of him?

Hastening to finish his preparations, Lervan smiled at himself in the handsome looking glass at his disposal and followed a haughty little page through the maze of passages and corridors that filled the palace.

"Great Thod," he joked to Sir Maltric, "I shall be lost in this place for a year."

Father Fornel walked on his right. "You will soon learn your way, my lord. The passages are linked by colors. Hues of red lead to the audience chamber and the royal apartments. Hues of green lead to—"

"Thod, yes," Lervan said with a yawn. "I'll catch on soon enough."

Folding his lips into a thin line, Fornel fell silent.

When they reached the cardinal's apartments, Lervan admired them very much, although the air was too stuffy and warm for his liking. The furnishings were magnificent, and he promised himself that he would make over his own rooms as soon as he had enough money. Already he knew that he never wanted to return home to Aiesliun. It was at the end of the world compared to Savroix.

And here, seated in a heavily carved chair, was the man

who offered Savroix to him. Lervan waited while he was announced in hushed tones, then strode forward in his easy, self-confident way.

Sweeping off his cap, he bowed low in the best courtly style, before kneeling at the cardinal's feet and kissing his ring. "My lord cardinal," he said politely, "how honored I am to meet you at last."

Thin and gimlet-eyed, the cardinal stared at Lervan without a smile, taking his time. Lervan didn't mind being looked over. He knew himself to be well built and fair visaged. Thod had favored him in all respects. He danced well, hunted well, jousted well. He had charm and understood how to enjoy himself so that life was always pleasant. And now, this man wanted to make him the next king. For that, Lervan was willing to stand on his head and caper like a fool if it would please Theloi.

"Well?" he asked at last, when the silence stretched out too long. He smiled at the cardinal. "Do I pass muster, despite my provincial clothing?"

"Perhaps." Theloi did not return his smile. His cold green eyes bored into Lervan as though he wanted to make the younger man squirm.

Lervan merely stared back at the cardinal, sitting there in his brilliant white robes, his diamond-studded Circle winking and flashing on its chain.

At long last the cardinal permitted himself a small, satisfied curve of his lips and indicated a nearby chair. "Will you not sit, my lord?"

"Thank you." Lervan seated himself and accepted the cup of wine a servant handed to him. The first sip made him sigh in pleasure. "This is very fine indeed, lord cardinal."

"Yes, I keep a passable cellar," Theloi said without much interest. "Let us speak plainly, my lord. You realize what's at stake."

"I have a chance to be the next king."

"A chance," Theloi stressed. "You do understand that nothing is settled, or certain, at this stage."

Lervan shrugged. "I'm sure his majesty and I will get along splendidly. Why shouldn't he like me?"

"I admire your self-confidence," Theloi said dryly. "There are, however, a few things you should do to advance your case."

Lervan finished his wine and hoped the servant would refill it. The servant, no doubt under orders, did not. "I am here, lord cardinal, to be advised by you," Lervan said.

"Very sensible. I understand that you indulge your carnal passions with little or no self-discipline."

A faint line creased Lervan's brow. "You make it sound like—"

"You seem to think that every maidservant in your father's household exists solely for your pleasure."

Lervan's frown deepened. "I—"

"You avail yourself of any female in the fields, stableyard, or nobleman's home. In short, my lord, you have no taste, no restraint, and no discernment."

Lervan shrugged. "Lord cardinal, I am a young man, and young men must have their pleasures."

"It is necessary that you win the hand of Lady Pheresa du Lindier," Theloi said sharply.

"Oh?" Lervan asked in quick interest. "Isn't she the one who—"

"Yes."

"Has she any beauty?"

"Yes."

Lervan smiled, his good humor restored. "Then that's very well. With the greatest delight, I shall woo her daily, if that's what you wish."

Theloi sighed and stroked his gray goatee a moment with a thin hand. "You do not seem to understand, my lord."

Lervan's smile widened. "Do not understand what, lord cardinal? The lady was betrothed to Prince Gavril, my cousin. I suppose that makes her a cousin of mine also."

Father Fornel cleared his throat. "Actually, no," he began pedantically. "The relation exists on the other side of the—"

"That will do," Theloi said sharply, and Fornel fell silent.

"And because she would have been the bride of the next king, and because she's the niece of the present king, she's Princess of the Realm, is she not? And that is why I should win her hand, especially since I'm to be the next Heir to the Realm."

Theloi was staring at him as though uncertain of what he saw. Lervan sent him a wide grin.

"It's very simple, isn't it, lord cardinal? Beneath all the intrigue and politics, things usually are."

"Nothing is simple," Theloi snapped. "The lady is your greatest rival for the throne."

"What?" Lervan laughed. "Impossible!"

Sir Maltric bent close to Lervan's ear. "A female can inherit the throne and rule in her own right, my lord."

Lervan twisted his head to gaze up at his protector. "I know, but really! It's so absurd. How could she lead men to war?"

"Her marechals would serve for her."

Lervan laughed again and shook his head.

"Pay heed," Theloi said coldly. "If you are to be advised by me, you had better learn not to argue."

Lervan forced himself to sober. "Forgive me, lord cardinal. I confess, I had not considered the lady as a claimant."

"She is, and a very determined one," Theloi said grimly. "She has thus far evaded my attempts to remove her from court. She has the king's favor, and she is highly popular with the people. I have hoped that her popularity would fade, but since her return to court she is cheered whenever she rides in public or visits the town."

"But if we are to be rivals," Lervan asked, beginning to feel puzzled, "of what merit is my wooing her? Should I not be better served in charming his majesty?"

"You will naturally bring yourself to his majesty's notice," Theloi said with exaggerated patience. "But we must think of all contingencies. If you fail—"

"Lervan de Waite does not fail!"

Theloi glared at him with those predatory eyes. "If you fail," he said coldly, "marriage to Lady Pheresa will bring you as close to the throne as is possible. And if you succeed in being named the king's heir, he will no doubt be pleased to see you wed to her. Either way, she is to be a key player in your strategy."

Lervan slapped his knees and rose to his feet. "Well, then, I must get started on my assignments without delay. Who will introduce me to the lady, that my conquest may begin?"

"I warn you, my lord," Theloi said in a voice that forced Lervan to pay attention. "You may feel as though it is your right to charm and flirt with all the ladies at court, and their maidservants besides, but you will refrain. You are to concentrate your charming wiles on Lady Pheresa alone."

Lervan frowned. "But I—"

"She alone. The lady is intelligent and sensitive. She has high morals and will not abase herself with a known ruffian and libertine. Take care you do not botch this."

"She sounds like a spinster with a squint," Lervan replied. "Those with high morals usually are the plain ones."

An ominous silence fell over the room. Catching Sir Maltric giving him a warning shake of the head, Lervan realized that perhaps his remark had been offensive. Any nobleman would have laughed at his joke, but these church officials had no sense of humor.

He bowed at once to the cardinal. "I beg your eminence's pardon if I spoke too freely."

"Your tongue will be your undoing," Theloi told him. "Take care, my lord! This is a serious matter. A great deal of effort and preparation has already been expended on your behalf. But it can be undone in minutes if you blunder."

Feeling chastened, Lervan endured a few more minutes of instruction and admonition before he was finally allowed to depart. He left the cardinal with a surge of relief, glad to escape.

"Great Thod, Maltric," he said, easing a finger between his neck and the edge of his tunic as they walked back down the corridor. "I feel like I'm a schoolboy again, with lectures heaped on my head from all sides."

"Too much is at stake, my lord," Maltric replied.

"I know. I know. But must we all be so serious and glum about it? I thought court was a place to make merry, to dance and sing and drink and love." He grinned. "Still, unless the lady has a face like a daub and wattle fence, it can't be too unpleasant, eh?"

Maltric's expression did not alter as he walked at Lervan's side. "I have no doubt that your lordship will enjoy himself very much."

Ahead, Lervan had spied a pair of ladies in pretty gowns and ringlets. Pleased by their curtsies as he walked past, he stared boldly at them, enjoying their blushes and quick glances. When his gaze met the blonde one's, he winked, and she giggled behind her hand.

Smiling, Lervan walked on, then pulled a dreadful face in response to Maltric's frown. "Don't scold," he said. "Am I not even to look at all that's offered to me?"

"I believe the cardinal would say no, my lord."

Lervan sighed. "Then Thod help me, but I hope I fall in love with Lady Pheresa at first sight. Otherwise, I'm doomed to offend someone."

Maltric stopped in his tracks and glared fiercely at his lord and master. "What ails you?" he whispered furiously. "Do you not see what's at stake? Do you not realize how close you are to having this entire realm placed in your hand? This is no time for joking, and no time to be a fool."

"I am no fool! Never call me that again."

"Then stop acting like—"

"Speak to me this way once more, Maltric, and I'll strip you of rank and knighthood," Lervan said angrily. He saw his protector change color and leaned forward. "I am no longer a boy, to be scolded this way. If anyone forgets himself today, 'tis you!"

Sir Maltric's face was wooden. "My lord," he said gruffly, "I beg your pardon. It's only that I don't want you to lose the greatest opportunity of your life."

"I shan't lose," Lervan said. "If I see the lady and love her, then she will be the light and radiance of my eye. If I hate her, she'll never know it. But rule this land, I shall. That, I swear to you."

"You can't swear something like that," Maltric whispered, his eyes full of loyalty and ambition. "You don't know how this will turn out."

"Ah, but I do," Lervan said, his temper restored. "It was foretold to me."

"Foretold!" Maltric echoed in astonishment. "By whom? And when?"

Lervan laughed and walked on, but he did not answer.

Chapter Eight

Sir Talmor shifted his aching hipbones on the hard bench outside Chancellor Salba's door and swallowed a sigh. He'd been waiting here for hours for his audience. When he'd ridden in yesterday, announcing that he brought urgent news from Durl Hold, he'd been permitted to report to an unnamed officer of the palace guards, who then told him to present himself to Lord Chancellor Salba first thing this morning. It was midday now, judging by the angle of the sun glimpsed through a narrow window and the rumbling hole in his belly. He'd eaten no breakfast, too nervous to swallow the hunk of crumbling bread and dried-up cheese remaining in Pears's saddlebag. Now it looked as though he could kick his heels here all day, starving and stiff from inactivity.

Thod's bones, but he'd never seen such a place as Savroix. The palace rambled in all directions, vast and beautiful to look at, chaotic and as busy as an anthill. Someone was always hurrying. Little pages wearing splendid livery ran here and there. Officials strode past. Courtiers lounged everywhere in groups, chattering and gossiping. The palace guards stationed at Lord Salba's door were relieved, and as Talmor watched the procedure he wondered if he'd still be here when the next shift came on duty.

Well, he was rapidly losing patience. Today there was to be a jousting practice. He'd hoped to attend and bring himself to the notice of some baron or chevard who might hire him.

A corner of his mind felt intense shame at being obliged to sell himself as a hire-lance. It meant starting over from bottom. After all his hard work and efforts to succeed at Durl, he did not enjoy finding himself beggared, with naught in either purse or belly, and a look of worry in his eyes that could not always be hidden. With the exorbitant prices the inns in the town charged for a tiny, partitioned-off mousehole fitted with a chipped basin for washing and a mattress of bug-infested rusks atop a wood-and-rope frame—never mind the high cost of horse fodder—he, Pears, and Lutel were camping in a ditch like vagrants.

"Sir Talmor!"

The young clerk bawled out his name, and Talmor jumped to his feet. Someone in the room snickered, and Talmor felt the edges of his ears grow hot. He strode forward as a knight should, however, and ignored the stares boring into his back from those not yet called.

"You are Sir Talmor?"

"Aye."

"The chancellor will see you now."

Nervously, Talmor followed the clerk through the tall door. To his surprise, a hallway lay on the other side of it. The clerk pointed, and Talmor walked forward alone.

At the opposite end stood another door, firmly closed, and another bench. No one was in sight to issue instructions. Talmor frowned, disliking not knowing the correct protocol, and hesitated only a moment. Giving his tunic and cloak a final twitch to be sure he looked his best, he straightened his shoulders and rapped on the door.

At a faint sound from within, he stepped inside a square chamber of spacious proportions. A large window admitted light and fresh air. At a large desk, two men were conferring over a sheaf of papers and maps.

Talmor walked halfway to the desk, stopped, and drew himself to attention. "Sir Talmor of Durl, my lord, reporting as sent for."

The discussion stopped in midsentence, and both men stared at him.

The chancellor was clearly the elder of the two, square of shoulder and heavyset, his beard streaked ginger blond, his brown eyes impatient beneath jutting brows. His tunic was pleated in tiny folds that made the silk shimmer, and he wore an important gold chain across his chest with the seal of his office dangling from it.

Now, he snapped the pen he was holding between his fingers and flung the pieces away. "Damne! Who the blazes are you? Who in Thod's name let you in here? How dare you interrupt?"

"Forgive me, Lord Salba," Talmor said with outward calm while inside his heart sank. He had erred, and at this court mistakes were not readily forgiven. "I am Sir Talmor. I was told to report here this morning."

"No one told you to burst in. Wait your turn, sir. Wait your turn!"

His gruffness reminded Talmor of Lord Pace. Shoving aside a pang of remembrance, Talmor drew on long years of experience with the irascible chevard and remained unruffled. "'Tis my turn, lord chancellor," he said quietly.

Salba blinked, turned red, and opened his mouth, but the other man standing beside him laughed unexpectedly.

"Well said, sir!" he applauded.

Salba turned on him. "Well said?" he repeated incredulously. "Kedrien, are you mad? He bursts in like an upland peasant, not even applauded, and you compliment these ruffian manners?"

"He's assertive and confident," Sir Kedrien replied. "He knows he's erred, but he's not groveling or cringing. What have you to say for yourself, Sir Talmor?"

Talmor faced him, seeing a stocky man of medium height

with a rugged face tanned from much time spent outdoors. He wore a rust-colored tunic beneath the distinctive green cloak of the palace guards, and the insignia of chevron stripes on the front of his tunic proclaimed his high rank.

Talmor bowed to him, not sure how to reply to the officer's ambiguous question. "Durl Hold is destroyed and its chevard dead, due to an attack from Vvordsman boat raiders. I—"

"You've already given that report," Sir Kedrien broke in crisply. "Chancellor Salba has received official dispatches from Durl, saying that the attack was devastating but not disastrous. Repairs are under way to strength the defenses, and Lord Pace is expected to recover from his wounds."

Talmor frowned. "The official report is untrue."

"Bosh!" Lord Salba said with a growl, glaring at Talmor. He leaned forward, thumping his desk with a forefinger for emphasis. "I have Lord Pace's seal on the letter. You lack any credentials. Why should I listen to you?"

"Anyone can use a seal," Talmor replied. "Does the handwriting match that of Lord Pace's previous reports?"

Sir Kedrien raised his brows, but Lord Salba's scowl deepened. "You ran away at first sight of the raiders and hope to cover your cowardice by reporting unfounded news."

Stiffening, Talmor set his jaw, and said quietly, "No, my lord. 'Tis not the way of it."

"And you insist on your tale, insist on it, despite an official report?" Salba asked.

Talmor met his brown eyes without flinching. "Aye, my lord. I was in the midst of the fighting. This"—he pointed to the gash, still healing, on his forehead—"came about when Lord Pace's hoard of saltpeter blew up part of the defense wall. I was knocked unconscious and had I not appeared dead, I would have been taken captive, along with many other knights, by these barbarians."

"Hah! So you played dead to save yourself."

Heat built up in Talmor's face. He struggled to hold his temper and glared at the chancellor. "No, my lord. I did not."

"How many taken captive?" Sir Kedrien demanded.

Talmor told him, including numbers of knights and villagers.

"How much of the hold was destroyed?"

"Much of it was burned, sir, and the damage to the wall makes it indefensible without extensive repairs. That, coupled with the gap in the seawall, means the force garrisoned there must use the old fortress atop the cliffs for the time being." Talmor frowned. "Especially since it's likely the raiders will return for more plunder."

"You were Lord Pace's adjutant," Sir Kedrien said. His eyes were alert and neutral, his voice stern.

Talmor faced him at attention. "Aye, sir."

"With the chevard gravely wounded—"

"He is dead, sir."

The officer frowned, and Talmor warned himself not to interrupt again.

"With the chevard gravely wounded," Sir Kedrien asked, "why did you not take command, as is your duty? Why have you come to Savroix?"

"The chevard is dead, sir," Talmor said firmly. "I was wounded in head and side. By the time I regained my feet, the fortress commander had taken charge. He and Lady Alda are in league, to conceal the chevard's death until the strongroom is cleared of its gold."

Chancellor Salba slammed a freckled hand on his desk. "What! Do you know what you are saying, sir knight?"

"I do, my lord. And I—I believe that when the gold is secured elsewhere, it will be reported that Lord Pace has died of his injuries and that the raiders have plundered his treasury."

"And this is how you serve the lady wife of a valiant chevard, a man you pledged your honor and loyalty to," Salba said in disgust. "Do you realize the force of these charges?"

Sir Kedrien frowned also. "Do you understand the penalty for false accusations?"

"Aye," Talmor said. "But my accusations are not false."

His heart was thudding in his chest. He would rather face a small horde of barbarian invaders than the prospect of being imprisoned and hanged for falsely accusing his superiors, but he'd known the risk the moment he set forth for Savroix. Riding all that way, telling himself over and over during the journey that he must do his duty, was one thing. Standing here facing ruin now was quite another.

His mouth felt dry as dust. He swallowed hard and forced himself to say, "I came to report treason, my lord. Had I stayed and taken orders, I would have been an accomplice to this scheme to rob the crown. My liege oath was made to Lord Pace, and his death broke that commitment. Until I find a new position, I am sworn only to the king. That is why I came here."

Silence fell over the room. Talmor stood stiffly, feeling sure his life was in the hands of these two men. The doubt in their frowning faces caused his courage to waver. Suddenly it seemed hard to breathe. What madness had he embarked on, he, an illegitimate son of a minor lord and a Saelutian enchantress; he, a landless knight, a hire-lance with nothing to his name but his weapons, armor, and immense ambition. Who would believe him? Why should they?

"And you stand by your report?" Sir Kedrien asked at last. "You swear to it, and will sign your name to it?"

"I do." Talmor swallowed. "And I will."

Salba scowled at him. "You cause a great deal of trouble for yourself, sir. Why not go away and hold your tongue? I can forget this conversation. Take hire at some hold far from here and be grateful for my mercy."

Talmor said nothing.

"Would you rather face prison?" Sir Kedrien asked. "Lady Alda can accuse you in retaliation, you know. Have you family and friends to support you if you're tried?"

Talmor thought of his father, whom he would neither name nor send for. "There's no one to help me, sir."

"Then you'd better think hard about this before you go further," Salba said gruffly. "Very hard."

How easy to accept his mercy and take this chance to flee, Talmor thought. But if he fled Savroix now, he would run forever, shamed by his own cowardice.

He had run away from Durl, to do right. He would not run away from Savroix, to do wrong.

Setting his jaw, Talmor lifted his gaze to theirs. "I do not withdraw my charges. They are true, and I stand by them."

Salba thrust a parchment at him. "Then sign your accusation of treason, damne!"

Talmor did not think his knees would support him if he stepped forward to take the paper, but they did somehow. He stared at the writing, and for a moment the words blurred and ran together. There was thunder in his ears and from a long distance away, he heard Sir Kedrien say, "Sign at the mark, if you can write."

Another insult. Talmor looked up sharply, some of his fear forgotten. "I am educated, sir."

"Then sign the paper, damne!" Salba said impatiently. "Don't fondle the parchment all day."

"If I may read what it says, my lord?"

Salba snorted, but Talmor read it from start to finish, making sure it conveyed the truth, complete and as he had stated matters. Dipping into the inkpot, he crossed out one line and rephrased it, ignoring the chancellor's squawk of protest. Then he signed his name with a styling that would have made his old tutor proud, finishing off with a flourish to hide the shakiness in his hand.

Putting down the parchment, he took a step back. Now, he thought bleakly, it is over. My life is finished, all for the sake of duty.

"You have courage, Sir Talmor," Sir Kedrien said while Salba sprinkled sand over the signature to dry it. "More than I expected."

Talmor kept his gaze rigidly on neither man. "Thank you, sir."

"Well," Salba said in a much altered voice. "Courageous, yes. It seems that we must also describe this man as honest and loyal."

The unexpected praise made Talmor blink. "My lord?"

Chancellor Salba's impatient scowl faded entirely. His brown eyes now twinkled although he did not smile. "I have here another report, sir. A dispatch came this morning from Lady Alda, saying that the chevard has expired from his wounds."

Disgust filled Talmor. He said nothing.

"I received, however, a prior report from another source, one which came by express courier mere days after the attack."

Talmor felt suddenly alert. "My lord?"

"Yes. His majesty keeps an eye on his holds, especially those at key defense points. The agent's report came much faster than yours, sir."

Hope was spreading through Talmor, yet he dared not believe too much yet. He frowned. "My servant had no horse, my lord. My own wounds slowed us yet more."

"Don't give excuses!" Salba barked, and Talmor fell silent. "Lord Pace did indeed die in the attack. All, in fact, is exactly as you described. His majesty's agent did not know about the scheme to steal the treasury, but that is being checked out now. 'Tis not the first time greed has driven folk past their good sense, sir, and it won't be the last."

"And what I just signed, my lord?" Talmor asked in relief.

"That will be used at Lady Alda's trial, once she's caught. Well done, sir. You stood for your duty despite all I could think of to frighten you into recanting. Truth doesn't frighten, does it?"

"Well—"

"Now," Sir Kedrien broke in briskly. "What do you intend to do with yourself, sir? You have delivered your report, and be assured that his majesty is grateful. What position do you intend to try for? And where?"

"There's jousting this afternoon," Salba added, "and plenty of lords about to impress with your skills."

Talmor bowed. "Aye, my lord. I thought of that." He shifted his gaze to the officer. "But I would prefer a different post than—"

"Yes, of course," Salba said heartily. "You'd risen as far as you could there at Durl, hadn't you?"

"Nearly, my lord. I hoped to become Lord Pace's protector."

Lord Salba chuckled, and Sir Kedrien smiled.

"Well, that's as may be," Salba said. "An ambitious man like yourself, young and in your prime, why, of course you want to look higher. And so you should. What say you, Kedrien? He's honest to the bone, loyal, and stubborn."

"He's proven that," Sir Kedrien said.

Listening to them, Talmor ached inside with a hope so sharp, so keen it hurt to draw breath. Could he dare reach for an officer's post in the palace guards?

Salba slapped his desk. "Well, then, the very thing for you is to get you a posting with the church knights. I'll see to it straightaway. Which order might you prefer?"

Talmor's hope crashed. Without realizing it, he frowned and took a step back. "Nay, my lord!" he said sharply.

Salba frowned back at him, his good humor fading in an instant. "What? What's this? You refuse a splendid offer like a churl?"

Hastily Talmor tried to school himself. "Forgive me, my lord. I do not wish to seem ungrateful."

"Fine way you show it," Salba said gruffly.

"I beg your lordship's pardon."

"So you should. Now then, it's settled. The order of—"

"No, my lord," Talmor said, less stridently this time, but his voice was absolutely firm. Inside, he felt tangled with a mixture of emotions—disappointment and horror being the strongest. "Thank you, but, no."

"Why not?" Sir Kedrien asked. "The church knights are among the ablest, most valiant warriors in Mandria's army. 'Tis a fine honor indeed to join their ranks."

"I know, sir," Talmor said miserably, knowing he could never explain. "I—"

"What ails you, man?" Salba demanded. "Are you not of the Circle?"

"Yes, of course I am, my lord. It's just—"

"What? What? Don't dither, fellow! Damne, have you lost

your wits? Speak up! They're not all celibate and spartan, you know. Some of the orders live quite well. Name your choice!"

Talmor knew the church knights were fine warriors, brave and favored by both crown and church. They were well paid, well fed, and well housed. But he'd never considered that route of advancement for himself, knowing he could not pass the spiritual examinations. The priests would uncover his darkest secrets, and he would never be allowed to join the their fighting orders. Instead, he might be executed as a heretic or at best driven away and forbidden to take up arms for any lord in the realm.

Drawing in a deep breath, Talmor battled to keep his thoughts and emotions under control. Realizing his fists were clenched hard at his sides, he forced them to relax. "I would prefer to join the palace guards, my lord."

Salba threw back his head and laughed, but the smiling interest on Sir Kedrien's face vanished, and his expression became blank and wooden. His eyes turned flat and cold with unspoken refusal.

"Damne, I took one look at you, sir, and knew you had ambition," Salba said, wiping his eyes. "Well, Kedrien? What think you?"

"Impossible," Sir Kedrien said.

Talmor stiffened, and it was his turn to look blank and cold. Inside, his pulse throbbed, and he did not have to soulgaze Sir Kedrien to recognize his bigotry.

"Now, now, Kedrien," Lord Salba said. "Don't be difficult, man. It's not the usual thing, of course, but—"

Sir Kedrien turned on him. "My lord, it cannot be permitted. Only the finest men, the best Mandria has to offer, make up our numbers."

"And is this young man not fine? Is he not valiant? Look at his shoulders and that strong, deep chest. You know he can wield a sword."

"I would have to see him in the field to judge his skills. I have no doubt they are adequate," Sir Kedrien said coldly.

"They are more than adequate," Talmor retorted. "As I will be happy to demonstrate."

"Gently, sir, gently," Lord Salba said to him in reproof. "Grow not too fiery here."

The rebuke was like a slap. Talmor made haste to bow in apology. But inside he felt a mix of anger and shame. It was always the same, he thought angrily. The same wall of prejudice blocked him again and again. Seething at the injustice of it, he threw caution aside.

"Let us meet on the practice field," he said to the officer. "I'll show you my skills."

Sir Kedrien's brows lifted haughtily. "Do you challenge me, sir?"

"Nay," Talmor replied evenly. "No challenge, except the chance to demonstrate my—"

The officer turned away from him with a shrug. "You see how it is, my lord. The lack of manners and discipline, the inability to take orders."

"Nonsense, Kedrien! Your sergeants can whip that out of him in a day. Why not accept the fellow if he wants a green cloak?"

Sir Kedrien's tanned cheeks darkened. "My lord, aye, I could put him in the bottom ranks and gladly so, on ability alone."

"Then do so, and let the matter rest."

"No."

Lord Salba's jutting eyebrows pulled together, and he glared at the officer while Talmor stood rigid with humiliation.

Sir Kedrien glanced at Talmor. "Must I go on with this or will you withdraw?"

Talmor felt as though he were on fire. Before he could master himself and answer, Lord Salba cleared his throat. "Go on, sir. Go on! Speak up!"

"Very well." Sir Kedrien frowned. "I object because he's intelligent and quick-witted. He's strong, and he's ambitious. He won't be content to stay in the bottom ranks, my lord. He'll want advancement, and that is impossible."

"Why?" Lord Salba asked.

Talmor wanted to close his eyes and hide, but he did not

allow himself to move. He stood at attention, rigid, furious, hating privileged men of good birth like Sir Kedrien who would forever keep the door barred against anyone different.

"He's of mixed blood, my lord."

"Aye, so he is. Not very obvious, though, is it? And surely not the first such man to creep into your ranks, for all your ideas of elitism."

Sir Kedrien's face reddened again at Salba's blunt comments.

"Now give way, Kedrien," Lord Salba said. "I know you like to think there's no one but sons of the finest families in your precious guards, but 'tis far from true."

"Officers are—"

"Oh, officers." Salba shrugged off the protest and let his brown eyes twinkle at Talmor. "He's paying you a high compliment, sir knight, for see how he believes you'll advance quickly? Very well. A guard you'll be. I'll sign your commission as soon as it's drawn up. In the meantime, report to the barracks."

The suddenness of it, after all Kedrien's protests, made Talmor dizzy. A smile spread across his face. "Thank you, my lord. Thank you!"

Salba smiled back. "You've done his majesty good service, and you deserve the reward you seek. That is all. Any page can direct you to the barracks if you know not the way."

"I'll give the man directions," Sir Kedrien said.

Together they left the chamber, with Lord Salba already digging through more papers and bellowing for his clerk. In the short hallway they paused. Talmor turned warily to face Sir Kedrien, whom he could have liked had not the door of bigotry slammed so harshly between them.

Sir Kedrien scowled. "I do not apologize for questioning you. The safety of the royal family demands that every man be true to the core."

Talmor kept his face frozen and did not make the mistake of offering additional reassurances of his loyalty. "I understand perfectly, Sir Kedrien."

"The barracks are through that gate, down past the stable-yard."

"I can find them."

"One last thing," Sir Kedrien said.

Talmor swallowed a sigh. "Aye, sir?"

"Report to Sergeant Goddal in Barracks Seven. Tell him to assign you to sentry patrol."

"Aye, sir."

Sir Kedrien's astute eyes searched his face. "If I thought for a moment you were part Gantese, or even Netheran, I'd have you out of here."

Talmor said nothing.

"You won't be assigned near the king," Sir Kedrien said harshly. "Put your ambitions aside, for you'll not advance."

"You make yourself very clear, sir."

"I hope so. As for any aim of one day becoming his majesty's protector . . . forget that as well."

Talmor blinked. So *that* was what Kedrien feared. He nearly reassured the man that such was not his goal, but then stopped himself. Kedrien would not believe him. *Let him worry,* Talmor thought grimly. *No doubt 'tis his own ambition, and he fears I shall use magic to block his way.*

He understood Kedrien now, saw through him as clearly as though he'd soulgazed the man. There was no point in trying to win Sir Kedrien's liking, or even his admiration, for never would the officer allow himself to grant either.

Talmor met Sir Kedrien's eyes. "If that is all, I'll report now to Sergeant Goddal."

"Barracks Seven," Sir Kedrien said.

Talmor walked away, feeling the officer's hostile gaze boring holes in his back, and wondered if every day would bring the same degree of bigotry and petty persecution. For an instant, Talmor felt wearied by it, knowing all too well how it could drag down a man's spirit, but then he straightened his shoulders. Efficiency and outstanding performance had long been his defense against prejudice, and he would use them again. He would prove his worth here at Savroix, no matter what it took.

Chapter Nine

Ten days later, the king returned to Savroix from his hunting trip. The royal party arrived with the usual fanfare of trumpets. His majesty rode in on a magnificent stallion, his hunting dogs dashing to and fro, barking in excitement. The falconers followed, bearing the large, hooded birds on wooden perches affixed to the front of their saddles. The huntsmen, garbed in foliage colors, rode with their curved horns slung over their shoulders, and behind them came the game wagons mounded high with trophies of pelts, antlers, and meat already dressed, seasoned, and salt-packed in wooden barrels.

As the king's cavalcade filled the main courtyard, members of the court came outside to welcome his majesty. Hearty greetings were called out on all sides. The Countess Lalieux, gowned beautifully in celestial blue, her curls arranged artfully around her face, waved and blew kisses to the king from a small balcony.

Smiling, Verence waved back to her before dismounting. Coated with dust and looking tired, he walked inside leisurely, with his lord protector at his heels.

Standing in the crowd of welcoming courtiers, Pheresa curtsied as the king passed. His gaze slid past her face without interest, then shifted back to her. He smiled at her but did not speak.

She saw the melancholy in his eyes, and knew that his hunting trip had not accomplished its purpose. The king still grieved for his lost son, and no amount of activity or distance could alter the grim results of last winter.

"The king looks well," Lady Carolie said beside her. Pretty and kindhearted, she was becoming a friend to Pheresa. Intending to marry at the end of summer, she stayed lit up with happiness. "I think his hunting has rested him, as usual."

Pheresa frowned. "I thought his majesty looked unhappy and tired. He is not well."

"Do you think he will cancel the summer ball?" Lady Carolie asked in dismay. "Are we to stay in mourning forever? Give up all our pleasures?"

"Hush!" Pheresa admonished her, as they followed the others back inside. "There can be no pleasure when his majesty is sad."

That afternoon, while the king strolled in the gardens and the court wandered with him in attendance, Pheresa was joined by her father.

Surprised, she curtsied to Lindier and allowed him to escort her to a bench surrounded by tall hedge. As she sat down, he clasped his hands behind his back. A cold, aloof man, the Duc du Lindier seldom gave his daughter much attention. Graying and afflicted with a stiff leg from an old battle wound, he had grown raddled from his life of courtly dissipation.

Today he seemed nervous and uneasy, which was most unlike him.

Pheresa sat with her posture perfect as usual, her wide skirts arranged prettily, her hands clasped in her lap. She stared up at him with a level, calm gaze, curious, but suspecting that he might be bringing her fresh trouble.

Frowning, the duc cleared his throat. "This Lervan de Waite fellow, have you met him?"

"No, of course not," she said, surprised by the abrupt question. "He has not yet been officially presented. How could I—"

"Oh, come, Pheresa, don't simper and play games. Officially at court or not, he hangs about, rides in the park, flirts with any girl he sees. Have you met him?"

"No, your grace. I have not."

"Would you meet him?"

"Before he's seen the king? Why?"

Her father's impatience grew more pronounced. "I think you know quite well why."

"Do you believe he has any chance to be named Verence's heir?"

"I think it very likely. He has looks, charm, wit, can sit a horse well, knows how to wear his clothes, and can handle weapons like a man."

Pheresa laughed. "And your grace thinks this makes him kingly?"

"If a man has the look and manner, daughter, very likely he has the heart as well."

She looked up at him, yearning for the affection he'd never shown her. "Do you value heart above intelligence?"

"Cleverness does not always win," he replied. "I do not often advise you, Pheresa. But you will have better luck using your beauty to make a good marriage than reaching for the throne."

Bitterness filled her, curling her hands into fists in her lap. If this was her father's notion of parental advice, she could do without it. She stared grimly out across the lawn, where the rest of the court divided itself into a game of ball and pins. Laughter carried on the air.

"So your grace opposes me as well. Do you support my mother?"

He snorted. "Never. Dianthelle's being absurd, indulging in fantasy and abandoning common sense. Take care you're absent when she gets her reprimand from Verence, for she'll turn on you in vicious temper."

"I thank your grace for the warning."

"Why not marry Lervan?" the duc asked her.

Surprised anew, Pheresa sent him a sharp look and found him studying her with eyes as opaque as stone. "Is he looking for a wife?"

"What man of good fortune and prospects is not? Consider it, daughter. Fortune favors him, and perhaps through him you may yet sit a throne."

"But he isn't—"

"Forgive me. I am being summoned," the duc said, and walked away from her without farewell.

She sat there a moment, frowning as she mulled over this strange little conversation. Her father was not known as an intriguer. He seldom plotted, unlike his wife. What, then, was he up to? Pheresa supposed everything he'd just said could be taken at face value. Perhaps he simply thought this Lervan had good prospects, as he'd said. Or perhaps Lord Meaclan's support was already stirring the deep waters of court.

"My lady! Come and play! We need you on our team." Laughing, Lady Carolie and her two sisters came skipping up, ribbons fluttering and lace awry. They grasped Pheresa by the hands and led her over to the lawn. Everyone applauded when she arrived, and there was no more time to think of schemes and convoluted plots.

A shower of rain ended the fun shortly thereafter, and the court scattered indoors to find other amusements. The king retired to his private apartments, and little murmurs of consternation ran through the court.

Lord Meaclan approached Pheresa casually after dinner. His wife was at his side. A plump lady with a good-natured smile, she curtsied to Pheresa, and said, "It is a tremendous honor to meet you at last. I have heard much of your beauty, and I did pray fervently last winter for your safe return."

"How kind of you," Pheresa replied with a reserved smile. She expected the woman next to question her about the Chalice or exotic details of Nether, but the lady fell quiet and let her husband take over the conversation instead.

"Have you heard the latest news?" he murmured, his eyes darting past her to observe the rest of the room.

She wondered who was staring at them, but her back was

to the company. Lips could be read from a distance, and Pheresa had learned to position herself to thwart such efforts. Lord Meaclan seemed equally adept. Although his face could be observed, he'd learned a trick of speaking from the corner of his mouth, and his lips hardly moved.

"I fear 'tis not good news," he added.

"What has happened?" Pheresa asked.

"You heard something, I am sure, of the sea raids on one of the northwest holds last month?"

She nodded, although she had no more information than that.

"A messenger came this afternoon with dispatches from the eastern border."

She frowned. "Trouble with Klad?"

"I'm afraid so."

"War?"

He smiled. "Nothing that grievous yet, my lady. Our information is that three of the Kladite chieftains have united forces to raid Mandrian pastures. Hard on the messenger's heels came representatives from the wool guild, with merchants demanding armed protection for the eastern trade route."

"The king will, of course, provide it."

"He has not seen them, nor has he heard their petition."

Her frown deepened. "Tomorrow—"

"Who can dictate when his majesty will grant an audience?" Lord Meaclan asked in exasperation.

"Surely the raids require swift action. Retaliation—"

He raised his hand in warning, and she stopped just as a baron joined them with an unctuous bow. Meaclan returned the man's greeting and, with a grave nod to Pheresa, moved away, drawing the baron with him. Pheresa realized she'd been given information ahead of the rest of the court. The privilege was rare, but it meant the minister of finance was keeping his end of their bargain by helping her all he could. Information, she knew, was sometimes as effective as a sword, perhaps more so. The question was, what could she do with it?

During the next few days, she watched and listened, but apparently the king took no action against Klad. Although he was no warmonger, he'd always been a vigilant ruler, watchful of his borders, protective of the trade routes that kept Mandria rich. Now, he did not seem to care. Rarely did he hold audiences. Often he shut himself away in private, seeing no one. Rumors spread through the court that his majesty was ill. His grieving seemed unnaturally prolonged, and the more foolish courtiers began to question Pheresa about what had really occurred in Nether. Had the king been harmed by evil spells? Was he trying to persuade the priests to resurrect Prince Gavril by some blasphemous means? Had his majesty turned to dark paths in search of unholy comfort? Why did he no longer care about his subjects? Was he going to grieve forever? Was he dying?

Impatient of such nonsense, Pheresa shook off their speculations and tried to dampen the worst rumors whenever she could. "Would you have his majesty forget the prince so quickly?" she said in mild rebuke to the Duchesse of Clune, a fat, particularly stupid woman. "Gavril is but two months in his grave, and the king loved him deeply. Give him time."

"But his majesty turns away even from Lalieux—"

"The king has changed mistresses before," Pheresa said curtly.

"You mean—"

"I mean nothing," she said, aware that a new rumor would commence at once. She did not want to cause trouble for the countess, but Lalieux was able to take care of herself, and at least speculation of this kind was better fodder for weak minds than political gossip that might do real harm.

But although she pretended all was well, she knew it was not. Worried about her uncle, she watched him sit listlessly at an afternoon presentation in which those newly arrived at court were paraded forth and introduced formally to the king. Lervan de Waite was among the presentees. Fashionably dressed and sporting a vivid jadecock feather in his cap, he bowed to the king, smiled without any evidence of nervousness, and offered a joke that made Verence chuckle. That so-cial triumph made Lervan immediately popular with the court, and he was soon surrounded by new friends and acquaintances, most of them ladies.

Pretending indifference, Pheresa looked him over. He was passably good-looking, although far less handsome than either Faldain or Gavril. His wit and charm seemed bountiful, judging by the way everyone around him laughed. He talked a bit too loud for her taste, and acted a bit too bold in his look and manner. She noticed how he eyed the ladies and how deeply he emptied his wine cup. Very thick and strong through the chest and shoulders, he was the type of man who would grow fat in middle years. Yet his cheerfulness was a welcome contrast to the king's gloom. When Verence retired early for the evening, the atmosphere lightened noticeably.

The Duc du Lindier introduced Lervan to Pheresa. Well aware that everyone was watching, including Cardinal Theloi like a thin little spider in one corner of the room, Pheresa curtsied to the young man and gave him her rather reserved smile when he bowed over her hand.

I do not like him, she thought.

Lervan straightened, his eyes meeting hers. She saw them widen a little, saw the quick flare of his nostrils. His smile showed genuine pleasure. "We meet at last, cousin."

She stiffened at the term and would have withdrawn her hand from his warm clasp had he not tightened his fingers. His gaze ranged over her in bold appreciation and lingered a moment at her bodice before returning to her face.

"How lovely you are. I have heard much of you, but still I was unprepared for how much your beauty eclipses the other ladies'." He bent his head and lightly kissed her hand before releasing it.

Despite herself, Pheresa felt a momentary shiver of physical attraction. At close quarters, she saw no cleverness in his face, only good humor and an easy readiness to smile. But there was something about him that was appealing. She found herself smiling back, forgiving him for what in another she would have found offensive.

"Your Aiesliun manners go too fast for me, my lord," she

said in her quiet, rather low-pitched voice. "We are not cousins, and you do not know me well enough to have the privilege of kissing my hand."

"Alas," he said merrily, cocking his head to one side and giving her a wink. "Since I arrived, I've had endless lessons in court manners and etiquette, and I believe I cannot remember half of it all. Why should I not call you cousin, for I wish you were my relation."

Her father murmured something and slipped away. To her surprise, Pheresa found herself enjoying Lervan and his silly prattle.

"Wishes, my lord," she replied, choosing to banter with him, "do not alter reality."

His mouth was mobile, with a habit of quirking slightly at one corner before he spoke. "And if we never indulge in dreams, princess, how can we change our circumstances?"

"I am not a princess."

"Not yet," he whispered, stepping closer. He gazed down intently into her eyes, so that she was momentarily mesmerized.

But someone else approached and spoke to them. The little moment shattered, and, with a blink, Pheresa glanced away. She was astonished by how audaciously he flirted. It was as though she found herself teetering on a precipice. Unwilling to fall, she stepped back. No doubt her father had been coaching Lervan, hinting of the suitability of marriage between them. She disliked such meddling, and had no intention of being rushed.

As for Lervan, this fine young lord had best learn he could not sweep her athwart with his charm. She curtsied slightly to him, giving him the respect due to a minor member of the nobility but nothing more. He might be playing on his prospects at present, but she knew how quickly the court flocked to a newcomer, and how quickly the court's favor could turn away whenever it grew tired of the novelty.

"Excuse me," she said, and walked away from him.

He hurried after her, causing people to stare. She heard the murmurs, saw the smiles of speculation. Flushing with annoyance, she turned on him. "Why do you chase after me?"

"Do not go so soon," he pleaded with her. "We were just getting acquainted."

"I retire early," she said. "Good night."

Again he hurried after her. The buzz of laughter and voices grew louder. She was blushing now, and that made her angrier than ever.

"Do not bounce after me like a puppy, my lord!" she rebuked him sharply. "I am finished with the evening."

"But I do not want you to go," he said, giving her that quirky smile. "Can you not stay a while longer and give me courage while I meet so many new people?"

Immediately she saw through him. He wanted her to introduce him about, as her father had introduced him to her. Drawing a sharp breath, Pheresa realized this man was not a fool after all. She must never again underestimate him. However, if he thought she was going to lend him consequence by turning herself into his closest friend and ally at court, he could think again. Despite his charm, she was not sure she liked him. At present, he remained her only serious rival for the throne.

She smiled at him warmly enough to rekindle the admiration in his eyes. He reached for her hand, saying, "Ah, that's better. I was feeling as though you did not like me much, my lady."

With equal smoothness she evaded his grasp and turned away. "You have such easy manners, my lord, that I cannot believe you ever to be at a disadvantage, whether the company is new to you or familiar. I believe you can manage very well without me. Good night."

Again she walked away, her head held high. This time, to her great relief, he did not come after her. But as she slipped out of the room, she glanced back and saw him at the center of a cluster of people. A cold little feeling of apprehension passed through her. She realized that he had that gift of instant popularity which she lacked. He seemed already at home, while her own natural reserve always made her hold back from people.

Was it wise, she wondered, to leave him to charm the court tonight? What might he do, what might he gain in her absence? Yet she knew she could not stop him from making others like him, even if she stayed glued at his side for the whole evening. And she was not yet ready to be swept into an alliance, no matter what Lord Lervan and her father plotted together.

Just as she started across the threshold of her rooms, she glimpsed something from the corner of her eye and looked back.

It had been a furtive shadow at the end of the corridor, but it was gone. She frowned, her gaze lingering on the spot where the figure had vanished. Man or woman, she could not be sure, but she felt certain she'd been followed.

Here in the palace it meant little. A shadow might be an admirer. It might be a spy or even an assassin. She sighed at her own fanciful notions and told herself it was probably Sir Brillon.

The thought of the church knight made her frown anew. She stepped inside rather hurriedly and watched as the door was shut.

"Bolt it," she said.

Her servants looked surprised. "But, my lady," Verine said, "we do not usually bolt your chamber door until after you've bathed and dressed for bed, and your posset is brought."

"I know that," Pheresa said impatiently. She still felt uneasy, and it sharpened her voice. "Bolt it. I want no bath tonight, and I'll have no posset either."

"You are sickening for something," Oola said. "Come and lie down."

"Leave me, both of you. Light the lamps and leave me. I want to be alone."

Her attendants exchanged troubled looks but obeyed. Oola loosened her laces, so that she could remove her gown unassisted if she wished. "You have only to ring for me, my lady, and I shall come and help you."

"Yes, now go away," Pheresa said.

When they were gone, Pheresa tested the bolts on both window and door just to make certain they were secure. She moved restlessly about her chamber, unable to settle herself, then finally unpinned her golden hair and brushed it out.

The long, slow strokes soothed her greatly. She could not explain why she felt so uneasy, except Lervan had disturbed her in a way she was not prepared for. Physical desire did not come to her as readily as it did to some.

She did not like the way Lervan's face kept returning to her thoughts or how flushed and restless she felt beneath her gown. He had kissed her hand. What would it be like if he kissed her lips or held her in his arms?

For the first time in her life she saw that a man could undermine a woman, sweeping away all her plans and intentions. How? How could a man do it? Was it his look, his smile, that quirk of his red lips? Was it the admiration in his eyes, the blatant invitation he issued so silently with his look and touch?

Her mouth tightened. She would not lose the throne to ordinary lust, she vowed to herself. No, Thod help her, she would not.

That night, dreams troubled her sleep, making her restless indeed. A dark mist crept constantly toward her, pursuing her no matter where she sought refuge in the palace. Ankle deep, the mist was a dark, narrow ribbon of menace that flowed snakelike through the galleries and corridors of Savroix in her wake. There were no people to help her. The palace stood empty, and her footsteps echoed as she ran here and there in search of help.

At last, she found herself in the throne room. A medallion of king's glass hung suspended from the ceiling. All the lamps were lit and shining. Red silk covered the walls in loose folds, like blood running down. The throne stood empty, waiting for Verence to come. She waited, too, breathing hard, knowing time was running out.

The king did not appear, but the mist did. It flowed beneath the door and aimed itself at her. Fearful of being cornered, she

ran to the private door used only by his majesty, but it was
bolted shut. She pounded on its thick panels and tried to call
out, but her voice was silent.

No one came. The mist kept flowing toward her, and when
she darted away from it, it widened and spread across the
room. Edging back, she stood pinned against the throne while
the mist slid beneath the hem of her gown. How cold and evil
it felt around her ankles. Shivering, she tried again to call out
for help, but her throat would give no sound.

Desperately, she knew she must break the law and climb
onto the throne. No one was permitted there except the
monarch, on penalty of death.

The mist curled deeper around her ankles, so cold she shuddered with pain. She retreated, and the throne skidded away
from her and toppled over. In trying to grab it, she fell herself,
hitting her jaw and one elbow most painfully. The mist engulfed her, spreading up her legs to her hips and waist. She
could not move in it, although she struggled to drag herself
clear.

She was held its prisoner, and now she sensed something
alive and malignant within it, something intelligent and cun-
ning. It had hunted her a long time, and at last it had her.

The mist spread across her body, making her heart jerk and
thud painfully. It touched her face, smothering her as she was
pressed down. She tried to struggle, but she was so cold, so
terribly cold and weak. Her mouth opened to scream, and the
mist flowed into it, tasting rotten and numbing her tongue. It
filled her whole being, making her a part of itself.

And she and the evil were one.

Pheresa sat upright with a gasp, breathing hard, shuddering
and spitting as though to vomit the mist out of her body. She
felt clammy with sweat. Her bedgown was drenched with it,
sticking to her skin. Her hair hung in a wild tangle in her eyes,
and she was clutching the sheet with both fists.

"No," she moaned. "No!"

A faint gray light illuminated the room. She found herself

in her bed, in her chamber, *not* in the throne room. She looked around, still breathing hard, and slowly came free of the nightmare. Realizing it had been a dream, no matter how vivid or real it had seemed, she lifted her hands to her face and began to cry.

Why did she continue to suffer such dreadful nightmares, she wondered, wiping at her tears. Was she not home in Savroix, far from the evil that had once held her prisoner? Was she not safe? Why did she continue to fear?

Perhaps it was not herself she feared for, she reasoned, but another. She thought about the empty throne and the empty palace. Surely such a dream reflected her belief that Verence must renew his heart and spirit. A demoralized king could not rule long. Already Mandria's enemies took advantage of his weakness to attack. If he did not meet these challenges soon, Mandria's problems would escalate into war.

Who dared tell the king that he was not doing his duty? Would Chancellor Salba speak bluntly to his majesty? Would Lord Meaclan? Would Cardinal Theloi?

Suddenly she felt certain that she must try to help Verence. She did not know what she could say to him, but she knew she had to offer what comfort she could. It was time the king made his peace with what had happened to Gavril.

Giving herself no chance to hesitate, she looked outside and saw that it was just now dawn. The air felt damp and cold, as though it might rain. She knew it was the king's habit to walk alone in his private garden at daybreak. If she hurried, she might be able to join him there.

Throwing on her clothes and hastily braiding her hair, she wrapped herself in a warm cloak, made sure she had her salt purse and dagger on her person, and slipped from her chamber as silently as a ghost.

The palace had not yet roused. Not even the servants were stirring. The passageways and galleries lay silent and shadowy, torches and lamps extinguished, ashes cold on hearths. The guards on duty slumbered or gazed blearily at her without challenge as she made her way outside. She knew that the only way she could enter the king's garden unseen was via a long, circuitous route along the rear wall of the palace. She would have to exit the safe enclosure of the walls and skirt the edge of the meadow between Savroix and the king's forest. The fog frightened her, and the world lay hushed and still in eerie silence, yet she did not turn back.

The elderly gatekeeper snoozing at his post by the small garden gates took bribes from anyone slipping outside for secret assignations, or so Lady Carolie had whispered to her with much giggling. Now, shivering as much from nerves as from the cold, Pheresa made sure her hood was pulled up to conceal her face before she approached the man. She handed him a coin in silence, and without a word he swung open the gate for her.

She ran, clutching her cloak at her throat, and flung herself against the wall past some bushes to stare back the way she'd come. Only the faintest rasp and clink of metal told her the gate was shut now. She waited, her heart beating fast, well aware of the possible danger she'd put herself in by leaving the safety of the palace walls. Her greatest fear was that Sir Brillon might be following her, and if he was, she'd just handed him the opportunity to abduct her.

The fog seemed thicker than ever here at the base of the walls. She watched and listened, but no figure loomed at her from the mist. She heard no furtive footsteps, nothing in fact save the measured cadence of the sentry walking the wall overhead.

Reasoning that the sentry could not see her if she kept near the base of the walls, she hurried on, keeping one hand on the wall for guidance. The rough-cut stones snagged at her fingertips. Her skirts dragged in the long grass, and she soaked her slippers in its dampness.

As she neared the turret corner, she slowed her pace and paused again to look back. But there was no sign of Sir Brillon. She began to relax, and told herself that she would never do anything as risky as this again. It seemed absurd that she could not simply request a private audience with the king, and yet all her petitions had been denied with the greatest politeness. Verence was interested in no one, wanted to talk to no one. He had isolated himself to a dangerous degree.

How, she wondered, did Lady Carolie dare slip outside the walls like this? Why did she, Sophia de Brit, Angelia, and even Verine take such risks? Could they not rendezvous with their lovers inside the palace?

"Of course," Lady Carolie had said once with a shrug, looking smug, while Pheresa stared at her in astonishment. "But it is twice as wicked and twice as fun to thwart the rules and meet in the forest. Someday, you, too, will risk all to meet your lover. Danger makes his kisses sweeter, you see."

Now, Pheresa waited while two sentries met at the corner, saluted each other, and marched away again. She crept warily past the stout door of the turret, then hastened onward. The fog thinned to mere patches, then thickened again so that sometimes she seemed to walk straight through a white wall of it. In the distance she saw the spire of the ruined church that had once belonged to the Sebein cult. She hated to look at the place and wished the king would tear it down. Nothing grew around the church, not even grass, as though the very ground was poisoned. By all she'd heard, only two walls and part of the spire remained of the evil structure, but now, wrapped in fog, the church looked intact in the dim, gloomy light, as though some dreadful spell had restored it. She even thought she glimpsed a light shining in its windows.

Blinking and rubbing her eyes, she looked again. There was no light. All stood dark and silent, and she told herself to stop letting her imagination frighten her so. The Sebeins were long gone, their cult stamped out and the members scattered. She'd do better to worry over whether the king would forgive her for intruding on his company like this. He could order her punished. He might even banish her from court.

Her rapid pace slowed, and she could hear her own harsh breathing. Perhaps she ought to go back to her rooms and bide patiently, letting Verence work out his troubles on his own.

But she did not retreat. Whatever prudence or common sense she possessed seemed to have left her. She felt an overwhelming instinct to talk to Verence without delay, as though a force larger than herself drove her onward.

Minutes later, her hand brushed not stone, but instead wood. She'd found what she sought, a narrow old gate that should lead into the king's garden. Designed originally to permit access to the gardeners, it looked long unused, for weeds and vines grew across it. She tore some of these away, then, with shaking hands, used her dagger to pry open the lock. As she pushed the gate open, it creaked loudly on rusted hinges. Squeezing through the narrow space, she pushed the gate shut behind her.

Her heart beat like thunder. Shoving back her hood, she wiped some of the moisture from her face and tried to brush away the grass stains and damp from her skirts. How disheveled and wild she must look. If the king did come, he would be offended by her appearance. She sighed, feeling as though the day was already a disaster.

After she settled herself on a bench by the fountain, she heard a gate creak open sharply and the sound of voices. Shooting to her feet, Pheresa strained to listen and recognized Verence's deep voice. He had come despite the foul weather.

Her heart leaped inside her breast. Suddenly she did not know what to say to him. She knew the urge to hide among the yews and not approach him at all, but this was no time to be a coward.

Squinting in an effort to see through the fog, she called out, "Your majesty! 'Tis I, Pher—"

Something tackled her from behind, pinning her arms to her sides and nearly knocking her over. Startled out of her wits, she cried out in fear, and found herself manhandled ruthlessly.

"Release me!" she cried. "How dare you—"

"Name yourself or die."

The dangerously angry voice that threatened her belonged to the king's protector. "Lord Odeil," she said breathlessly, aware that if she was not quick his dagger would be in her ribs. "'Tis Lady Pheresa. No assassin. Please let me go."

She was released so suddenly she nearly lost her balance.

He spun her around to face him, making her dizzy, and as the fog momentarily thinned she saw his scarred, wizened face looming over her.

"Ah, so 'tis," he said, much less fiercely. "What in Thod's name are you—begging your majesty's pardon," he called out, his tone abruptly changed as footsteps approached them. "Lady Pheresa, sire. Alone with no escort."

"Alone?" Verence said in surprise.

He, too, loomed out of the fog, wrapped in a dark, hooded cloak. She curtsied to him, her face burning, and wondered how in Thod's name she could explain her fears and worries to him. Her nightmare seemed foolish now. And how dared she presume to advise him? She must take great care.

"How came you here?" the king demanded. "This is my private walk, where I am never disturbed."

"I know, majesty," she said hurriedly, afraid he would dismiss her before she could explain. She sank down at his feet. "Forgive me, I beg you. I am much worried about you. I thought I would—"

"Leave us," the king said to Lord Odeil.

The protector bowed, but did not obey. Instead, he stared at Pheresa. "She is armed in your presence, majesty."

"Armed? How so?"

Lord Odeil reached for Pheresa, but she needed no prompting. Rising to her feet, she produced her small dagger from her pocket and held it up.

Verence took it from her and laughed hollowly. "Mercy of Tomias, Odeil, would you fear this little toothpick? She would never harm me."

"Your majesty, 'tis forbidden to carry weapons into your presence."

"Forgive me," Pheresa said. "I have made it a habit never to be without my salt and dagger. I forgot to leave both behind." She bowed her head, trembling. "Now have I offended you twice, sire. I can only offer my deepest apologies and beg for your mercy."

Verence stared down at her. She gazed into his peculiar eyes of blue and green, and saw sadness cloud them.

"Salt, niece?" he said gently. "You carry salt? Even here at Savroix?"

Tears stung her eyes. "I'm sorry," she whispered.

He gave her back the dagger and gestured dismissal at Odeil. With a snort of disapproval, the grizzled protector trudged a short distance away. Although he disappeared into the fog, Pheresa knew he did not go far.

"Salt," the king repeated dully. "Have you not yet put off your fears? You are safe here, you know. Quite safe."

She did not believe it. "I tell myself so, but I cannot put my little protections aside. Forgive me for recalling misfortune to your majesty's mind. 'Twas not my intention to do so when I came here."

"You have given offense," he said, but his voice was gentle. "I will hear no requests, child. I receive no one here. Although I forgive your intrusion this once, you must promise never to repeat such behavior."

Desperate to avoid dismissal, she said hastily, "Sire, you mistake me. I come seeking neither a favor nor the granting of a petition. I fear for your health, and no one will let me talk to you, or do what I can to ease your troubles. You are not yourself, sire. I—I knew no other way to reach you than this."

The king placed his hand lightly on her head. "Ah, Pheresa, what a gentle and kind heart you have. Do you truly worry so much about me?"

"I do, sire."

His hand fell away, and he sighed.

She stepped closer. "How may I help you? How can I comfort you?"

"Nothing can help. I think daily of my son's last moments. If only he had not lost his soul. The thought of it torments me past all bearing."

"Sire, please," she said, fresh tears spilling down her cheeks. She clutched his hand, shocked by how cold it was. "Dwelling on it cannot lift your sorrow. You must trust in Thod's mercy."

"There is no comfort in Writ," the king murmured, drawing his hand from hers. "It carries only condemnation for the poor boy."

"Gavril made many mistakes," she said. "He did much that was wrong, very wrong. But he was not evil, sire. Does not Thod know what lies truly within our hearts? Who is to say what happens between a man and his Maker at that moment of confrontation?"

"Would you blaspheme, Pheresa?" the king asked gently.

She shook her head, but she felt angry at the church for having failed her uncle in his search for answers. "Nay, sire. But I would urge you to consider the teaching of the Circle before Reform. Read the old texts and find comfort there."

"Turn aside from Tomias? Take care, my girl."

"I have found comfort from the old writings. Where does the Chalice of Eternal Life come if not from before Reform? Where does the Circle come? Think of it, sire! We were all joined once, before Reform divided us. Oh, I do not urge your majesty to throw away the teachings of Tomias. I would not dare! But—but even Tomias studied the old texts before his revelation."

The king stood silent for a long while before at last he spoke. "Never utter such things in public, Pheresa," he said sternly. "You would destroy yourself faster than you think possible."

The warning chilled her. She stared at him, wondering if she'd gone too far. Would he denounce her to the church? "I've never said anything like this before to anyone. But since I sipped from the Chalice, I've had many questions and new thoughts. I—I thought your majesty would understand."

"Bring no trouble on yourself, Pheresa," he said. "Would you suffer interrogation and purging? Would you be flogged, your tongue cut out?" Tears glistened in his eyes. "Mercy of Thod, I lost Gavril to the darkness, and now to see you in danger as well, I—"

Breaking off, he shook his head.

Astonished to see him so unmanned, Pheresa reached out her hand. "Nay, sire, nay! I didn't mean to—"

"Hush," he said, turning away. "Say no more of this. I shall pretend I heard none of it."

"Of course, sire."

"Pheresa," he said harshly, "swear to me that you will not become apostate. Swear it!"

She curtsied, feeling frightened by his fierceness. "I swear."

"Perhaps Theloi is right. Perhaps you should be cloistered at once, yet I cannot bear to lose you so soon."

She felt as though he'd just struck her. Horrified, she lifted her gaze to his. "Dearest sire, do not send me away. I am unfit to be a saint. I—I want to remain here. Please, please—"

"Would you beg and grovel, Pheresa?" he broke in with annoyance. "Where is your dignity, your comportment? I like this not, this new behavior, this coming to me without permission, looking wild and dirty, and babbling anathema. Is nothing to remain pure and clean in this world? Are all things good and right coming to an end?"

Her face puckered unhappily. She was making things worse with everything she said. "What must I do to reassure and comfort your majesty?" she asked, forcing her voice to sound calm.

"Stop meddling in matters of state. Stop alarming church officials. Stop trying to be what you are not."

Tears stung her eyes at his rebuke. What did he want her to be, she wondered bitterly. Was she to go back to being shy and timid? Was she to remain only an ornament, pleasing to look at but empty inside?

Overhead, a bird began to twitter sleepily in a tree. Fragrance from exotic blossoms suddenly scented the air, and the fog grew noticeably thinner. Pearly coral suffused the sky. The garden, moments before shrouded in mist and shadow, was suddenly gilded with sunlight. Verence shoved back his hood, and his face looked gaunt and drawn as though he had not slept.

"I beg your majesty's pardon," she said miserably. "I have failed you, and did not know it until now."

He gave her a fleeting smile. "You're young, child. 'Tis

only natural that you make mistakes. But learn from them. Learn from them, and do not plunge yourself into folly, as Gavril did."

"I fear for you, sire. You have many years yet. Will you not live them? Can you not bring your heart out of the grave and know joy again? And if not joy, then at least the knowledge that Gavril went forth to save a life. My life." She sighed. "If anyone should feel the burden of responsibility or guilt, 'tis I. Had I not drunk of that poison—"

"Hush," he said. "You mean well, child, but don't assume his guilt for him. He willingly embraced evil and threw away his soul. Nothing changes that. And no prayer, no vigil, no ancient text can comfort this father's heart. Somehow the king failed him. And so I brood and search my memories for what went wrong."

"Perhaps," she said softly, "all the wrong lay in him."

Verence's head snapped up. "Nay!" he said sharply. "As a babe, he was sweet and good, such a fine little fellow, so brave and stalwart. He could ride a pony when he was but four years old. How he would crow and shout and pretend to joust with a stick in his hand. He—"

Breaking off abruptly, Verence buried his face in his hands.

She stared at him a long while, saddened to see that all her sympathy had only brought him more pain. Yet this broken, grieving man was not the king she knew and admired. Frowning, she tried one last time. "You have lost your son, sire. Will you lose Mandria also?"

"Pheresa—"

"Will you leave the holds undermanned? Will you go on ignoring the pleas for help from your borders? Will you allow barbarians and savages to insult this realm and do nothing? How can you—"

"Enough!" he shouted, turning on her.

So fierce did he look that she sank into a startled curtsy. He glared at her, his eyes blazing with life now.

"So you will tell me how to rule my own kingdom," he said in a voice like thunder. Lord Odeil came running up in alarm, only to stop and retreat once more. Verence never noticed him as he went on glaring at Pheresa. "You go too far. You dare too much!"

She'd wanted to revive his spirit, but it seemed as though his fury would mean the end of her. Wanting to shrink up into a tiny ball and hide, she was desperately sorry she'd opened her mouth. "Sire, I—"

"Silence! I've loved you like a daughter. I've thought so well of you, but nay, you are like your mother, always so certain that your way is right. You are determined to interfere, to meddle, to poke your nose where you are not wanted. You have no knowledge of what it means to rule. None!"

"Sire, I—"

"How dare you tell me what I should do. I thought you the best of my court, a maid sensible and worthy, honorable and good. You are no better than the rest, jackals all, greedy to see my majesty dead and gone."

"No—"

"You want my throne, girl. Admit it! You worry at the problem like a dog with a knucklebone. Scheming and plotting for the crown, always the crown. How you've changed, and 'tis not to your credit."

"Please! Your majesty misunderstands."

"You care nothing for me," he said bitterly. "Just as you cared nothing for Gavril. How superb you are at pretending emotions you do not feel. So lovely and perfect, so saintly of demeanor, yet you are proven to be grasping and ambitious. You plighted troth with Gavril only to be queen. Admit there was no other reason. *Admit it!*"

Aghast, she found herself saying, "I thought I loved him at first. I did truly want to please him, but I—"

"You wanted to be queen. You rejected an alliance with Nether because you still want to be queen here. Confess to it, Pheresa. I know what lies within your greedy heart."

Tears spilled down her cheeks. His words raked and wounded her. She did not know how to answer such rage as this, such icy contempt. She'd never guessed he felt this way about her. She'd never realized the resentment that festered in his heart.

Knowing that anything she said now would only be turned against her, she bowed her head in silence and refused to answer. Let him take that as admission if he wished, she thought miserably. He would only spurn her further denials.

"No more," he said. He shook his head, and his face was bleak indeed. "No more."

She lifted her tear-streaked face and met his angry gaze. "Blame me, sire, if you wish," she said, knowing she was finished at court. "But I did not put Tanengard in his hand. I did not overlook his faults and absolve him of blame every time he practiced his cruelty on those who could not strike back. I did not excuse him or coddle him. I did not force him to offer me marriage; he did so only for reasons of spite and jealousy. And I did not persuade him to ignore Faldain's guidance when he plunged us straight into Nether's trap. Everything else, yes, I will confess to. But none of that."

Verence turned his back on her. "Leave."

The dismissal was final. Her knees were shaking, but somehow she managed a curtsy. He did not acknowledge her as she withdrew, backing step by shaking step from him until she turned, half-blinded by tears, and fled down the path. The sky was golden now. Dew glistened across the garden, filling it with a shimmering radiance. She saw none of the beauty as she ran back to the little gate, yanked it open with both hands, and whipped through it. She pulled it shut with a slam and ran on through the rough grass across the meadow.

Out here, the air hung sweet and heavy with the scent of dew-laden grass. The fog still lingered in low-lying spots, tendrils of it hanging in the air. She ran through them, heedless now of anything save her own sobs, and thought only of hiding herself in the woods, where she could cry unseen and unheard. Stumbling at the edge of the woods, she caught herself against a tree and gripped it, weeping.

Why had she gone to him? She wished she'd left everything as it was, for now all was ruined and broken. The king blamed her, hated her. His scorn hurt still. Now she understood why he'd avoided her company, why he'd refused to see her. He wanted no comfort from her, for he despised her. She

wished she'd known from the start. She would never have returned to Savroix at all.

Swiping angrily at her eyes, she ducked her head and
pushed herself away from the tree, walking rapidly, without
heed for the twigs that snagged her cloak and gown. She
stayed near the edge of the woods, skirting them, for now that
she was here she found she did not want to venture deeper.
Still, she hardly cared where she walked, as long as she did
not return to the palace.

She was aiming vaguely for the park when a figure suddenly sprang out from behind a thicket, rushed at her, and
caught her harshly by one arm.

She screamed and shrank back, striking out with her fists
before she even glimpsed who it was.

The man was clad in a dark robe of coarse cloth, hooded
so that she could not clearly see his face. Fearing that at last
she'd landed herself in Sir Brillon's clutches, she jerked back
with all her strength, trying her best to wrench free.

His grip tightened so harshly she feared he might break her
arm. Crying out in pain, she struck out again, hampered from
kicking him by her long skirts. In the struggle, his hood fell
back, and for the first time she clearly saw his face.

He was the man in her nightmare, the one who'd attacked
her in her dream's bedchamber before she pelted him with salt
and drove him away. Astonished and horrified, feeling the
blood drain from her face, she stopped her struggles abruptly
and stared at him.

He smiled at her, and it was a fanatic's smile. He said, "At
last, Pheresa, you have come to my hand, as I bade you. From
dream to reality, you have come, enspelled by me, ready to do
my bidding."

Shrinking back from him, she screamed.

Chapter Ten

"Pheresa!" the man said, his eyes glowing with fervor. His face was as white as marble, gaunt and beardless. "Be at peace, good lady, and fear me not, for I come to offer you everything you desire."

"Release me!" she shouted, still struggling. "Let me go, assassin! Let me go!"

"Cease your cries and bide quietly. I am here to give you aid."

"Ruffian," she said scathingly, panting in her effort to pull free. "Unhand me at once!"

"When you are quiet and will listen, I shall release you."

"Do so now! I warn you that if you do not—"

He laughed at her threat. "What soldiers do you command, good lady? Where is your protector? What authority have you?"

Bitter and furious, she fell silent.

"Ah, that is better. Will you now heed what I have to say?"

She remembered the dream where he'd come to her chamber and attacked her. Only it hadn't been entirely a dream.

And had he truly worked a spell on her? What else could have compelled her so strongly to venture outside the walls this morning? What had compelled her to speak so rashly to the king, wrecking her future with foolish, heedless words?

As she gazed at this stranger, she felt a cold clutch of fear. Her heart began to pound, and she thought her knees would buckle.

"What are you?" she whispered. "What do you want?"

"I am Kolahl. And it lies within my power to give you the throne you seek. That interests you, yes? Oh, I see that it does. Come and walk beside me, good lady, and we shall talk of these matters."

She dug in her heels, resisting with all her might as he tried to lead her deeper into the woods. "I'll go nowhere with you. You're naught but an abductor or assassin. No doubt you're in league with Theloi!"

"The cardinal and I have no dealings," Kolahl said angrily. "Quieten your fears, and listen."

She abruptly pushed at him and twisted her arm. Although it felt like her wrist might break, she managed this time to get free. Staggering back, she whirled around and ran for the meadow. If she could get into the open, she thought, one of the sentries might see her and give her aid.

Kolahl caught up with her in two paces, gripped her by the back of her cloak, and spun her around to pin her against a tree.

She cried out, and he shook her so roughly the back of her head bounced against the trunk.

"Hush, I tell you! Hush and listen. There is little time before you are missed, and I have much to tell you."

"Let me go!" she insisted, struggling.

He slapped her hard. Her head buzzed with pain, and her knees failed her. She would have crumpled at his feet had he not held her propped against the tree.

"Forgive me for being harsh, but you force my hand," he said, sounding exasperated. "If you do not quieten, I shall be required to employ dark arts to make you listen. That, I do not wish to do. Not here where we might be seen. It is too dangerous."

She barely understood him. Pain engulfed the left side of her face. Her head throbbed and she wanted to be sick. Somehow, she managed to fight for self-control. Now that her initial panic was over, she felt more afraid than before. *Who is he? Who is he?* The question would not stop circling through her mind, but she had other things to think about first, chiefly escape.

Kolahl's eyes were dark and compelling, filled with a fervor that scared her, for he looked even more fanatical than Sir Brillon. He smelled of herbs, bitter and burned. His hands, still gripping her hard, were filthy, the nails rimmed with black.

"Pheresa, you have come to my hand, as I compelled you. But put aside your fear, for I mean you no harm," he said urgently, glancing over his shoulder before he turned his gaze back to her. "I can give you all that you desire. I can give you the throne."

She frowned, hating him. "Don't lie," she said harshly. "My chances are finished. I doubt I ever had any. I've made a fool of myself, and now I'm to be banished from court."

"Are you certain of this?"

"Oh, yes. You'd better ensnare another victim, for I'm of no use to your wicked plans."

"You know nothing of my plans," he said with a smile. "And why are you so certain they are wicked?"

She frowned, realizing belatedly that he was working some kind of mysterious influence over her senses. What was she doing, standing here meekly, confiding in him? Swiftly, she averted her gaze from his and refused to meet it again. She trembled in his grasp and tried desperately to think what she should do.

"Are you ready to listen?" he asked.

It occurred to her that as long as he talked it was likely he would do nothing else. The delay would give her a chance, however slim. Well, then, she would let him talk, she decided, and surreptitiously slid her hand toward her pocket.

"What do you want?" she demanded.

"I am Sebein."

She gasped, but such was the terror that flashed through her she could not utter another sound. How in Thod's name, she asked herself, had she fallen into such trouble? It had been a Sebein member who ensnared Gavril, training him in the use and control of the tainted, evil sword Tanengard. No doubt, thanks to that contact with Sebein evil, Gavril had taken his first, early steps toward madness. And now she found herself in the clutches of this creature, a subscriber to darkness so abhorrent she could not bear to think of it.

She fought off a bout of dizziness. *Keep your wits,* she told herself desperately, and reached in her pocket for salt.

"Come, do not feel such terror," Kolahl said to her now. "Look into my eyes and see for yourself that I will not harm you."

She frowned, fighting the urge to obey him. *Don't look,* she told herself.

"You think me evil, but truly I am not. Pheresa, I can help you. I can put wondrous powers at your disposal. I can clear a path before you, lead you to all you desire. Tell me what it is that you want, Pheresa. What do you thirst for, as a plant thirsts for water? Tell me, Pheresa. Tell me."

His voice was gentle, hypnotic. Her lips parted, and her throat made a strangled noise. She closed her eyes, terrified at having come so close to answering.

"You want to be queen," he said to her. "You were destined to rule this land, good lady. It has been foretold."

Tears stung her eyes. "I don't believe you," she whispered.

"As queen of Mandria, you will control the most powerful kingdom in the world. All men will bow down to you. Great jewels and tribute will flow into your coffers. Your name will be revered across the land. Do you not want it, Pheresa? Do you not yearn for it?"

"I—I want to serve. I want to do my duty to—"

"Service. Duty. What are these things but dust and ashes? Do you not crave more, good lady? Do you not want accolades? Do you not want the people's worship?"

She stiffened with shock. "No! That's blasphemous! How dare you suggest anything like that."

He smiled. "I see into your heart, Pheresa. I see much hurt. How deeply the courtiers have hurt you, misunderstood you, insulted you. They scheme against you and talk lies behind your back. You can punish them when you are queen. Would you not like that? Would you not like to crush all your little enemies?"

"N—no."

"And you want friends, loved ones, people around you whom you can trust. I can give you allies, Pheresa. I can turn stubborn hearts in your favor. Would you not like to have friends, loyal and true only to you?"

She frowned, astonished by what he said. How did he know such things? "Everyone wants friends."

"Yes." His dirty fingertips gently stroked her cheek, and she shuddered. "The king has maligned you today. He has broken your heart. But think of the satisfaction of having his throne. Such sweet and ultimate revenge. Don't you want it?"

She battled with herself. He would have her speak treason, she warned herself. She must fight him, with all she had.

"What do you want?"

He smiled. "Very little. The simplest act on your part would bring a wondrous result to my people. You know how we of the Sebein are persecuted throughout Mandria. We are hounded, driven out, stoned wherever people find us."

"The k-king has ordered it," she said.

"But when you are queen, Pheresa, you can order a halt to such cruelty. I have traveled to many lands, and I assure you that nothing anywhere compares to Mandrian bigotry. We are forbidden to practice our religion here on pain of death. Do you know how brutal that is? Our teachings require us to serve. Our blood burns within us to obey the teachings, and yet we cannot. You cannot imagine our suffering."

"I cannot help you."

"Oh, but you can, Pheresa." He spoke persuasively, his dark eyes compelling her. "You know that your mind is filled with doubts. Wisely, you have begun to question the precepts of Tomias. You are ready to be reborn, Pheresa. Drinking from the Chalice was but the first step. Now you must shed your old beliefs, your old convictions. Embrace what is new and right and good."

"I shall not renounce my faith," she said shakily.

"Ah, but have you not already done so?"

"Nay! I have not!"

"The king might say otherwise."

"How do you know this?" she demanded. "How came you to spy on us this morning? Where hid you?"

"You have angered many officials, and already made yourself enemies among the churchmen. If you can question Tomias and the teachings of Reform, good lady, you can open your mind enough to grant us mercy. That is all we ask."

She felt cold to the depths of her soul. Kolahl knew too much. He somehow could peer into her heart and mind and see all that was bad and petty in her, all that was shameful and base. He triumphed in it, and yet Writ said that a good man governed his heart against wicked urges. It was not taught that to be good meant having no wickedness at all. 'Twas one's behavior, she assured herself, not one's temptations that made the difference.

"I will not renounce my faith," she said angrily.

"We do not ask that," he replied, but she knew by the way his eyes tightened that he lied. "Simply show us mercy. Allow us to return and practice our ways openly, without harm. We ask no more than that. Of course, should you ever wish to learn our teachings, we would rejoice."

"I suppose this is how you corrupted Gavril," she said furiously. In her pocket her hand closed on the salt purse. "You promised him something he wanted, then you destroyed him."

"We did nothing but teach him the arts of swordplay—"

"He knew those. Nay, you twisted his mind, taught him to embrace darkness. That is what you worship. And what you want me to worship. You are evil, and I will not help you. Never! No matter what you promise."

Kolahl's smile vanished, and his expression grew cold and harsh. "Will you be queen without us?"

She trembled, but met his cruel eyes. "I will not be queen."

"Indeed not. You angered the king this morning. What chance have you now of being named his heir?"

Her disgust grew. "If the Sebeins possess such mighty powers, why do you not use them to reinstate yourselves? Why do you need me?"

Kolahl frowned. "Mock not what you do not understand."

"No, I don't understand it. How can you persuade the king to favor me? You've failed to make him end official persecution of your cult. You're just a shadow, whispering evil in my ear and hoping I'm foolish enough to believe your ploy."

Anger twisted Kolahl's features. He released her arm and drew back to slap her again. This time, however, Pheresa was ready for him. Pulling out her salt purse, she flung the contents in his face.

He screamed, reeling back, his hands clapped to his face.

She ran into the open before he caught up with her and grabbed her by one arm. She turned on him, striking hard with the little dagger. The tip raked him from shoulder to elbow, slicing cloth and bringing blood.

Crying out, he swung at her with his wounded arm, splattering his blood across her face and gown. Ducking the blow, Pheresa stumbled, grabbed up her skirts, and ran for the palace walls. She screamed for help at the top of her lungs.

Kolahl came pounding after her, gaining rapidly, and she screamed again.

A sentry on the wall peered down at her from the crenellations, shouting a question.

"Help me!" she cried. "In the name of Thod, help me!"

Something hit her back with terrible force, driving her to the ground. Stunned, she could not seem to breathe properly. Neither could she move, not even when Kolahl began to drag her through the tall grass. Vaguely she heard more shouts and the sound of running feet.

She closed her eyes a moment, then there was a struggle over her, violent and brief. The next thing she knew she was being lifted in someone's arms.

Terrified, she cried out.

"You're safe now," a stranger's voice said.

Opening her eyes, Pheresa gazed into a handsome face with skin tanned dark gold. His wide-spaced eyes were the color of a flask of honey shelved in the sunlight, and his black hair fell in loose curls across his brow. He wore the tunic and green cloak of the palace guard, and in his powerful arms she knew that she was safe.

He cradled her closer to his strong chest. "My lady, speak if you can!" he said urgently. "This blood on your gown. Is it yours or your attacker's?"

"Sebein," she murmured as darkness engulfed her senses. "A Sebein . . ."

Horrified, Talmor stared down at the maiden now lying limp and unconscious in his arms, her blond hair shimmering like gold, then turned his gaze to the dead man lying at his feet. What had sent a Sebein assassin to harm a maiden this lovely, this innocent? He stared down into her face, entranced by the pale perfection of her skin and the dark curve of her lashes against her cheeks. She was the most beautiful girl he'd ever seen.

How little she weighed despite the volume of her skirts and long cloak. Blood splattered her cheek and gown. Her cloak was half torn off one shoulder, and her slippers were ruined. Her skirts were soaked wet and dirty, and her hair hung in a wild tangle, falling out of a loose braid. Yet there was no question that she was a lady of the court. Even so, she looked sweet and gentle, unlike so many of the women here. He felt a surge of protectiveness so powerful it staggered him.

"My lady," he said, giving her a little shake to rouse her. She did not stir, and indeed her face was too pale and still.

Freeing one hand, he pressed it to her throat.

Her pulse was racing and wild. He wiped away a smear of the blood and sniffed it. A stink of copper and something feral made him grimace and wipe his fingers clean. Not her blood, but the Sebein's, he told himself. The air felt strange and unsettled, as though a spell had been thrown. Talmor frowned, suspecting it might have hit her. If that were so, she needed assistance quickly.

By now a squadron of guardsmen led by Sir Pem, the duty knight, came running up to surround him.

"What's happened?" he demanded. "Is she dead?"

"No, but she may be wounded."

"Aye," the duty knight said, frowning at her. "Bloodied, ain't she? And been fair mauled by the look of her."

"Fought her way free of attack," Talmor said, nudging the corpse with his foot. "When I saw her, she was running with a dagger in her hand, screaming for help."

"And this ruffian was in pursuit?"

"Aye."

One of the guards rolled the dead man onto his back.

"Before she swooned," Talmor said grimly, "she said he was a Sebein."

Everyone reached instinctively for their weapons and stepped back from the corpse. Sir Pem looked very grim. "The lot of you, fan out and start searching for any more of them. Lors, you and Itienne head for the old church. Check it out, but take no chances. If you find anything, shout for the rest of us."

Nodding, the men scattered to begin a search. Young Waltem picked up a small dagger from the trampled grass and came running back with it. "Look, sir!" he cried. "Got blood on it."

"Give that to me," Pem said gruffly, wrapping a cloth around it with swift dexterity. "Not much of a weapon."

"The lady's knife, no doubt," Talmor said. He hoisted her higher in his arms, impatient to go. "Where do I take her? The infirmary?"

The duty knight frowned over her, studying her face again. Suddenly he blinked and gave a low whistle. He looked up sharply and met Talmor's puzzled gaze. "Great Thod!"

"What? Do you recognize her, sir?"

"Aye." Pem backed away. "I'm thinking that's Lady Pheresa du Lindier, niece of the king."

Talmor felt hollow with astonishment. "The Lady of the Chalice?"

"Get her inside, quickly."

"Aye, sir."

"I'll pass the word that all the gates are to be secured at once. Damne, the commander will have our guts on a string. How'd she get outside? Bribed the back gatekeeper, I'll warrant. Damned old fool." He glared at Talmor worriedly. "There's going to be an uproar, and we'll take the blame for it, damn our souls. Talmor, jump to it!"

Talmor headed for the corner turret as fast as he could carry the lady. Despite the chilly morning air, he was already sweating. Thus far, he'd managed to fit in and perform his lowly duties without much difficulty. Sir Kedrien had kept his dislike to himself, it seemed, although Talmor knew his sergeant had orders to ride him hard. Now, he could not help but come to official notice, carrying in the king's niece. He'd have to make a report. There would be an investigation, just as Pem said, of how she'd gained exit at this early hour without being noticed or stopped. If a maidservant wanted to go frolic in the woods, well enough, but a lady of this rank and importance had no business being outside without guards or attendants or companions. Whom had she gone to meet?

The idea of her sporting with some dandified courtier made Talmor scowl. Swiftly, he yanked his emotions back under control. It was no business of his what she did, unless her folly brought him under review for dereliction of duty. Realizing he could be blamed for the whole matter, if someone wished to be unjust, Talmor frowned and quickened his pace.

He climbed the twisting turret stairs until he reached the walkway atop the wall. Holding the lady with the greatest care, he carried her at a rush into the palace proper and was heading for the wing of private apartments when a stern voice brought him up short.

"You there, guard! What are you about, slipping your wench back to her bed?"

Talmor turned around and found himself face to face with a steward. He glared at the man. "It's the Lady Pheresa, fool. Attacked and hurt."

The steward gawked, his face turning bone white. "What?"

"Quick! Show me where to take her."

With a blink, the steward regained his wits and hurried down the corridor. "This way!"

Together they rushed along. Only the servants were stirring as yet, and few of those were in sight. The steward hailed a sleepy little page and gave the boy a rough shake by one shoulder.

"Get the physician. Make haste, boy! Send him to Lady Pheresa's apartments."

Round-eyed, the boy ran to do as he was told.

"Down here," the steward said, pointing.

Talmor rounded a turn in the passageway, went up a short flight of stairs, and came to a door bearing a coat of arms. The steward knocked urgently while Lady Pheresa moaned and stirred in Talmor's arms. He realized he was clutching her too tightly in his concern and gentled his grip. Her eyes fluttered open, soft brown within curling lashes, then closed. She looked paler than ever.

He feared he had taken too long to get her assistance. Did anyone here know how to counteract a Sebein spell? "Her priest?" he asked. "Her personal chaplain? He must be summoned as well."

The steward continued his barrage of knocking, and at last the door was opened by an indignant woman wrapped in a shawl and still heavy-eyed with sleep.

"Go away, you stupid man!" she scolded. "Have you no regard for my lady's—"

Catching sight of Lady Pheresa lying limp in Talmor's arms, she loosed a muffled shriek. "Oh, sweet Tomias, she's dead! My lady's dead!"

"Quiet," the steward said roughly, pushing his way in. "Here, guard. Bring her this way."

Talmor shouldered past the servingwoman, who was moaning into her hands. "Not dead," he said curtly. "But hurt. The physician's been sent for. She'll need her chaplain as well."

"My lady! My lady!" the woman cried, ignoring him as she rushed ahead, bleating and fluttering her hands in dismay.

She opened the door at the other end of the little sitting room
to reveal a small, but splendidly appointed bedchamber.

There was no time to gander about. Talmor laid his burden
gently on the bed and smoothed her golden hair back from her
face. Even disheveled and splattered with blood, she looked
beautiful. So fragile, so vulnerable, so exquisite. Gazing
down at her, he found himself enchanted by the pale dusting
of freckles across her delicate nose.

"My lady! Oh, my lady!" Another woman joined the first,
both bending over her and weeping.

Talmor thought them useless and exchanged a look with
the steward, who rolled his eyes.

"I'll see what's keeping that boy," the steward said.

"Get the lady's chaplain," Talmor insisted.

The steward frowned, looking aghast. "You really think
there's need for her to receive final unction?"

Realizing he'd been misunderstood, Talmor opened his
mouth, but the steward said brokenly, "Poor sweet lady. And
after all she's gone through."

The elder of the two women raised her head. "She'll not
die, not in my care. Quick, there's a fire to build and water to
fetch."

The steward bowed. "I'll see it's done," he said and off he
hurried.

"Let's get her out of these wet clothes. You, out," the
woman said to Talmor.

He clamped his powerful arms across his chest and refused
to budge. "I stay until her ladyship is safe," he said. " 'Tis my
duty."

Gray-haired and plump, the woman was not cowed by
him. Putting her hands on her ample hips, she said, "You can
guard my good lady out there, at the door, as is seemly.
There's no need for an oaf like you in here."

With a last look at Pheresa, he retreated to the corridor. By
then the court physician had arrived, looking flustered, and
several gawkers followed. Talmor stayed on guard sternly,
thwarting the courtiers who sought admittance. He knew the

idle curiosity in their faces, knew they wanted only to stare and gossip.

More people came, sighing when a priest in official robes of white and yellow hurried in. A woman began to weep, and the chatter quieted for a moment before a buzz of new speculations began. Two men laid a wager on how fast the lady would die, and Talmor gritted his teeth against the urge to bash their heads together. He kept his place, rigid and grim, ignoring all that was said and done by the spectators.

Then a commotion could be heard in the distance. People turned to look, and a page ran up crying a warning that the king was coming.

Talmor stiffened, his heart suddenly thudding in his chest with excitement. As yet he'd been given no duty that brought him close to the king. Now, at last, he was going to see his majesty.

Seconds later, heralds pushed through, parting the crowd. The king, his protector, and his entourage strode through, ignoring the bows and curtsies. Talmor stepped aside from the door, coming to full attention and saluting as he'd been taught.

The king swept past him without a glance. His protector followed. The rest of his majesty's companions, including a handful of guardsmen, waited outside.

Two of the guardsmen gave Talmor a nod. "Return to your post."

He knew a momentary sense of rebellion. Was he not to know how the lady fared? But he could not argue against orders.

Saluting, he strode rapidly away. Inside, he felt as though he'd been knocked asunder, and barely knew what he was doing as he returned to his station on the wall and resumed sentry duty until midmorning, when he was relieved. "Report to the guardhouse," he was told.

"How goes the search?"

His relief shrugged and spat. "Demon's luck, as usual. If there's any more, they've gone. Like chasing smoke, them Sebeins and their black arts. You keep your Circle good and tight around your neck and get yourself to the guardhouse on the double, like I said."

The guardhouse was a square brick structure located in the midst of the barracks. As Talmor approached, he passed a detail of guardsmen clad in mail and hauberks standing at attention in double rows before Barracks Four. A sergeant was inspecting them, bawling out orders for a more detailed search.

Grimly tightening his mouth, Talmor stepped through the open guardhouse door and found it abustle with activity. An officer had rounded up the barracks sergeants and was briefing them with a curt series of orders. Security of the entire palace had been tightened. The main gates had been shut, and no one was to go in or out until further orders, no matter what the personage's rank. Talmor glanced at them swiftly, but Sergeant Goddal was not among them.

Instead, he saw the man standing before Sir Kedrien and Lord Nejel at the rear of the room. Goddal was nodding to what the officers were saying.

When Talmor came up, Sir Kedrien, as bleak and as angry as Talmor had ever seen him, scowled. "About time," he said curtly.

Talmor saluted woodenly. "Sir Talmor reporting as ordered."

Goddal squinted at him. Grizzled and worn, with the scars of a veteran, the sergeant's head came only to Talmor's shoulder, and most of his teeth were missing, but he was as fierce as a gamecock with a reputation of being the toughest sergeant in the force.

"You!" he said sharply. "Make your report, and be quick about it."

Talmor spoke succinctly and well, omitting no detail of what he'd observed, heard, and done. Sir Kedrien listened stone-faced while Lord Nejel grew round-eyed with astonishment. Sleek and privileged, with wavy blond hair and an air of fashion despite his rust-colored hauberk and green cloak, Nejel was reputed to be fair and just with all his men. Sometimes he overlooked minor transgressions, and he was considered something of a devil with a lance on the jousting field. Talmor took heart from his presence. With Nejel present, perhaps he would not be blamed after all.

"A gate to the king's private garden was found unlocked," Sir Kedrien said harshly, his eyes boring into Talmor. "Did you know of this?"

"No, sir."

"Are you not a sentry, assigned to watch that stretch of wall?"

"Aye, sir."

"Then it's your responsibility. Why was that gate unlocked?"

Fighting his anger, Talmor swallowed hard. Despite what Sir Kedrien said, the gates weren't his responsibility, and he didn't even rank high enough to be allowed off the wall to patrol the grounds. Sir Kedrien knew that, and this grilling was unjustified.

"Sir Talmor! I asked you why that gate was unlocked."

Pulling Lady Pheresa's dagger from his belt, Talmor unwrapped the dainty weapon, still smeared with dried blood, and held it out. "It belongs to the lady, sir. If you look at the tip, you can see that it's newly bent."

Sir Kedrien scowled. "What has this to do with—"

But Lord Nejel examined the dagger. "By Thod! Are you suggesting the lady picked the lock?"

"It's possible, my lord."

"Extraordinary."

Sir Kedrien glared at him, then shifted his gaze back to Talmor. "Do you presume to blame your dereliction of duty on the lady, sir?"

"No, sir."

"Then state the truth. Quickly!"

Talmor drew a swift breath. "The truth is that I don't know why the gate was unlocked, unless the lady picked it. Why she would do so, I cannot guess. Why she was outside the walls, I do not know. I did not see her exit, and—"

"No, you did not," Sir Kedrien said, breaking in. "The

gatekeeper admits he took a bribe from the lady at dawn and allowed her to exit. Saw you any of this?"

"No, sir."

"Were you asleep?"

"No, sir. The fog—"

"No excuses! You—"

"Kedrien," Nejel said in gentle protest. "Have done."

Sir Kedrien turned on him, red-faced. "Yes, my lord. If you coddle him, he'll lie readily."

Nejel looked at him calmly. "I do not expect this man to lie, but hysterical accusations will avail nothing."

Tight-lipped, Sir Kedrien walked a short distance away and stood, visibly fuming. Nejel swung his gaze back to Talmor and gave him a little smile. "Now, Sir Talmor. Let us see what we can sort out. How thick was the fog this morning?"

"It started rolling in shortly before dawn," Talmor replied. "At daybreak, it was waist-high or more and thick enough to keep visibility down to an arm's length at its worst."

Lord Nejel nodded. "Atop the wall, you'd not see much of the ground, then."

"No, my lord."

"No. We found the lady's tracks along the base of the wall. She was clever enough to know a sentry couldn't see her at that angle."

Talmor frowned, his glance shifting momentarily to Sir Kedrien before he snapped his gaze back to the officer in front of him. "Interesting, my lord."

"You told Sir Pem that she said a Sebein attacked her. Did she say anything else?"

"No, my lord."

Sighing, Nejel clasped his hands behind his back and scuffed his boot back and forth. "This is a most peculiar business. The lady is not in the habit of slipping outside the walls. Indeed, I believe she's kept herself mostly indoors since her return, as is proper for her circumstances. Why should she go to the king's garden by such a foolhardy route? And why was a Sebein lying in wait for her when she tried to return? I do not like it, Sir Talmor. It smacks of a trap. Somehow, the lady was lured out into danger."

Frowning, Talmor wrestled a moment with his conscience then said, hesitantly, "There's something else, my lord."

"Ah, yes. I thought there must be."

Talmor glanced cautiously Sir Kedrien's way, and told himself he was a fool. "She was spell hit at the end of the struggle."

Nejel's eyes popped. "What? What say you?"

"Aye, my lord. I saw little of what happened. By the time I reached her, she was unconscious, and the Sebein was attempting to carry her off. I dealt with him swiftly, of course."

"Pity you didn't leave him alive," Nejel said. "We could have questioned him."

Talmor dropped his gaze. He'd struck hard and efficiently, the way he would have attacked a rock adder.

"The assassin didn't attempt magic against *you*, I suppose?" Lord Nejel asked.

Talmor's gaze snapped up. He was aware of Sir Kedrien listening intently. "No, my lord."

"And this—er—spell," Nejel said. "Are you certain it struck the lady?"

"I saw her fall in midstep as though struck from behind. The air smelled burned around her, and her swoon seemed most—"

"I see," Nejel said uncomfortably. He glanced at Sergeant Goddal, who scowled and spat on the floor.

"So you know about things like that, do you?" the sergeant asked.

Talmor forced himself to face Goddal's suspicious eyes. "Magic has a stink to it, sir. It reeks in the air, afterwards."

"So it does, but not all the young pups these days know that. You an uplander?"

"I've served north of here."

"Aye, at Durl. That don't answer my question. You're mighty shifty about where you come from, Talmor. What—"

"Never mind all that, sergeant," Nejel broke in impatiently. "Let's stick to the point. A highborn lady very dear to this

court and land has been grievously attacked and injured
within sight of the palace walls. The king's spies are already
at work unraveling whatever plot was laid to harm her, but the
guards are responsible for making sure no Sebein has slipped
inside the palace itself. There's been too much laxness, and no
more will be permitted."

"Aye, my lord," Goddal said stiffly.

Nejel looked Talmor over. "You're to be commended for
saving the lady's life. Well done."

Talmor saluted. "Thank you, my lord."

Dismissed, he headed outside to find something to eat, but
Sir Kedrien caught up with him.

"Wait!" he ordered.

Warily, Talmor faced him, wondering if he'd finally
proven his worth to this man.

Sir Kedrien's eyes remained harsh and unfriendly. "What
meant you by all that nonsense about magic and spells?"

"Nothing, save that the lady should be tended with special—"

"Her well-being is not your concern! You'll say no more
about this to anyone. Is that clear?"

"But—"

"I suppose it amuses you to spread slander about the king's
niece."

"No! I—"

"She's been no victim of magic," Sir Kedrien insisted, red-
faced. "You're not to say that she is. The Lady of the Miracle
is not to be besmirched with such rumors."

Angrily Talmor opened his mouth, but Sir Kedrien raised
his hand.

"You have your orders. If I hear anything of this matter
spread among the barracks, I'll have your head on a trencher.
Am I clear?"

Seething at Sir Kedrien's unfairness, Talmor held himself
at stiff attention. "Aye, sir. Very clear."

"And don't expect a reward from the king—or the lady—
for your actions today."

"No, sir."

Scowling, Sir Kedrien strode away, leaving Talmor boiling with resentment. In that quick exchange, Sir Kedrien had managed to cheapen Talmor's actions and motivations. Did he never leave off his suspicions and fears, Talmor wondered.

Muttering to himself, Talmor walked on.

Chapter Eleven

Pheresa came awake with a sudden jolt of awareness. She sat up with a muffled cry, only to be pushed down by gentle hands.

Voices murmured soothingly to her: "You're safe, my lady. Safe now. Be easy."

Bewildered, Pheresa turned her head to find Oola smiling at her. She realized she was lying in her bed, propped up on a vast quantity of pillows, wearing a pretty bedgown, her hair brushed and shining loose on her shoulders. It was night, for shadows filled her chamber beyond the circle of lamplight. She did not understand what had happened or how she came to be here. The last thing she remembered was fighting for her life against Kolahl, so how . . . was the argument with the king, the ambush by the Sebein in the woods, her flight . . . was it all yet another nightmare?

Pressing her hands to her face, she began to weep, unable to bear such uncertainty. She felt as though she must be going mad.

"My lady, hush. Do not cry. My lady, please." Oola pulled

her hands away and wiped away her tears. "Here, sit up and look around you. You're with friends, my sweet. Safe and sound again. And you have a special visitor who wants very much to see you smile."

Pheresa blinked, her eyes a little dazzled by the light. The air felt warm, almost stuffy, and she realized there must be several people standing around her bed, people she could not see for the shadows.

"I don't understand," she said weakly. "I thought I was—"

She broke off and frowned, while Oola stroked her brow. Then the woman glanced up and moved back from the bed with a curtsy.

Another figure emerged from the shadows. He sat down on the chair Oola had vacated, and Pheresa saw that it was Verence himself, smiling down at her.

Her frown deepened, and fresh tears sprang to her eyes. They'd quarreled. He hated her. He'd said such terrible things.

"Dear child," the king said softly, taking her cold, slender hand in his large one. "What a fright you have given all of us. Promise you will take no more foolish risks with your life."

"Majesty," she said, her voice trembling.

He smoothed back a strand of her hair. "Oh, yes, I was angry, but that is past. Take none of it to heart, for the king would not have you distressed this way. I care for you as though you were my own child."

She stared at him, drinking in his words, his forgiveness. Her fingers tightened on his, and he smiled. Timidly she smiled back. "Then it all happened?" she asked him timidly. "'Twas no dream, there in the garden?"

"No dream, I regret to say."

She began to cry. "I'm sorry. I'm so sorry!"

"Hush your tears," he said kindly, lifting her chin to make her look at him. "You are infinitely precious, and I had nearly forgotten that. Never again must you encounter danger. 'Tis a protector you need."

"But if I'm to leave court, I do not need—"

His finger crossed her lips to silence her. He shook his

head, and the jewels in his crown flashed fire. "Speak no more of that. It pleases me to keep you nearby. You will remain at court, and you will have a protector."

She dropped her gaze. "I thank your majesty."

"Have you a champion in mind?"

In silence she shook her head.

"Then I shall order a tourney to be held, with the victor to take the position. Provided he's suitable, and the look of him pleases you, sweet lady."

Hardly able to believe her ears, she smiled. Somehow, despite the disaster in the garden, Verence was kind again, himself again. She dared not question such a swift change of heart too closely, and was so glad, she longed to throw her arms about his neck and laugh.

Verence chuckled at her expression and glanced around at the others. "Ah, that has caught her fancy," he said in satisfaction.

A man in physician's robes came forward. "Perhaps enough excitement for now, majesty."

Verence stood up. "As soon as you've fully recovered," he said to Pheresa, "the tourney will be held."

"And will your majesty preside over the event?" she pleaded. "Will your majesty choose a proper warrior for me from among the victors?"

The king hesitated with a frown. Pheresa held her breath, and not a sound came from anyone in the room. A rueful look stole into Verence's eyes. He shook his finger at her, his mouth twisting half between amusement and annoyance.

"How can I resist the entreaty in those pretty eyes? Very well, I agree to your wheedling. And afterwards, there will be feasting and a ball. Does that please you, child?"

Her eyes were shining now. Clapping her hands, she smiled up at him with the full charm of love, admiration, and gratitude. "Indeed it does, sire. Your majesty is too kind."

"And you have the wiles of a vixlet." He cleared his throat. "Sleep now, and grow well quickly. I cannot bear to see you ill."

He departed, and most of the people in the room followed.

Pheresa lay quietly on her pillows, pleased and radiant while Oola fussed over her, bringing her a tray with coddled eggs and steaming broth to tempt her appetite, chattering about the gifts various courtiers had brought.

"You can look at them tomorrow if you feel up to it," she said.

"But I am not sick," Pheresa protested, shoving her tray aside. "I don't know why I swooned, except I was so frightened."

"Being attacked by a fiend is enough to frighten anyone out of their wits," Oola said, plumping her pillows fiercely. "Now you lie down and get your rest. You've had a nasty shock, and the physician says you're to make no exertion until you're stronger."

"But I—" Pheresa frowned, as more memory returned to her. "Did Kolahl harm me in some way? I thought he stabbed me from behind. It hurt so much, then I fell."

Oola looked frightened a moment before she pinned a big smile to her lips. "Nay, child. You suffered no wounds, no cuts. What fancies you speak! Now here's something the physician wants you to drink."

Pheresa twisted her head away from the cup of nasty black liquid. "No potions. I don't want it!"

"Be a lamb and drink it down. You'll not get better until you do."

She was tempted to hurl the cup away, but at last she swallowed part of it. The foul taste made her shudder and gasp. At once she felt her eyelids grow heavy and knew she'd been drugged.

She glared at Oola. "I don't want to sleep. I have to know what—"

The door opened to her room and a slight, solitary figure came through the shadows to her bedside. Believing it to be another physician, she opened her mouth to protest this free coming and going through her private apartments.

But when the newcomer stepped into the light, she saw that it was Cardinal Theloi.

Surprised and displeased, she gripped the coverlet, struggling to hold her heavy lids open. "You!" she whispered.

He made no immediate answer and instead gestured dismissal at both Oola and the physician. They obeyed without hesitation or protest.

The door shut behind them, leaving Pheresa alone with this man who was her enemy.

He studied her dispassionately, his falcon's eyes cold and keen. "So you have persuaded the king to end his deep mourning," he said quietly, his voice precise. "The realm owes you a tremendous debt, my lady."

She smothered a yawn, fighting the sleep that crept over her. Her head felt so heavy. It was so hard to stay focused on the cardinal's face. Had he just complimented her, she wondered. It seemed that he had, but she mistrusted her hearing. She murmured something indistinct.

Theloi bent over her. "You have survived and eluded more snares than I believed possible, but I'll catch you yet, my lady."

Her eyes drifted shut despite her efforts to hold them open. "No," she whispered in defiance.

His fingers brushed her cheek. "The game is not yet over. I have infinite patience, as you will learn."

Her lips parted, but she heard no more of his soft-spoken threats. She slept.

Lutel came running into the sluice room, where Talmor was shaving his jaws with a blade of finely honed bronze. Despite the tiny windows set high along the walls on all sides, the place tended to be dark and damp, smelling of mildewed toweling, wet tunics left hung up to dry, and the harsh lard soap that either sat in soggy lumps in puddles of water on the washing table or else were dried hard and fast to whatever surface they'd been left on. A handful of other knights and servants moved groggily about in the early-morning light. In the far corner, Sir Carlemon was pomading his hair with a loudly scented hair oil imported from Thod knew where while his squire held up a small, square looking glass to aid him. Talmor grimaced and tried not to breathe more than he had to. He'd smelled fish oil more appealing than Carlemon's pomades. And before breakfast, it was particularly foul.

"Sir Talmor! Sir Talmor!" Lutel called out excitedly. Despite orders, he was running, heedless of the men who cursed him or of the slick spots on the wet floor that sent him slipping and careening. Somehow he kept his balance, long skinny arms flailing, evaded the irritable swat of Sir Pem, suffering this morning from ale-head, and came panting up to Talmor with his freckled face aglow. "I've news, sir! Ye'll never guess it, no matter how clever ye be."

Talmor wiped the remaining bits of lather from his face and decided his mustache was trimmed enough. Putting away his blade, he gave the boy an indulgent look. "More news of the tourney?"

Lutel's face fell. "Ah, damne, ye've heard already."

"Nay, I haven't," Talmor said, relenting with a laugh. He clapped the boy on his thin shoulder. No matter how much food they poured into Lutel, the boy never fattened. "Hand me my tunic and speak your news."

Lutel obeyed happily. "There's five more knights arrived in the night to enter the lists. Aye, and one's the champion of his hold."

"Is it Sir Nuin?" Carlemon asked, wiping his hands clean and tossing the towel aside.

Lutel shook his head, and Talmor gave him a sharp nudge with his elbow. "Answer the man properly, boy."

"Nay, sir. I heard not that name."

Carlemon grunted, eased on his tunic, and strolled out. By now Talmor was dressed. Leaving Lutel to gather up his kit, he stepped outside into fresh golden air, already growing warm after a cool dawn. They wheeled away from the privy line and headed for the hall to eat.

Talmor said idly, "Five more makes a total of how many entrants? Forty?"

Lutel was bouncing awkwardly with every step. He wore new leggings, a secondhand gift from Pears, and they were too long and too wide for his skinny legs. "Most like there be more than that now, sir. The lists have been opened to guardsmen, and I thought ye'd want to know—"

Talmor stopped in his tracks and met the boy's dancing eyes with grave intensity. "Is this the truth?" he demanded. "No lies or foolery?"

Lutel pointed at the line already forming outside the guardhouse. "It were just announced, sir. I ran to tell ye."

"Thod's bones," Talmor said. He smiled and gave the boy a nod. "Well done!"

Leaving Lutel behind, he hurried over to join the line, and although he tried to act casual, he could not conceal the pulse of excitement hammering through his veins. A chance to win the post of Lady Pheresa's protector. The very thought of it set his mind racing. His weapons were in good order, thanks to Pears's diligence. He'd grown rusty with lance work. His duties, lately doubled with assignments to shifts on both sentry work and grounds patrol, left him little spare time for practice on the jousting field, but he'd correct that. There were three days left before the tourney opened, hectic days for guardsmen, for the palace and town had swelled with visitors, including combatants and spectators, and more people continued to arrive.

Talmor frowned, mentally weighing the problem of whether he should stand the cost of fitting his charger with new shoes or purchase a tourney shield. The latter would be expensive, especially with prices inflated for the tourney and fair. He supposed he could use his palace-issue shield, although it was a bit short to thwart a lance. Better to see his horse decently shod, for in a joust a stumble could see him dead.

An elbow dug into his spine, and he glanced over his shoulder to see a guardsman with broken teeth and a crooked nose grinning at him. "So you got the word, eh, Talmor? Good fer you. Thought you'd turn up."

Talmor smiled with more good nature than he actually felt. He'd taken plenty of ribbing for his part in rescuing Lady Pheresa. It wasn't often that a guardsman of sentry rank got his arms around a highborn lady. The fact that he'd carried her all the way into her bedchamber had sparked ribald talk for days. It infuriated him for these coarse, unlettered men to make sport of the lady's name, but he knew better than to show his anger. He was no longer an officer, he had to remind himself. It was not his place to shut them up, no matter how often his fists involuntarily clenched.

"The word is that the king wanted no less than fifty knights in the tourney, so they're letting ten of us compete," the man with the broken teeth said. He winked. "Can't let us all go in, eh? Who'd mind the crowd then?"

"Ten," Talmor said thoughtfully. His gaze went to the head of the line.

"I done counted. You make eight, and I make nine." The fellow grinned broadly. "We're all right. There's four officers I see ahead of us."

Sir Kedrien, Talmor saw now, was second in line. Talmor's brows drew together, and he felt a hot surge of angry determination. If he met Kedrien face-to-face on the jousting field, for that brief time they'd be equals. Talmor intended to break Kedrien, break him and defeat him and shame him at arms.

When his turn came, he stepped up to the table and signed his name on the line. Lord Nejel stood nearby, watching the proceedings. He grinned at Talmor, and said with good cheer, "I thought I'd find you here. What luck that you weren't on duty and could enter."

"Aye, my lord. Thank you."

Sir Kedrien turned at the sound of their exchange and glared at Talmor in red-faced displeasure. "What are you doing here?" he demanded sharply. "You've no business entering."

Talmor set his jaw. "The lists are open to any guardsman, of any rank, sir. I—"

"You're late for duty. Consider yourself fined—"

"Excuse me, sir," Talmor said, his voice clipped, his muscles rigid, "but I chose to sign up rather than go to mess. I don't report for duty until the bell rings."

Sir Kedrien's eyes were flat and hard. "Get out."

Talmor saluted and strode out briskly, his heart thumping with anger. At least today, he'd had a chance to stand up for himself, he thought. But Sir Kedrien faded quickly from his mind as he hurried across the courtyard to assume his post. Instead, he thought of Lady Pheresa, with her long eyelashes and the sweet curve of her mouth. By some miracle he'd been given the chance, however slim, of vying for the honor of serving her the rest of his days. And by Thod, he meant to win.

Chapter Twelve

The fanfare of trumpets marked the start of the tourney. Escorted into the royal box by her attendants, Pheresa found the king already there, attended by his marechals, ducs, and favorites. Lervan, clad in a yellow doublet with slashed sleeves, his cap at a rakish angle on his light brown hair, the absurd jadecock feather curling out from it as usual, had taken a position higher in the stands. Several other young nobles stood laughing with him as he described something with sweeping gestures. Princess Dianthelle, dressed for hunting, looked bored and dissatisfied. The Countess Lalieux, exquisitely gowned, nibbled bonbons daintily from a plate held for her by an attendant and fanned herself with a handkerchief.

The trumpets sounded again, and Pheresa saw the contestants riding into the arena behind the heralds. The tourney was to take place over the course of three days, with jousting first, followed by combat on horseback, followed by hand-to-hand sword fighting on foot.

The spectators cheered and applauded Pheresa's arrival, and Princess Dianthelle cast her a sour look.

But although she might feel flustered at being late, Pheresa kept her expression serene. She wore a gown of celestial blue, cut low and plain across the bodice, then filled in with ruchings of delicate lace. The sleeves were long and slender, emphasizing the grace of her arms, and ended in points at her knuckles. A scarf of silk gauze covered her hair to protect it from dust, and the long ends trailed artfully over her shoulders. Her haste had brought a most becoming blush to her cheeks.

Verence broke off what he was saying to one of the dignitaries to greet her with a smile. She curtsied deeply to him, giving him her apology, which he waved aside.

"Nothing can begin without you. 'Tis for you to start the proceedings at your leisure."

This gracious statement embarrassed her more, for it only emphasized her discourtesy in coming so late. She knew better, however, than to repeat her apologies, and instead asked, "Then, if it please your majesty, shall I permit them to commence now?"

The king looked around at his company. "We are commanded to take our places, it seems."

Everyone laughed and seated themselves in evident good humor. Pheresa's blush deepened, and inside she wanted to sink with mortification at her own gaucheness. What was wrong with her today, she wondered. As a rule, she ordered her life well, appeared on time, kept her person and her clothing tidy, said the proper things at the proper moment, and was skilled at maintaining her composure under the most trying circumstances. Today, however, everything seemed awry. The tourney was bringing a change in her life, for to have a protector of her own gave her not only a measure of safety which she welcomed, but also tremendous consequence. She knew wagers were running as to whether the king now intended to name her his successor. She could sense the anticipation and tension gathered around her, and indeed she felt it herself. More was happening here than a tourney in her honor. Yet she had enough sense to realize that few things at court were as they seemed. She dared make no assumptions, and tried once more to calm the wild rush of her senses.

Seated on the king's left, a tremendous honor that made Dianthelle's mouth pinch at the corners, Pheresa was glad of the canopy's shade against a blazing sun. She pitied the contestants milling inside the enclosure. It looked very hot inside the arena. One of the heralds was wiping perspiration from his face. Another fanned himself with his cap. The knights, glittering in polished armor, rode excited horses caparisoned in armor cloths of bright colors and patterns. On the wooden stands, the common folk shouted, clapped, and cheered, while pennons fluttered in the fitful breeze and the trumpets blared again.

At the king's nod, Pheresa lifted her dainty handkerchief high.

A sudden hush fell over the crowd. The heralds looked up. Everything seemed frozen, waiting for her signal. The power in that moment rushed to her head. It thrilled her and alarmed her, for she realized how easy it was to become drunk on such a feeling, drunk and unwise.

Swiftly she dropped her hand. A great shout went up from the people, and the contestants galloped thunderously from the arena. While the heralds shouted the rules of the opening round, the first two knights took their places opposite each other in the jousting list. Armored, their faces hidden inside their helmets, they readied their lances while their eager horses pawed and strained at the bit.

The shout came, and they charged each other. There was a great crash, and the man in green and orange went tumbling off the back of his mount. Cheers rang out. It was a most satisfying opening round, quickly and cleanly won.

As she watched, Pheresa felt a wave of hostility coming from someone. Not mere dislike or scorn, but something darker, something terrible and dangerous. Closing in, breathing on her, reaching out to her in some mysterious way.

Another crash, another tumbling knight. Fresh cheers went up, and startled, Pheresa clapped with the others. The feeling of danger ebbed, and she gasped, her eyes filling with tears that she blinked quickly away. *Soon,* she told herself, pretending to laugh at Lalieux's witty remark, *soon I shall have a protector. Please, Thod, keep me safe until then.*

Two days later, staggering a little as he walked down into the cool stone chambers beneath the jousting stands, Talmor pulled off his helmet to let the air bathe his sweating face. All he wanted was to drink an entire pail of water and collapse somewhere.

Pears walked close beside him, muttering under his breath and pointing out the way through a maze of passageways thronged with knights, squires, and nobles. It was the last day of the tourney, and today's contest was hand-to-hand combat. Thod's bones, Talmor thought to himself, swiping his sleeve across his brow, but it was mortally hot. He'd won the contest of lances on the first day, and yesterday he'd acquitted himself well enough until felled in the final round. He was determined to gain another victory today, for unless he demonstrated, beyond all question, that he was the man best qualified to serve as Lady Pheresa's protector, someone like him, with mixed blood, would never be chosen.

Now, as Pears ushered him into a small chamber fitted with a stone basin and a pair of benches, he dropped his helmet and pushed back his mail coif. He was beginning to regain his breath a little. Pears brought him water, and he took the dipper, gulping down its cool contents greedily before drawing his sword.

"Check the edge. Be sure I haven't nicked it."

Scowling, Pears took the weapon and sighted down the blade with an expert squint. "Be a wonder, won't it, after ye walloped the gate?"

Talmor had to laugh. "The fool shouldn't have run and cornered himself against it."

"Ye scared all the growth out of that boy, damn 'im." Pears shot a disapproving look at Talmor. "Just because that great brute Sir Maldriard is scaring the piss out of the lesser ranks don't mean ye have to do the same."

Being compared to the brutish knight, who'd almost hacked off a man's arm in one of the opening rounds, brought Talmor's dark brows together. He dipped himself another drink, then bent and pulled off his hauberk and mail shirt with a wince.

He was battered, with dark bruises liberally staining his face, torso, and arms, and more to come after today's fighting.

"Your hauberk is cut along the side," Pears said in alarm. "Damne, but I didn't see that thrust strike home."

Talmor grinned. "That's because he missed."

Pears held up the mail shirt and waggled his fingers grimly through the severed links of mail. "Not by much."

Talmor showed him the tear in his undertunic. It was a battered, smelly old garment, sweat-soaked and hard-worn. Some of the padding was spilling out in places.

Shaking his head, Pears unbuckled the straps and peeled it off before picking up a pail of water and pouring it over Talmor.

Shuddering with pleasure, Talmor slicked back his hair with his hands and sank down on a bench. The contest had halted for an hour to permit a rest period. There were two rounds remaining. He, Sir Kedrien, and Sir Maldriard had made it to the end. One of them would have to fight both rounds, back-to-back, depending on the luck of the lots.

Pears dug through the leather pouch where he kept remedies and the tools with which to make small repairs. "I'm sorry, sir. I've no camphor and culleinwort left."

"Thod be thanked," Talmor said fervently. "I reek enough now from your ointments."

"'Twould numb the scrape on yer knuckles, but I've used it all on them bruises."

Flexing his hand, Talmor shrugged. "Just see to my sword."

Pears flung the hauberk over his arm and picked up the sword. "I'll run to the armorer and see what he can do."

"The sword's important. My mail isn't. I doubt there's time for both."

Pears looked suddenly fierce. "By Thod, he'll make time."

Dashing out, he jostled in the doorway momentarily with a man in a herald's tabard.

The herald, followed by two escorts, halted before Talmor and held out a small leather bucket. "The others have drawn, sir."

Talmor drew his lot. It was white, not red, which meant he must win the next round in order to advance to the final one. He stared at it in numb disappointment, wondering which of the two men he was about to face.

The herald handed the lot to his assistant, who made a written notation on a piece of parchment. "Sir Kedrien also drew white. That means you and he will fight next. Sir Maldriard drew red, and awaits the victor of your contest."

Voices came from the doorway. Talmor saw several curious faces gazing in at him. He made sure his own visage betrayed no expression at all before these professional wagerers, but inside he felt cold fingers of dismay. Two more rounds to fight, not one. Assuming he could defeat Sir Kedrien, who no doubt meant to trounce him to prove Mandrian superiority. He wasn't sure if he had enough strength left in his arms to make it. Sir Maldriard, humiliated before all by his defeat with the lance, had already publicly sworn revenge and declared that if he didn't meet Talmor today in armed combat, his challenge would be issued as soon as the tourney ended.

"May I enter?" a soft, educated voice asked.

Glancing up, Talmor saw an elderly courtier in an old-fashioned tunic and leggings, soft shoes on his feet and a thinsword belted around his somewhat portly waist. He was accompanied by a young priest in yellow robes. Two burly church knights stood at his back.

"Forgive the intrusion," the nobleman said with a placating smile. "I know you are not to be disturbed, but I hoped to speak to you privately."

Talmor wanted to be left alone, but he could not be discourteous to a lord. He rose stiffly to his feet, and gave the stranger a wary bow.

The courtier smiled and waved his hand at his men. All of

them withdrew, and the rickety wooden door was closed, leaving Talmor and his visitor together.

"Forgive me if I make no introductions. Names are unimportant."

Talmor frowned. His sense of uneasiness was growing. To hide it, he began to pace slowly back and forth. He had to keep himself from stiffening up too much, but the exercise also helped keep him up and ready for whatever might come.

"Have you come to offer me a post at your hold?" he asked.

The courtier laughed. "Alas, I have not. You are an able fighter, but I am no chevard."

"What then?"

"You are an impatient man, sir."

"I haven't much time." A burst of laughter came from the passageway outside. Talmor ignored it, keeping his gaze on his visitor.

"Are you going to win today, sir knight?" the courtier asked. "You look as though you might. I must say that you are a magnificent warrior, wonderfully trained."

Talmor inclined his head to acknowledge the compliment and said nothing.

Again the courtier laughed. "A cautious man, I see."

"If you seek to bribe me into throwing the contest, I won't do it."

"So blunt, my good sir. So crude!" The courtier made a little tsking sound and shook his white head. "Nay, indeed not. I think you will win, and if you do, I want to be the first to approach you."

If he squinted his eyes, Talmor glimpsed something dark and shadowy around this man, something very wrong, and wholly at variance with his mild, cultured, smiling demeanor.

Talmor frowned. "What do you want?"

With a flourish, the courtier closed his fist, then turned it over and opened his fingers. Thick disks of gold lay on his palm. They were larger than Mandrian coinage, and heavier.

Crossing his arms over his chest, Talmor scowled. "Keep your gold. I'll not take it."

"But I want you to win," the courtier said with a smile. "This is simply an extra inducement, in case your energy has started to flag."

"What else do you want?"

"Your loyalty in the years to come. Your information."

Talmor's eyes narrowed. The man looked Mandrian. There was no trace of Gantese narrowness to his skull or features. His skin was too pale to be Saelutian. "Who pays you?" he asked sharply. "The Kladites?"

The courtier's smile vanished. "I shall ignore your question. Your rough manners are insulting, but even those will I overlook. Come, sir, let us strike a bargain."

"Get out," Talmor growled.

"I'm offering you a fortune," the courtier said sharply. "Regular payments in exchange for information whenever you're asked for it. You're a fool if you turn this down."

"My name is fool."

"Insolent cur!" the courtier said angrily. Pocketing the gold, he glared at Talmor. "You should be thinking of your future. How many years will you toil as a sentry, earning little beyond your room and board? In the end, what will you have to show for it? Nothing! I offer you security, a chance to build wealth without—"

"Get out," Talmor said. He stepped forward, and the courtier retreated, scowling and angry, with a bang of the door.

Swearing beneath his breath, Talmor glowered and paced a rapid circuit of the small room before leaning over the stone basin and dumping water over his head.

It felt cool and refreshing. It seemed to clear away some of the stink of treason and dishonor from the chamber.

Something hard and heavy walloped his back, driving him headfirst into the water. Gasping and spluttering, he jerked up his head and whirled around without straightening, driving his fist deep into his attacker's belly.

With a grunt of expelled air, the man went staggering back, and Talmor charged him, using his impetus to drive him hard into the wall. The club dropped from the man's hand and thudded on the stone floor. The attacker, a peasant with a coarse, pockmarked face beneath a fringe of ill-cut hair, clutched himself and groaned.

Talmor bent and scooped up the club. The moment he touched the wood, a surge of fury slammed through him, and he felt a kind of madness. He wanted to hammer this man with it, beat him, pound him to a pulp.

Astonished by this brutal, surging, violence, this lust to strike out and murder, Talmor swung the club high before he realized what he was doing. With an oath, he hurled it in the far corner. It clattered against the stone wall and fell, rolling across the floor.

Breathing hard, Talmor shuddered and rubbed his stinging palm back and forth across the other. He glared at the peasant, who looked at him now with fear.

"A magicked club," Talmor said in accusation. "Who made it?"

Rising to his feet, the peasant uttered a curse, and Talmor drove his fist hard into the man's belly. Doubling over, the man retched dryly, and groaned. Talmor gripped his filthy hair and jerked up his head, observing that he'd turned a sickly gray hue.

"Who made it?"

"Dunno!"

"Who gave it to you?"

"Dunno!"

Talmor hit him again.

"Dunno!" the man said desperately this time, holding up his hands in surrender. "Gave me a piece of silver for the job. Told me where to go. That's all I know! Swear it!"

Pears came in, looking curious, then alarmed. Tossing down Talmor's sword and mail, he drew his dagger. "What's amiss here?"

"An assassin out to crack my skull," Talmor said grimly.

Pears's face turned red. He put the point of his dagger right in the peasant's sweating face. "By Thod, I'll fix you—"

"Never mind that," Talmor broke in. "Run and fetch the guards. Tell them this fellow wields a magicked club."

It took a moment for that to sink into Pears's brain. He frowned at Talmor with dawning horror. "A magicked—you mean a—"

"Exactly what I said. Don't touch it!" Talmor said sharply. Pears stopped in his tracks.

"Fetch the guards," Talmor repeated. "Hurry! I've little time before I go back to the arena."

Running into the passageway, Pears set up a shout. Guardsmen arrived in short order, bursting in and looking around with their hands on their sword hilts. At the sight of Talmor, holding the peasant pinned against the wall, they relaxed and grinned.

"Here's our champion," one said. "Victor over a—"

"Take care," Talmor said grimly. "That's his club over there. We need a priest to destroy it."

"A club against Talmor's sword," the other guardsman said. "I'll wager silver on that contest."

Both men laughed. In the distance a trumpet sounded, and Talmor released his prisoner with an angry shove.

"He won't say who hired him to break my skull, but he was paid handsomely for the job."

The guardsmen sobered immediately, while the peasant held up his grimy hands and began to blubber for mercy.

"Dunno who it was, sirs," he said. "Dunno we's to hit one of yer—"

"He won't say how he came to be using a magicked club," Talmor went on, "but it's dangerous. Don't touch it."

"Magicked!" one of the guards said in astonishment. "But that can't be. It's not—"

"—possible?" Talmor broke in, exasperated with such ignorance. "I tell you it's enspelled with evil."

The trumpet call came again, and he swore. "I leave the matter in your hands, for if I don't go now, I'll forfeit to Sir Kedrien."

"Get to your contest. We'll lock up your man. And luck to you, but my bet's on Sir Kedrien," the guardsman said, and grinned. "No offense."

"None taken."

Talmor hesitated, wanting to make sure they handled this properly and knowing they didn't believe what he said about the club. It lay there on the floor, looking innocuous, but it was quite deadly. *Who?* he wondered furiously, but there was no time to investigate.

Pears pulled his hauberk on over his head, tugging it down ruthlessly. Picking up his sword belt, Talmor strode out of there quickly, swearing with every step. "We've got to find out who's behind this," he said to Pears. "I thought it was—"

The roar of the crowd drowned him out. He came up the steps into the hot sunshine and walked down the alley between the two sections of stone stands. Pears was skipping along at his side, trying to buckle his sword belt the way he liked it.

Talmor flexed his shoulders. "As soon as the contest begins, get back down there and see that those louts don't mishandle the club. It's dangerous, and the fools don't believe me."

"Ain't no one hereabouts believes in spells and magic," Pears mumbled with a frown. "Just as well, damn 'em."

Talmor paused at the gate and stared out across the arena, where the heralds were already bawling out the announcements over the cheering of the crowd. "See to it."

"Aye, sir."

Pears hastened away, and Sir Kedrien came up beside Talmor at the gate. Busy fitting on his helmet, the officer did not speak, did not even glance at Talmor. He radiated grim determination so strong it took no soulgazing to tell Talmor what lay in his heart.

As their names were called and the gate was swung open, Talmor said, "Luck to the best man."

Sir Kedrien shot him a glare. His eyes were stony. "You'll never serve her," he said, his voice soft and furious. "I've sworn I shan't let the likes of you defile her with your presence. It's abominable that she should be required even to consider you."

"We are all the king's subjects," Talmor said mildly, but

his jaw felt tight. He knew those around him were listening with big ears.

"Take heed, for I'll give you no quarter."

"I ask none," Talmor replied.

Ducking his head, Sir Kedrien strode ahead of him, his hand already gripping his sword hilt, his back rigid.

Talmor had been taught that in combat one used anger for energy, but one also kept a cool head. He would use Kedrien's ire against him, he thought.

He walked into the arena more slowly, and heard the crowd cheer him. Keeping his hand off his sword hilt as was courteous until the round started, Talmor held himself like a champion.

He hurt, dammit, and he was weary. He was tired of being the butt of Sir Kedrien's derision and petty bigotry. At last the chance had come to end this man's power over him.

The herald rode up to him. "Draw your weapon, sir."

Talmor obeyed.

The other herald gave the same command to Kedrien, who yanked out his sword. The blade glinted in the sunlight, and he held it with strength and confidence, flourishing it a little to stir up the crowd.

"Salute the king."

Both knights turned to face the royal box, where servants were busy plying large fans made of woven splints and bringing drinks to his majesty and companions. Together Talmor and Kedrien lifted their swords high, then swung them down in perfect unison.

The crowd applauded, and with quickening heart, Talmor turned to face his opponent. They carried no shields and no other weapons besides their swords. The midafternoon sun felt brutal. Not a single breath of wind stirred in the enclosure. The heat was shimmering on the sand, and he felt as though his mail and helmet had become crucibles for melting him alive.

The herald's flag flashed, and with a roar Kedrien charged, swinging his sword aloft. He came at Talmor hard, pent-up anger behind every blow. Talmor parried skillfully, aware of how Kedrien meant to attack him. He could read the man's stance and footwork. He caught the telltale glint and shift of Kedrien's eyes behind his visor. Every trick he tried, Talmor was ready for him. At first they went at it hard and fast, keeping the crowd on its feet.

The heavy broadswords clanged steadily. Sure of his weapon and confident in his skill, Talmor made no charges, no feints. He was content to stay on the defensive at first, letting Kedrien tire himself out and reveal all his tricks. They had never fought each other before, but Talmor had watched Kedrien on the practice field and understood his patterns. He liked to attack swiftly, taking no time to measure his opponent. He was quick, very quick, and deft in the wrists. He handled the broadsword at times almost like a thinsword, making his blade flash brightly when it caught the sunlight. The crowd loved the action, cheering his flourishes. Clearly he knew how to compete in a tourney and win the approval of a crowd.

Talmor's experience lay mostly in battle, where the opponent mattered more than the crowd. He defended himself, doing no more than he had to at first. Their blades locked together, and, with a grunt of effort, Kedrien twisted the guard of his sword against Talmor's.

Standing there braced and straining against each other, Kedrien glared at Talmor. "Fight me, damn you!"

Talmor didn't answer, but he shifted his weight suddenly and broke the lock. He retreated swiftly, leaving Kedrien to stagger in order to keep his balance, then feinted close, giving Kedrien an almost playful slap with the flat of his blade.

Laughter broke out from the spectators, and Kedrien's eyes narrowed behind his visor. Cursing, he charged Talmor again, and again Talmor defended himself. Kedrien's next blow, however, came so fast and with such power that Talmor almost wasn't quick enough to catch it. Steel clashed against steel, and Talmor grunted with the effort to parry the blow. He heard Kedrien's wheezing breath. The heat was taking as much toll on them as the fighting.

Now, Talmor thought to himself.

With a lightning shift of his feet, he took the offensive in midblow, shifting his swing without warning and catching Kedrien off guard. His blade bit deep into Kedrien's arm, gashing through the mail and bringing the bright redness of blood.

Kedrien staggered, but managed an awkward parry that was enough to free him from Talmor's attack. Talmor pressed him hard, pounding him with every blow. As though executing a drill, he backed the weakening Kedrien across the arena, one part of his mind gauging the amount of blood now dripping steadily from Kedrien's arm.

As they neared the wall, the spectators there sprang up, some leaning over dangerously close, others yelling and waving their caps. Talmor glimpsed Sir Maldriard watching behind the gate in his black surcoat, his swarthy, black-bearded face grim. There was no doubt he was observing this contest closely to learn all he could about the fighting style of his next opponent.

You won't learn all my tricks, Talmor thought grimly.

Kedrien swung low at his legs, and Talmor jumped back to avoid the blow that could have crippled him for life. The crowd booed, but the move had broken Talmor's steady attack. Kedrien rallied with courage and hurled himself back at Talmor, hammering at his blade with a strength born of sheer will and courage, nothing more. He was spent, losing blood, and they both knew it was only a matter of time.

Talmor had no intention of dragging this out. He was gasping for breath. Sweat burned his eyes. Conscious of the next, much fresher and stronger opponent waiting for him, Talmor moved to end this contest. He parried two exchanges, waiting for the right moment. As soon as Kedrien gave it to him, he surged forward with a mighty blow at Kedrien's head.

The officer was caught with his weight on the wrong foot. He tried to shift back, seemed unbalanced, yet wrenched his sword up to parry Talmor's blow.

Talmor's blade shattered without warning, lethal shards of steel flying in all directions even as the jolt of impact shuddered through his wrist up into his forearm. Caught off guard, he could not right himself fast enough, and the flat of Kedrien's blade slammed into him, driving him to the sand.

Disbelief was already filling him before he hit the ground hard enough to jolt his teeth together. Dust clouded up, stinging his eyes. He tried to roll, but Kedrien's foot stamped on his back, pinning him down.

"A victory for Mandria!" Kedrien said hoarsely, puffing hard between every word. His sword tip rested on the back of Talmor's neck, pressing there hard enough to make Talmor wonder if he would shove it through.

Blazing resentment filled Talmor. He lay still, betrayed by his own weapon and sheer bad luck. Raging with disappointment, he lifted his gloved hand in surrender.

It was over.

Chapter Thirteen

Attendants came racing up while the herald called out Sir Kedrien's name as victor of the round. Talmor was helped to his feet. Someone pulled off his helmet to give him air. He coughed, gulping in deep breaths, and shook his head at the inquiries. He was too spent, too angry to talk. Right up until the end, he knew the contest had been his. Victory had been within his grasp, yet there strode Sir Kedrien, lifting his hands to the cheering crowd while his squire tried to bind his wound.

Scowling, Talmor reminded himself that *almost* was never the final reckoning. It was win or lose here, and he had lost. All his effort, valor, and skill had been no match for the cast of fate against him. He told himself he had done his best, yet wondered what he had overlooked, what detail he had missed, to allow this terrible luck into his life.

He picked up what remained of his sword and with a curt nod of thanks accepted the pieces handed to him by one of the lads. The blade had broken in the middle, about where he'd nicked it earlier.

This, he thought bleakly, was what he'd overlooked. A weakness in the sword, and he'd given it no thought, no attention beyond dispatching Pears to take care of the nick. He'd been too tired to examine the blade himself during the rest period, preferring instead to depend on his squire. Pears was an excellent man, but dependence was wrong. Dependence opened the door for mistakes. He should have paid the matter more heed, given his weapon the respect it deserved. But, nay, he'd been too distracted by his fatigue, by the attempted bribe, and then the attack, to focus his thoughts on anything else. Had Pears even been able to have his sword attended to by the armorer? Talmor could not remember, and that made him angry at himself.

With his helmet clapped under his elbow, he forced himself to walk out of the arena as Maldriard stepped in. Plenty of knights crowded around Talmor, clapping him on the shoulder in commiseration.

"Thod's teeth, what hellish bad luck," Sergeant Goddal came up to say. "Lost half my wages on you, damn all."

Looking like a whipped dog, Pears brought water. Talmor drank long and deep as the trumpets sounded and the herald began the last announcement. Wiping his face with a corner of his surcoat, he pushed back his mail coif and motioned for Pears to loosen his gorget.

"Oh, sir," Pears whispered. "I thought the blade was sound, damn it, or I'd never have put it back in yer hand. I swear—"

Talmor shrugged. "I do not blame you."

Pears bowed his head, and silently took the broken pieces from Talmor's hand.

By then Lutel had appeared, elbowing his way through the crowd to stare up at Talmor with stricken eyes. "That win belonged to ye!"

Talmor shook his head at both of them. "Put it aside. It's over and done," he said, gulping more water. "I knew the blade felt off in the last round after I hit the wood. I should have used another sword, and I chose not to. Thod's will stood against me today."

"Morde," Pears said, his voice choked. "I had the smith grind out the edge, just as ye bade me. I never dreamed he wouldn't check it for further damage, damn 'im."

A roar went up, and Sir Pem showed up to grip Talmor by his arm, pulling him away from his servants. "Let's watch this. Sir Kedrien's got to win, for the honor of us all!"

They climbed into the stands, squeezing in although there wasn't much room among the jammed bodies. Talmor cheered for Kedrien with the others, for no matter what lay between him and the officer, he wanted Sir Maldriard defeated.

Sir Pem leaned forward, shouting instructions as though they were on the practice field. "Keep your guard up, man! Higher, damne! Watch him. *Watch him!* Ah, no!"

A groan went up from the crowd as Kedrien staggered back. Talmor's brows pulled together and he felt a suddenly terrible foreboding. "He's letting too much blood. Maldriard won't give him quarter."

"Nay, he'll have to. Only honorable thing to—"

Someone screamed.

Talmor's gaze whipped back to the fight in time to see Maldriard's sword plunge into Kedrien's chest. The crowd gasped and groaned, and for a moment all seemed frozen. Then Maldriard pulled out his sword, letting Kedrien crumple at his feet. He stepped away from the body, swinging his bloody weapon high in victory.

A few ragged cheers rose for him, but most of the crowd stood hushed, many craning their necks to see if Kedrien would stir. Already the heralds were spurring their horses across the arena, and several guardsmen in green cloaks ran across the sand to kneel beside their comrade.

Gently they lifted him up, and Talmor saw Kedrien lift his hand in a feeble wave. Clapping broke out, and people cried, "He lives! He lives!"

But Talmor knew no one could survive so mortal a wound. He and Sir Pem exchanged somber looks.

The latter swore. "Maldriard's a whoreson. Damn his eyes!"

A sudden wave of coldness moved through Talmor, and he had a vision of himself out there, fighting to the death with Maldriard. If his sword had not broken when it had, would he now be the dying man carried from the arena? He felt as though death had skimmed past his shoulder. Defeat had spared his life today, he thought; of that, he was certain.

The men of Barracks Seven appeared from the crowd, singly or in small clusters, and together they followed their fallen officer off the field. Still feeling shaken, Talmor went with them.

In the surgeon's pen, Sir Kedrien was laid on a table. Blood stained his surcoat, and a cloth had been draped over his face. Knights stood everywhere, many bowing their heads in grief.

Lord Nejel arrived, his face grave as he stood a moment beside his friend and comrade. When he lifted his head, tear tracks glistened on his cheeks. Compressing his mouth, he joined Talmor's side.

"It couldn't be helped," he said quietly, something raw in his voice.

"Couldn't it?"

Nejel's gaze shot to his. "Do you think you could have defeated Sir Maldriard the Black?" he asked sharply.

Talmor opened his mouth, but Nejel didn't let him answer. "He would have won today, whether you or Kedrien faced him. Thod spared you. Be glad of your blessing and speak not against our Maker's will."

"My lord, I—"

"Not now," Nejel said. "I've heard something of what happened to you during the rest period. We must talk of it."

"Aye, my lord, but—"

"Not here," Nejel said, gripping his arm in warning. "Make haste, man, and ready yourself to go before the king."

Talmor stared at him in frustration. There was so much to discuss and report, yet he had no time. Grimacing, he bowed to the commander and left. Pears and Lutel trailed him anxiously.

An official hurried up to Talmor. "You are summoned to

appear before his majesty as soon as you're clean and presentable. Make haste."

Talmor stared at the long, immense expanse of the palace stretching ahead of him, thinking of the king who would see him, and of the lady he longed to serve. This day, this long, difficult day, was far from over. The objective he sought was not yet won, and if he meant to prevail, he had best turn his attention to what lay ahead instead of what had just happened.

He went straight to the sluice room behind the barracks and stripped off his clothes before Lutel threw a bucket of water over him. Then another. Scrubbed with soap, his bruises and welts complaining, he submitted to the dousing, then dried himself and stepped into the leggings Pears held for him. He put on his dress-issue tunic with the guardsman crest embroidered on its front. His green cloak was fastened at his throat, his gauntlets thrust into his hand. Pears secured Talmor's belt.

Frowning, Talmor fingered the empty scabbard hanging at his side. He felt lost without his weapon. The sword had been plain and serviceable, not even custom-forged, but it had served him well for many years and he was sorry to lose it.

"Hurry," the official said.

Pears looked Talmor over and hastily ran a wooden comb through his wet hair. "Thod's luck be on ye, sir," he said softly. "Do us proud."

Talmor sent him a ghost of a smile and followed the official away. Inside the palace, he was hurried along through galleries of breathtaking grandeur. Clusters of courtiers stood about, attempting to look nonchalant, yet their curiosity was palpable. Talmor felt their stares as he strode by, heard their murmured wagers on whether he would be chosen.

When he reached the audience hall, so grand, so immense with its tall pillars and arching ceiling, Talmor's steady stride faltered. A huge lump filled his throat, and his mouth felt as dry as dust.

His heart began to hammer. *Please, Thod,* he prayed. *Let the lady choose me.*

Watched by many, he and his escort walked up the center

of the audience hall. Talmor's keen ears picked up the buzzing whispers and idle talk.

The throne, magnificently carved with its tall back and massive arms, stood empty. Staring at it, Talmor felt a convergence of great power—old power—around the throne. Here was Mandria's heart, its center.

Awed, he found himself rooted there until the official plucked at his sleeve.

"Hurry," he whispered.

Past the throne they exited the audience hall and walked through a passageway lined with guardsmen on duty. Magnificent tapestries hung on the walls, and there were furnishings of tables and finely carved chairs, none of which seemed to serve any purpose.

Through another door, opened for him by a bowing servant, Talmor found himself in a small, crowded antechamber. Lacking windows and lit by dim lamps, it felt like a cave.

The tapestries on the walls smelled musty. Too many men, clad in finery that put Talmor's simple clothing to shame, were already crowded in here. Talmor saw Lord Nejel among them, smiling in encouragement. He also saw Sir Maldriard, standing head and shoulders above the others. The knight looked huge and sinister. His black hair was sleeked back from his low, heavy brow, and he wore a fancy doublet of black cord cloth, its sleeves slashed to reveal lining of yellow silk. Sir Silvrie, victor of yesterday's contest and a rugged individual with curly gray hair and a jaw like granite, stood as far away from Sir Maldriard as possible in the room's close quarters. He wore a blue tunic and a fine, soft red cloak. He was fingering his sword hilt nervously, and gave Talmor a curt little nod of acknowledgment, which Talmor returned. Maldriard glared at Talmor and gave him no courtesy at all.

Confidence radiated from the man, along with a fierce sense of satisfaction. Staring at him, Talmor began to frown. Was Maldriard simply pleased with today's outcome, Talmor wondered, or did he feel certain of the ultimate victory?

The door opened, and several officials and lords of the

court stepped into the next room. The three champions of the tourney were held back.

"You will wait here until you are called," an official instructed them. "Come into his majesty's presence as you are announced. Singly, mind! Not together. Do not stare at his majesty. Do not speak unless you are spoken to."

They bowed to him in compliance.

The official frowned. "Those of you who are armed, remember that this is not customary in his majesty's presence. There are guards on duty, and his majesty's protector will watch you closely. Keep your hand off your weapon, sirs, at all costs. To do otherwise is to threaten the king, and such treason will be dealt with harshly."

Sir Silvrie released his sword hilt and cleared his throat nervously.

As soon as the door shut, leaving the three of them alone, Maldriard turned on Talmor.

"You are not to be chosen," he said. His voice was heavy and gruff. Although he was the best dressed of the three, it was obvious to Talmor's nostrils that he had not bathed. "You are in league with the darkness or you could not have unhorsed me the first day."

His verbal attack made Talmor stiffen. Staring up into those hostile dark eyes, Talmor said nothing.

"Aw, let it go," Silvrie said nervously. "The contests are over."

Maldriard ignored him and went on glaring at Talmor. "You should have been beaten hard."

With a start, Talmor soulgazed him, and knew the truth in an instant. Maldriard had been behind the peasant's attack today. Had paid for it, certainly. Clearly, Maldriard felt a measure of bafflement and frustration over its complete failure.

Talmor's eyes narrowed, and a little smile curved his lips. Seeing it, Sir Maldriard scowled even more.

He took a step toward Talmor, who instinctively reached for the weapon he did not carry. A roaring began in his ears. If it was a fight Maldriard wanted, he . . .

Frowning, Talmor drew in his breath sharply. Was he mad

to be thinking of brawling here and now? It was unlike him to lose his temper this way. Yet he found himself longing to tackle the brute right now, consequences be damned.

Realizing another's will was trying to force his temper past prudence, Talmor withdrew his emotions behind a shield of calm aloofness. There was magic at work in this room, weak magic but capable of causing mischief.

Wary now of the trap he'd nearly fallen into, Talmor felt certain other dangers lay in wait for him.

"You are mixed blood," Sir Maldriard said, still trying to provoke him into a brawl that would see him hustled from the palace forever. "You do not belong. You use what is forbidden, and you cheat."

The accusation made Talmor curl his hands into fists at his side. He held his tongue, but with difficulty.

"See?" Maldriard said to Silvrie. "He does not say it's a lie. He confesses that it is truth."

Talmor's temper grew hot, but he held himself silent, glaring at the man.

"He is unworthy of our company," Maldriard said. "He is a baseborn cur and—"

"Hold your tongue," Talmor said, his voice cold and clear.

Sir Silvrie stepped between them. "Stop it, you fools! You cannot fight in here."

"He cannot fight anywhere without his magic," Maldriard said. "He is a cowardly knave, hiding behind tricks and—"

"I was attacked with a magicked club," Talmor broke in. "Let us discuss that."

"A magicked club?" Looking unworried, Maldriard shrugged. "There is no such thing. Only swords can be spell forged."

"Hush!" Silvrie insisted. His eyes darted from Maldriard to Talmor. "You're mad, both of you, talking of such things. 'Tis said the palace is full of spies. You will get us condemned."

Maldriard never took his eyes off Talmor. "You cheated, or you could not have unhorsed me," he stated flatly.

Talmor was not surprised by Maldriard's evasion. He wondered if Maldriard had intended the attack merely as revenge, or was some larger plot at work? If the latter, then Talmor told himself that Maldriard was merely a tool, mouthing what he'd been told to say.

"You cheated," Maldriard said, more loudly. "No one defeats me."

Normally, Talmor would have taken that statement from no man. Hot with anger, he struggled to hold his tongue.

"You are a cowardly wretch. Do you fear to defend yourself?"

Thod's bones, Talmor thought angrily, how he ached to teach this arrogant brute a lesson. But he also knew that protectors could not issue or accept challenges. Maldriard was still trying to trick him into disqualifying himself. Talmor went on holding himself silent and aloof, although it made him appear cowardly.

"You say nothing. You admit it," Maldriard taunted him.

"I admit nothing," Talmor replied with all the calmness he could muster. Had he chosen to cheat, he could have shot the black knight from his saddle with fire. *That* would have been cheating.

"We are alone here," Maldriard persisted. "You can admit it."

"I was trained to joust by a master," Talmor said coldly. "Why don't *you* admit that my skill with a lance surpassed yours?"

"You are a bastard dog, kicked out of your father's household," Maldriard said. He let a slow smile spread across his face. "I know Etyne."

Talmor stiffened. His gaze locked on Maldriard's and could not break away. Although his expression stayed cold and blank, inside his mind was spinning. He felt cold, unable to think. Ruin, always so close, loomed over him. *Not again,* he thought miserably, remembering how many times he'd started over. *Sweet mercy of Tomias, not again.*

Maldriard chuckled deep in his throat.

Somehow Talmor rallied his courage and faced the knowledge in the man's eyes. "Say anything you please, but who will believe your tales? 'Tis the lady who chooses today. I doubt she will want you, stinking of combat and showing the manners of an oaf."

Maldriard's dark eyes flashed with contempt. "If you believe the lady chooses, you are a fool," he said, and turned away.

Silence fell over them all. Although he was grateful that Maldriard had finally shut his mouth, Talmor could not still his worry. How much did Maldriard know? What combination of lies and truth would he say to discredit Talmor before the king and Lady Pheresa?

He knew nothing, Talmor tried to reassure himself. Etyne would not have told him much, if anything. Their father had taught them all to keep silent about Talmor's curse. *"Family matters belong within the family,"* Lord Juroc always said. *"Nothing must come back against the family."* And although Etyne, Porhal, and Amic—Talmor's half brothers—had all hated him, they feared their father's wrath more. No, he did not think Etyne had spilled old family secrets to Maldriard. Whatever the brute had learned, it had not been from that source.

Of greater concern was this possibility that the lady would not be allowed to choose for herself. If not she, then who? And based on what criteria? How many plots and intrigues swirled around the lady's future?

The door opened, making them all start.

"Sir Maldriard."

Sneering, the black knight cast an arrogant look at Talmor and the other man before he stepped through the doorway. The door shut, and there was an eternal wait.

Talmor's nerves knotted his entrails. He felt a terrible sense of foreboding, as though danger was closing in around Lady Pheresa. If Maldriard had sold himself to a master who meant the lady no good, was a spell at work even now to persuade her in the black knight's favor? Talmor rubbed his jaw, trying to keep himself from rushing to the door and battering it open with his fists.

The door opened, and he was grateful he'd stayed where he was.

"Sir Silvrie."

The man in blue cleared his throat, pulled his hand from his sword hilt, and hurried through the doorway.

Again the wait seemed endless. Talmor wanted to pace about, but he forced himself to stand still. He'd done all he could, he reminded himself, and now his future rested on the decision to come. Fretting would not accomplish anything.

Great Thod, he prayed. *I am in thy hands.*

The door opened, scattering his thoughts.

"Sir Talmor."

Chapter Fourteen

"Sir Talmor."

Talmor strode inside like the officer he had once been. None of his nervousness showed. He bowed first to the king, then to the lady, who stood with her back to the tall windows. Her face remained in shadow, while sunlight streamed in behind her. He wanted to look at her and determine what she was thinking, but he dared not.

Then she stepped away from the window and walked over to stand beside the king's throne. She wore green today, the green of the sea on a cloudy day. Her face looked pale and tired. Her eyes, brown and uncertain, studied him, then moved restlessly from face to face.

Talmor took his place beside Sir Silvrie. Several ministers of the council, a cardinal in robes of dazzling white, and a marechal numbered among the courtiers permitted to observe these proceedings. Lord Nejel stood out of the way, smiling pleasantly, his eyes keen and interested.

Slender, beautiful, vulnerable, Pheresa slowly blushed from being the center of so much attention. She needed him,

Talmor told himself. The air hung thick with anticipation, possibly even an undercurrent of menace. Talmor had to ask himself if there was a single man present who did not want either something from her or something against her.

The king—handsome and magnificently dressed—smiled at his ease, as though unaware of the tension in the room. A young man in a brightly hued doublet, wearing an ornate feather in his cap, bent low to murmur in the king's ear.

His majesty chuckled, and all eyes turned to the monarch. "Lervan," he said merrily, slapping his knee, "you delight me with these sallies. Share your jest with the whole company."

Grinning broadly, the young lord repeated his joke. Talmor did not listen. His attention was focused on Lady Pheresa, and he noticed the quick flash of resentment in her eyes when Lord Lervan stole the attention.

Talmor knew the barracks gossip, which said Lervan hoped to be named the king's heir instead of Lady Pheresa. Something about him seemed insincere to Talmor, who disliked him on first sight.

Everyone laughed at the end of Lord Lervan's tale, the king more heartily than the rest. "Now, dear lady," he said to Pheresa, and she hastily curtsied. "Let us turn our attention to the matter at hand. These champions have fought hard and valiantly, proving themselves to be stalwart men both competent with weapons and courageous in the face of danger. What say you to them? They are the best of our realm, the most able fighters, each willing to serve you to the death."

While she hesitated the cardinal joined the king. He was a thin, slight man with a gray goatee and cold green eyes.

"Sire," he said, "surely it is too much to ask the lady to decide. Let a warrior choose for her. Her own father, perhaps."

Beaming, the marechal came forward. Talmor eyed him narrowly, not much impressed by the Duc du Lindier. Obviously he had been a handsome, athletic man in his youth, but was now bloated from too much drinking and other indulgences, a warrior no longer.

"Now then," Lindier began, smiling at his daughter. "A

protector for you, my dear, will seldom be called to defend
you on horseback. I believe that prowess with a sword is the
most critical qualification."

Sir Maldriard puffed out his massive chest. Lady Pheresa
gazed up at the black knight with visible dread.

Talmor frowned, never taking his eyes off her. *I am true to
you,* he thought at her with all his will. *I will never betray you,
will never fail you. I will keep you from harm, even if I die for
it.*

She blinked, tilting her head. Her gaze shifted in his direction, then away.

His heart squeezed with hope, for he felt certain she had
sensed his message. He held himself still, his heart thudding,
and dared not breathe.

"You make excellent sense, Lindier," the king announced.
"Your assessment is quick and to the point. Lady Pheresa, do
you agree with your father?"

"N—no," she stammered, and blushed to the roots of her
hair.

Everyone stared at her. Despite the high color in her face,
she did not shrink under their scrutiny, not even when Maldriard scowled at her.

"A protector should be able to excel in many things," she
said.

The king's protector, standing behind the throne, permitted
himself the faintest glimmer of a smile. It vanished the moment he caught Talmor looking at him.

"A protector should also be less visible than the person he
guards," Lady Pheresa continued. "And possessing some
measure of refinement suitable for court."

Maldriard's face looked thunderous, and his meaty hands
clenched with ill-concealed ire. Lord Odeil moved his hand to
the hilt of his weapon.

"Let his majesty have final say in this matter," the cardinal
urged. "Let the king choose."

Lady Pheresa shot a look of annoyance at the cardinal,
then turned back to the king in appeal. "Sire, I could never

protest your choice on my behalf. Thanks to your generosity, I am given this tremendous opportunity."

"But you wish to choose for yourself," Verence said with mild amusement.

"I do, sire."

"Then state your choice."

She frowned, hesitating while she looked Sir Silvrie over. Talmor's heart seemed to stop. Her gaze shifted to Lord Odeil, and he guessed she wanted to consult with the protector; however, while the man was on duty that was impossible. Tempted to cast his thoughts at her a second time, Talmor never took his eyes from her.

At last her own gaze met his, and her frown deepened. "This man," she said, almost unwillingly, and pointed. "Sir Talmor."

His heart leaped with triumph, and he smiled. Scowling, she turned away from him at once.

Everyone else tried to talk at the same time, and Maldriard's gruff voice rose over the rest.

"He is unfit! I do protest. This half-breed bastard from—"

The king gestured angrily. "Silence!"

At once the guardsmen surrounded Sir Maldriard, but the knight thrust some of them back. His face was ablaze with anger. "Hear me! He used sorcery to—"

Lord Odeil moved with astonishing speed and put his dagger blade at Maldriard's throat. The knight roared, but by then the guards held him pinned. "You heard the king's order," Odeil said, pressing the blade enough to make a trickle of blood run down the black knight's throat. Maldriard froze, his eyes squinting with fury. "Take him out."

Maldriard bellowed and heaved against the men holding him, but he was marched away. As the door closed, Talmor heard him still shouting his slander. But here in the privy chamber, no one was listening.

"Sir Silvrie," the king said, and the man in blue bowed. "You fought well and conducted yourself with honor."

"Majesty," the man murmured, looking gratified.

"You may withdraw," an official said to him. "Your prize

awaits you at the gatehouse. Be sure you collect it when you ride out."

Silvrie smiled and bowed again. "Thank you, sire."

He departed, looking content, while everyone turned to Talmor.

He stood at attention, trying to keep his joy and relief from flashing across his face. He had never known a prouder moment.

The king smiled at him. "Well done, sir. Well fought. And, I hope, well chosen."

Talmor bowed. "Thank you, majesty."

"Now, who is your sponsor?"

Lord Nejel came forward. "The man serves in your majesty's guards. As his commander, I sponsor him."

"Can you vouch for this man, his worth, his honor?"

"Your majesty, he serves in the guards, surely the most valiant of all your majesty's warriors."

The king looked impatient. "Glibly said, Lord Nejel, but I would have facts."

Nejel gave Talmor a nod. "I suggest the man speak for himself."

Verence stared at Talmor, who drew a deep breath. "My father is Lord Juroc of Templan Hold."

Verence's gaze grew interested. He leaned forward. "My southernmost hold."

"Aye, majesty."

"That explains why you can fight so well. Juroc's men are the best trained in the kingdom."

Wishing his father could hear the compliment, Talmor bowed.

"You are a natural-born son?"

"Aye, majesty."

Verence leaned back. "Enough said. I find no fault in Lady Pheresa's choice. Swear the man to his vows, and see that he is granted the authority he requires."

Talmor's throat swelled with emotion. He knelt swiftly and repeated the vows given to him, swearing on Writ, his honor, and the holy Circle.

Lady Pheresa made her obeisance to the king. "Your majesty's kindness on my behalf overwhelms me."

Looking pleased, Verence took her hand a moment, then left with most of his courtiers and officials trailing after him. Only Lord Lervan and the official who had escorted Talmor earlier lingered behind.

She shot them both a look of dismissal. "That is all."

The official bowed hastily. "I shall await Sir Talmor outside."

He went out, but Lord Lervan circled Talmor with his hands clasped at his back. The fellow looked strong and quick, but he would run quickly to fat, Talmor thought. He eyed Lervan in return, noting he was about Talmor's own age. They were much the same height, too, but there the similarities ended. Talmor did not like the fellow's smirk or the bold, speculative way he ran his gaze over Lady Pheresa.

"He's strong, my lady," Lervan said, looking Talmor over the way he might a horse. "Well favored in face and form. You've chosen for looks, of course, and who can fault you?"

She turned bright red. "Think what you please, my lord," she replied in a low voice. "But do not say such things at my expense to others."

Lervan winked. "Your secret is safe. Oh, how you sigh and look impatient. I am keeping you from getting acquainted with him."

"Leave off these fancies and teasings," she said stonily, while Talmor yearned to knock the smirk off Lervan's face. "Your humor, my lord, has never been in poorer taste."

"Alas, the lady is not amused," he said with a mocking grin. "Since your protector's company is preferred to my own, I'll away." Laughing, Lervan bowed to her. "But let us bargain, sweetest cousin. I'll make no jests at your expense if you'll promise to dance the *spinnade* with me at tonight's banquet."

With a frown, she nodded. Lervan sauntered out, and Talmor unclenched his jaw. However, thanks to Lervan's remarks, the atmosphere in the room was now constrained and ill at ease.

Talmor contented himself with letting his eyes feast on her beauty, especially on how the sunlight shone red spangles in her golden hair. Desperately, he tried to think of something to say, then reminded himself that he must not initiate conversation. He was sworn now to her service. Her every command was his to obey, without question.

She stood before him, studying him in silence, then slapped him hard.

The force of her blow rocked his head back a little, and his cheek stung fiercely. Taken aback, he stared at her open-mouthed.

Her eyes flashed fire. "How dare you!" she said furiously. "Did you work some spell on my mind, seeking to influence my choice? Did you? I was on the verge of choosing Sir Silvrie, but then your name came from my lips. What magic do you possess?"

He blinked, his mind athwart as he tried to find a way to answer without lying.

"Who trained you in the usage of such powers?" she demanded. "Answer me!"

It would be fatal to lie. He knew that, and his spirits sank inside him, for he believed she would reject him as soon as he answered. "My lady," he said carefully, "I did but fill my mind with the strong desire to serve you. Were you not—sensitive—you could not have heard my thoughts."

She stiffened, her eyes ablaze. "How dare you accuse me of having magical powers of my own! I do not, sir. I do not!"

"You misunderstand—"

"And now you dare correct me? Indeed, you are an oaf, with the greatest ignorance of your place."

His face was burning. "Forgive me," he forced himself to say, bowing his head. "I'm but a knight, willing to serve, but ignorant indeed of the manners your ladyship requires. May I begin anew?"

"You will answer my questions, with no more evasion," she ordered.

"I am half-Saelutian. My mother was unknown to me, but if I possess any special sense or ability, 'tis due to her."

"There is much sorcery in Saelutia."

"Aye, my lady. I have heard it to be so."

Her mouth compressed to a thin line. "Are you a *sorcerel*?"

"No!"

"Did you work magic on me to influence my choice?"

"No."

"What magic did you use to unhorse Sir Maldriard in the joust?"

"None! 'Twas skill at arms, my lady, no matter what that blackguard claims."

She lifted the Circle she wore around her neck and held it out. "Swear this."

He knelt and kissed the holy object. "I ply no trade of sorcery. I used none in the contest. I used none today. This do I swear."

Lady Pheresa walked away from him, leaving him kneeling there on the floor. "My Circle did not burn you. It seems you speak the truth."

He rose to his feet. "I do not lie, my lady."

"But you do not speak freely either."

His gaze dropped. She was astute, this beauty. This was not the conversation he'd dreamed they would have. "My lady, my blood is mixed. In Mandria that is often considered a crime. Of course I have secrets, but I intend you no wrong. I have pledged my total loyalty to your service. I would die for you."

"So would any protector pledged to my service."

"Nay, my lady. I—"

"You are different?" she broke in, her voice haughty and imperious. "Why?"

He stared at her, his ears roaring, unwilling to answer such a bald question. If he admitted the full truth of how much he loved her, she would have to dismiss him. "I care for your safety," he said at last. "I do not serve from a mere sense of duty."

"Emotions in a protector are forbidden," she said.

"Aye, my lady. They'll never interfere."

"Easily said, sir."

"I swear it on my word and honor."

Her cheeks grew pink. "I warn you, sir, that if you think with your loins and not your wits—"

"My lady!" he protested in acute embarrassment. "I—"

"Quiet! 'Tis not your place to interrupt. I hope that you will learn your duties quickly, for I will not permit further insubordination."

He had not expected her to be so fierce and defensive. Realizing she was too frightened to trust him, he gentled his expression all he could. "My lady," he said quietly. "If I am a little dazzled today by the—the honor of serving you, 'tis only natural. It will go no further. I pledge to you that I shall forever guard you with all the courage and loyalty I possess."

She stared at him in silence, her brown eyes troubled and still uncertain. He saw how she yearned to trust him, but could not.

He would have to prove his loyalty to her, he told himself, and was determined quickly to win her trust. He would have to serve her patiently, demonstrating that he had no link to her enemies.

Plunging her hand into her pocket, she drew out a small leather purse, which she threw at him.

Catching it, he hefted it on his palm in puzzlement. It had weight, as though it held money, but there was no clink of coinage.

"Do you know what that is?" she asked.

Loosening the drawstring, he peered inside. "Salt."

"Do you know what it's for?"

His gaze met hers with utmost seriousness. "To keep Nonkind at bay."

She turned pale, and her lips parted a moment. "Know you how to sense their presence? Before they materialize to attack, can you feel them?"

"I do not know, my lady. I have never faced Nonkind before."

Worry burned in her eyes. "Can you recognize a Gantese

agent? Many are in disguise, looking harmless, yet lurk here with evil intent."

He frowned, thinking of the courtier who'd offered him the bribe earlier today. "Perhaps. I think I—"

"You cannot think! You must *know*!" Whirling away from him, she began to pace. "Lowland Mandria thinks itself safe from such dangers, but it is not. The evil will come against us any way it can." She paused, frowning at things he could not see. "It does already."

Talmor watched her, so beautiful in the sunshine spilling in through the windows. This lady, he thought in admiration, was no fool. But she was very, very frightened, and with good cause.

"Sometimes, my lady, I can sense trouble to come," he said slowly. "My instincts are very keen. Perhaps I can learn to detect the presence of these Nonkind."

"Do so. Learn by any means you can," she commanded.

He bowed to her, beginning to hope. "And your ladyship will retain me, even if I am not wholly Mandrian?"

"What does that matter, as long as I have a man I can trust to guard my back?"

Her answer, with its lack of prejudice, stunned him. He realized that initially she would have distrusted even Sir Silvrie, had he been chosen.

He loved her all the more. In that moment, he became her slave.

"And will your ladyship forgive me for letting my hopes of serving fill my mind so strongly that I—"

She gestured impatiently. "Have done. Use your powers in my defense. But remember that if ever you turn them on me, I shall report you to the church, and to his majesty."

The threat was clear enough. He bowed in acknowledgment, then she suddenly frowned and stared at him very hard.

"I have remembered . . . you're the man who saved me from the Sebein attacker."

"Yes, my lady."

Her face lit up momentarily before she schooled her features once more. "I thought I had seen you before. Then I believed you were working some mischief on my mind. Why did you not say so at once?"

He remained silent, and she sighed.

"Of course you could not. It was your duty, and men— some men—do not boast of such things."

"Yes, my lady."

She nodded, but her previous hostility had dissipated. "Very well. We've talked long enough. Is there someone to instruct you in the duties of a protector?"

"I understand the duties. Am I to commence immediately?"

She hesitated, obviously unprepared as yet for his presence in her life. He could see her thinking. Was she shifting living arrangements among her attendants, he wondered. Ladies usually depended on their male relatives to keep them safe and did not go about with protectors at their back.

"You have fought long and hard these three days," she said at last. "The morning will be soon enough. A steward will determine how you're to be housed."

He thought the delay unwise, but he dared not argue with her. "I come with a squire and a servant, my lady."

Her brows lifted in surprise. "Indeed? For a sentry-rank knight, you are well supplied in dependents."

"I was not always a sentry."

"No doubt. Even the natural son of a chevard has advantages in life, does he not?"

Talmor quelled a swift little thrust of bitterness and did not try to correct her. As he left, he felt her gaze following him out and guessed that she was still curious about him. Would she ask her questions directly, he wondered, or would she seek information from others? He hoped he had convinced her to trust him today. If not, then she remained vulnerable to whatever mischief her enemies might use to divide them.

The following week, with the excitement of both the tourney and fair fading, it was announced that the court would move to Aversuel, the king's summer palace among the cool, rolling

mountains of the eastern lake country. The hot weather had
come early this year, and already Savroix grew unbearable.
Pheresa was issuing packing instructions to Oola when a page
with a saucy little face brought her a summons.

Pheresa put aside her list of things yet undone to hurry to
the looking glass. "Oola, will this gown do?" she asked in
frustration. The heat made her apartments swelter, and she felt
too hot and tired to bother changing her attire. "What on earth
can his majesty want at this time of day?"

"No doubt he seeks your ladyship's advice on the hiring of
that new minstrel," Oola said. "The one with the squint eye
who sings like a divine being." She smoothed a wrinkle from
Pheresa's skirts. " 'Tis a pretty gown. And not too crumpled."

"What a mercy I did not change after this morning's
madrigals," Pheresa said, glad to see that no dirt smudged her
face. She'd been rummaging in the back of an old chest in
search of reading scrolls.

Now, she adjusted her necklace, tucked up a wayward
strand of hair, and picked her way through the litter of half-
packed chests and belongings strewn about in precarious
piles. "Keep at this, Oola. I'll return shortly."

Oola curtsied. "Yes, m'lady."

As soon as Pheresa emerged from her bedchamber, Sir Talmor left the tall window where he'd been standing and fell
into step behind her. Still uncertain that she was dressed well
enough to visit the king, she fussed with her hair while Talmor preceded her out into the corridor. She saw him gaze both
ways with his alert, keen eyes, then he moved aside smartly
for her to take the lead again.

She hurried forward, thinking of all the myriad details still
to be done before they departed in the morning. She'd never
been to Aversuel, and the prospect of going there excited her.

As she rounded the corner of the passageway and stepped
out into one of the public galleries, she stopped fidgeting with
her hair and pulled her flustered expression into one of calm
serenity. Having Sir Talmor at her back was a tremendous
comfort. Already she did not know how she'd ever survived
without him. He was incredibly organized and efficient; al-

ways ready at her beck and call, anticipative of her needs, watchful, and alert. She felt safe with him nearby, knowing that very little missed his quick eyes. Despite his size, he was light on his feet, graceful and lithe in his movements, rather like a large predatory cat. His worth had already been demonstrated, for he had routed Sir Brillon completely, pouncing on the church knight yesterday morning when Pheresa was on her way to chapel. The two men had exchanged sharp words, but Sir Brillon stalked her no more. Getting rid of the Qanselmite had taken a great load from her shoulders.

She felt in merry spirits today, filled with anticipation about the journey to come. Smiling a little as she sailed through the rooms and long galleries, she found it no longer an ordeal to walk past the watchful faces. She no longer had to pretend to be courageous; Sir Talmor's presence gave her both confidence and a feeling of security. Serenely, she entered the king's section of the palace and approached the clerk hovering on duty in the main passageway.

"Ah, Lady Pheresa," the man said before she could state her business. "His majesty bade me escort you straight to his privy chamber."

She was surprised, but kept her expression neutral and pleasant. Several courtiers lounging nearby heard and sent her speculative looks. She ignored them. There was always speculation, always gossip. She'd learned to discount it all. The king had acquired the recent habit of sending for her on impulse. At first, she'd been excited and hopeful, but each time it seemed he wanted only to ask her advice on a trinket for his mistress or some other trivial matter. Now she treated these summonses as commonplace.

In the privy chamber, Verence was laughing as usual with Lervan.

She could never see them together without a pang of jealousy. It looked more and more as though Lervan was going to be Verence's choice. She wondered why his majesty bothered to hire jesters at all when he had Lervan beside him. Still, the king's melancholy had gone, and if Lervan's jokes were the reason, she supposed they should be grateful. Casting a critical eye over yet another new, fashionable doublet, she wished Lervan did not wear such bold colors. But it seemed he wanted to be the center of attention wherever he went.

She was announced, and curtsied deeply.

"Ah, Lady Pheresa!" the king called to her, holding out his hand in good humor.

Smiling, she went to him. "How may I serve your majesty?"

"These damned boat raiders continue to nibble at the western coast," he said with a fretful sigh. "I wonder if I should postpone the move to Aversuel while they venture so far south. Will they think the king fearful? Will they think the king flees from them?"

Astonished that he was actually asking her advice on a political matter, Pheresa kept her wits, and said, "Nay, sire. If they hear your majesty has been affected by them to such a degree, they will feel heartened enough to continue their raids. Leave Savroix well-manned, but let not your majesty defer his pleasure."

Smiling, Verence clapped his hands. "Splendid reasoning. Hear that, Lindier? Your daughter has a head on her shoulders."

"Indeed she has, sire," the duc replied with a smirk.

"Salba, do you not find the lady's answer sound?"

The chancellor bowed. "Yes, of course, majesty."

"Meaclan?"

The minister of finance added his agreement to the rest, and shot Pheresa a look that made her blink in sudden anticipation.

Verence was beckoning to a page, who brought forth a small cushion and placed it on the floor. "Kneel on this, child."

Realizing something momentous was happening, Pheresa's heart began to thud. She knelt on the cushion and struggled to stay calm.

Verence's unusual blue-and-green eyes gazed down at her so solemnly that she felt her face flame. Enrapt with hope and excitement, wishing she had taken the trouble to change into her very best gown before coming, she stared up at him.

"Pheresa," he said, "you have proven yourself worthy in every way, passing all my tests. No matter what the circumstances, you keep a cool and logical head. Your patience I know to be long and steady. Your loyalty to the king and your sense of duty to Mandria go unquestioned."

She bowed her head, clutching her hands together, trembling now.

Verence beckoned to Lervan, who sauntered over with a broad grin. He looked so pleased with himself, Pheresa thought. Indeed, *both* men wore smirks on their faces.

Her father was also smiling, and as her eyes met his, he gave her a little nod of approval. Suddenly suspicious, she felt her heart lurch, and everything seemed suddenly awry. *Fooled again,* she thought in dismay. Lervan would not be happy if he thought she was about to be named successor. Verence had not sent for her today to make her his heir. 'Twas a marriage he planned. She felt sure of it.

"What a pretty couple," the king said, beaming at them both.

Still kneeling on the cushion and feeling at a distinct disadvantage with Lervan looming over her, Pheresa grew angry. Lervan was sending her sly little looks of admiration and pleasure, and while his expression might please her vanity, she could not master her larger disappointment.

"What say you, dear child?" the king asked. "Find you not this cousin to be handsome and pleasing company?"

Lowering her gaze lest Verence see her distress, she murmured something agreeable. Lervan moved even closer to her, his leg brushing her shoulder. Confused by his proximity, wishing the king had asked her privately first, she fought the urge to burst into tears and told herself not to be a fool. She could not go unmarried forever, and whatever the king arranged for her she dared not refuse.

Her mind began to turning rapidly. She did not love Lervan, but what did that matter? She was no longer a naive and foolish girl, dreaming of romance. People of her rank married for advantage and alliance, not love. She instantly saw that there would be advantages to a union with Lervan. His birth and rank were acceptable. He had wit and a certain degree of charm. He made amusing company, and was it not better to wed a man with the gift of laughter than a sour temper or arrogance?

Struggling to be sensible, she told herself all this, and knew that he was not what she wanted.

But the man I want is forever denied to me, she thought bleakly, and shut Faldain from her mind.

" 'Tis decided," the king said abruptly. "You, Pheresa, will be my heir and successor. From this day forth, you are Princess of the Realm."

Her gaze snapped to him, and she forgot all about matters of love and marriage. She could not believe what she'd just heard and reeled from the unexpectedness of it. "M-majesty?" she stammered.

He laughed and flicked her cheek with his fingertip. "I am well pleased with you, niece. I find you worthy in all respects."

Her throat was suddenly so full she could not find her voice. It had come at last. Just when she'd nearly given up, all she'd dreamed of and longed for was finally happening. It seemed like a dream, yet Verence was touching her shoulders in official blessing, and the courtiers present looked on in solemn witness.

There would be a royal investiture, she thought in a daze. A ceremony of tremendous pomp. She would be given a small crown, and the church would bless her publicly.

She was so breathless with awe and joy that she felt faint. Yet she realized the king was no longer speaking. Somehow, she must regain her wits and find her tongue.

"Majesty, I shall do my best to honor and fulfill all—"

He laughed again, cutting off her confused speech with a gesture of satisfaction. "Yes, yes, dear princess. You may say all that later. Rise now and give me your full attention, for there is a little condition that goes with this honor."

Some of her soaring happiness checked, and she grew wary as she rose to her feet. "Indeed, sire?"

"What say you to Lervan as husband and consort?" Verence asked. "I find it a good match, and 'twill solve the problem of these little factions that have sprung up in recent months."

"Consort, sire?" she asked carefully, trying to keep her wits about her. "Not joint monarch?"

Lervan's gaze narrowed at her question. Something unreadable flashed across his face.

"Consort," Verence replied, and smiled at Lervan.

The young lord smiled back at him with a bow.

Pheresa wondered if Verence had noticed the disappointment in Lervan's face, so swiftly concealed. It seemed not. Well, let him be disappointed, she thought with a new surge of confidence. Lervan was getting a generous prize indeed, more perhaps than he deserved, and he need not be greedy. The power and position so suddenly bestowed on her made her feel giddy. She studied Lervan through new eyes, aware that if they married, she would always outrank him. The supremacy in the marriage would be hers, not the reverse, and this pleased her. A year ago, when she'd hoped to win Gavril's notice, she'd prepared herself to live in submission to a man she did not love. Now, 'twould be Lervan's duty to please *her*, and in these circumstances she believed he could. His charm glowed at her, his eyes laughing as they stared into hers with open admiration. Liking the way he looked at her, she felt a new blush heat her face.

If she wanted the throne, she must take Lervan, she thought. The king had made that clear. Well, the decision was not difficult. When the day came that she was queen, Pheresa told herself, she alone would rule. And the most charming, affable, free-spirited man at court would be her husband.

It gave her a very good feeling indeed.

She smiled with a sudden radiance that made all the men in the room blink and look at her with new attention.

Lervan seemed particularly dazzled. "Beautiful," he whispered.

Her smile grew even brighter, and she turned it on the king. "I am honored and delighted by your majesty's wishes. Naturally I agree."

"Splendid." A visibly delighted Verence took her hand and placed it in Lervan's. His touch was very warm, and she swallowed a little convulsively. He stirred her. She need not deny it.

"What say you, Lervan?" the king demanded.

Blinking as though roused from a dream, Lervan tore his gaze away from Pheresa's face. He bowed deeply, his finger sliding playfully along her palm. "Your majesty has rendered me the happiest, and most grateful, of subjects."

Verence nodded. "Then it is settled. The announcement will be made tonight, and we'll banquet past dawn. Let the feasting and celebrations begin!"

The officials gathered around, in a babble of noise, to wish them joy.

Lindier kissed Pheresa's cheek. "The perfect settlement, a solution earnestly wished for. My deepest felicitations, daughter."

"Will you tell Mama?"

He looked disconcerted, but before he could answer Verence shot them both a wicked little smile. "The king will inform his sister of the news in private. Her tantrum will be like a tempest, spouted with much fury, but quickly spent. Thod willing, she may even leave court for a while and give us all peace."

Pheresa felt less confident that her mother would recover quickly from disappointment, but she was glad she would not have to face Dianthelle.

Lervan, busy accepting bows and good wishes, now leaned close to her ear. "Let us escape, my beauty, and run away to the gardens."

She caught her breath at his audacity, marveling that he would flirt with her in front of both the king and her father. But they looked indulgent, and the king nodded his permission.

"Come," Lervan said. "If we may be excused, sire?"

"Use my private garden, but tarry not too long," the king told him.

They hastened for the door with more speed than Pheresa considered dignified.

She glanced back, and found Talmor, looking more serious than usual, following her. Lervan frowned at her protector. "We've no need of you, sir. She is safe with me this day."

"Come to the gardens in a half hour, when we are finished with our stroll," Pheresa told Talmor, conscious of the other men's little grins to each other. "You may escort me back at that time."

Talmor bowed in the silent obedience proper for a protector, but the deep disapproval in his eyes gave her a momentary qualm. Was there something amiss with Lervan, something she should know?

Nay, there could not be, she told herself. Of course, Lervan was a silly man, given to too much laughter and song, but did she not deserve the reward of both? Was it not time, finally, to make merry and enjoy herself? She felt ready to seize life with both hands.

Lervan whispered an outrageous compliment that made her laugh aloud. Pushing the last of her doubts aside, she hurried off with him, and did not look back.

PART II

Chapter Fifteen

Two years later

Sitting in bed, Pheresa nibbled at the delectable breakfast pastries without much appetite. This was supposed to be a joyous morning, filled with happiness, but it was not. She felt angry and disappointed, and could not persuade herself to stop caring.

Lervan had a new mistress.

It was not yet public knowledge, but soon the gossip would spread, yet again, and soon she would have to pretend to ignore it, *yet again*.

Her hand clenched on her spoon in an urge to throw it across the room. Damn the man. If only they hated each other, everything would then be simple. They could go their separate ways, keep to their separate friends and activities, and expect nothing from each other but civil courtesy on state occasions when they had to appear as a couple.

But, alas, she did not hate her husband. In fact, she liked him too well, longed for him too much, missed his absences too often. And he—sunny of temper, blessed with endless charm—brought a warmth and happiness to her life that she had never achieved on her own. She needed him, and craved his company, for he gave her something she'd been starved for all her life. But although her feelings ran deep, it seemed that Lervan's were shallow. He was equally delighted to be with her or with any other woman who caught his fancy.

Lady Carolie came bustling in, sparkling with happiness in a pretty blue gown that matched her eyes. "Good morning, your highness!" she sang out as she curtsied. " 'Tis cool at last. No more of that wicked heat, Tomias be thanked. Will you—"

"Not now," Pheresa said, shoving her breakfast tray aside. None of the food pleased her. She looked at Carolie, so happy in her own marriage, already the mother of a fine little boy. At her throat sparkled a beautiful yellow diamond, a gift from her doting husband.

Sour bitterness filled Pheresa's heart. Had Lervan showered her with gifts, now that she finally carried his heir? Nay, not he. At last night's banquet, given by a delighted King Verence to honor the royal baby to come, Lervan had smirked and preened and accepted congratulations as though he were the happiest man in the realm. He'd made a show of kissing Pheresa's hand, of choosing the daintiest morsels for her to eat. He'd told jokes, laughed loud and long, and sent her fatuous smiles. Fuming on the inside, smiling serenely on the outside, Pheresa resented his hypocrisy. In truth, after two years of marriage and frustration, she was breeding only because she'd been forced to consult an old crone in an out-of-the-way herbalist shop. Then she'd set about the humiliating course of seducing her own husband, winning him to her bed the night of the Harvest Ball. Oh, he was passionate that night, all she could wish for. His kisses were sweet, and his endearments tender. Lying in his arms in the dark, she'd dreamed of conquering his capricious heart and commanding his faithfulness at last.

But within days, he had strayed again, and despite his sweet compliments and passionate embraces, Lervan had not shared her bed these many weeks since.

Now he had a new mistress. The thought of it made Pheresa's stomach curdle.

"Why the frown, highness?" Lady Carolie asked. She gestured for Pheresa's tray to be removed, and her lovely violet-blue eyes took note of what was eaten and what was not. "Have you no appetite? 'Tis said the stomach misery is a sign of a hale and healthy child."

"My misery has naught to do with the babe," Pheresa said. She knew she sounded cross and petulant, emotions she seldom betrayed, but this morning she did not feel like pretending. She was tired of the insults Lervan dealt her. "There are other problems which beset me today."

Sympathy crossed Carolie's face. She smoothed her hand across the rumpled silk coverlet. "I know, highness. I am so sorry."

Dismay filled Pheresa. She stared at Carolie, hating her friend's pity as much as she felt grateful for her understanding. But if Carolie knew, the whole court knew.

"I hate him!" Pheresa burst out, her throat choked with tears.

"Oh, my sweet lady, do not distress yourself so. He is a man, and men exist to break women's hearts."

"Your husband does not treat you so ill."

A strange look crossed Carolie's face. "I am much blessed, your highness. But then, I married to please myself with no duty to fulfill."

Pheresa's frown deepened. "Sometimes duty is poor comfort."

"Of course, your highness. But this is only a flirtation. No one believes him to be serious. After all, he obviously adores your highness."

"Does he?" Pheresa mused aloud. "I wonder."

"Oh, but he does," Carolie reassured her. "I have seen the way he looks at you. There is such tenderness in his eyes, such affection." She sighed. "He is such a handsome man, is he not? So manly. He cannot help but draw the eye of every lady present in whatever company he joins. But his feelings for your highness are too obvious to be mistaken."

Pheresa pleated the coverlet between her fingers, unable to meet Carolie's eyes lest she betray her hunger to hear more assurances. Although she wanted to believe whatever lies she was told, Pheresa could not blind herself to the truth forever.

He had never before dallied with any one woman this long.

A mere flirtation was not the same as taking a mistress. She did not know which was worse, her hatred of his infidelity, especially when she was finally expecting his child, or her humiliation in not being woman enough to keep him from straying.

"Do not weep," Carolie said, as Pheresa bowed her head, her shoulders shaking. "Please, your highness. It is foolish to distress yourself. It means nothing. You know that."

"I know nothing of the kind," Pheresa said harshly. "The woman's name is Hedrina. What have you heard of her?"

"Almost nothing." Carolie fetched a comb and began gently to run it through Pheresa's unbound hair. "'Tis said she's dark, not fair, and comely enough but not out of the ordinary."

"Do not lie to me."

"I repeat only what is said."

Frowning, Pheresa compressed her lips. According to her spy's report, Hedrina was the niece of some obscure baron. Newly arrived, she was living in town, and not yet received at court. She was described as a stunning beauty, lush and curvaceous, with masses of black hair and eyes of darkest blue. The report said that Lervan had met her at a noble's house in Savroix-en-Charva immediately after the Harvest Ball, and that he had remained captivated by her since.

Anger flashed through Pheresa. She pulled the comb from Carolie's hand and threw it across the room. "My robes, quickly!" she ordered. "I will dress."

Carolie ran to throw open the doors to Pheresa's sitting room. She summoned servants and issued orders while Pheresa climbed out of bed and began her morning toilette. By the time Pheresa had bathed and been dried by Oola, the ladies of the wardrobe and ladies of the bedchamber had assembled themselves in line by order of importance behind Carolie, who served as first lady in waiting.

The ceremony had never seemed to take so long, Pheresa thought, fuming inwardly. Laughter rippled through the room, and she winced before forcing a smile so they would not guess anything was amiss.

But Carolie knew, and some of the others did as well. Pheresa caught their speculative glances. Some pitied her. Others enjoyed her disquiet. Pheresa longed to scream at them all.

Hurry! Hurry! she wanted to say. *Finish your duties, and let me go.*

But she could say no such thing. She'd always believed it an unseemly abuse of privilege to denigrate her courtiers or behave discourteously in their presence. But today, she felt she would burst if she did not speak to Lervan immediately. She would have it out with him, she decided. No hinting, no polite civility. She seldom exercised her higher rank to bring him to heel, but she knew now that she'd made a mistake in giving him too much freedom.

"Enough," she said, twitching her skirts from Oola's hands. She glanced at her reflection in the looking glass, then turned to her attendants. "Thank you," she said.

It was the formal dismissal she always used. They curtsied and filed out with rustles of silk and little clackings of their slippers.

Pheresa barely waited for the door to close behind them. "Summon a page," she said to Lady Carolie. "I wish to speak to Duc Lervan immediately. Tell him to meet me in the—"

"Your highness has forgotten," Carolie interrupted softly. "His grace is hunting today with the king."

Remembrance of the appointment slowly quelled Pheresa's temper. She walked over to her windows and gazed out across the gardens, which were ablaze with late-summer flowers. Far away, sentries marched atop the walls, and a flock of sparrows flew suddenly past her window to land in the stone gutter and squabble. Her eyes filled with stinging tears. Without even trying, Lervan could make a fool of her. Why did she let him, she asked herself bitterly. *Why?*

To occupy her morning, she wrote a brief message to Lervan, requesting him to come to her as soon as he returned from hunting. Then she set about reading her correspondence and sorting out which letters were to be saved, which answered promptly, and which ignored. Taking up her pen once more, she wrote to her mother, informing Dianthelle of the happy event and asking her to stop spreading rumors that Pheresa was barren.

Following a midday meal, Pheresa set forth on the daily walk her physician had prescribed. She chose to stroll the eastern gardens, which had been redesigned to please her. The paths meandered between beds of blooming flowers, and bees droned in the warm, still air.

Her entourage of courtiers accompanied her, the women chattering, the men talking with equal idleness. There was a laziness to the day that soothed Pheresa's tension. Autumn was coming. The astrinas were nearly spent, and some had already gone to seed, much to the delight of tiny, yellow-and-black birds who clung precariously to the fragile stems and gorged themselves on seed heads. The sunlight shone golden and soft. She slowed her pace, relaxing in the peacefulness of this mellow afternoon, and thought of her baby. What would he be like, if he were born a man-child? Would he be strong of body and foolish of heart, like his father? Would he be nervous and far too serious, like his mother? What would his life be like in all the years to come? She smiled to herself, indulging in daydreams of a little boy with golden curls running to sit on the king's knee, teasing sweets from the palace cooks, racing his pony across the grounds with a dog bounding behind. Or would this child be a daughter, slender and solemn-eyed, her nose buried in scrolls of poetry and adventure?

There would be other children, Pheresa told herself with steely determination. She would see to that. What was important now was to remember how good her life was. She needed to consider her many blessings and dwell less on her problems. Lervan could be corrected. She would make sure that this Hedrina creature was never received at court. It could all be dealt with, and life would go on pleasantly.

"Your highness! Make way, there. I must get through to the princess. Your highness!"

Everyone turned in surprise, and Pheresa saw a man, cloaked and spurred, running across the garden toward her. He trampled across the flower beds, first annoying, then alarming her.

Sir Talmor stepped slightly in front of Pheresa, vigilant as always, but by now she saw that the messenger wore the insignia of a king's equerry.

"Let him through," she said.

The man was out of breath. Little rivulets of sweat ran down his face, and he looked white with shock. As he knelt and lifted his eyes to hers, she saw that he'd been crying. Something inside her grew still and frozen.

"Speak quickly," she said. "What news do you bring?"

"Your highness," he gasped out. "The king . . . the king is dead."

She heard his words clearly, with no mistake, yet they made no sense to her. Around her, everyone stood silent in shock, and in the distance she heard a keeback's plaintive *kee . . . kee . . . kee* through the forest. It was so strange that she should be able to hear a small sound like that, so far away, while everything here close to her seemed muffled and silenced.

The messenger bowed his head. "Oh, Thod!" he cried in anguish. "What a black day this is."

Frowning, she attempted to rally from the shock. A dozen questions ran through her mind at once, confusing her. "How?" she asked, feeling stupid and slow. "When?"

"We'd coursed a fine buck in Waiseun Forest, the first sighting of the morning, and he gave us splendid sport. Aye, how well the king did ride, all out, like he used to in the old days. He whooped every time his horse jumped a fallen log. We had a hard time keeping up. And the buck was a wily one, wise and old and full of tricks."

Pheresa wanted to shake the man. What in Thod's name did she care about a deer? "Go on, man," she said impatiently. "Tell it!"

"The buck led us well, but after the king's arrow went into him he tired rapidly and went down soon after. We drew up to rest our horses and watch the huntsman pull back the dogs. His majesty was laughing and saying what fine sport it was. He c-called for wine." The man broke down a moment, then stiffened his shoulders. "It was brought to him in a stirrup cup, but before he bent down for it, he—he twisted in the saddle as though a stone or arrow had struck him."

"What?" cried out elderly Lord Pelane from among the courtiers. "Do you mean to say his majesty was shot?"

"We thought so at first, by the way he stiffened and cried out in a loud voice. He fell before any of us could help him."

"Say you that an arrow brought him down?" Pheresa demanded in horror.

"Nay, your highness. We only thought it. But there was no mark on him." The equerry lifted stricken eyes to hers. "He is dead, my lady. The physician says his g-great and noble heart failed him."

Around her, people were weeping openly. Lord Pelane stood with his hand across his eyes. Lady Carolie sobbed in the arms of her sister.

Pheresa stood frozen and numb with disbelief. It could not be real, she told herself. The king could not be dead. By now another messenger should be coming to say the king had only swooned, and did not lie dead in Waiseun Forest. She could see Verence so clearly in her mind's eye, revived by now, sitting up and demanding wine.

But such fancies were only tricks in her mind, she realized. The messenger kneeling at her feet had no reason to lie. Yet how could the king's heart fail? There had been no sign of illness in him, no hint of weakness.

Verence had ruled Mandria since before Pheresa's birth. She could not imagine anyone but him on the throne. He'd been so heroic, so bold, so full of vigor and health. Last night he'd laughed and caroused with more energy than usual, drinking deep and even dancing with Pheresa so boisterously she grew dizzy and had to stop.

Even if she could not believe it, there was no way to deny it. Verence had ridden out at dawn with vim and spirit. He would not ride home.

It was Sir Talmor who knelt first, Sir Talmor who said in his deep voice, "Long live the queen."

Her courtiers and friends looked startled, but they quickly knelt around her, each of them repeating the words.

Pheresa accepted their homage numbly, while from the chapel a bell began to toll solemnly. *The king is dead,* she thought. *I am the queen, the queen, the queen. Dear Thod preserve me, for I rule Mandria now.*

People began streaming out into the gardens, guardsmen and ministers and courtiers and servants. Some wailed in honest grief. Others called out prayers. Still others shouted her name. In the growing confusion, Pheresa was conducted swiftly back into the palace, to be met by her chancellors and highest officials, all looking very grave. One by one, they knelt to her, pledging their allegiance and loyalty.

Then she was led to the throne in the privy chamber. She sat down, her heart hammering wildly, her face aflame with a rush of emotions she could not describe. There were guardsmen everywhere, as though someone feared for her safety during this transference of power.

A bishop came and spoke to her at length, saying a prayer over her that she did not hear. She was talked to, and asked to make decisions about whether the army should be ordered forth to support coastal and eastern holds before the terrible news was sent to all corners of the realm. She could not think, could not assimilate it all. Her head was buzzing. She felt cold, and when the royal seal was solemnly placed in her hand, she gripped it with such white-knuckled determination that her hand soon ached.

And when she could take no more discussion of treaties or how to avert possible war or funeral preparations or the schedule for her coronation seven months hence or speculation on what illness had felled the king with such sudden finality, she rose to her feet. The babble fell silent as she stood there, white-faced and shaking.

Without a word, she fled the privy chamber, half-blind and trembling, forcing her way out without heed for where she was going. Although she sought the privacy of her own apartments, instead she found herself steered into the passageway leading to the king's chambers. She stumbled across the threshold in a kind of dazed horror.

Two sitting rooms, an immense bath, a dressing room as large as her entire apartment, and the royal bedchamber. How spacious, nay, vast everything was, how lofty the ceiling overhead. The bed, enormous and canopied, with heavy hangings embroidered with gold thread, stood in the center of the room with a low fence around it and ample room for the courtiers who usually came each morning to observe the king when he rose from slumber and took his breakfast.

Instinctively she tried to retreat, for no one wandered unbidden into the king's private apartments. He would be brought here, she thought wildly. His body would lie in state in this bed, and the court would file through, observing the final rites of passage before the state funeral.

But it seemed she was mistaken. Her servants were already at work arranging her belongings. She saw her sewing box, her lute, her case of poetry scrolls, her clothes chests. Everything lay scattered and disordered, and confusion reigned between her servants bringing her belongings in and the king's staff hastily taking his possessions out.

"No!" she wanted to cry out. "Do not remove his presence like this. Do not strip him away!"

But her throat seemed incapable of uttering a sound. The servants stopped their work to curtsy to her, and dismay filled her as she realized she could not seek refuge here, nor anywhere. Her head felt light, and she longed to lie down in private for a few minutes of rest. She needed to weep for Verence, needed to grieve, but she could not do so openly.

In despair, she turned to Sir Talmor, who stood, as always, just behind her.

He bent his head to her at once. "What may I do?"

Gratitude swept through her. He always understood what she needed. He never wasted time with foolish questions.

Her eyes filled with appeal, and then she frowned and shook her head in silent answer. Slowly, she turned back to the servants, all of whom stood staring at her with shocked eyes and pale countenances.

She stood silently in the vast bedchamber and forced herself to face the realities before her. How suddenly life altered its course. When she first came to court—young, naive, and ambitious—she'd worked hard for the prize she wanted. She'd survived court intrigues, poison, imprisonment, and war on foreign soil. She'd had her heart broken and learned to love again, learned to feel passion's force and its sweet aftermath, learned to live with the kind of hurt that nagged and festered. She'd felt life quicken inside her womb and in the new year she would know the wonder of bringing forth a babe into the world. And now, a man she'd admired and respected, a man she loved more than her own father, would smile at her no more, would dance with her no more, would lose his temper, shower her with gifts, and defeat her at chess no more.

Her throat began to ache. How she longed to hear Verence striding through the passageway. But he would not come in shouting for his slippers, or his bath, or his wine cup, or his supper. His return would be silent, cold, and still.

With stinging eyes, she thought of this morning, when she'd been so angry at Lervan for treating her ill. And now, Lervan did not matter at all. He was a tiny speck, a single detail among a myriad of others, and she must move past him to the new world that awaited her.

Queens do not cry, she thought to herself while she fought to hold back tears. *Queens do not hide in their rooms to indulge in weakness and tears. I must never run away like this again.*

Oola came cautiously, almost fearfully, across the large room and curtsied very low. "Is—is the queen ill?" she whispered.

Pheresa blinked and lifted one hand to her cheek. Her face

was dry. Her eyes were still stinging, but she had vanquished her tears. "No," she managed to say. "The queen is well."

She retreated into the passageway, then lifted her chin and squared her shoulders. Back she walked to the privy chamber.

The conversations there broke off at her sudden entrance. Everyone bowed, and Pheresa walked through the clusters of men to reseat herself on the throne. Her hands gripped the carved arms as though she would never let go. She could feel her heart racing beneath her breast. Her head was still aching, but she ignored the discomfort as she stared at the men before her.

No longer was everything a blur. She still felt overwhelmed and unsure, but now she was determined not to show it. They had seen weakness in her already, she thought. It made for a poor start, but she would remedy her mistake. They would never see weakness again.

As for Verence's council, whom in it could she trust? Her gaze went first to Meaclan, for he had proven himself a worthy ally. And Chancellor Salba could be relied on, although he was getting old. Who else, she wondered, would give her the advice she needed and not take advantage of her inexperience?

In her absence, a courier had arrived with dispatches from one of the holds. Was all well there, she wondered, or had another raid struck at her coast? How much longer until the season grew too cold, and the seas too rough, for these attacks?

Panic swept over her anew, but she held it back and, with a sigh, took a little courage from Lord Salba's sympathetic gaze. "Let us begin afresh, my lords," she said to them all. "We have all suffered a great shock, but we must strive to continue in a manner that does honor to my uncle. Let us go slowly and deal with one matter at a time."

They bowed, and she searched their expressions for hints of who would prove to be friend and who would prove to be enemy. The greatest challenge of her life had begun.

"Lord Salba," she said, "you will determine which matters are most pressing and which can wait."

The old Duc de Clune stepped forward with a jerky bow.

White-headed and stooped with age, he spoke gruffly, "Perhaps best if the queen waits for Duc Lervan to return. No need in being hasty with these matters. Her majesty will need—"

"Her majesty seeks the guidance of her counselors," Pheresa said in an icy rage. She glared at Clune, determined to quell his suggestion at once. "The queen does not need her consort's advice or assistance."

Silence fell over the room, and Pheresa's angry gaze swept their suddenly wary faces. She recalled that Clune had always caused Verence trouble, and the old duc was wasting no time in giving her the same attention. She would have gladly booted him from the room had it been possible. At least, she told herself, he was not foolish enough to argue further.

But she knew more trouble along this line was to come. Anger curled inside her, burning through her stomach. Lervan again, she thought. How could the man manage to stay at the center of so much trouble?

Her gaze returned to Lord Salba. "Please commence."

Along the narrow, filthy streets twisting through Savroix-en-Charva's heart, a cloaked, hooded figure hurried through the deepening, late-afternoon shadows. Now and then he paused, pressing himself into the dark recess of a doorway to peer back the way he'd come.

No one followed him.

He hastened on. In the Street of Knives, he passed ragged men grinding new edges on daggers and fish knives, swept past shops selling blades of all kinds, dodged the peddlers hawking wares, and ducked around a corner into the darkest, gloomiest, oldest part of the city. The noise behind him grew fainter. No one walked this unnamed street save he, and he quickened his pace, counting doors beneath his breath until he came to the seventh past the corner.

He stopped, glanced around furtively, and rapped on the weathered door in the prearranged signal.

Seconds later, he was admitted by someone who kept well back in the shadows. The cloaked man hurried through a passageway to an open door, and descended a flight of rickety wooden steps into a dank, cold cellar. It stank of mildew and rats. When he stepped onto the uneven stone floor, his boots crunched on black beetles scuttling in all directions.

He paused, letting his eyes adjust to the dim light in this gloomy place. Across the cellar, a figure emerged from the shadows and beckoned to him.

Hesitating, the cloaked man put one hand surreptitiously on his dagger as he obeyed.

The figure waiting for him was a Gantese agent, short in stature, with a narrow face and eyes that burned like coals. His robes were brown and old, much stained by wear and travel. He smelled of ashes, and his hands were filthy with soot as he lifted them in a foreign gesture of greeting.

Halting just out of reach, the cloaked man felt his heart pounding.

"Is it done?" the Gantese asked. His voice was a harsh, ruined whisper. "Is it satisfactory?"

"It's done," the cloaked man replied. His own voice sounded steady and firm, surprising him. He drew in a sharp breath. "The king is dead."

The Gantese's smile revealed a row of pointed teeth. "Then our *sorcerel*'s work has pleased you."

"Aye . . . and those I represent."

A filthy hand was extended, and the cloaked man drew out a very heavy purse and surrendered it. He realized he was sweating. Inside, he felt a queer sort of illicit exhilaration. He'd done the forbidden, the unthinkable, and gotten away with it.

Somehow, he kept himself from smiling. "All gold Mandrian dreits, as agreed."

The Gantese held the purse with both hands and bowed. "And the second payment?"

"You'll get it, when the time comes. Not before!" the cloaked man said sharply.

Without a word, the Gantese withdrew into the darkness. Breathing hard, the cloaked man turned around and hurried up the creaking, swaying steps faster and faster until he reached the top. He burst through the doorway, then collected himself, realizing he did not want to be thought a coward. Squaring his heavy shoulders, he strolled to the door and put his hand on the latch.

No one stopped him. He let himself out and stood a moment on the filthy little street, drawing in great lungfuls of fetid air. The sewers in this part of town were disgraceful, he thought, wrinkling his nostrils. Something, no doubt an animal such as a rat or a dog, had obviously died close by. He glanced about but did not see a putrid, swollen corpse. Nor did he remember such a ripe stink when he arrived.

Whatever had dragged it forth, the stench drove him away, for who wanted to linger in such horrid squalor?

Pressing a corner of his cloak across his nose and mouth, Lervan hurried back the way he'd come.

Chapter Sixteen

It poured rain the day of Verence's funeral. Across the city, cathedral bells tolled his death knell. The procession wound through the streets while people knelt and wept for the good king who had ruled them so wisely. At the conclusion of the long funeral mass, Pheresa rose to her feet, encumbered by the heavy weight of her gold-embroidered gown, train, and cloak. Wearing a small diadem in her hair and carrying a small, gilded scroll of Writ, she placed her gloved hand on her husband's arm and walked slowly up the aisle while the priests chanted a recessional. As she left, she saw the Countess Lalieux, mistress to the king, heavily veiled and seated in a box pew in the company of her elderly husband. Pheresa's step never faltered, but she reminded herself to issue the lady's dismissal from court on the morrow.

There would be other changes, she thought, but now was not the time to think of them.

In the vestry they halted, waiting there while the great bell finished tolling the years of Verence's life. At last, quiet fell over the church.

The heavy doors were pushed open, letting in a gust of rain-dampened air. Outside it was still pouring. Water gushed from stone drain spouts, streamed down the steps, and swelled into a lake in the stone-paved square, where the royal coach was being maneuvered into place.

Out there, crammed into the square, stood the people of the city—common folk, shopkeepers, servants, and serfs. Soaked to the skin, they waited, grieving for the passing of their king and ready to greet the coming of their new queen.

Pheresa drew a deep breath, preparing herself. At her side, Lervan had been standing with bowed head, apparently praying. Now he lifted his head and shot her a small, private smile.

"I'm glad to see the end of this," he murmured, his relief evident. "Such an endless stream of bleak duties. Now we can get on with our lives."

"I thought you were fond of Verence."

"Aye, my dear. But he is gone. Must we grieve and wear long faces forever? These past few days have tired you too much. Now you can take some much-needed leisure. Perhaps you would like to retire to Aversuel for a month or so."

"Impossible," she said.

Inside the nave, the recessional chant ended, and people rose to start filing out. It was time to go. She nodded to a cleric waiting at the door. He gestured to church servants, who went out into the rain and unfurled a canopy of stout cloth to shield her.

While the small pages struggled to take charge of Pheresa's heavy train, Lervan smiled at her with the crooked little quirk of his lips that she loved most of all.

"I'm thinking only of you," he said. "A change of scenery will do wonders for your health."

"There is too much to do," she replied, striving to keep irritation from her voice. "I know your grace means well, but this is no time to be idle."

"'Tis a perfect time. You need the rest. I do not like to see my lady wife looking so thin, pale, and worried." His hand squeezed hers gently. His eyes held nothing but concern and affection.

Had she not known him to be still enthralled in the clutches of Lady Hedrina, Pheresa might have believed him. As it was, she felt a cold knot of resentment. Did he take her for an utter fool? Withdrawing her hand from his, she started for the doorway. "My duties do not permit me to go."

"Duties . . . what duties?" he asked. "A round of stuffy meetings, your signature on documents . . . what of it? Is not your greater duty to our child?"

She stopped on the threshold and glared at him. "What mean you by that?"

He smiled at those waiting for them to come out and leaned close to her ear. "We're delaying the proceedings—"

"Speak plainly," she retorted, taking no step forward. "You imply I am endangering the—"

"You work too hard. I mean no more than that," he said soothingly. "You are under too much strain. This should be a tender time, a time for us and our family-to-be."

Hope leaped inside her. Wondering if this meant he was ready to give up his infatuation with Lady Hedrina and return to her, Pheresa almost smiled at him. "Does your grace truly mean that?"

"Of course. I am willing to undertake your onerous duties while you go away for a short time."

Angry disappointment swept her, and on its heels came alarm. She stared at him, feeling a peculiar coldness drain through her face and body. *Liar,* she thought savagely to herself. *What are you up to?*

The answer to that question was obvious. Flooded with resentment, at that moment she felt such fury she wanted to strike him. Instead, she stood there, making everyone wait, while she battled to master her emotions.

"My dear, do not take me amiss. I—"

She would not look at him. "I think I understand your grace perfectly."

"My dear—"

She walked away from him, out into the driving rain. The servants struggled to keep her dry with the canopy that was popping and jerking in the wind. Overhead, the bells began a joyous ringing in her honor, and the palace guardsmen standing clustered at the foot of the steps lifted their swords in salute.

"Long live the queen!" they shouted.

A cheer went up from the people in the square. Pheresa lifted her hand to them, and Lervan did the same. He was smiling again, she noticed, obviously enjoying the adulation and attention. Tall, splendidly dressed, and hale, he grinned at her as though they hadn't just quarreled.

"They cheer you well, my dear. The people love you."

She waved again to the crowd and allowed Sir Talmor to assist her into the coach. Lervan climbed in with her, shaking droplets of water from his cap and dabbing his face with his velvet sleeve. She sat facing him, wondering if he realized he had just plunged a dagger of suspicion and despair into her heart. Clearly he remained besotted with his mistress, and now he was trying to persuade Pheresa to leave Savroix so that he could bring Hedrina to the palace.

I must never trust him again, she told herself sadly, and the coach rolled forward.

That night, Lervan returned to the palace just minutes before the huge gates were closed. He had dined in state with Pheresa before making his excuses and slipping away to Hedrina's charming little house to sup again. She had transformed the place into a bower of sensuality, where every pleasure was offered. Her wine was Saelutian, of the finest quality. Her boudoir was swathed with hangings of diaphanous silk gauze, muting the lamplight into a golden shimmer of soft radiance. Thick carpets covered the floor, and the settee where he lounged was draped with a magnificent lyng fur imported from Nether.

Hedrina, her thick black hair unbound and spilling down her back, met his arrival with lips glistened with honey to make her mouth taste sweet. She wore only a silk robe of the same intense blue as her eyes, and when she pressed herself to him in a kiss of greeting, he could feel her naked, lush body beneath the thin cloth.

It had been a pity to leave early. He hated going. Every time he left her, it was as though he carried an ache inside him. She fascinated him as no other woman ever had. He thought of her constantly, dreamed of her, yearned to bring her here to the palace, where she belonged, where they could be together as much as they wished. He thought of Hedrina's honeyed mouth, her lush breasts, the silken perfection of her skin. Even now he could smell her perfume on him, and he longed to go back to her.

"May I take your grace's horse?"

The gruff voice of a stableboy brought Lervan's thoughts back to the present. He dismounted, tossing the reins to the boy, and strode inside the chapel wing of the palace. Sir Maltric followed grimly on his heels. Waves of silent disapproval flowed from the old protector. Lervan ignored him. Long ago he had discovered that he would never satisfy or please the man's rigid standards, nor need he try. Pleasing himself was what mattered, and Lervan had become a master at it.

Admitted at once to Cardinal Theloi's apartments, he tossed his cap aside, bowed to the cardinal, and kissed his ring before taking a chair and thrusting out his long legs with a sigh.

"Thod's teeth, but what a day," he said, and perked up as a servant brought wine. He admired the cardinal's cellar, which was almost as good as Lady Hedrina's.

Theloi, his narrow face looking weary at this late hour, sat in a massive carved chair and watched Lervan with glittering green eyes.

"Was your grace's evening a pleasant one?"

"Indeed, yes," Lervan said with satisfaction. "Has your eminence ever eaten spiced grapes? What a delicacy of—"

"I did not make this appointment with your grace to discuss food," Theloi said coldly. "Have you approached the queen yet about withdrawing to Aversuel?"

"Aye. She won't agree to it."

A little silence stretched between them, while Theloi's eyes grew even colder. "Does your grace care to go on?"

Lervan drained his cup with a smack of his lips and leaned back in his chair. He was growing sleepy now. A long day of ceremony and ritual at the funeral, a fine supper, a great deal of exercise in Hedrina's bed, and a generous quantity of wine was enough to tire out the best of men. He hoped Theloi was not going to make this a long, tiresome discussion.

"I put it to the queen that she looked tired and ill, that she needed rest, and that she should think of the child she carries."

"Exactly the approach I suggested," Theloi said with a nod of approval. "Go on."

"None of it swayed her. Damne, the woman is astonishingly stubborn. How she can look so soft and womanly and be as hard-hearted and clutch-fisted as a usurer is beyond me. She will not retire to Aversuel to have the baby. She will not allow me to lighten her burden by taking on any of her royal duties. She will not increase my allowance, saying we must keep the coffers full in case of war. She will not agree to receive Lady Hedrina at court. In short, your eminence, she is impossible!"

Theloi leaned forward. "Did you suggest taking on her duties?"

"Aye, of course I did."

"That was foolish."

"Foolish or not, it seems a reasonable suggestion. Why shouldn't I share the throne? Am I not kingly material? I am no less highborn, of no less renowned lineage than she. Am I to stand behind her like a lackey all my life, bowing and scraping to her?"

"Your grace had best curb such annoyance and exercise patience," Theloi said in warning.

"So you have told me before. I *have* been patient with her, but I do not like the way she speaks to me now, or looks at me. I am not her lapdog, and I will not be forced to attend her constantly, as she seems to wish."

"You are her majesty's consort. To serve her is your duty."

Lervan frowned. "I was promised more, and we both know it."

"It will take time."

"Aye, so you keep saying. But when is she to understand how much she owes me? Were it not for me, she would still be waiting for that throne she loves so much. Waiting years for a robust king to age and linger."

Theloi shot to his feet. "Quiet! Has your grace lost all wit and sense? Say nothing of that, not even here."

Lervan glanced around. The room was empty. Even Sir Maltric stood outside the door, which was too thick for their voices to be overheard. Shrugging, Lervan toyed with his empty wine cup. "Where can it be safely discussed, if not here?"

"It must not be mentioned, ever," Theloi said with a gesture.

Lervan frowned. "Then it becomes buried in secrecy and time, lost eventually from memory, forgotten, and denied. I will not accept that, not between us. I carried the bribe to those—"

"Hush!"

"And you supplied the gold. We are guilty together, and we are yoked together," Lervan said fiercely. "Thanks to you, I have committed treason with an enemy I never thought I could accept as ally. Thanks to you, I have risked my life. You promised me a share of the throne for that, eminence."

"And you will get it. But it takes time. The queen is nervous and unsure at present, imagining plots and enemies around her. Eventually—"

"Do we wait until she gains experience and grasps power securely?" Lervan asked scornfully. "Far better to force her to agree now, when she is breeding and easily confused."

Theloi shot him a look of contempt. "And how did your grace fare today in gaining her agreement?"

"Damne, have I not just said she would not yield?"

"Exactly."

Lervan did not at all care for the cardinal's mocking smirk. He shifted irritably in his chair and told himself that court in-

trigue involved more trouble, more risk, more discomfort, and
more toadying to little men he disliked than he'd ever expected. He did not believe the effort was worthwhile, not if it
meant he had to go on waiting endlessly for what he'd been
promised.

"'Tis impossible to persuade her," he said in a huff. "She
is like a mule."

"Were your grace to give her more of the attention due a
wife, she might be more quickly persuaded. A woman in love
is generous. A woman scorned and humiliated becomes jealous and vindictive. I warned your grace long ago, when you
first came to court, that Pheresa would not accept libertine behavior."

"She has no choice," Lervan said defiantly. "I go my way
and leave her to do as she pleases."

"The queen does not please."

"Well, if she had affairs, by Thod, she might be considerably less sour!"

Theloi stared at him coldly. "While she carries your
grace's child, she expects special attention from you. Give it
to her, and she will share the world with you."

"I think not. She's grasping and ambitious. She enjoys giving me orders and seeing me jump like a trained monkey."

"Put your petty resentment aside, and make an effort."

"I do. I have!" Lervan said in exasperation. "But she is
never satisfied. It's like being strangled by a vine, pulled
down and wrapped tight by her incessant neediness. She gives
nothing. She only takes."

"Getting rid of this new mistress would appease her
greatly."

Lervan shot to his feet. "Never! I refuse. It's out of the
question."

"Then forget your bid to rule Mandria."

Glowering sullenly, Lervan turned away from Theloi.
"Hedrina is mine," he muttered.

"Your grace, think of what is at stake."

Lervan wanted to close his ears. The very thought of for-
saking Hedrina stirred up a panic inside him. He'd never

loved a woman the way he did her. The more he saw of her, the more he wanted her. It had become a craving, a force that he could not resist. Nor did he wish to. Giving Hedrina up now would be like cutting out his heart. He refused to consider it. Even so, a tiny corner of his mind asked, *What if Theloi is right? Do I really want to sacrifice the throne for Hedrina?*

But he swept such doubts away. There had to be a solution. He would find a way to keep Hedrina *and* share power with Pheresa.

"The queen is going to fail," he said, turning back to the cardinal. "She's all bluff, you see. She acts serene and confident, but it's fakery. She doesn't believe in herself, doesn't believe that she can do what she's set for herself. Why, she doesn't even believe she's beautiful."

Theloi said nothing.

"She'll fail," Lervan repeated with assurance. "She's busy now demonstrating to one and all that she's clever and shrewd. She's learning as fast as she can, trying to take an accounting of every detail, and exhausting herself. She'll collapse from the strain, then she'll be forced to come to me for help."

"Are you so sure?" Theloi asked.

"Aye, of course I am. Your eminence forgets I am married to the lady. I see a side of her no one else does."

"And this is your grace's strategy?"

"If I wait for anything, I wait for that. And, to put it plainly, I think better of my strategy than yours."

"You have made her distrust you," Theloi said in disgust. "Such a mistake is—"

"I'll not woo her while she fattens and swells," Lervan said firmly. "Let her bear the child and grow comely again, then I'll charm her anew. If I choose."

Theloi compressed his lips, but said merely, "I believe we are finished tonight, your grace."

Lervan bowed to him, but made no move toward the door. "There is a final matter."

"Yes?"

"The queen will not increase my allowance. 'Tis irksome, as I have twice as much entertaining to do now that I am consort. My wardrobe needs replenishing, and I want larger apartments. I find myself already in debt, and have no wish to fall deeper in the clutches of the usurers."

No sympathy crossed Theloi's face. "I doubt the queen will reward your grace's infidelity. Perhaps she feels that a fatter purse in your grace's pocket would only be spent on your mistress."

Lervan flushed, but kept his temper. "Perhaps," he agreed through gritted teeth. "But I want more money. Since the queen is a clutch fist, I think my increase should come from church coffers."

Theloi's green eyes narrowed. "Your grace is mistaken."

"Oh, I do not think so," Lervan said airily. "After all, a flunky could have dealt with the *sorcerel* rather than myself. You wanted me directly involved in our treason, so that I would remain beneath your thumb."

Theloi's expression grew stony.

Lervan nodded to him. "You see, I may act the cheerful fool, but I am far from being one. I know why I was sent to deal with those foreign devils, why I had to risk their magic and evil ways, and why I had to carry the payment to them. All the risk fell on me, while your eminence has remained safely hidden from view, like a spider in its lair. But if I went to the queen and told her some of the truth, that a plot was laid against Verence to bring him down—"

"If I fall, so does your grace," Theloi said in a tight, dangerous voice.

Lervan laughed. "Oh, but I wonder. For the lady loves me still, and might forgive my sins were I to throw myself on her mercy. And the lady likes you not at all."

Theloi went pale. He stroked his gray goatee while his eyes grew fierce and predatory. "Have we come now to threats, your grace?" he asked in a very soft voice. "Have we forgotten how I sponsored your grace's cause, so that the king invited you to court and grew to like you?"

"I've forgotten nothing," Lervan said. "Thanks to you, I

came to court. Thanks to my own wit and efforts, I found the king's favor. I seek no quarrel tonight, eminence, only gold to line my pockets. After all, a consort needs heartening from time to time, does he not?"

As he spoke, he cocked his head to one side and grinned, but Theloi did not smile back.

"Oh, come!" Lervan said heartily, holding out his hand. "What good comes of black looks and resentful hearts? I want money. I care not whence it comes."

"Very well," Theloi said. "I shall authorize a fund for your grace."

Lervan's grin widened, and he bowed with a flourish. "Your eminence is too kind."

Theloi went to his desk and picked up a quill pen. He wrote hurriedly, splattering ink, and signed his name with an angular loop. Tossing down his pen, he turned to Lervan with the paper in his hand. "Take care, your grace," he said in a cold, hostile voice. "Remember who your true friends are and how unwise it would be to make enemies where you are in most need of allies."

Lervan eyed the paper avidly. Already his head was swirling with plans of how to spend his new largess. Hedrina would look magnificent in sapphires. He would commission a necklace, a stunning necklace, to adorn her lovely throat. Aye, and there would be other jewels to lavish on her, for she must be rewarded for making him so happy. He supposed he would have to give Pheresa a trinket as well and buy a cup of the finest eldin silver for the baby's gift. But first there was a new horse he wanted, and he must have new clothes, for surely Pheresa would not wish her consort to look shabby. His style would now lead the court, so he would have to employ the very best tailors.

Theloi cleared his throat, and Lervan hastily pulled himself from his daydreams.

He smiled, laughing a little, and bowed again. "Thank you. I was sure we could come to terms. We always work well together, you and I."

With a frown, Theloi handed over the writ of authority.

Lervan took it with no more than a cursory glance, rolled it up, kissed it with a laugh, and tucked it safely away inside his doublet.

"Be at ease," he said to the cardinal as he strolled to the door. "I shall give the queen some of the petting she craves, and see if I can't lighten her heart a bit. From time to time."

Theloi's eyes narrowed. "Your grace plays with fire."

"Nay, my lord cardinal," Lervan replied. "I was born under the luckiest of stars."

With a saucy salute, he walked out.

Chapter Seventeen

In the chill of an autumn night, Talmor awakened suddenly and completely, every sense instantly alert. He lay still, listening hard, as he sought to understand what had awakened him.

There was only silence. The small alcove where he slept in earshot of the queen held his bunk, a stand for washing, and a chest for his possessions. He had no window of his own, but he could see moonlight slanting into the queen's bedchamber. He lifted his head warily, alert for danger.

No servant stirred to answer some private need of her majesty. No lamp had been lit, no low murmur of voices disturbed the slumberous quiet.

Yet something was wrong.

His unease grew, swelling into a feeling of urgency, as though he needed to take action *now*. Something was coming, he realized. It was coming soon, and he must be ready.

What was this danger, he wondered. Why did it feel so powerful, so menacing? Why was he consumed with the urge to awaken the queen and run?

He rose silently from his bunk and pulled on his leggings swiftly before belting on his dagger. Barefooted, he eased into the enormous chamber—fully as large as the great hall in his father's hold—and padded silently over the wooden floorboards to the windows and peered out.

He saw a glow fill the west horizon, brightening rapidly like daybreak, except the sun did not dawn in the west. Pressing his face to the glass, Talmor watched ruddy light fill the night sky. He was disbelieving at first, then sure.

Striding back to his alcove, he finished dressing, quick and efficient in the darkness as he'd trained himself to be, and tiptoed through the servant's door to wake Pears.

Coming awake with a jerk, Pears threw off his blanket and knuckled his eyes. "Sir?"

"Trouble," Talmor whispered softly. "Send Lutel to the guardhouse for news."

Returning to the queen's bedchamber, Talmor stepped over the low fence and walked quietly up to her bedside. For an instant he hesitated, then pulled aside a portion of the bed hangings, and said, "Majesty, wake up."

She stirred but did not awaken.

"Majesty."

"Go away," she mumbled. Then with a start, she sat up. The coverlet slipped off her shoulders, exposing the pale cloth of her bedgown.

He realized he'd frightened her, looming over her in silhouette against the moonlight streaming across his shoulders. "'Tis I, Talmor," he said quickly.

She released an unsteady breath and rubbed her face with her hands. "I—I was dreaming. I thought . . ." She shook her head and looked at him with more alertness. "What is it, sir?"

"Savroix-en-Charva is on fire, majesty."

"What?" She jumped out of bed and hurried over to the windows, where the ruddy glow continued to spread and brighten. Pheresa pushed open a window, heedless of her physician's strictures against the evil humors of night air, and leaned out into the cold darkness. "What has happened?" she asked, her voice muffled. "How can this be?"

With the window open, Talmor now heard sentries calling out. He frowned at how slow they were to give the alarm. A call to arms should have already been issued, the entire barracks roused and assembling.

In the far distance, the bells of the cathedral began to ring, calling to the palace for help.

"This is dreadful," the queen said. "Some accident, a fire allowed to spill from its hearth. An overturned kettle of hot oil—"

"Nay, I think not, majesty."

She turned to stare at him. In the moonlight, wearing only a voluminous bedgown and her hair hanging over her shoulder in a long braid, she looked like a little girl, vulnerable with surprise and innocence. It made him ache to look at her, but he had long ago taught himself to shut away that part of himself, deadening it to all feeling. He deadened it again now.

"What mean you, Sir Talmor?" she asked. "What say you?"

"Trouble comes. I know not what kind, but it could be . . . boat raiders."

"Vvordsmen?" she whispered, her hand stealing to her throat. "Sweet Tomias, I pray you are wrong."

"I think I am not."

"Have you knowledge? Certainty? Have you sensed something?"

She gave him no chance to answer, but swung around and shouted to summon her servants. In moments, lamps were lit and sleepy women appeared. "My clothes!" she ordered, cutting across their queries. "I will dress at once."

"But, your majesty, the ladies of the wardrobe are not assembled—"

"Thod take the wardrobe!" she shouted, stamping her foot. "The city is on fire, and I have no time for protocol. You, Verine, summon the duty captain to me."

As the servants scattered to obey her, Pheresa turned back to Talmor. "I will send the guards to defend the town."

"The palace guards may be needed here," he said grimly.

She gasped. "You don't think they would dare attack the palace?"

"Aye, I think it."

"But this far inland?"

"Majesty, we are less than a league from the town harbor. The harbor defenses have obviously been breached, or they would not be sacking the town as we speak."

"I pray you are wrong, sir, and 'tis only a fire gone out of control."

He understood that she wanted reassurance, but Talmor was not a man who believed in denying problems.

He tried to be patient as he said, "Majesty, consider that every raid this year has ventured farther south. What navy have we to repel them from our shores or to protect the richest, most desirable port city in the realm?"

"But they—"

"The coast is gentle here, with many beaches and places to land. They need not confine themselves to the town. Your majesty's palace offers them the greatest loot of all."

"Savroix attacked," she said in disbelief, heading for her dressing room. "'Tis impossible."

Talmor stopped arguing with her. He feared her ministers and officers would probably maintain the same foolish view. A small, well-fortified hold could be defended, even sieged, but Savroix sprawled forever. Its walls were mighty, but there were gates everywhere, even ground-level doors in the turrets. The guards were trained to keep order within the palace complex, not defend the palace against the attack of a large force.

That was the job of Mandria's standing army, an army now scattered to points east and west to support the beleaguered border holds.

A perfect campaign, Talmor thought bitterly, *obviously planned by a master strategist. Small, vicious strikes intended to lure the army farther and farther away from Savroix, which no doubt had always been the main target.*

And at Savroix's center was its queen. He felt a terrible sense of fear and foreboding squeeze his heart. On no account must she be taken hostage.

A furious pounding on the door made him whirl with his hand on his weapon. Pheresa emerged from her dressing room in the hauberk made for her as monarch. She wore it over a long tunic that was split for riding. A servant followed her, carrying her boots, while another opened the door.

The duty captain, accompanied by two sergeants and Lord Nejel, trooped inside, boots thudding on the wooden floor. They saluted the queen.

"Majesty," Lord Nejel said, "I bring grave news."

"You may report it, my lord."

"The town is under attack. The older sections have been torched. There is looting and pillaging going on, although the town constabulary have been mustered."

"Can they repel such an attack?"

The duty captain frowned, and his gaze flashed to Talmor's for a moment. Lord Nejel never took his gaze from the queen's. "Nay, majesty."

Pheresa's chin came up. "Dispatch a force of fighting men immediately to assist them."

Talmor frowned, knowing she had just sent those squadrons to probable death in a futile waste of limited manpower.

"Aye, majesty." Bowing, Lord Nejel glanced at the duty captain, who saluted smartly and strode out. The sergeants followed him, but Nejel remained behind. "I have ordered extra guards stationed at your majesty's door for protection."

She nodded. "And extra guards for my consort?"

"Of course."

"Thank you, my lord. I rely on you and your men. Whatever the town needs, it must have."

He bowed and left her, and Pheresa slowly rubbed her forehead a moment before she turned around and met Talmor's gaze.

Her cheeks grew pink. "You think my gesture is futile."

" 'Tis not for me to question your majesty's orders."

"Damne!" She stamped her foot. "Give me no courtier's answer, sir!"

"A muster of guardsmen against a barbarian horde?" he retorted. "What chance have they?"

"My guards are superb fighters. They—"

"There's a chance they can harry the attackers enough to let some townspeople escape death or capture. That is the only gain possible."

"You sound very sure, sir. Do you foretell the future as well?"

"I have met Vvordsmen in battle, majesty," he replied grimly.

"Aye, so I have heard. But how can you stand here making dire predictions and gloomy pronouncements when you know not how large a force they have? Unless you go out there, to stand and observe their numbers and their movements, how can you say what they will do or how victorious they will be?"

He crossed his arms. "I am a fighting man, majesty. I know that no warrior, wherever he comes from, would dare attack Mandria's heart without a sizable force."

"But 'tis the dead of night!" she cried out. "What infamous behavior, what calumny do they practice, to ignore all—"

"Your majesty has heard the reports of other raids. Vvordsmen attack, day or night, whenever conditions favor them."

She flung out her hands. "By all accounts these boat raiders are monsters, savages without mercy, and vicious killers. They destroy all they touch." She turned her gaze to the window. "They are destroying my city now . . . and perhaps . . . my palace next?"

"Not if a stalwart defense can be put in place," Talmor said in a bracing voice. He wanted the queen to face the danger, but not be overwhelmed by it. "There's time enough, if quick action is taken. Foremost, there is your majesty's safety to consider. We—"

"I must summon my council," she said. Courage returned to her brown eyes, and her voice sounded stronger now. "They will advise me. In the meantime, messengers must be sent to my marechals."

While she issued a string of orders, the alarm bells of the

palace began to peal, rousing everyone. Talmor was thinking fast and hard.

Burning the town was a stroke of genius, for it would panic the populace and render them helpless before the marauders. But more importantly, it was obviously a lure for the palace's defense forces, for if the queen's tender heart incited her to send too many of her guardsmen to defend the town, Savroix itself would be left at the mercy of a second strike force, which had probably landed elsewhere.

No report had as yet come of such a tactic, but Talmor felt certain that was the strategy. He knew that were he the attacking commander, he would divide his forces in such a manner. From which direction would the raiders strike Savroix? And how could he best get the queen to safety? He knew she must not remain here.

Pheresa was now hurrying for the door. Talmor strode after her, determined to stick close. He had more than invaders to worry about. Any potential assassin lurking within the palace might choose tonight to strike her down, taking cover in the chaos. Worried and alert, Talmor closed in on her heels, nearly treading the hem of her tunic, and never took his hand off his sword hilt. With her escort of guards, she swept through the private passageway between her private quarters and the privy chamber.

Her council—groggy-eyed, haphazardly dressed, and deeply alarmed—assembled themselves within minutes. Chancellor Salba, limping heavily, arrived just after the queen.

"The army is too far away to reach in time," he said without preamble.

Her face turned white as his announcement sank in.

"We are exposed and vulnerable," he continued, "and the enemy knows it."

Pheresa did not sit down. Instead, she paced back and forth before her throne. Her military garments emphasized her pregnancy, and her hauberk—worn previously twice to inspect the palace guards—had not been laced tightly. The changes in her body had affected her stance and gait as well.

She was not as graceful as before, not as postured. Tonight, in her ill-fitting clothes and her hair haphazardly braided, she looked like an ordinary woman, tired and frightened, her customary serenity in ruins. As she paced, her slender hands kept touching the mound of her belly as though for reassurance.

Talmor's sense of impending danger grew, and he saw little need to stand about and discuss the matter. He felt convinced that the longer the queen stayed here, the greater her danger became. And she, burdened with child and at her most physically vulnerable, did not seem to understand that it was too late to meet now to develop a strategy. The entire palace defense was structured on having an army nearby. Without the army, they had nothing, and this meeting was futile.

He noticed the other men's worry. Some of them, at least, had the wit to realize they were wasting time. But had any of them the courage to so inform the queen?

Duc Lervan breezed in tardily with his usual self-confidence. Garbed in hauberk and leather leggings, still knuckling sleep from his eyes, he bowed to the queen with a flourish.

Her whole face lit up. Uttering a glad cry, she held out her hands to him. Watching him press his fingers to her cheek and murmur to her, Talmor glowered. He loathed Lervan, heart and soul, and despised the man for his hypocrisy, lying, and infidelity. Each time the queen grew angry with her husband, Talmor rejoiced inwardly. Of late, she had looked strained each time she found herself in Lervan's company, and Talmor hoped she would banish him from court.

But now, tonight, she was smiling up at the scoundrel for comfort, still as bound to him emotionally as ever. The sight of it made Talmor boil.

He checked his temper, putting it into that dead place inside him as he had done for the past two years. He was not permitted to judge or express his opinion. He remained in the background of Pheresa's life, and he never forgot his place. But tonight, he had never found it harder to stay in control of himself, to curb his tongue, or to keep himself from shoving Lervan away from her. The blackguard was not fit to grovel at her feet, and what effect did he think he achieved, appearing in battle garb like a theatrical mummer, strutting about and mouthing brave words that only wasted the air?

Clearly relieved by Lervan's presence, the queen now asked her husband's advice. Talmor retreated to the side of the room where the other protectors stood, and took his place beside Sir Maltric. The older man glanced at him and grunted an acknowledgement. Talmor nodded in reply. They were not friends, not even allies, save in their common purpose of protecting the royal couple.

While the council debated and discussed the best measures to take, Talmor leaned toward Maltric.

"We've got to get them away," he murmured.

Maltric's eyes, wise with experience, met his. "We'll do as they decide."

Talmor's hands curled into fists. His heart was racing with the need to take action. Thod's bones, but he could not bear to stand here while talk wasted the precious time left to them. She was listening to Lervan, full of theory and bravado, and drinking in everything he said. Annoyed by the consort's pomposity on matters he did not understand, Talmor scowled at the floor. He was tempted to break into the discussion and start issuing orders that would do some good, but such a flaunting of his duties was impossible. If he was dismissed from the queen's service for interrupting, who would protect her majesty?

News came, none of it good. The town continued to burn out of control. A guardsman arrived, accompanied by his sergeant. Soot-stained and bloody, his green cloak in tatters, the guardsman announced that four squadrons had engaged the enemy but were forced to fall back.

The council roared in outrage, and Lervan was loudest in condemning such cowardice.

Talmor's temper grew hot, and both the messenger and sergeant turned red and tight-lipped.

Pheresa, perhaps sensing that it was unwise to insult her own palace guards, raised her hands to quell the noise and turned to the messenger. "Savroix's guardsmen are the bravest fighters in the realm," she said. "What drove them back?"

"Outnumbered," the messenger replied, still red-faced. "Eight to one. Damned marauders keep coming, waves of 'em. Boat after boat after boat."

Lervan stepped forward. "What does it matter if there are thousands of them? Guardsmen of true valor retreat before no one. They should have fought on and—"

"'Twas certain suicide, with no hope of stemming such a tide," the knight said angrily. He wiped some of the blood from his face with the back of his hand. "Our commander ordered us back, saying we're needed to save the palace."

"Nonsense!" Lervan retorted. "The palace is not in jeopardy. 'Tis only loot they want, and soon they'll be gone. We are in no danger here."

An awkward silence fell over the room, and several of the councilmen exchanged glances.

The queen saw the looks and her face turned pink, but she returned her gaze to the messenger. "Can the guard not rally at the guild halls and hold the city from that point?" she asked.

More looks were exchanged around the room. Talmor fought to keep from frowning in embarrassment, for the queen's question betrayed terrible ignorance, not only of the situation but also of how battles were fought. Dismay spread through him, for the duc consort was a fool and the queen untested. Talmor felt chilled by the prospect of the realm being in such inexperienced hands. *Someone must advise her,* he thought, sending a fierce look Lord Salba's way. *Someone must speak up, and quickly.*

The silence made Pheresa's face redden more. She looked from face to face, her posture stiff now as she obviously realized something was wrong. "You give me no answer, sir knight," she said at last. "I asked if there cannot be a rally at the guild halls?"

"The enemy numbers too many for a rally, majesty," the guardsman said. "The guild halls and warehouses were the first to burn down."

Her face drained of color, and several of the ministers shook their heads gravely.

"This is monstrous," Lord Salba said. "Monstrous! These looters are not content to steal, but they must also destroy—"

The Duc du Lindier strode in, geared for battle with his breastplate shining and his plumed helmet held under his arm. Looking every inch a marechal tonight, he saluted the queen. "I regret to inform your majesty that another force of barbarians has landed at Telvier Point," he reported. "At least a thousand men, if not more. They are marching on the palace, and at least half of those looting the town are now marching on us from the south. If your majesty has sent any forces to defend the town, I suggest they be recalled at once."

Pheresa's face was white. "Merciful Tomias, what are we to do?"

Lervan squared his bullish shoulders. "We shall fight, my dear. More guardsmen must be sent out at once. They'll never enter the park—"

"Nonsense!" Clune sputtered with a stamp of his foot. "Divide our forces and how is the palace to be protected? Defense is—"

"Majesty," Lindier broke in, staring urgently at his daughter, "messages have been sent by courier to your armies, but it will take days before they respond. The palace guard is not sufficient to hold off a force of this size, although I know they will fight to the last man."

"Come, your grace, you're frightening the queen unnecessarily," Lervan said.

Frowning, Lord Salba gripped his chain of office with a white-knuckled hand. "Do you really fear the palace will fall?"

Lindier, who in his younger days had been proclaimed Mandria's greatest marechal, stood there grimly. Gone were his cynical, world-weary expression and wine-blurred voice. He looked alert and implacable, veiled in past glories, a warrior tonight rather than an aging, dissipated courtier.

"My lord," he replied to Salba, "our counting is no doubt faulty in the darkness. For all we know, there are even more boats coming, more Vvordsmen landing. This is war, not a raid, and we lie ripe for the taking. We must prepare ourselves for the worst."

"Impossible!" cried out Lord Fillem. "This is Mandria. This is Savroix. We rule the world. No other realm dares to presume, knowing our forces are the most valiant and will surely rally—"

"Do you expect a miracle to fall from Beyond and save the palace?" Lindier said harshly. "We have no army. We cannot defend!"

"But the guardsmen—"

"—can hold off attack long enough for evacuation . . . *perhaps*. Nothing more. 'Tis impossible, with the forces at hand, to withstand what comes against us tonight."

Scowling, Meaclan now chose to speak up. "For the past ten years I've warned against underfinancing the army. And now—"

"Never mind what we should have done," Clune interrupted gruffly. "If it's flight, then let's to it!"

No one made a move to leave the privy chamber. Pheresa's eyes were huge with fear and despair.

Salba lifted his wise old head and looked at Talmor. "Sir Talmor, you have fought these raiders in the past. You alone in this room have had direct experience with them. Tell us what you know."

All eyes turned to him. Talmor drew himself erect and stepped forward. Although the old chancellor had asked the question, it was to the queen that he spoke his answer: "The Vvordsmen are ferocious fighters who do not fear death. They follow no standard rules of battle. Chivalry? They know none. Mercy? They give none. If you think it's possible to strike a bargain with them, you delude yourself. They will not do it. They fight until they have what they came for. Their losses mean nothing to them. They don't even collect their own wounded or dead. As for prisoners, they take them only for slaves. Those captives deemed unsuitable for their purposes are killed."

Shocked silence fell over the room. The queen stared at

Talmor with her lips slightly parted, and her hand tightened on her husband's arm.

Lervan gave her a comforting pat and gestured dismissively at Talmor. "If you mean to bring our spirits even lower than they were before, you've succeeded. What encouragement are we to find in your words?"

"'Tis the truth, your grace," Talmor said quietly.

"Well, say no more of this gloomy talk. You are frightening the queen, and undermining the courage of these good men."

"It is necessary that all present understand our foe," Talmor said. Unable to restrain himself any longer, he turned to Lindier. "Your grace, if we abandon the idea of defending the palace and instead concentrate our—"

"Be silent!" Lervan snapped. "The marechal requires no advice from you. Resume your place, sir!"

Talmor refused to back down. "Then will your grace advise the queen to flee while there is still a chance of getting her to safety?"

"No!" Pheresa said in wide-eyed alarm. "I will not run away."

The council all began talking at once, and Talmor, increasingly conscious of time running out, despaired of accomplishing anything.

Pheresa kept shaking her head at every attempt to persuade her. "Nay, I cannot abandon my people simply to save myself."

"If your majesty is captured and held hostage for ransom," Lord Salba said, "what could be more devastating to Mandria?"

Stubbornness reddened her face. "I am no coward, my lord. I will not retreat."

"The palace will fall," Lindier said. "The queen's safety cannot be guaranteed."

"I will not run away! And the palace will not fall. I will speak to the men and rally their courage. Mandrian knights are worth ten thousand Vvordsmen. My guards can hold off these invaders."

"Pheresa, have sense, for Thod's sake!" Lindier said in exasperation. "Savroix cannot be defended. You must give the order for the court to flee while there is still time."

"For the sake of your majesty's unborn child and heir, fly to safety," Lord Salba urged her.

Talmor, watching her, thought she was about to concede, but then she stiffened. "All Mandria will say that at the first sign of trouble their new queen fled. All Mandria will say the queen is a coward and unworthy to rule."

"All Mandria will say 'tis better to have a queen alive and safe than a fool held for ransom," Lindier muttered.

She glared at her father, but only he dared say aloud what all of them were thinking.

Meaclan stepped forward. "Your majesty *is* Mandria. The palace is not. The palace can be rebuilt, but your majesty is all that is most precious and vital to this realm."

She stared at her minister of finance, and Talmor knew hope that she would listen to this man if no other. "My lord," she said to Meaclan, "let both servants and courtiers depart if they wish. I will not prevent them from seeking what safety they can find. But how can I abandon them? Is my royal duty not here?"

Lord Salba stepped forward. "But, majesty, no one can depart unless the queen leaves first."

Her eyes widened, and contrition filled her expression. She bowed her head. "Oh. I—I had forgotten this. Forgive me in thinking only of my pride. I would not preserve it at the expense of other lives."

Lervan kissed her hand. "No one questions the queen's bravery."

She managed a tremulous smile for him. "It's just that everything inside me hates the thought of abandoning Savroix to these barbarians. To flee, leaving the palace open—"

"Nay," Lervan said at once. "I shall remain behind to command the guardsmen."

"You!" Fresh alarm filled her face, and she clutched him. "Oh, no! You must not risk yourself."

"I assure you that if the danger presses too close, I shall

run for my life. The guardsmen and Sir Maltric will keep me safe."

"But, my love—"

Talmor turned away, unable to go on listening. Quietly he went to the door and issued orders for the queen's household to pack essentials and exit the palace via the east gate. Meaclan and Clune also dispatched orders for the immediate evacuation of their personal households.

By the time Talmor returned, the matter was settled. With tears in her eyes, Pheresa agreed to leave her consort behind to defend Savroix, delaying discovery of her flight for as long as possible.

"Splendid," Lindier said in approval. "The men will fight all the better knowing one member of the royal party remains behind for them to protect."

Pheresa opened her mouth, but her father continued: "And they will be heartened to know their queen is safely away, out of danger."

She sighed. "Inform the men that the queen honors their courage."

Lindier turned to Talmor. "Protector, heed this. Two companies of men will travel with her majesty for her protection. The queen's barge can take you upriver—"

"But, your grace—"

Lindier lifted his hand to quell Talmor. "Retreat as you deem best to protect her. I recommend that you go as far as Scice, perhaps, or even Aversuel. Just get her out of harm's way."

Talmor had no intention of taking the queen to either town. Whoever had planned this attack was well informed, perhaps even guided by a traitor within the palace. Those were the first locations anyone bent on capturing the queen would search. As for trying to flee on the royal barge, he refused to even consider an action so ill-advised. The Vvordsmen's boats were shallow-keeled, more than capable of going upriver from the harbor. If they overtook the queen's enormous, slow-moving barge, defending her would be difficult indeed. Nay, he'd already formed a different plan. But without argument, he bowed to the marechal. Let the man think he agreed with him. Anything to get the queen moving away from Savroix.

"Aye, your grace," he said crisply.

Dismissing her council, Pheresa turned to bid a tearful farewell to Lervan and pleaded with him to take care.

Looking excited by the danger, he grinned at her. "Morde a day, my dear, as the uplanders say. I'll show these savages what Mandrian knights are made of, damne if I don't."

Lindier broke in on such bravado. "Fear not, Pheresa. Lervan will get safely away in time. I shall see to it personally."

She smiled gratefully. "Thank you, Father."

Lord Salba bent his head close to Talmor's. "There are secret ways beneath the palace, many of them designed for such contingencies as these."

"Aye, my lord," Talmor said. "When I was a guard, I occasionally patrolled the catacombs."

"I warn you, sir, that if you go that way you put the queen's safety in the hands of the priests."

The old man's eyes held a significant warning, and Talmor nodded. "Understood."

"There is an alternative," Salba said and placed an iron key in Talmor's hand.

Talmor's fingers closed over it. His heart was pounding. Swiftly, he glanced past the old man to see if anyone had noticed their exchange. The other men were dispersing. Clune, Talmor saw, was already gone. No one was paying him and Salba any attention.

He looked into Salba's eyes. "Where—"

"There is another way out of the palace, known usually only to the king and someone he trusts."

Talmor's breath caught in his throat. "Known to King Verence, and now . . . only you?"

Salba nodded.

"The queen does not know of it?"

"Her majesty has much to learn," Salba said in a soft voice. His brown eyes were intent on Talmor. "What danger lies in this path, I know not. Perhaps none. 'Tis so secret it has hopefully been long forgotten. It leads into the forest."

Excitement leaped inside Talmor. "Perfect."

Salba's hand closed on his wrist in caution. "I pray that it proves so. Keep her majesty safe, sir knight."

"I swear it with my life," Talmor answered.

A shout was raised outside the privy chamber. Talmor stiffened, and he and Maltric reached for their swords as one man. Those few still remaining in the room stepped back as Talmor and Maltric rushed for the door. Reaching it first, Talmor eased it open.

A page came flying up the passageway, shouting, "My lords! They're coming! They're coming! They've reached the park."

Cursing, Talmor spun around and looked back at Pheresa, standing within her husband's arms. She was weeping, and Lervan was dabbing at her tears, murmuring endearments to her.

Jealousy twisted inside Talmor, but there was no time for that. With no pretense of courtesy he walked up to the queen and interrupted what her husband was saying.

"Your majesty, there is no more time. We must depart."

"Your majesty," Salba said, "I beg a final word with you."

"Come, chancellor," Lindier called to him from the door. "Leave them to say their farewells in private."

Salba frowned, looking frustrated, but Lervan, it seemed, had finished with the queen.

He kissed her cheek hastily, flourished a bow, and with a jaunty wave strode out with Lindier. Salba limped after them, but instead of leaving, he shut the door swiftly on their heels and locked it.

Pheresa and Talmor exchanged a quick look. She frowned. "My lord, I—"

Salba hurried back across the room. "Your majesty, quickly."

He reached behind a tapestry. Talmor heard the creak of a hidden door swinging open. A scent of mustiness rolled into the room.

Pheresa was staring. "What is this passage? Where does it lead?"

Salba came out from behind the tapestry. His ginger blond hair was ruffled on one side. "It leads, your majesty, outside the palace."

She took a step back. "To the catacombs? To the clutches of the priests? I thank you no, my lord!"

"There's no time to argue. Your majesty must hurry."

"The priests are not my friends! Cardinal Theloi—"

"Even Theloi does not know of this passage. The king and I alone held this secret."

Talmor attempted to shoo her toward the passageway. "The queen must hurry—"

"Where does this lead?" she asked Salba suspiciously.

"Your majesty, I assure you that—"

"Where, my lord?"

Lord Salba sighed. "To the ruined church of the Sebeins."

"What?" Her gaze flashed from him to Talmor. "Know you of this?"

Talmor's own suspicions were aroused. He glared at the chancellor. "You said this passage led into the forest."

"Does not the forest lie behind the ruin?"

Pheresa was sputtering questions, and with a scowl Talmor tried to soulgaze the old man. But Salba's brown eyes slid expertly away from his. Talmor sensed nothing from him, as though something shielded the chancellor's thoughts and emotions.

"Nay, majesty!" Salba said urgently. "Put aside your fears. 'Tis no trick. On that, you have my word."

"But what connection lies between the throne and those—"

"The passageway happens to emerge there. Nothing more. That's why the old ruin has never been pulled completely down."

"But the Sebeins—"

"I cannot explain all the secrets now. There are worse evils in this world than theirs." With a placating gesture, Salba unlocked a massive wooden chest and began taking out documents hurriedly. "They won't be there. Your majesty need not fear that I'm delivering you into their clutches. Time grows short. Your majesty must not tarry. Come!"

Pheresa still looked doubtful, even angry, but Talmor knew it was a risk they must take. Pocketing the iron key, he picked up one of the lamps. Holding it aloft, he stepped cautiously into the narrow passageway and ducked to avoid a curtain of spiderwebs. He saw a small landing, with a flight of steps leading down in a tight, steep spiral. Talmor detected no danger lurking nearby. He glanced back at the queen, who looked very frightened and unsure.

"Come, majesty," he said.

Despite her obvious fear, it seemed she still trusted him. Her eyes met his in appeal. "Say you that it's safe?"

"Safer than any other way out," he replied.

She stepped through the secret door, and Lord Salba hurriedly thrust documents and a small velvet pouch into her hands.

"Thod keep you both," he said gruffly, and slammed the door on them.

Talmor heard the bolt shoot home, and they stood there, locked out of any possible retreat.

Chapter Eighteen

Pheresa hesitated on the narrow landing with cobwebs tickling the back of her neck. Her head was reeling with the speed of events, the amount of danger so close. She did not feel that she'd had time to assimilate the shocks of tonight, and now to find that the Sebeins could gain access into the palace anytime they chose both stunned and infuriated her.

She felt frozen, unwilling to move, her ears roaring and her heart a tempest. All this time, she'd believed that Verence loathed the Sebeins, but had there in truth been some secret alliance? Was it similar to the agreement posed to her by Kolahl two years ago? How many secrets about Verence's reign had she yet to discover?

"Majesty, let us hurry—"

"Nay, Talmor," she said sharply. She was filled with an acute reluctance to descend into the darkness. "I cannot trust this. I fear we shall meet with disaster."

His golden brown eyes met hers. "We are committed."

Pheresa shook her head. "Find another way for me to exit.

Break the lock if you must, but I cannot willingly put myself into Sebein hands."

A frown creased his brow, but he did not argue. Sliding past her in the cramped space, he lifted the lamp higher in an effort to find the catch or mechanism that would allow them back inside the privy chamber.

As Pheresa pressed herself closer to the roughly mortared wall, her gaze fell on the items Salba had handed to her at the last minute.

The documents featured archaic lettering and illuminations drawn in vivid inks across the top and sides of the pages. Each bore the royal seal stamped in heavy wax. With widening eyes, she recognized the charters of rule, Mandria's most precious deeds. Here also was the Treaty of Blood, much creased and worn, almost falling to tatters in her hands, which signified the unification of upper and lower Mandria. And she found the proclamation of her investiture as heir, with Verence's bold signature, followed by her own small, shaky one.

The last item she held was a velvet pouch containing the royal seal. Wrought of gold, it rested heavy and substantial in her hands, perhaps the most tangible symbol of her position and power.

Realization of what Salba had done made her swallow hard. In her fear and confusion, she'd forgotten these precious items, but Salba had made certain they remained in her keeping. *To be captured with her?* She frowned at the thought. *Or to be kept safe?*

"Stop," she said to Talmor.

He turned to her at once.

She met his calm, intelligent eyes with new hope. "My lord chancellor has not betrayed me. I shall go on."

What emotion—relief or exasperation—flickered in Talmor's gaze? The expression was gone before she could be sure. But being Talmor, he drew his sword in silence, making neither argument nor complaint over her momentary indecision, and descended the steps ahead of her.

Tucking the documents safely inside her garments, Pheresa made certain the drawstrings of the seal pouch were tied securely to her belt. Keeping one hand on the pouch, she eased down the steep steps one at a time, her other hand braced on the wall. The steps were so narrow her entire foot could not fit on them. The shadows and uncertain lamplight made it difficult to see where she was going. Her balance, already ungainly from her pregnancy, was unsteady.

At last she sat down and lowered herself from one step to the next, around and around, until she grew exhausted. Dust fogged over her, stirred up in a little cloud by the drag of Talmor's cloak over the steps ahead. She fought against sneezing. The stairs seemed endless, and all the while she was thinking angrily, *This is how Kolahl entered the palace, slipped along to my chamber, invaded my dreams. 'Twas no spell at all, no magic, but instead this dreadful passage. If I survive to return, I shall have it blocked up, and the ruins pulled down and buried.*

After an eternity, the spiral stairs finally ended. The air was cooler here as they headed along a crude passageway.

In places, it grew so narrow she found it difficult to slip through. They came to more steps, a straight flight this time, not a spiral. She went down them slowly, again using the wall to brace herself, while Talmor hurried ahead to light the way.

Now the air felt very cool indeed. There was an unpleasant smell of dampness and mold, and now and then she had to duck to keep from bumping her head on a support beam.

She began to feel caught in a nightmare, some fantasy that could not actually be happening. She could not be creeping through some dank, beetle-infested tunnel beneath the ground, cut off from her friends, her ladies in waiting, her attendants, her courtiers, her palace guards.

Yet when she had to crouch on her hands and knees to crawl through a space where part of the passage had fallen in, she found the grit on her palms real enough. The sting of perspiration in her eyes was real. The feather-soft run of a spider across her hand was real.

She jerked back, flinging the spider away, and held in a scream.

Talmor glanced back, the lamp glowing in his free hand.

He looked worried but unafraid. His black unruly hair hung over his brow, and a cobweb lay draped across his left shoulder.

He helped her to her feet, steadying her. She glanced down at herself, seeing her garments were now filthy. Some of her hair had escaped its loose braid and was hanging in her eyes. She shoved it back in sudden anger.

She was the queen, not some hapless refugee to be forced from her bed in the dead of night. What trick of fate was this, to send her fleeing for her life down this unknown passageway into an uncertain future? She had no attendants, no servants, no clothes other than what she wore on her back. Chain mail was heavy and most uncomfortable to wear, chafing her in spots. Her boots were designed for riding, not walking, and she was beginning to rub a blister on her heel. And once they emerged from this endless tunnel, supposing they eluded any possible Sebein traps, what then? Where was she to go? Was she to spend the night outdoors in the cold and damp, waiting until the battle was over and the invaders thwarted before she crept back to survey the damage? That these barbarians, these unlettered thieves, should be able to bring her to such a state at all infuriated her.

Mandria was the mightiest, richest kingdom in all the world. Its superb army was unequaled. It worshiped Tomias and served Thod. Pilgrims journeyed yearly to the shrine of Tomias's birthplace in Olmiere. Culture and art abounded under the patronage of educated nobles. She had intended her court to be a center of knowledge, and only yesterday she had met with architects to discuss the design of a great library she intended to build.

How, then, did she—the symbol of so refined a civilization—come to be fleeing ruffians who were burning her city and storming her palace?

A terrible coldness settled over her as she realized that since the day Verence had chosen her as his successor, she had been living a fantasy, believing herself at the pinnacle of life, superior to every other living creature. Adulation on all sides was so easy to believe, so easy to succumb to. She'd been a fool in that way, letting it all go to her head, forgetting that life is never certain, and all that is golden and perfect is a fleeting gift from Thod, not a daily right.

This, she thought, *is the reality. This danger. This fear. This anger at having been caught unawares by a wily and clever enemy. I thought I had learned this lesson in Nether, but I forgot it. I must never forget it again, if I live through this night, I must never take my power or my high estate for granted again.*

Talmor stopped so abruptly in front of her that she nearly careened into him. He stood very still, his head held at an angle as though he were listening.

She listened, too, but heard nothing. Alarmed, she suddenly feared this dark, unwholesome place and reached into her pocket for her salt purse. Despite the confusion it had been that she chose to carry with her rather than her jewels.

"What is it?" she whispered. "A Sebein trap?"

Her protector glanced back at her, and she saw the lamplight shimmer across the golden surface of his eyes. He looked in all directions, then, without a word, he handed her the lamp and crept forward, holding both sword and dagger in his hands. As always, she was struck by the lithe, predatory way he moved, like no other man of her acquaintance. She imagined a giant lyng cat, flexed and ready to spring, powerful muscles rippling beneath fur. His alertness and intensity made her wonder what he sensed, heard, or knew that she could not determine for herself.

Unwilling to be left behind, she followed him.

He shot her a warning look and shook his head. "Stay," he whispered.

"I am no dog, to be commanded thus," she retorted, but kept her voice soft as well. "What lies ahead? Magic? A spell—"

"The end of our path, I think." He hesitated, glancing above them. "Wait here."

Fear made her cold. She drew her dagger and found breathing difficult. "Sebeins?"

"Nay, there are no Sebeins here. Their doings are long since faded away."

"If only I could believe that."

He eased forward again, glancing over his shoulder only to add, "Please stay here while I check ahead."

She obeyed, although she did not want him to leave her. Where their narrow passageway ended at a stout door, Talmor inserted an iron key into the door's rusty lock, struggled with it a while, and finally turned it. He pulled the thick, ironbound door partway open, slipped past it, and vanished from sight.

She hesitated only a moment, then tiptoed forward to peer past the door.

A small cellar lay beyond. Clearly it was a musty, long-unused place. Dust-coated cobwebs hung from the beams overhead. An overturned table and some broken stools were the only evidence that anyone had ever been here. Along one wall stood an altar of pagan design. She frowned at it fearfully, but saw no artifacts of heathen worship left there.

Talmor's footsteps tracked across the dusty floor, clear evidence that no one had come here for a very long time. On the opposite side of the chamber rose a flight of rickety wooden steps. Talmor stood at their base, half-crouched and listening. A rat squeaked somewhere, and he spun about with his dagger raised to throw before he stopped himself. He glanced at Pheresa, frowned, and eased one foot onto the bottom step.

The whole structure creaked and trembled under his weight. He hesitated, then returned to her. Taking the lamp, he put it out, plunging them into darkness.

She stood squeezed between his muscular bulk and the wall, and imagined that her thumping heart could be heard. "What—"

His fingers touched her lips, and she fell silent.

"The stairs lead up into the open. Our light can be seen," he explained softly. "Wait here in the passage until I return."

"Where do you go?"

"To find our horses."

He pressed a slim, heavy object into her hand. She realized

it must be the key, and her fingers closed around it convulsively.

"Have patience and wait here," he said. "I'll be as quick as I can, but if anything goes wrong, bolt the door."

Impulsively she gripped his sleeve. "Take care," she whispered.

He hesitated, then eased himself through the doorway and was gone. Pressing herself harder against the wall, Pheresa bit her lip and tried to hold her fear at bay. She listened to the creaking of the steps as Talmor climbed quickly from the cellar, then all grew very quiet. The darkness pressed around her, and she smelled the unpleasant stink of mice.

Her body was trembling with fatigue, and she lowered herself to the ground. Ah, how she ached, especially her feet and low back. Cold air poured into the passageway through the open door, making her shiver. And the waiting grew long indeed.

Doubt crept into her mind. Would Talmor desert her? Had he been killed? Or taken captive?

Numbed with exhaustion and worry, she fell asleep, then woke with a start, disoriented and anxious. The cold darkness oppressed her, and she dared stay there no longer. For all she knew, hours could have passed. Whatever had happened to keep Talmor from returning, Pheresa understood that she was now responsible for her own safety. If she could get away, she must try.

Cautiously, she crept from her hiding place. All was silent and still in the cellar save her ragged breathing. She had never felt more alone.

She started for the steps, which were dimly illuminated by a shaft of waning moonlight, then hesitated and glanced back. The passageway led straight to her throne. If the enemy came here, found this passage . . . Pulling the iron key from her pocket, she went back to lock the door.

Resting her forehead a moment on the rough planks of the door, she felt as though she'd just cut off her own way of retreat.

But there was no going back, she told herself. She'd

known that from the moment she left the privy chamber. Whatever lay ahead of her now must be faced with courage.

She ascended the rickety steps slowly and cautiously, and at last emerged into the tangle of fallen beams and scattered rubble that comprised the ruined remains of the church. Only two walls and part of the tower still stood. She gazed around, fearful of shadows and starting at sounds, and listened to the terrible din of battle coming from the palace. Perhaps she hadn't waited as long as she thought. Talmor would be furious if he returned and found her gone. But the prospect of returning to that dark concealment in the Sebein lair daunted her. She hesitated, and found herself gazing instead at the forest. Talmor's plan, she recalled, had been to take refuge among the trees first until her company was assembled, then slip away under cover.

But if she went into the forest, how would he find her?

Fire suddenly blazed from an upper window of the palace, and she heard screaming war cries so wild and savage she took an involuntary step back.

With pounding heart, she knew she was hearing Vvordsmen. Another window shattered, and orange flames burst free. She stared in horror and rage, tears running down her face, and saw a band of men running atop the walls. Her guardsmen met them in a clash of swordplay. But the barbarians overwhelmed her valiant men. She saw a guard's body topple from the ramparts, and another, and tore her gaze away.

Fear drove her now. She saw another band of Vvordsmen running across the meadow between her and the palace walls. Although they were not headed in her direction, she knew they might decide to explore these ruins. Her hiding place was no longer safe.

Yet to venture away from the ruins into the open where anyone could see her was to court disaster. Forcing herself to remain calm, Pheresa thought hard and realized if she were careful and quick, she could keep the ruins between her and the invaders while she ran for the trees.

And if the woods were full of the enemy? That thought nearly paralyzed her with fresh fear. She rallied herself, refusing to delay as she picked her way out of the ruins. She must take the risk, she told herself, and trust to Thod to keep her unseen.

Stones and bits of rubble lay hidden in the tall grass. She tripped and stumbled, just managing not to fall. Breathing hard, she collected herself, then hurried onward. She wanted to run, but dared not take a chance with the uncertain footing. Holding her stomach cradled protectively with one arm, she glanced back at the palace, but the ruined tower blocked her view.

She hurried awkwardly toward the trees, supporting her stomach as best she could. It seemed an endless distance. Her feet rustled in the grass, and her breath came short and fast. It took all her willpower to resist looking back.

Hurry, she told herself. *Hurry.*

Finally, she reached the forest and stumbled into a trot. She looked back once, her braid bouncing on her shoulder, and saw a blaze of fire break through the palace roof. People were screaming and throwing possessions from the upper stories. In that moment, Pheresa forgot her own troubles.

"Dear Thod, in thy mercy," she prayed aloud, "help them and keep them in thy hand tonight."

Making the swift sign of the Circle, she hurried deeper into the forest. Branches grabbed at her face and sleeves, but she forced her way onward, pushing deeper into the undergrowth and inhaling the pungent scents of broken twigs, leaves, and the damp, rotting vegetation. She slowed to a walk, pressing on despite her weariness, until she could no longer see the palace or hear more than the faintest sounds of battle. She had escaped, but she felt no relief, no sense of triumph. Stumbling at last to a halt, she hugged a tree trunk, pressing her hot face against the rough bark, and wept.

Chapter Nineteen

The snap of a twig behind her, and the sound of running footsteps suddenly close, was all the warning she had.

She whirled around just as a shadow tackled her from the darkness. Her head slammed against the tree trunk with a painful thud, and a man's body pinned her there. She tried to cry out, but his hand closed over her mouth, muffling her sounds. She felt the links of his mail sleeve scrape her cheek, and understood that he was Mandrian. The barbarians, she'd been told, wore no armor.

Relief swept through her, and she stopped struggling. Her captor took his hand away, and she could breathe freely again. Still, she knew that although her captor was no boat raider, she remained in danger.

Steely fingers gripped her arms and pulled her away from the tree.

"Have you nothing to say?" said a rasping voice she recognized at once.

A tide of despair washed over her. "Sir Brillon."

"Aye, majesty. I'm honored you know me, even in the dark."

"You will unhand me, sir," she said regally, trying to hide her fear. "You have no business accosting me this way."

His grip did not slacken. "Your majesty should have sought help in the catacombs. By now you'd be safely on your way upriver. But I'll protect you—"

"I have a protector—"

"What, that coward? He's run away," Brillon told her with a gargling sort of chuckle. "He saw you as far as the ruins, did he not? Aye, I knew he had you stashed in the cellar."

"How did you know?" she demanded. Since Talmor had been in her service, she'd seen no more of the Qanselmite and believed him transferred to another post far from Savroix. "How come you to be here now? Why have you followed me?"

"I have my orders," he said, his tone queer. "All this time I have stayed nearby, waiting for my chance."

She could feel his hot breath on her cheek. Rigid with disgust, she leaned as far away from him as she could. But he only pressed closer.

"I swore myself to serve the Lady of the Miracle," he whispered hoarsely. "I can find you anywhere, in darkness or day. I sense your presence always, as clearly as though I see you. I have performed the rites necessary to be your most devoted acolyte."

"Withdraw, sir!" she said, so repulsed she could barely speak. "Release me, and withdraw!"

His grip only tightened. "I am sworn to you. Since I was given charge of your safety on our journey back from Nether—"

"That was years past," she said sharply, trying to recall him to sense. "And a temporary duty only."

"You were holy then, purified by the Chalice, and so divine in your beauty that your radiance was almost unbearable for mortal men to view. How innocent, how perfect you were. And never had you any inkling of how I kept you from harm—"

"You are dreaming," she broke in, wanting to stop this

tirade. "'Tis my protector, Sir Talmor, who guards the queen's safety."

"The queen," he said bitterly. "You could have been canonized, worshiped, adored by all who made pilgrimages to see you. You could have remained pure and holy and perfect."

His hand slapped her prominent belly, not hard, but she flinched in startlement. "Now, see what you have become. You have debased yourself, allowed a man to defile you, in order to seize worldly goods and honors."

Fury suddenly burned away her fear. She wrested her arm free and cradled her stomach protectively. "How dare you speak to me this way! My husband—"

"Husband?" he echoed harshly. "Nay, majesty, defiler! Know you how many lovers he has taken? Know you his drunkenness, his lewd acts, his—"

"Silence!" she screamed, forgetting the need for caution. "You go too far! The duc has remained behind, bravely risking his life to defend my palace, and you are not fit to—"

"He spoiled your purity," Sir Brillon broke in. "Destroyed you, when you could have been forever our Lady of the Chalice. And now you defend him, defend his blasphemy."

She took an involuntary step back, certain he was mad and knowing she could not run from him.

"I was never a saint," she said desperately, trying to break through his delusions. "I was never what you believed me to be. You have woven a fantasy for yourself, Sir Brillon, and you must stop it. 'Tis the Chalice that is holy. I never was."

He reached out and touched her face with his fingertips, making her shudder. "Such modesty," he whispered sadly. "Despite all that has befallen you and changed you for ill, you retain that."

"You must go," she said. "The queen gives you permission to withdraw."

He stepped closer, and again she backed away, her heart thudding faster.

"Sir Talmor will return at any moment," she said, wishing desperately that it was true. "He will see to my safety. Your concern is unnecessary."

Sir Brillon continued to advance. "Poor, misguided lady," he said. "Defending your craven protector just as you defend your defiler of a husband. I will take you far from here and restore all that is good in you. I will give you back to the Chalice, and see you cleansed with rites of purification until you—"

"No!" she shouted.

Whirling around, she fled, but in two steps he caught her from behind. She struggled, terrified of him and worried that harm would come to her baby. She had no strength to match his. His arms held her fast, and although she kicked and fought him, he marched her through the forest toward an unknown destination. He muttered and chuckled to himself, truly mad, and she feared what he meant to do. In her mind, she prayed hard for courage and the chance to get away. *Oh, Sir Talmor,* she thought desperately, *what has become of you?*

A branch whipped her face, and the stinging pain gave her strength to stomp hard on Sir Brillon's instep. For a second his grasp loosened. She stabbed hard with her small dagger, but the point glanced harmlessly off his mail. Growling something, he gripped her wrist with crushing strength. She flailed out with her other hand and smacked him across the face.

He struck back, his fist like a hammer. Pain shattered her face, and she went reeling back, lost in a cloud of agony and shock.

Vaguely she felt his arms catch her before she hit the ground. He scooped her up, and although she tried hard to swim back to full consciousness, she could not seem to escape that which pulled her down.

I must not faint, she told herself desperately, certain that if she did, she would be this madman's prisoner forever.

And then she knew nothing at all.

Talmor, having succeeded in gathering his squire, servant, and the few members of the queen's household who were to accompany her, pushed Canae through the milling confusion. Courtiers ran in all directions, clutching bundles of possessions too precious to leave behind. Wagons were still being loaded, and guardsmen hurried back and forth, shouting in vain efforts to organize the chaos. Talmor knew it was only a matter of time until the Vvordsmen sent a boat here to cut off the exodus at this river landing.

Cursing beneath his breath, he thought of the queen left behind in her dark hiding place. *Thod keep her safe for a few minutes more,* he prayed, and pointed his little group toward the eastern road. "Follow it if you can to the first crossing," he said to Pears, "then take the north turning. If Thod is with me, I'll rejoin you soon."

"But, sir—"

Lifting his hand, Talmor spurred his horse away, heading back to the Sebein ruin. Galloping through the trees away from the curve of the river, he leaned low over Canae's whipping mane, aware he'd left the queen too long. If only Pears and Lutel could keep their horses and the wagon from being stolen, all might yet be managed.

At that moment a Vvordsman war cry sounded, and a group of them leaped from the bushes into his path. Canae reared in fright, and Talmor barely had time to count five of the savages as he drew his sword and met their attack.

They were naked to the waist, their eyes glowing orange and yellow-green in the darkness. Howling and brandishing their spiked clubs and curved swords, they came at him, but Talmor's weapon was quick and sure. He struck off a head, and swung his sword around just as a hand gripped his cloak. Twisting in the saddle, Talmor cut off the man's arm. Screaming, the Vvordsman fell back, his blood splattering in a wet arc. One tried to spring at Talmor from behind, but Canae kicked him away. Another lunged at the horse, trying to cut Canae's throat, but Talmor leaned forward recklessly in the saddle and struck him down. Wheeling the furious charger, he spurred Canae toward the remaining man, who tried to attack. Talmor rode him down, letting Canae trample him, then with a leap, horse and rider were back on their way.

He fended off two more such ambushes before he was able to veer out across the meadow. He no longer bothered to stick to cover. The main brunt of fighting was at the palace, and from the sounds of battle and the fire blazing from some of the windows, the barbarians had managed to storm the walls successfully. Part of Talmor was enraged and wanted to go back to fight the enemy, but the rest of him knew he belonged with the queen.

Worry about her drove him to spur Canae faster. He hoped she'd stayed where he left her. Surely she had sense enough to do that.

But when he dismounted at the ruins and went hurrying down the swaying steps into the dark cellar, he came to an uncertain halt and listened intently.

All was still and silent. He knew at once that she'd gone. He felt no sense of her presence anywhere nearby.

Alarmed, he found the passageway door locked, and although he called out softly to her, hoping she remained on the other side of it, there came no answer.

Cursing, he forced down his worry and wondered if she had gone back into the palace. Nay, surely she would not be that foolish. If she had, he could not help her, for he could not get through the door.

But if she had left the ruins . . .

Turning around, he stared at the steps leading up into the open air. How long had she waited before she emerged? A part of him admired her for such courage, but the rest of him wanted to break her neck. Thod take the woman. Couldn't she stay put for an hour?

He found himself prey to all sorts of fears and imaginings about the many possible ways she could come to harm.

Ruthlessly he suppressed them and forced himself to clear his mind. *Sanude, help me now,* he thought and closed his eyes. The lady had her faults, like any living creature, but she did not lack for valor. If she believed herself abandoned, she would not cower here in hiding indefinitely. She would take action, and she would go . . . outside.

He opened his eyes, feeling the pull of some instinct now. Swiftly he went back up the steps and glanced around, trying to see the ruins, meadow, and forest through her eyes. They had talked of taking refuge in the forest until she could be re-united with her household. That's where she had surely gone.

Swinging back into the saddle, Talmor headed into the forest. He soon slowed, for the undergrowth was thick, and in the darkness he could find no trail.

He tried to determine how far a frightened, pregnant woman could go. Every few minutes he halted Canae to listen. The forest lay still, its denizens hiding tonight. Behind him came the sounds of battle, fierce and distracting, and with a frown he focused his senses forward.

The next time he reined up to listen, he heard a woman cry out.

It was Pheresa's voice, and the sound of her in trouble pierced him like a knife blade. He spurred his charger, his sword already in hand, and came bursting into a small clearing lit by the fading moonlight. There, he saw an armed man carrying the unconscious queen.

"Hold!" Talmor shouted.

The man—garbed in a white surcoat—turned, letting the queen slip to the ground, and drew his sword. "Give way!" he shouted back. "She's mine now."

Blazing fury took possession of Talmor. He heard nothing, cared about nothing, except saving her from the clutches of this abductor. Swiftly he jumped from the saddle and ran across the clearing to meet the other man's charge.

Their swords clanged through the forest, a grunt springing from Talmor's lips at the force of their exchanged blows. The church knight tried to lock swords and force his down, but Talmor disengaged and with a swift swing of his wrists, sent his blade flashing at the man's head.

The church knight parried the blow, and sparks flew between their blades. Back and forth they fought, furious and well matched. Talmor was the stronger man, but his opponent was seasoned and wily. He used tricks that nearly caught Talmor unawares, and when Talmor thought he had the man pinned, the knave eluded him. Like all church knights, he knew how to fight dirty, and he grew more and more ruthless.

With each blow of his sword, he grunted out a line of Writ, calling on Thod and Saint Qanselm to strengthen his arms.

Then Talmor, retreating to give himself room, tripped over a tree root and fell sprawling. The Qanselmite yelled in triumph and charged him, sword blade flashing in the moonlight. Talmor was ready for him, however, and as he lunged, Talmor twisted his blade and sent the church knight's weapon flying from his hands. The sword landed in the shadows, gone from sight, and with a terrible oath the man pulled his dagger.

By now Talmor was up and ready. Still swearing, the man crouched low on the balls of his feet, swinging his dagger from side to side like a peasant fighter.

Honor required Talmor to sheathe his sword and use his own dagger, but just as he moved to do so, the knight leaped at him. Talmor twisted on his back foot, risking losing his balance, and swung his sword up in time for his opponent to impale himself on it.

Beneath the shifting tree canopy, moonlight shone down, and Talmor recognized the man at last.

A terrible gargling noise came from Sir Brillon's throat. He sagged, his weight pulling down Talmor's sword. Talmor drew his weapon back, and Sir Brillon collapsed on the ground, thrashing a little.

Talmor knelt beside him and pressed his hand to the man's shoulder. "You fool," he said quietly. "You should have never challenged me."

Sir Brillon shuddered beneath his hand. He reached up and gripped Talmor's wrist as though to push him away. His fingers were bloody and slick. "She was to be a saint," he said through a groan.

"She is a woman," Talmor said, "and a queen."

"Could have saved her," Sir Brillon whispered. He gagged and choked a moment, then his fingers dropped from Talmor's wrist.

Standing up, Talmor cleaned his weapon, then hurried to Pheresa's side. He gathered her in his arms, propping her gently against his knee, and touched his fingers to her throat.

Her pulse beat strongly, and something tight and anxious inside him relaxed.

"Majesty," he said urgently, pushing her hair back from her brow. How soft and fragrant her tresses were. He lifted a curl to his lips and kissed it, then ruthlessly brought himself back under control. "Majesty, wake up."

She stirred, moaning a little, then stiffened and tried to pummel him with her fists. He gripped her hands, holding them harmlessly against his chest. "Majesty, 'tis Talmor. You're safe now."

Her eyes opened, and her face looked pale and ghostly in the dimming moonlight. "Talmor," she whispered. "I thought—"

"Forgive me," he said, soothing her. "Everything took longer than I intended. If you're not hurt, let us go from here quickly."

She looked around, then lifted her hand to her temple as though still dazed. "He followed me, came out of nowhere. I thought he—"

"Sir Brillon is dead," Talmor said grimly. "The queen need not fear him again."

In silence she dropped her hand and gazed across the clearing where Sir Brillon lay. Helping her to stand, Talmor steadied her as they walked slowly to the horses. He helped her to mount Sir Brillon's horse and shortened the stirrups for her.

"'Tis queer, riding astride like a man," she said, then fell silent again while Talmor smiled to himself in the darkness.

"Shall I lead your majesty's horse?" he asked.

"Nay, sir!" she said sharply, sounding more like herself. "I've been well rattled this night, but I'm not yet helpless. You—"

"Soft," he said suddenly, hearing a noise. "Someone's coming."

She gasped, but made no other sound. Talmor climbed quickly into his own saddle and drew his sword. A party of men tramped past a short distance away, but did not notice them. When they were gone, Talmor let out his pent-up breath and only then noticed that the queen was weeping.

His heart turned over inside him, but she pulled herself straight and gathered her reins. Clearly, she wanted no comfort.

"Is this all we have?" she asked in an unsteady voice.

"Nay," he replied gently. "Unless they've come to harm, my men are with your attendants. We're to join them on the road."

Pheresa nodded with a sigh. "I fear for my people," she said, gazing past him in the direction of the palace. "Every scream and outcry pierces my heart. I fear for my consort."

Jealousy curled sour and angry in the pit of Talmor's stomach. "We have but one way to defy these invaders now," he said quietly, "and that is to keep your majesty from their clutches. Don't you realize that someone at Savroix surely advised them on the perfect time to strike? Do you not wonder that your majesty's army has been sent out of range? 'Tis but part of a daring plot."

"But if I leave, then I give them everything," she said angrily.

He felt tired, and forced himself to find the patience to go through this argument one more time. "Everything but the queen."

She sighed. "Betrayal . . . 'tis unbearable to think about."

"Then think about your majesty's countermove."

She said nothing, and in silence they turned their horses northward.

Chapter Twenty

In Pheresa's opinion, Sir Talmor's selection of Vurdal as their destination was a master stroke. Thod bless him for his cleverness, she thought, for he knew that were she united with part of her army, she would find herself surrounded by trustworthy allies. Vurdal was a garrison town in central Mandria not far from where the Charva River curved to divide the upper and lower halves of the realm. The countryside was flat and featureless, with practice fields and parade grounds for training purposes on three sides of the village. Normally, Vurdal would have been swollen with knights in training, the air alive with the clash of arms and trumpets signaling for maneuvers. But the garrison stood at one-third its usual force, the rest having been ordered to the coast less than a month before.

Pheresa sighed. Talmor had done his best. Until their arrival last week, neither of them had known Vurdal's forces had been reassigned. During the journey, she'd clung to hope by assuring herself that once she reached Vurdal, she would have not only refuge, but an army to lead to Savroix's rescue. Instead, she'd found cruel disappointment.

Exhausted from strain and hard riding, her womb filled with pains she tried to conceal during the journey, Pheresa could do nothing but put herself and her small, bedraggled party into the hands of the garrison commander.

Considerably startled, for he'd had no advance notice of her majesty's arrival, the commander had hastily installed her in the best rooms available—his own—and summoned the garrison physician to attend her. She had been ordered to bed for several days of rest.

Feeling herself at the end of her strength, Pheresa sank gratefully into exhausted slumber, but within two days her health improved enough for her to feel anxious for news.

She sent forth letters and messages, and summoned the commander daily for reports regarding what had befallen Savroix.

She imagined her beautiful palace lying in smoking ruins, its wealth and treasures plundered, its art destroyed by barbarian hands. During these days when she had nothing to do save fret, she regretted not going to Scice as her father had recommended. From there, she could have returned to Savroix quickly. Here at Vurdal, she was too far away.

As a distraction, her attendants—including her court physician, two lackeys, Lady Carolie, Oola, and the Countess Adema de Muliere—sought her supervision in inventorying what they'd managed to save. The countess guarded many of the queen's jewels, sewn to her petticoats and hidden in the seams of various articles of clothing. There were two chests of royal clothing, some of it mismatched and quite unsuitable, the queen's lute, her favorite pillows, a case of literature scrolls, her writing implements, a flask of perfume, and a strongbox of money. It was better than nothing, Pheresa kept telling herself, but it was not very much.

At last a letter arrived from Lord Salba. The chancellor informed her that the palace still stood, thanks to the efforts of her consort husband. She cried aloud when she read these opening lines of good news, laughing in her relief, feeling tremendous pride in her husband.

But then she read the rest of the letter, and her laughter

turned to a frown, then a scowl, then horror. Lervan, despite his promise to defend Savroix to the last man, had instead surrendered the palace to avert its total destruction. He had given it up during the first onslaught. Pheresa doubted she'd ridden even a quarter league away that night before the seat of her government lay in the hands of the enemy.

Oh, the shame of it was like poison burning a hole through her, a hole that could never heal. She *knew* she should have stayed there and defied the enemy. Savroix would not have been surrendered had she remained in charge. Nay, even if the palace had fallen in defeat 'twould have been better than this ignoble end. *Given* to the barbarians, the gates opened willingly, *by Lervan's order.*

· And she had trusted him to do what was right and honorable in her absence. Standing here in her borrowed quarters at Vurdal, she ate the bitter seed of self-blame. Savroix had been her responsibility, and in her first true test as a monarch she had failed.

And would being taken prisoner have been a nobler act? The thought only made her angrier.

Yes, she told herself, easy enough now to think of what she should have done. Hindsight was always so certain and never knew the confusion of the moment, the urgency, the need to make instant decisions without benefit of experience or knowledge. Well, she could be honest with herself now, honest enough to admit that she'd known Lervan to be a boaster and weak of character where it most mattered. And yet, like a fool, she'd blinded herself to his faults, forgiven them, overlooked them, perhaps even ignored them, because she wanted to pander to his vanity and ego by giving him something to be proud of, some way to achieve glory for himself. She'd fallen under his spell too many times, trusting him because she wanted to depend on him, because she needed someone who would not fail her. She'd bestowed the gift of responsibility on him, because she wanted him to admire her.

As though, she thought bitterly, admiration could ever be bought.

Savroix lay in the hands of a Vvord king called Mux, a

pale-skinned man with orange eyes and a child's scalp hanging from his neck for a talisman. The very thought of it made Pheresa grind her teeth together. She longed to race back to Savroix and confront her fool of a husband, but as yet she could not without placing herself in the enemy's hands.

On the following day more news came, informing her that most of her council and perhaps half of her courtiers had escaped. The rest remained at Savroix with Lervan, who reputedly was feasting with the enemy, offering them the honors of full Mandrian hospitality. Pheresa burned with the shame of it.

Lervan has betrayed me in the past, has betrayed our marriage, she thought miserably. *Why shouldn't he now betray our kingdom?*

Bowing her head, she wept.

In the following days, as the autumn season grew colder, she received no reply to her appeals from King Faldain of Nether. She told herself it was too soon to expect an answer. Nether was far away, a dangerous land for travelers. The courier might have been waylaid, killed, or even become lost. But if her letters got through, she was convinced Faldain would advise her well, and she said so to Talmor repeatedly, drawing comfort from saying it aloud. Her protector, in his quiet way, replied little, watching her pace and fret to no avail. She told Talmor that there could be no doubt of Faldain's courage or battle experience. And his honor was inviolate.

"He sounds like a paragon of perfection," Talmor replied.

"You believe none of what I say, but I speak the truth about him," she said, wrapped in memories of her good friend. "He will come to me."

"This king of a foreign land, does he obey your majesty's summons like a dog called to heel?"

Flushing in annoyance, she let Talmor's impertinence pass, and said stoutly, "Never has Faldain failed me. He will not fail me now."

But while she waited for Faldain's response, she received more news from Savroix, all of it bad.

The official report: King Mux had left Savroix, taking his

army horde with him. Duc Lervan was being hailed by the townspeople as their savior and praised as the consummate diplomat.

Lord Meaclan's report: Duc Lervan had ordered the treasury room broken open so that he could bestow *half its contents*—including crown jewels, gold plate, and coins—on Mux. Only then had the barbarian king departed, leaving the palace soiled and looted, the very throne room defiled.

Pheresa crumpled Meaclan's letter in her hands, so intensely angry at that moment she could not breathe. Her ears were roaring. "The fool," she muttered aloud. "The stupid, stupid fool!"

Oola, who was tidying the room, paused in her work to look at Pheresa in concern. "Majesty?"

"Go away!" Pheresa said angrily. "Go at once!"

Oola curtsied and hurried out, leaving only Sir Talmor present. Quietly, he stood near the door, leaning his powerful shoulders against the wall. His golden eyes watched her in concern.

Pheresa looked at him with despair. "Lervan is hailed as a hero. Well, he has bought his heroism at a very dear price. How could he have been so stupid?"

"What has his grace done now?"

She told him, withholding none of the sorry tale, and saw bleak contempt enter her protector's eyes. "Aye, all that," she said angrily. "Does he not realize they will only return, again and again, for more gold?"

"Of course they will return. He has rewarded them well for their attack."

Tears stung her eyes, and she averted her face, clenching her hands tightly so that her nails dug into her palms. *Queens do not cry,* she told herself angrily.

"We must return to Savroix immediately," she said. "I fear there will be no quick remedy to hand for all that is awry."

Talmor looked as though he would say something, but then he bowed. "I'll announce your majesty's order."

But the following morning, while they were still preparing for departure, the garrison commander sought out Pheresa.

His weathered face looked grave beneath its fringe of gray hair.

"Your majesty," he said, "I am informed by Marechal du Lindier that Duc Lervan has proclaimed himself King of Mandria."

The scroll she'd been trying to read fell unheeded from her fingers. She felt numb with disbelief. She could not even speak.

Lady Carolie and Countess de Muliere rose to their feet. The countess dropped her needlework, and Lady Carolie's face went white. Sir Talmor, standing in his customary place behind Pheresa's chair, took an involuntary half step forward so that he brushed against the back of it. She hardly noticed their reactions. The room seemed to be shrinking around her. She was glad her companions were close by. Fearing she might swoon, she held herself furiously rigid until the moment of weakness passed.

Clearing his throat, the commander bowed. "Er, perhaps I'd better read what it says. These are not *my* words, majesty."

"Please go on," she said, her mouth so dry she could not swallow.

"Well, er, it says, 'Because of the queen's cowardly desertion of her people and subsequent abdication of her throne, his grace, Duc Lervan, consort and prince, does hereby assume the throne and all sovereignty over the realm of Mandria—' "

"Stop," she said wearily. "Read no more of it."

"I am sorry, your majesty." The commander was a gruff, plain-spoken man, accustomed to bawling orders at trainees, and clumsy with courtly ways. He stared at her now in visible distress. "I am ordered to escort you back to Savroix at the earliest opportunity."

It was as though she teetered on the brink of a precipice and could fall at any moment. The roaring in her ears grew louder. She felt a wave of heat sweep up through her, as though to burst her skull into pieces, then it ebbed again, leaving her cold and rigid in her chair.

"What," she asked the commander in a voice like ice, "do you intend to do?"

He stiffened, slapping a hand to his sword hilt, while Sir Talmor watched him like a falcon. "I intend to serve my queen."

His loyalty was a gift, made even sweeter because of the treachery she had just discovered. Her eyes blurred, and she struggled to keep her dignity. "The queen is grateful."

He bowed. "This dispatch came in the royal courier pouch, but it bears no official seal. Therefore, I cannot be sure that it is a legal document, or that it hasn't been substituted for genuine orders by enemy hands."

She frowned, thinking of the royal seal safely in her possession. She had that, and the ring of state, which was on her finger. She also had the charters, as well as the heir's crown, which Verence himself had placed on her brow when she was invested as Princess of the Realm. Those things, along with her personal jewels and two purses of money presently hidden in her chest of linens, were all she had in the world. Pheresa realized that until now she'd believed she was preserving such precious artifacts from loss or harm. But in fact, they might prove to be her most powerful legal weapons.

Never had she expected Lervan to depose her. She'd not seen the ambition in him, the hidden greed ready to take her trust and twist it into personal gain. Why had she been so blind?

"What are your majesty's orders?" the commander asked.

Pheresa forced herself to think. She said to herself that if this commander remained loyal to her despite Lervan's perfidy, then others would as well. She was not beaten yet. She would not give way tamely and let herself be taken back to Savroix as a prisoner. She would not allow herself to be judged and found wanting, to be accused of failing her subjects and duty. These months before coronation were a new ruler's most vulnerable time, and although she'd been deposed already, she did not intend to stay that way.

Lifting her chin high, she said, "I want escort northward, to upper Mandria. You, commander, will say that the queen departed Vurdal before you received your orders."

With relief flickering in his eyes, he bowed. "Your majesty—"

"If anyone questions you, you may also relate your suspicions regarding orders sent to you without an official seal."

"Aye, your majesty."

Pheresa's gaze went to Lady Carolie. "Is the packing finished?"

"Almost, your majesty."

"See that it's completed immediately. We cannot delay another hour." Pheresa rose to her feet. "Commander, give me as escort all the men you can spare."

"It shall be done."

As the commander walked to the door, Talmor followed him. "Her majesty is not fit to ride. Can a carriage be provided?"

The commander looked doubtful. "There's none at hand. Had I known in time, I could have ordered the smith to craft something out of a wagon, but—"

"A second supply wagon then," Talmor said.

"Aye, of course." The commander looked past him at Pheresa, bowed quickly, and left.

Lady Carolie hastened in, looking flustered and unhappy. "I've given the orders. Will your majesty give me leave to write a letter before we go?"

"Nay. See about your duties. You can write when we're safely at Thirst."

Carolie curtsied, but dismay was spreading across her pretty face. "Thirst Hold? But that's so far away!"

Pheresa nodded. "We may meet cold weather so far upland," she said to Talmor. "Make certain everyone is supplied with a warm cloak and extra blankets."

"But must we go so far?" Carolie asked. "The journey will be long and slow—"

"What of that?" Pheresa asked impatiently. "I must issue a call of allegiance to my upland lords. Lervan's hand will not reach me at Thirst."

"Your majesty puts herself at Faldain's mercy," Talmor said doubtfully.

"I can trust him," Pheresa retorted.

Carolie looked increasingly distressed. " 'Tis said there is much danger in upper Mandria. And they have such strange ways and customs. Must the queen go so far—"

"We have more to fear at present in lower Mandria than in upper," Pheresa said. "Why do you dawdle and refuse to obey your queen? Is the canker of treason to spread among my closest companions as well?"

Carolie burst into tears. "No, your majesty! Oh, no!"

She hurried from the room with her face buried in her hands.

"She is worried about her husband," Talmor said quietly. "There's been no word as to the baron's fate, or her son's."

Pheresa sighed, already regretting that she'd been so harsh. "Of course. I have prayed for the baron's safety, but her child is safe at their estate, and well she knows it. I cannot afford to indulge her desire to go home, not when my crown—indeed my life—are at stake."

Talmor said nothing, and Pheresa shot a fierce look at the countess. "You have my permission to withdraw."

The countess curtsied slowly, picked up her needlework off the floor, and went out.

Pheresa turned on Talmor. "Well, sir? You stand here frowning. Have you objections to my orders, too?"

"Nay, majesty."

She knew him well enough to see that he had doubts of some kind. That annoyed her, for it made her wonder if she was erring again.

"Something troubles you. Speak, sir!"

He crossed his arms over his chest. Stalwart and quiet, he looked worn from the strain of recent days. A pang of worry touched her, and she wondered for the first time if he even slept at night or instead stood guard over her slumbers. When did he eat? He never absented himself when she dined alone from a tray, and insisted on personally checking her food. Was he taking proper care of himself? Did his squire and servant see to his needs adequately? A monarch usually employed two protectors, yet she'd never considered anyone else but him at her back. She realized now that she'd been unfair in using him so harshly. And Talmor, so quiet, so dependable, so loyal, never complained.

"Will you not say what you are thinking?" she asked again, less sharply.

He hesitated still, but when his gaze at last met hers, there was no wavering in it. "Does the queen realize that when she crosses the Charva and appeals to the upland lords against lower Mandria, there will be—"

He broke off, frowning.

She stared at him in growing impatience. "There will be trouble. Yes, of course." Then she suddenly understood his meaning, and something cold passed through her bones. "You mean there could be civil war."

"Upper versus lower."

Defiance spread through her, and she tossed her head. "It will not happen. The realm is unified, and it will stand for its rightful monarch."

"I pray unity will hold under the strain of this conflict."

She shook her head, unable to believe that lower Mandria would support the coward Lervan had proven himself to be. "Lervan has a few supporters now, but he hardly speaks for the entire realm. Am I to stand aside and let him usurp me?"

Under knotted brows, Talmor's eyes met hers in grave warning. "As long as the queen understands the costs if she takes this course."

"Is there aught else I can do?" Pheresa asked rather shrilly.

"I'm no adviser, majesty," he said.

"No." She frowned, hugging herself against the dreadful vision conjured up by his words. Verence, and his father before him, had worked long and hard to bring the two halves of the realm together. She thought uneasily of the Treaty of Blood in her possession. It had been forged at a dreadful cost. Families had been torn asunder. Lands had been confiscated. Punishment had been harsh indeed to bring the rebellious Edonia to heel. What if Talmor was right, and she broke that uneasy union apart? Yet what else could she do?

"Faldain will advise me," she said, clinging to that assurance, and ignored Talmor's exasperated frown. "He understands the problems of upper Mandria, and he knows what it's like to be betrayed. He will give me the answers I seek."

"This king is not Mandrian," Talmor said doubtfully. "He has not your majesty's concerns at heart."

"You do not know him!"

"He has his own realm to think of. Would a foreign king not welcome division in Mandria, and take advantage from—"

"Nay, sir!" she said angrily. "Faldain is my friend and a man of honor. He saved my life. He saved Verence's life. He found the Chalice when it was lost and restored it to his people. Were he not a man of pure heart and unquestioned valor, he could not have even touched the sacred relic without grave harm. There is no finer man alive than he. I trust him absolutely."

A little silence followed this ringing speech. Overheated with defiance, Pheresa drew a quick breath and looked down, embarrassed now by the ardor that had filled her words. Talmor's amber eyes took on an expression she could not read, and the line creasing his brow deepened.

"This Faldain is the man your majesty would have married," Talmor said slowly.

It was as though he had peeked into the most secret corner of her heart. It was the last thing she'd expected him to say, and she felt exposed, suddenly raw.

She glared at him in fury. "Who told you that? Faldain is married, as am I. Think you that I go to meet him for some other purpose than saving my realm? How dare you!"

Talmor's expression grew stonier, his gaze remote and fierce, so that for a moment he seemed to be almost a stranger. "I do not criticize the queen," he said in a colorless voice.

Scowling at him, she realized too late that her own angry defensiveness had given her away. It was as though some madness seized her, making her horrid in all that she said and did. She wanted to lash out at everyone, punishing those around her as she longed to punish Lervan.

She opened her mouth, but queens did not apologize. She

had to be a sovereign now and somehow hold on to her realm, even when everything seemed to be slipping from her fingers.

"Go outside and leave me to myself," she whispered, and it took tremendous effort to speak calmly.

Talmor was still looking at her in a peculiar way. *Is he disappointed in me?* she wondered, and felt fresh anger wash over her. *He has no right to judge me, no right at all.*

"Your majesty—"

"Stop questioning my every command!" she shouted. "Obey me!"

He bowed, his mouth tight, and left without another word.

Pheresa whirled around and ran to the window for fresh air. Gulping in deep breaths, she realized she'd been shouting at a man who could not answer back. Shame at her behavior flooded her, and she picked up a pen case and hurled it across the room. Then she put her hands to her face and let the scalding tears fall. Her anger was something wild inside her, clawing and horrid. And Talmor was wrong about Faldain, very wrong. There must be a good reason why he had not replied to her letters. He was a true friend, and he would not fail her. There was nothing wrong in wanting his wise counsel, and Talmor was a fool if he believed otherwise.

Biting her lip, she hastily slammed a mental door on further consideration of what Talmor thought.

She must keep her concentration on Lervan instead, and think of nothing else save his black treachery. She wanted to hurt him, as he had hurt her. She wanted to punish him. Dear Thod, how she wished herself a man this day, so that she could ride home and challenge Lervan to fight. He had besmirched her honor. He had made her think of another man, a man she had once loved, with a degree of regret so deep and strong it was unbearable. He had made her quarrel today with two of her most faithful companions, obliging her to face their censure and disappointment.

How could she have been so deceived by Lervan's handsome looks and charming manners? He had told her the things a woman most longs to hear when she lies in the arms of her husband, and in gratitude she'd tried so hard to please his unfaithful heart. It shamed her now, bitterly and deeply, to think of how desperately she'd worked to pander to him. And all the while, he'd been waiting for the perfect opportunity to steal from her everything that mattered.

She would never forgive him.

Never.

Chapter Twenty-one

The last time she'd come by Thirst Hold, Pheresa had been desperately ill, kept alive only through a precarious spell. Long had she been curious about this remote hold, where both Faldain and Gavril had been fostered and come to manhood, for Thirst stood wreathed in legend. Here was where the evil sword Tanengard had been forged. Here was where a Nonkind shapeshifter had nearly killed Gavril until Faldain saved the young prince's life. Here was where Faldain had been adopted by kindly Chevard Odfrey and later had proclaimed himself rightful King of Nether.

Pheresa sat wrapped in a fur-lined cloak in the lurching, slow-moving wagon, hardly feeling the cold and discomfort. In rising anticipation, she squinted against tiny needles of intermittent sleet.

"We're nearly there," she said to Lady Carolie, sitting huddled under a cloak and a blanket, her pretty little nose red with cold. "At any moment, I'm certain we'll see the walls."

"I hope so, your majesty," Carolie replied through chattering teeth.

The road rounded a bend and emerged from dense forest into open country. A flock of black-winged keebacks broke from the trees, noisy and sudden, and Pheresa saw the hold at last.

Nothing prepared her for how bleak and impoverished it looked.

Flat marshes teeming with waterfowl seemed to stretch out forever beyond tall levees of packed dirt. Fields were small and muddy, the village a mere cluster of pathetic hovels peopled with ragged serfs who watched her ride by in suspicious silence. And beyond, standing between village and the marshes leading to the river, rose the gray stone walls of Thirst.

How small it was, how grim. Most nobles in lower Mandria had expanded their fortresses into stately villas or grand homes that displayed their prosperity, softening the harsh lines of old castles with new architectural styles. Here, no one had altered the formidable walls, thick, squat turrets with arrow slits, or the stout gates with an old-fashioned portcullis hanging behind them.

Thirst showed no pretensions to being anything other than the fortress it was, and even at this distance it looked primitive. Pheresa was reminded that this was a land where Nonkind beasts roamed and struck the unwary. This was a land of brutally cold winters, hard men, and considerable danger. She recalled Prince Gavril's disparaging remarks about his fostering time at Thirst Hold, how horrid and backward it was, how much he had hated it. For the first time, she began to understand what he meant.

Her excitement died, and she stared ahead in silence, while Lady Carolie looked dismayed, and the countess frowned.

"It's not at all welcoming, majesty," Carolie said in a small voice.

"'Tis at the end of the world," the countess said with a sniff of disgust.

"You judge too harshly," Pheresa said, but then fell silent. In truth, it did look awful, the kind of place that had no amenities at all. She found herself longing for a warm fire, a cup of mulled wine sweetened with her favorite spices, and a bath in hot, scented water. From the look of it, Thirst would be awash with drafts of icy air, have old rushes on the floor instead of carpets, and would be run by a clutch of ignorant louts. Faldain had loved it. Verence had been furious to lose it. And Gavril had hated it.

For perhaps the only time in her life, she found herself in agreement with her dead cousin.

The sleet stopped, and rain began to drizzle instead. The wheels of the wagon were already struggling through mud that sucked and clung.

Sir Talmor rode up alongside. "Sir Ninquin has sent a rider ahead. Look yon. They're opening the gates."

Pheresa saw. As she pulled up the hood of her cloak to shield herself somewhat from the rain, she heard trumpets sounding a welcome. It was a tinny, ragged little fanfare, nothing like what she was used to at Savroix.

But then she saw the flags of the hold flutter on a sudden gust of wind. And Nether's bold pennon of green and white unfurled proudly.

Gripping the side of the wagon, Pheresa leaned forward behind the driver while her weariness fell away, and her heart felt light again. "He's here!" she said, turning to smile at Lady Carolie and Sir Talmor. "Faldain is here and awaits my arrival. I knew he would not fail me!"

Lady Carolie's eyes widened. "The king himself attends your majesty's bidding?"

Pheresa tossed her head with renewed confidence. "Did you think he would not?"

"Of course, majesty." But there was a sly little smile that curved Lady Carolie's lips as she spoke.

Their welcome was warm. Once inside the gates, the riders of her escort milled around the wagons, while geese and chickens scattered out of their way, squawking, and stableboys hurried out into the rain. Servants of all kinds appeared from nowhere, to stand and stare. Pheresa was assisted to the ground. The rain began to fall harder, and she had a confused impression of stone walls, snug, well-tended barns of wood, and a well-swept stableyard.

A tall knight wearing a surcoat in Thirst's colors bowed to her in greeting. "Your majesty is most welcome," he said. His firm voice was clipped in the manner of uplander speech. "I am Sir Bosquecel, commander of this hold, and am bid by my lord and master to escort you inside."

Again her heart gave that absurd leap. Smiling, she extended her gloved hand to Sir Bosquecel in warmer greeting than was her wont. "Thank you, sir. Then King Faldain is in residence? I saw his pennon flying, but could not be sure."

The man bowed again. "Aye, majesty. This hold is well honored to receive your grace, and all here bid you welcome and good cheer."

Still smiling, she deigned to look around her at the serfs and servants, many of them still gawking with their caps in their hands while the rain soaked them through. When she smiled and nodded to the little crowd, they cheered her.

Well pleased, Pheresa allowed herself to be escorted into a paved courtyard. Here, she saw a tiny chapel, a turret, a small, walled garden with an unruly tangle of vines spilling over its gate, and the stone steps leading up into the keep. Its door stood open, with a liveried steward standing in the welcoming rectangle of light.

She walked inside, her leather slippers crossing an ancient stone threshold worn down in the center, and was taken immediately to a warm fire burning with fragrant apple wood. Seated in a comfortable chair, her feet resting on a carpet, she accepted a cup of warm cider.

She sipped the stuff cautiously, found it agreeable, and drank it down. When she was warm enough, she allowed her cloak and gloves to be taken away, and well-mannered servants escorted her and her party up a broad spiral of stone steps to chambers that were plain in furnishings but supplied with both hearth and well-placed braziers. Glancing at the massive wooden bed with its odd shutters instead of hangings, Pheresa wondered if sleeping inside it would not be like trying to sleep inside a box. Still, it would be less subject to drafts than a bed with the customary draperies. She saw a writing table adequate for her needs, a tiny alcove for washing, and an adjoining suite of rooms for her attendants. Satisfied, she nodded, and the steward released an audible sigh of relief.

"Where is your master?" she demanded, anxious to see Faldain without delay.

The steward wore a silver collar with Thirst's coat of arms engraved on it in the ancient custom. "Hunting, my lady. I mean, your majesty."

"Hunting!" she said in disappointment, and spun around so that her skirts billowed wide. "Can men think of nothing else?"

The steward bowed. "'Tis but an hour left before twilight. We expect his grace back anon."

"When he arrives, inform him that the queen has arrived."

The man bowed and hurried out, as though glad to escape. Pheresa swiftly quelled her disappointment and turned to Lady Carolie. "I shall have time to put off these travel clothes and dress myself more becomingly. Have Oola see to it. And tell her to hurry."

Lady Carolie went to do her bidding, and Pheresa's swift calculation of which of the few gowns in her clothes chest were suitable for the occasion was interrupted by Sir Talmor.

"If I have permission, I'll withdraw for a short time."

"Yes, of course," she said at once. "See to your needs, Talmor. The queen is well fixed here for the present."

He frowned, his unruly hair falling as usual over his brow. "I want to familiarize myself with the hold and these passageways, majesty. It won't take me long."

The door closed in his wake, and she stared after him with a little frown. All the way to Thirst, he had been a little stiffer than usual in his manner, distant, his thoughts seemingly far away. Yet, if anything, he was more efficient than ever. But although she could not fault his service, he was not himself. No doubt he was tired. She reminded herself to add another protector to her service. Perhaps Faldain had a knight he would be willing to spare for such duty.

Her smile returned, and she set about making good use of the hot water provided for her.

Eventually she put on a gown of dark green velvet, chosen because it was Thirst's colors, but sadly creased despite Oola's efforts to improve its appearance. Fuming, her slippered foot tapping while the countess gravely fastened an emerald necklace around her throat and Carolie hung matching earrings in her ears, Pheresa felt she had never looked more dowdy. Her hair was coiled about her head stylishly enough, but there were no jeweled pins to fasten up her golden tresses, jewels that would flash fire with every turn of her head. She had pearls for her hair, but they did not go with her gown. There was no scarf of fine silk gauze to drape over the back of her hair in soft, artful folds. Her slippers were pretty, beaded things, but they did not match her gown, and they pinched her swollen feet. Her fingers had grown so plump she could no longer wear her rings.

She told herself that Faldain would be appalled when he saw her, this fat, ungainly creature in a creased dress and inadequate jewels. She wanted to charm him, delight him, and render him sorry he'd ever rejected her, but that wasn't going to happen tonight.

She frowned in distress, then suddenly laughed at her foolishness. 'Twas not his heart she needed to captivate now; 'twas his cooperation and a quick agreement to give her his army.

For she had decided on the perfect way to avoid creating civil war in her realm. If she moved against Lervan with a Netheran army, she would not be asking Mandrian to fight Mandrian. It was a simple, and therefore perfect, solution.

A knock on the door made her whirl around with her heart thudding too fast. It was not Faldain who entered, however, but a slender man with a light brown beard and smiling hazel eyes. She recognized him at once with pleasure, but could not recall his name.

"Sir Thum du Maltie, majesty, at your service," he said with a flourishing bow.

She smiled at him, pleased to see the courtier manner here

in this backward place. "Sir Thum, yes, of course. How good to see you again. You look well. 'Twould seem that Nether agrees with you."

"Aye, your grace. But 'tis good to stand on Mandrian soil tonight."

She pretended to misunderstand him. "I thought Thirst belonged to Nether now."

"Well—"

She laughed, relenting. "Forgive my pranks, good sir. I know what you meant. Have you had any chance to visit your family?"

"Not yet." His thin face, freckled and rather serious, lightened briefly in a smile. "We but arrived four days ago. There is always much to be seen to when his grace comes back to Thirst."

"You must make Faldain relent and give you leave to visit your people."

Sir Thum inclined his head. "May I escort your majesty to the Hall? A feast has been prepared in your honor, and I am bidden to see to your entertainment until his grace can join us."

She nodded graciously, and put her fingertips on the back of his hand as he led her out. Sir Talmor fell into step behind them, and Sir Thum's protector followed him. They went downstairs at a slow, dignified pace. As they descended, a quartet of hounds came bounding up to meet them, uttering excited little barks, and were quickly shooed away by an energetic page in a plumed cap.

Music was playing in the distance, and Pheresa heard the hubbub of many voices talking at once. The doors to the Hall opened before her, and she was struck by a rush of light from blazing torches and a terrible racket that fell silent abruptly as the knights assembled within caught sight of her.

She realized that Faldain kept the old ways here, in this old-fashioned hold, for lord and knights ate together in common, with even a long trestle table set up at the rear of the Hall for the servants. There were rushes strewn on the floor in here, clearly the most ancient part of the keep. Pikes, swords, and archaic shields adorned the walls, and proud banners hung from the massive rafters above.

The knights parted to make way for her, and every man present went down on bended knee in her honor as she walked the length of the Hall to the head table.

There, she was seated in the place of honor, to the right of a tall, beautifully carved chair. Sir Talmor stood behind her, watchful and wary among so many strangers. The Hall was cold, and a whistling draft seemed to be pouring right down the back of her neck. She kept herself from shivering by an act of sheer will.

Although this place was crude, the faces staring at her were loyal ones, weathered and pocked and scarred from old battles. These were experienced fighters, warriors to the last man, not puffed-up, primping court daisies. She gazed out at them, warmed by their simple allegiance, and gave them a smile.

Their faces lit up, and they cheered her loud and lustily. Then a staff was rapped on the stone floor, and new quiet fell over the company. A name was announced, but Pheresa's ears were buzzing, and she heard nothing. She clenched her hands together hard in her lap and stared at the man striding up the length of the Hall toward her.

Yes, it was the same easy stride. Those were the same powerful shoulders. He still stood head and shoulders above most men, his black hair flowing to his shoulders, and held back from his rugged, manly face by a narrow circlet of gold. His pale gray eyes flashed to hers, and she felt a rush of emotion she could not name.

"Dain!" she cried out in gladness, and behind her Sir Talmor stiffened.

Faldain came up beside her, clad in blue and gold, his garments made of rich fabric but plain of adornment as had always been his custom. His long, tapering fingers wore but an ornate seal ring and a plain iron ring of marriage.

The sight of the latter sent a pang through her, and she tempered herself swiftly, bringing her feelings back under control. Clutching her Circle with a swift mental prayer for forgiveness, she forced herself to hope that he was as happily married as she was ill matched.

Smiling, she held out her hand to him. "Faldain," she said warmly, "how well and stalwart you look. The years have treated you kindly."

He bowed over her hand, his own warm and rough with calluses. "Aye, 'tis good to see a friend, even if that friend comes in need."

Her fingers tightened on his. "The need is great. I—"

"Ah," he said, his gaze moving past her. "The feast is being brought in. Let us dine!"

With the order, he seated himself and banged his cup lustily on the table. The knights sat down on the benches and began banging their cups in unison, filling the air with such a racket Pheresa thought her skull would crack. She sat there, astonished and disapproving, while a line of servants carried in platter after platter of venison, roast, and pig. There were huge bowls of taties and carrots and turnips and knobby root-like vegetables called poldacs. There were apples baked to a deep red hue and sprinkled with sugar and spices. There were ale and mead and cider. There were pastries filled with savory meats, pastries filled with cream, and pastries filled with fruits and spicy sauces.

It was all plain food, served on platters and huge wooden bowls, most of it still hot from the kitchens, and surprisingly good. Long bored by the artistic creations of her palace chefs, in which every night her supper was teased into the shape of some mythical creature, complete with dyed feathers and jewels for eyes, Pheresa found that she liked plain, hearty fare. Here at Thirst, pork looked like pork, and venison looked like venison. The baby kicked as though it approved as well, and she ate until she hurt; but it was a good ache, and she did not regret it.

After the food, toasts were given, with each man trying to outdo the next. The music was simple and old-fashioned, piping and fluting in merry jigs. She watched the dancing, but soon grew bored by the entertainment. There were few ladies present, and they all looked too awestruck by her to offer her any conversation. She knew they were eyeing her clothing with avid gazes, and more than ever her appearance displeased her, but Faldain seemed not to have noticed.

When she caught his eye, he leaned toward her with a polite smile, and she said with great seriousness, "We must talk. I have little time."

"Aye, I know it," he replied softly beneath the swirl of the music. "But tonight 'tis neither the place nor time. In the morning, my lady, you shall have all my attention."

Annoyance pricked her. She realized that she was wasting her time tonight.

Yawning behind her hand, she rose to her feet. "Your majesty, I shall retire," she announced.

Faldain stood up swiftly, and the music came to an abrupt halt. He bowed to her. "Rest well. Sir Thum will see you safely to your door."

She gave him a perfunctory curtsy, displeased with how smoothly she'd been given a dismissal, and walked away with her head held very high. Her attendants hurried to her, but graciously she allowed Lady Carolie to remain behind and went out with only the old countess at her heels. Sir Thum walked beside her, saying little as he escorted her back upstairs.

At her door, while Talmor opened it and walked inside first to check the premises, she sent Sir Thum a look of appeal. "I must speak to him in private. My concerns are most urgent. Will he listen?"

"Aye, your grace," Sir Thum said quietly. "He will. I'll come for you in the morning. Good night."

With a bow, he was gone. Pheresa's frown deepened. Pleasant courtesy aside, she had the impression that Faldain was not eager to offer her the aid she sought. As she walked slowly into her chamber, she felt unsettled by thoughts of his cool reception and failure to give her his complete attention. Another matter occupied his thoughts, she believed, and she did not like being forced to wait her turn.

Was not the throne of Mandria of the greatest importance? She sighed, forcing herself to consider the matter from a per-

spective other than her own. Perhaps Faldain did not care all
that much what became of her.

"No," she muttered aloud. "I cannot believe it!"

"Majesty?" Talmor asked.

With a glare at her protector, she turned away, holding out
her arms so that the countess could begin undressing her. Talmor exited without a word, and when she was in her bedgown
and safely shuttered in the queer, creaky old bed, she lay shivering beneath the fur blankets, and felt afraid.

In the morning, she found Faldain's study a small room with
inadequate windows that let in both sunshine and a great deal
of cold air. Faldain faced her across a desk littered with parch-
ments, scrolls, old musty ledgers, and assorted maps. His dogs
sprawled next to the hearth, snoring. Outside, she could hear
an altercation in the stableyard, and somewhere a pig was
squealing.

In silence they stared at each other. This morning Faldain
was dressed in a tunic of soft gray, with leather leggings and
riding boots already splashed with mud. She knew, by the
scent of wind and horse on him, that he'd been out early. His
pale eyes were keen and alert as they met hers.

"Now, Pheresa," he said without preamble, dispensing
with all formalities, "I've received a spate of letters from you
this past month, all urgent. Your situation is dire, I agree, and
growing worse, according to the reports I receive. What is it
you want from me?"

"Your army."

He blinked at that, and stubbornness entered his face. "I
think not."

"Dain, I am in desperate trouble. My throne is in jeopardy—"

"Your throne, my lady, is gone. This husband of yours—"

"He is a scoundrel, a betrayer!" she said angrily, pacing
back and forth. "Lervan commits treason. His claim lacks any
legality—"

"He possesses the throne. That's claim enough."

She whirled around with a glare. "What mean you by that? I will not accept Lervan's usurpation."

"You may have to."

She could not believe what Faldain was saying. She'd expected sympathy and an instant offer of help, not this cool appraisal in his eyes.

"Where, Pheresa, is *your* army?" he asked, resting his hand lightly on his sword hilt.

She stared at the weapon, suspecting it was magically endowed. There was something slightly different about Faldain this morning, as though wearing the sword made him carry himself more erect, more kingly. With his hair braided back warrior-style today, he looked remote and foreign, especially with his prominent cheekbones and slightly pointed ears. He had changed much since she last saw him. No longer was he a raw boy, fresh from his first hard-won battles. This was a man who stood before her, a king in obvious command of himself and his realm. All these years, she'd pitied him a little, imagining him struggling to hold his impoverished, much-troubled kingdom together. Yet this morning he looked calm and at his ease, while she—monarch of a prosperous kingdom—stood here as a supplicant in terrible trouble.

"Will you not answer?" he asked, jolting her from her thoughts. "Where is your army? Why have you no supporters?"

"I do!" she said defensively. "That is, I would if I could get word to them. But—"

He cocked his head to one side. "Where is your army?"

"Fending off Klad raids and seafaring barbarians!"

"And why did you fail to keep a standing army close to Savroix for its defense?"

She angrily averted her gaze from his, yet there was no point in lying or evading his questions.

"Because I thought no harm could come to Savroix," she said, her voice hard and brittle. "Because the border holds needed additional men."

"Was this your idea, or the advice of your ministers?"

"My protector thinks it the work of a plot."

Faldain's brows shot up. "He is a man of intelligence."

"Of course he is," she said impatiently. "Faldain, I—"

"In my experience, when a throne is at stake, enemies can be very patient indeed," he said. "They lie in wait for years, sometimes a generation, before they strike. And sometimes their reach is long."

"What does that matter?" she asked impatiently. "A solution must be found, and quickly. I must get my throne back before Lervan's foolish claim is made a reality."

"Then summon your army to you. Call up your church soldiers," Faldain said, rearranging the maps on his desk. "You have vast resources at your disposal. Why not avail yourself of them?"

"Are you saying you will not help me?"

"You have an army, Pheresa. You do not need mine."

"But my army is not with me."

"Then claim it. Go to it. Make your appeal directly to the men."

She stared at him in bewilderment. He made it sound simple, and she knew it was not. A rush of emotion nearly overwhelmed her. "I—I—you do not understand the situation."

"Explain it."

"The church has opposed me since the miracle when I was healed by the Chalice. I cannot depend on church knights for aid."

"This is serious indeed."

"Of course it is! I would not have come to you for help had I not been desperate. I—I think my father also supports Lervan. I cannot be sure, but I sometimes suspect it."

"Is he still a marechal?" Faldain asked in surprise. "I thought him too old."

"He has not been replaced. Of course, he spends most of his time at court instead of in the field. The other marechals are stationed across the realm. I"—she looked down in sudden shame—"I have not met them."

"Forgive me, my lady, but this is slack work indeed."

Her head snapped up. "I have not been queen long, sir! There has not been time."

"Not time to secure the absolute loyalty of your primary generals?" he asked without masking his scorn. "I wonder at your priorities."

"Mandria is not like Nether," she said defensively. "We are secure, peaceful, not constantly at war with all sorts of dangers. Except of late. I expected to meet these men on the day of my coronation."

"It looks doubtful that you'll see a crowning."

Tears stung her eyes, and she turned away. "I thought you to be my friend," she said, hurt and angry. "You, who have had no easy time with your own reign, can surely understand my plight."

"I do understand it," he replied, his tone softer now. "What I do *not* understand is how you come to be in such a mess. Your own husband, Pheresa. What sort of cur did you marry?"

"If a man lies and charms all who meet him—if a man professes to esteem, even to love the one bound to him in the sight of Thod . . . if a man swears his allegiance, yet has no honor, no truth, no loyalty in him . . . how can a person suspect until it is too late?"

Tears broke from her despite her efforts to hold them back. She pressed her hands to her face, and Faldain was suddenly before her, his hands gripping her shoulders.

"Ah, Pheresa, my dear friend," he said softly. "Do not weep. I hate to see your tears."

She clung to his chest for comfort, grateful that at last she could let her emotions out. "I need you. I need your help," she said, her voice muffled against his chest. "You are the only one I can trust. You can drive him out, send him running, and get back my throne."

Gently, Faldain pushed her back from him.

She stared at him woefully. "You are the only one who can save my realm from disaster."

"Nay."

"But you can! You're the best warrior in all the—"

"I'll not invade Mandria with my army," he said harshly, and turned away from her.

"But, Dain—"

"We have a treaty. I'll not violate it."

"The treaty binds our realms together in friendship. If one is threatened, is not the other obliged to help?"

"Aye, against a common foe. But not this."

"Lervan is my foe. I want him punished for what he has done. He opened Savroix to the barbarians. He let them pillage it and gave them all that they wanted. He has shamed Mandria, and shown the world that we can be cheated and humiliated by anyone bold enough to dare."

Faldain frowned. "And to punish this man who has wronged you, you would summon a foreign army across your borders."

"Aye, I would! I will bring war to Lervan. I will teach him to dare reach for my crown. I will make him pay for what he has done!"

"And what will Mandria pay?"

She stared at him, her fury slowly ebbing. "I don't understand."

"What will Mandria have to pay? What glory is there in having a foreign army—a Netheran army—bring Mandria to heel?"

"Not Mandria," she corrected him swiftly. "Lervan."

"Can the two be separated?"

Her anger surged over her like a tide, swift and hot. "*I* am Mandria!"

"Pheresa, put aside your emotions and think like a queen."

"How dare you! I—"

"Hear me! You're angry at this husband of yours, and with good reason. He's caused you no end of trouble, and he's a craven rascal besides. Paying off invaders does no good, for they'll come back for more."

"I know," she cried. "I think him a fool."

"But you must deal with him, not I."

"And so I shall, once you've driven him from Savroix."

"You must drive him out. I cannot do it for you."

"But you are my only hope."

He stared at her and slowly shook his head.

Bitterness filled her mouth. She could not believe him so unsympathetic, so selfish, as to refuse her.

"Don't you see?" he asked. "If you would be queen, then face the man down. Drive him out. Rally your lords and knights to your cause, for without them you have nothing."

She stood there, feeling cold and alone as she faced the harshness of what had to be done. "Then I have no choice but to call for the support of my upland lords and lead them southward."

"Are you mad?"

Her eyes flashed to his. "I have no choice. You have said it."

"I said rally your—"

"Are the uplanders not my men?"

"If you pit upper and lower Mandria against each other, you will start civil war. Lervan's actions—no matter how foul—do not warrant such retaliation."

"Do not defend him!" she said, so angry she did not care what she said. "You think him better suited to rule than I. Why? Because he's a man, and you are a man?"

"You twist my words. You deliberately misunderstand me," Faldain said coldly. "That's a dangerous road."

" 'Tis easy to stand here, far north from the trouble that besets me, and make your judgments. I thought you my friend, not a coward."

Faldain stiffened, and fire now glittered in the depths of his pale gray eyes. "I have given you sound advice," he said after a moment of silence. "If you will not heed it, 'tis your choice."

"What good is advice if you will not back up your words with action? I need troops, sir, not speeches."

"Then return to Vurdal and call forth your troops. Summon them, hold by hold, and make them crown you there. Be bold, Pheresa, and assert your rights as sovereign. If you stand aside in modest, womanly fashion, remaining quiet, looking pretty, and acting helpless, by Thod, you will soon find yourself without any supporters at all."

She stared at him, her pulse throbbing in her throat, and

hated him for what he said to her. "If I retreat to Vurdal, then all is lost. They have orders to take me prisoner and conduct me to trial for abdicating my throne."

"Then find another garrison and make your stand," he said in exasperation.

"I shall do it here," she said, then gave him an inquiring nod. "With your permission."

"You'll not suck Thirst into your troubles," he said fiercely.

"Thirst is a Mandrian hold!"

"Thirst belongs to me, and while I rule it, it will remain neutral."

"Thod rot your bones!" she cried, her patience at an end. "Will you turn me out now and leave me wandering without shelter?"

"Don't be a fool. You may shelter at Thirst as long as it pleases you. With the deep cold coming on, you will not be able to travel, and when your child is born you will need a place of safety."

She bowed her head in thanks, hating the need of his hospitality.

"That much I can do, and gladly," Faldain said, "but I will give you no men. Nor will you ask Sir Bosquecel for any Thirst knights after I depart."

A little stunned, she said, "You're leaving? But when?"

"This afternoon. My business here is finished, and I cannot be gone from Grov for long."

"What is your haste? I have hardly seen you."

Faldain looked at her sternly. "Surely we have discussed this matter enough. Lingering will not change my mind, and you, no doubt, have more important matters at hand than old reminiscences."

She felt a tide of heat spread from her throat to the roots of her hair. "In the past, you were kinder to me."

His eyes softened momentarily. "Forgive me. My tongue has grown rough and blunt. It never did have much polish to it."

"Aye, I remember well. But even without courtly manners,

you were kind then. I knew I could rely on you for anything I required."

" 'Tis a kindness I offer you now," he said with a frown. "Perhaps in time you will come to recognize it."

"Do you not remember when you had nothing, Dain?" she asked in desperation. "When you ached to claim your rightful throne, but you had no supporters, no army of your own? People laughed at you, and you were sore tried. I thought you would remember, and have sympathy for me now that my plight is similar to yours."

He turned away, his keen eyes gazing out the window. "Aye, my lady. I remember well," he said quietly. "I had to find my own way and prove myself worthy of my throne before any would serve me. So must you find your path."

"I know what to do. I just need your help."

He shook his head. "Pray for guidance, Pheresa. Put aside your anger and listen to what is right."

"But—"

"I'll not invade Mandria. I'll not break our treaty and the good faith that lies between our realms with such an invasion, not even at your bidding. That is not the solution for your troubles."

She stamped her foot in frustration and felt the baby kick inside her. "And where, pray, am I to find this solution? Where am I to turn?"

"I cannot say. Trust to what is right, and keep your honor."

"Why not advise me to retreat to a nuncery and devote myself to a life of prayer?" she asked scornfully.

"I'm sorry," he said. "I wish you well, but I am not the answer you seek. Were it help in driving out these Vvordsmen now, then I—"

"Thank you," she said woodenly.

That was that. She went back to her rooms in a daze, feeling bewildered, furious, and betrayed yet again. It had never occurred to her that he would not help her.

Sir Talmor, his tanned face grave, walked behind her, and when she reached her room he opened the door and hesitated, blocking her entry.

"I—I am sorry, majesty," he said in quiet sympathy. "I know you were counting on his support."

He should not have spoken to her that way, and for Sir Talmor it was a most unexpected breach of protocol. She stared at him, but was not angered—not even offended—by his pity. Instead, all she felt was deep sadness.

"I am not beaten," she said in a low, determined voice. "I will not accept defeat."

"Whatever you choose to do, I remain your man," he said.

His loyalty quickened her heart, and she tried to give him a smile of thanks. "I know it. I rely on you."

He stood taller. "What, then, is to be done?"

"I shall summon all the upland lords to me. They are plain men of good sense. I know they will not support Lervan when mine is the legitimate claim. They are my one remaining hope."

"I'll see to it at once, majesty."

She busied herself writing letters to each chevard, and by the time she was finished and ready to dispatch them, noise from the stableyard made her look outside. She was in time to glimpse Faldain striding forth to his charger. He mounted his steed with graceful economy of motion, flinging his cloak out of the way as he settled himself into the saddle. At the head of his armed escort, flags flying, he galloped away, while his people cheered and waved farewell.

As she watched, she felt a bitter lump in her throat and implacable purpose in her heart. He was a friend no longer, and she had discovered today the true worth of the treaty between their lands. He had not even troubled to bid her good-bye. She wondered why he had bothered to meet with her at all.

But no matter what he said, she was not beaten yet. She would not yield her crown without a fight. She would find an army, and she would somehow bring battle to Lervan the coward.

That she swore on all she held sacred.

Chapter Twenty-two

Dawn . . . gray and cold. Her heart . . . bleak and cold.

Three days after her ill-fated meeting with the chevards of upper Mandria, Pheresa walked across the deserted courtyard of Thirst Hold with Sir Talmor a quiet shadow at her heels. Wrapped in a heavy cloak, with her hood pulled up, she shivered in the icy air and wondered why she had ever come to this dreadful place. She remembered the cold all too well from the time when she was a prisoner in Nether. She remembered how, when she returned to Savroix, she'd sworn she would never look at snow again. Yet here she walked in this cold, friendless place. Why in Thod's sacred name had she ever sought help up here?

She paused at the entry to the chapel, saying nothing, while Sir Talmor pushed open the door for her. He went inside first, and she followed impatiently, giving him no time to tell her the way was safe.

The interior of the chapel glowed with votives, and she smelled incense. As plain and primitive as the rest of the hold, the chapel had little to recommend it. Crude religious murals were painted on its walls. The altar was modest at best, featuring a brass Circle instead of gold. The pews were only rudimentary benches built from wooden planks. Damp and cold, this small place of worship did not feel welcoming; but as she could find no comfort in her sore and angry heart, it was time to seek solace in prayer.

She caught Sir Talmor looking at her with concern. The memory of last night flashed through her mind, and she frowned.

She'd dined in her room, too heartsick to eat in the communal Hall and unwilling to face Sir Bosquecel after he had asked her, albeit courteously, if she planned to winter at Thirst. He said he needed to know so that additional supplies for her comfort could be laid in before the deep cold. What he so obviously meant was, *When will you go?* Mortified, she had as yet given the man no answer, but there it was, another problem that must be dealt with soon.

And after she finished toying with her food last night, pushing bits of it about, unable to swallow more than a few morsels, Sir Talmor had knelt before her and offered to take her to Saelutia.

" 'Tis warm there, always, on the isles," he said, his honey-colored eyes searching hers. "The breeze blows soft, and in the afternoons rain showers clear the air, so that the evenings are cool and fragrant with the perfume of flowers."

She sat rigidly in her chair, her heart drumming inside her, unable to look away from his eyes. His voice, calm, deep, and quiet, mesmerized her.

"The people are not fractious," he went on. "They are gentle folk, quiet and restful. Their ways would seem queer to your majesty at first, but it would be a haven—"

"Do you miss your mother's people so much?" she broke in, unable to bear the temptation. "Are you so unhappy in Mandria?"

"Nay, majesty. I know little of the islands, save that they are very beautiful. I have only visited them once, as a boy."

"But you would like to live there." She frowned, feeling an

unexpected sense of loss. "Do you wish me to release you from service?"

"Nay!" He jumped to his feet in affront. "I seek no release. Thod's bones! Does your majesty think I am so poor spirited as to quit when all stand against you?"

She stared at her hands, which were clenched in her lap. She knew what he meant; alas, nay, she did not. She knew nothing anymore, for nothing was as it had been. Nothing could be relied on. Lies lay in everything.

The silence drew out too long until the air between them became awkward and wrong. She would not look at him. She feared that she would weaken and agree to the temptation he offered. How easy it would be to surrender her troubles and let Sir Talmor take her to a sweet and gentle exile. How easy to let everything fall from her hands and struggle no more.

He retreated from her, standing at attention with his hands clasped at his back. The fire on the hearth burned behind him, so that his face lay in shadow. "Your majesty has misunderstood," he said stiffly.

"Have I?" she countered. "The upland lords will not serve me. They have called me an uncrowned queen, and they will not pledge their swords in my cause. They say they will seek Edonian independence rather than fight to hold this realm together. And you offer me exile, sir. I am to leave my realm and my people to fend for themselves. I am to throw it all away, choosing a dignified exit, rather than see even the pittance of power still remaining in my hands wrested from me entirely." She looked up at him. "Have I misunderstood, sir?"

He was angry. She saw the blaze of it in his eyes, in the quick flare of his nostrils, but his extraordinary self-control held firm.

"I beg the queen's pardon," he said with a bow, and retreated.

At that moment she hated him for not daring to quarrel. Her pent-up emotions needed a fight. She wanted to scratch and yell and throw things. She wanted to release all that churned inside her, but Talmor never let the barrier down between them. He never forgot she was queen. He would not argue with her, equal to equal, and she was left alone with nothing save her bitter dignity.

Now, this morning in the chapel, with dawn's light falling gray and dim through the ocular window overhead, she met his golden eyes briefly before shifting her gaze away. She remained angry with him; it was easier to be angry than to face the truth.

His bronzed face showed no expression at all beneath his unruly curls. His mouth remained clamped in a tight line.

"You have the queen's permission to withdraw," she said. "I wish privacy in my prayers."

Bowing, he retreated to the door, standing where he could stop anyone who tried to enter.

"Nay," she said sharply. "Withdraw, sir. I have no need of you here."

He looked at once alarmed. "Majesty, I do not advise—"

"The queen has not asked for your advice. Leave, sir!"

"Majesty—"

"What will harm me here in Thod's house?" she demanded, tired of his constant presence, tired of never having true privacy. There had been a time when his devotion, his admiration, had supported her. Now, they created a burden she could no longer endure. She wanted to be alone; here in Thod's eyes she wanted to be weak. Not a queen, deposed and lacking allies, but a woman in trouble. "See to your breakfast, sir, and return in an hour."

Although disapproval furrowed his brow, he made no more protest. "As your majesty commands," he said, and left her.

She sighed, turning toward the altar just as the priest, no doubt having been roused by their voices, pattered in. He was a short, nearsighted creature, his tonsure in need of a shave, his robes crumpled as though he'd slept in them. She accepted communion before sending him away.

Prayers would not come. She frowned, closing her eyes to force them, but her heart remained too angry, too knotted with resentment and bitterness to be soothed. Even the ritual of communion had eased her only momentarily. She felt as though the Circle of Thod's love had broken to bits around her.

"Lead your army," Faldain had said. *"Make them follow you."*

It seemed she did not know how. She had spoken rousingly to the chevards who obeyed her summons. She had greeted these gruff, hard-faced men with their mud-splattered leggings and serviceable swords and thought to stir their blood by speaking of injustice. She had urged them to join her cause in regaining her throne.

But there had come no cheers. Their suspicious faces had not lit with enthusiasm or support. Their eyes measured her when she spoke of Lervan's betrayal, and she knew they felt contempt for a woman both gullible and trusting, a woman who had been given a throne and lost it.

"Merciful Thod," she prayed aloud now, lifting her gaze to the Circle hanging above the altar. "Why have I failed? What must I do? What must I become, to win these nobles' hearts?"

No answer came to her restless, unhappy mind. All she knew was that two choices lay before her. She could go into exile, living forever on someone's mercy, or she could find another way to force Lervan off the throne. But what? She'd tried every avenue she could think of, and nothing had worked. Was she to acknowledge herself beaten? Was she to give up?

Her clasped hands dropped and she frowned. No, she thought angrily, she was not ready to quit. Verence had entrusted her with his realm. He had put the kingdom in her hands, not Lervan's. She must find a way.

But the answers she sought were not going to come to her in this chapel. Restlessly, she climbed to her feet and caught the priest peering at her from the shadows.

Realizing he must have been spying on her during her prayers, she frowned and suddenly wanted to escape, to get away from the constant stares and prying eyes. Since she'd become queen, she'd never been entirely alone. This was her chance to get away.

Exiting the chapel, she crossed the courtyard, clutching her cloak hood about her face to keep it hidden. Servants were stirring now. The gate leading out to the stableyard had been opened, and sentries were calling out to each other as they changed shifts. The air smelled like snow, and pewter-gray clouds hung low overhead. It looked like poor weather for riding, but she knew of no haven in the hold where she would not be sought and found by someone anxious about her welfare.

Reaching the stables, she ordered her courser saddled.

"Am I to saddle yer protector's horse while ye wait, yer grace?"

"No. I wish to mount my horse at once. Will you assist me?"

"Aye."

With a saucy grin, the stableboy lifted her into the sidesaddle. Hampered by her large belly, Pheresa crooked her right leg in place across the pommel while the boy fitted her left foot into the single stirrup.

"Will yer grace be wantin' someone to lead the mare at a nice, quiet pace?"

Pheresa gathered up the reins in her gloved hands. "No, I ride alone this morning."

" 'Tain't safe to go out alone past the fields—"

"Thank you for your warning. Stand away."

She wheeled the mare away from him, knowing she was being foolish and not caring. She rode through the stableyard and across the bailey. It was full now of peasants coming in from the village to bake their bread in the hold ovens. The smithy had opened up, the hot fire of his forge blazing away. A flock of geese waddled across her path, honking, as a little girl herded them with a stick. Shoats squealed, as a pair of boys carried them hastily around a corner of one of the barns, and from the kennels the dogs were barking for their breakfast.

She rode out beneath the portcullis, jostled on all sides by a group of pilgrims who were leaving after having spent the night safe inside the walls.

A sentry shot her a startled look, and someone called after her, but Pheresa pretended not to hear. Trotting clear of the pilgrims, who had begun to sing in ragged harmony as they headed for the road, she kicked her frisky little mare to a canter and headed toward the marshland. Little flakes of snow stung her eyes. All she could see ahead of her was open land and blessed solitude. And if bandits accosted her, or Nonkind monsters leaped at her, what of it? She'd become nothing to this world, to this kingdom she had once considered her own. Tears welled up hot and blurry in her eyes, and she hated herself for feeling self-pity. She must escape such a worthless emotion, push past the anger, confusion, and self-doubt. She was tired of living in a muddle, of trying to cope with one crisis after another without any chance of succeeding. The air whipped back her cloak from her shoulders, and her hood slipped down. Suddenly, she found the cold bracing, even exciting. In this bleak landscape she felt stripped clean of wealth and trappings and honeyed lies and intrigue. There was honesty here, brutal, yes; but the simplicity of this remote countryside appealed to her. She knew a fresh surge of determination. She would find a way. Somewhere, out among the marshes and the forest, there had to be an answer that she could find.

Or she would not come back.

Talmor stared at the priest. "Gone?" he repeated in alarm. "What mean you?"

"The queen left not a quarter hour after you took your leave," the priest told him. "I gave her grace communion and thought she meant to—"

"Where did she go?"

The priest looked bemused, and with an impatient mutter Talmor strode out of the chapel. He knew he should not have left her, no matter what she ordered. It was his duty to stay near. Now she could be anywhere in the hold. He hoped she had decided to return to her chambers for breakfast.

She had not.

Lady Carolie and the countess exchanged alarmed looks, setting up a clamor of questions that he retreated from swiftly.

Outside in the passageway, he grabbed the shoulder of the first page he came to and sent the boy running to fetch his squire. By the time Pears caught up with him, an oily rag still in his hand, Talmor had checked the Hall, the kitchens, the solar room, the study, and the upper storerooms. No one had seen her.

"Sir?" Pears asked, puffing as he caught up with Talmor. "The boy said ye wanted me right away, but a damned fine time I've had in finding ye."

"Where's Lutel?"

Pears frowned, folding his rag in on itself to protect its oily center and hitching up his belt. "Well, then, if it's him ye wanted why didn't ye—"

"Tell him to check the stables, quick and quiet," Talmor ordered. Worry jabbed him so he could hardly speak. *Where could she have gone?* He met Pears's eyes. "The queen is missing."

The squire's annoyance fell away. "Morde a day! What infamy is this?"

"Nothing but her own low spirits," Talmor said, drawing a swift Circle. "At least I pray so. I must find her, but let no alarm be raised as yet."

Pears raced away to do as he was bid. A moment later, however, he came back with Sir Bosquecel at his heels.

The tall, gray-haired commander nearly always wore a serious expression, but this morning he looked grave indeed. "Good morn, sir!" he said. "The gatehouse reports that a lady rode out of the hold an hour past without authorization. We fear the queen—"

Talmor swore. It was as he had suspected. She'd planned that sojourn in the chapel simply to rid herself of his company so that she could strike out alone to Thod knows where. Glaring at the commander, he demanded, "Why didn't you report this sooner? Why the delay?"

"I was just informed," Sir Bosquecel said. " 'Tis baking day, and most of the village is coming in and out—"

"Thod smite your baking day," Talmor told him, and headed downstairs.

Sir Bosquecel followed on his heels. "Forgive me. The sentry says he thought at first it was the queen, but she had no escort and no protector, so he assumed she was one of the ladies in waiting sent to fetch the village midwife."

Talmor paused halfway down the steps and scowled over his shoulder. "Sentries have no business thinking. No lady of the bedchamber would ride out herself."

"Aye, that I know. I'll see the man is properly reprimanded when he comes off duty."

Talmor hurried on, uncaring how Bosquecel disciplined his men. The guards at the gate never should have let Pheresa get past them. His worry grew, almost strangling him, and he quickened his pace as he made for the stables.

He found Pears ahead of him, with Lutel busy saddling Canae. Drawing on his gloves and taking cursory note of the snow now falling, Talmor cursed again beneath his breath and glared at Sir Bosquecel. "Was any notice taken of which direction she went?"

"We'll ask at the gate," Sir Bosquecel said grimly, and turned to issue orders.

In minutes, he and Talmor were mounted, joined by a party of Thirst knights and the huntsman, an individual who wore a soft green cap and carried a horn slung across his shoulder.

"Fear not," Sir Bosquecel said quickly, as Talmor frowned at the huntsman. "He's got a nose like a hound. He can track anything."

"Her trail'll be fresh, sir," the huntsman said.

Talmor took no assurance from what they said. He spurred Canae across the bailey, the cold wind cutting through him like blades of ice. Snow was falling rapidly now, beginning to whiten the ground. It would obliterate her tracks in minutes, he knew, and felt his heart lurch.

They paused at the gates to question the guards, who had little to add. Talmor opened his mouth to blister the sentry, then found his eye caught by Sir Bosquecel and held his tongue. With an effort he reminded himself that these men owed their primary allegiance to King Faldain, not Pheresa. Minding her was his responsibility, not theirs. He told himself to be grateful they'd noticed her departure at all, especially since they didn't actually recognize her.

That thought stirred pity inside him. That the queen should be brought so low as to be abandoned by all who should have leaped to serve her, to pass unrecognized in a crowd of peasants. Thod's bones, but that dogsbody of a husband had much to answer for, and one day Talmor intended to see that he did. But right now, with her babe growing large in her and drawing down her strength, she needed friends and comfort around her now, not betrayal and calamity.

"Here's her tracks, sir!" the huntsman called out.

Talmor trotted over to join the man, who was eyeing the trampled ground expertly.

"See the track, sir? A dainty hoof and well shod."

Talmor saw the tracks, and gave thanks that despite the snow the ground was not yet frozen. She had headed for the marshes, and the river. A dreadful, nameless fear swarmed up through him, but he clamped it down, refusing to give way.

"Let's hurry!" he said, and spurred Canae forward.

They followed her trail until it ended in marshy ground. Splashing Canae impatiently through the reeds and water, Talmor let the huntsman search for the broken trail while he stood tall in his stirrups and squinted at the horizon. The river lay ahead beyond this finger of marshland. Spurring his horse up atop a levee, he found himself on a stone-paved road leading to a bridge.

"Ho, there!" he shouted, waving at the guards on duty there. "Has a lady ridden this way?"

"No, sir," the guard replied crisply, his gaze shifting past Talmor's shoulder to Sir Bosquecel. "We've had merchants and travelers, anxious to get ahead of the snow, but no womenfolk."

"Damne," Sir Bosquecel said. "Where to now?"

Talmor began to feel more than worry, more than dread. Something ominous tingled along his spine, bringing a rushing sense of urgency and the conviction that he must find her at once. He stared past the river at the forest of Nold, telling himself that despite her depressed spirits, she would not venture there and put herself and her unborn child in such danger.

"She doubled back!" came a shout.

In relief, Talmor spun his horse around. Down the side of the levee he went, Canae snorting as he slipped and lurched, then galloped through the mud in the direction the huntsman was pointing. The man held aloft a broken reed and a snippet of velvet cloth.

Talmor grabbed it. "'Tis hers."

Back and forth they cast in the marsh, with no sight of her. Talmor kept shutting away images of her body floating in the water among the reeds, and tried to still his worried thoughts in order to catch some sense of where she might have gone.

His gaze kept returning to the forest. "Is there any other way across the river besides the bridge?"

"Aye, there's an old fording point," Sir Bosquecel said with a frown. "But why would her majesty go that way? She knows better than to venture into the Dark Forest."

"In truth, sir, I know not what she would do this day," Talmor said frankly. "After the council—"

"Aye," Sir Bosquecel said quietly, his eyes knowing. "That was a bad business."

"So's this," Talmor said, staring at the trees once more. He felt uneasy every time he looked in that direction. Hesitating, he turned his mount toward the ford, where the river ran shallow over gravel. "I mean to look on the other side."

"You'll be trespassing in clan territory," Sir Bosquecel warned him. "The dwarves don't like it, and they'll—"

A scream rose in the air, a woman's scream. Although distant, it had a piercing quality that lifted the hair on the back of Talmor's neck. He recognized it immediately as Pheresa's voice. The fear and horror in it were all too clear. When it fell silent, he felt as though a javelin had gone through his chest.

"Thod's blood!" Sir Bosquecel said. "Is that her?"

Talmor drew his sword. "To the queen!" he shouted, waving at the men. "Make haste!"

Chapter Twenty-three

Canae galloped across the ford, sending up a spray of water. Urging him up the bank, Talmor went hurtling into the trees only to slow down as he encountered dense thicket like nothing he'd ever seen before. The men with him rode fast and close, weapons ready. Talmor noticed how they watched all directions, even from above. That sent a chill through him, for he had not considered attack from the sky. These Nonkind monsters must be horrible indeed, and if one had caught Pheresa . . . he scowled and ducked beneath a branch, refusing to think about it.

The forest closed in around them, walling them off with foliage of bright crimson and gold hues. Angered at having to slow down, Talmor hacked at bushes and vines with his sword, trying to cut a way through.

"Hold, sir," Bosquecel said softly. "You can't force yourself through the forest. Look for the trails."

"We must get straight to her," Talmor said. His keen ears caught the faint sounds of shouting, and he thought he heard the clash of weaponry. In fresh alarm, he kicked Canae forward.

The horse reared, nearly entangling him in vines snaking among tree branches, and a moment later the huntsman came up beside him. "Easy, sir," he whispered, holding out his hand. "Crashing through the undergrowth will warn them sure. What hear you?"

"Fighting," Talmor said grimly. His heartbeat was like thunder in his ears. He felt heat coiling through him, and for an instant he longed to burn the forest down. Yet he knew he must master himself. Emotions clouded the mind and created errors of action or judgment that could be fatal. Struggling to distance himself from his worry, he pointed in the direction they must go. "That way."

The men of Thirst spread out in loose formation until he lost sight of many of them. They trotted through the trees, ducking low branches and finding ways around the densest undergrowth. Talmor had never been in a forest like this, so choked with saplings and thicket, so nearly impenetrable he could not see any distance. Focusing on the sounds of fighting ahead of him, growing steadily louder, he kept going grimly in Pheresa's direction.

Pears rode near his flank, muttering curses and prayers under his breath. Talmor glanced at him. "Mind you keep yourself back from the fighting, for you've no armor."

Pears cast him an unreadable look, his eyes worried. "Bless ye, sir. How many years have ye given me that same warning?" But he nodded his obedience just the same.

Another scream rang out, and the way ahead opened into a clearing. Talmor saw a band of dwarves surrounding Pheresa, and his heart leaped to his mouth. The filthy dwarves, armed with knives and javelins, were of various heights and ages, some no taller than her stirrup. With shrill cries, they swarmed her on all sides, some of them climbing up her stirrup and tugging at her long skirts as though to pull her from the saddle. Screaming and shouting back curses of her own, Pheresa slapped at their hands and clung to reins and saddle, kicking some of them away as she struggled to stay mounted. Her little mare reared up, nearly unseating her, and with a roar of fury Talmor charged forward.

"For the queen!" he shouted, waving his sword.

Canae thundered from the trees in full charge, sweeping through the outer cluster of dwarves in a single swath that trampled some to the ground and knocked others off their feet.

The men of Thirst poured into the clearing from all sides, shouting, "Thirst, Thirst, Thirst!"

Talmor's sword sliced off a dwarf's head, sending it rolling like a ball, and a moment later he reached the queen.

She was bedraggled and wet from the rain, her hair falling in her eyes. A long scratch bled on her cheek. Wild-eyed, she stared at him as though he were an apparition, and shouted something in a voice so choked with fear he didn't understand her.

He leaned over, reaching out to put an arm around her so that he could pull her onto his horse, but she fended him off.

"No, no! Don't kill them. They're—" Then her eyes flared wide, and she screamed, "Talmor! Behind you!"

Something hit him from the side, nearly knocking him from the saddle. As he reeled and fought to keep his balance, he smelled an overwhelming stench of death and decay. Twisting about in a desperate effort to bring up his sword, he found himself staring into a gaping maw filled with enormous fangs. It belonged to a creature from a nightmare—a dog; nay, a wolf; nay, larger than that with black-scaled, glistening hide instead of fur. Its red eyes glowed into his, and he felt frozen as though time itself had stopped. He had never seen anything more hideous, more terrifying, but in that instant he knew exactly what it was.

"Hurlhound," he whispered.

His body felt boneless. His fingers had gone numb, and only by the grace of Thod did he keep his grip on his sword. He was staring straight into the dripping fangs of death, or something infinitely worse, and a lesser man coming face-to-face with a Nonkind monster for the very first time might have stayed frozen until it slaughtered him. But Talmor had never lacked courage. He rallied his wits in a split second before the monster sprang at his throat. Talmor dodged. The beast's head struck him hard in the ribs without doing any true harm. With a grunt, Talmor swung his sword around and hit the beast with a one-handed blow. His blade skidded harmlessly across the hurlhound's flank. Astonished, for his sword should have broken the creature's spine, Talmor recovered swiftly and jabbed the creature's throat with his elbow, knocking it back as he struck again with greater force.

He put the strength of his body behind the sword this time and managed to cut the animal. It bled, with blood that splattered and hissed on the wet leaves underfoot. The dwarves, shouting in their incomprehensible tongue, attacked it from behind, jabbing it with their javelins until it turned on them.

Talmor spurred Canae hard, reining the horse around. The war horse reared, screaming fury, and struck the hurlhound with his forefeet. Talmor heard a snap and crunch as Canae broke the hurlhound's back. Howling, the beast fell to the ground, then snarled and snapped at the dwarves who surrounded it. While they pinned down its thrashing forequarters with their javelins, one of the dwarves thrust a slim bar of eldin silver into the creature's snarling jaws, saying words of incantation at the same time. A dreadful howl erupted from the monster as it thrashed even harder, then it exploded into bits of ash and smoke.

Astonished, Talmor saw another hurlhound lying pinned on the opposite side of the clearing. The knights of Thirst were circling a third beast, which snarled and turned to face them before they grimly hacked it to pieces.

In that moment of respite, Talmor turned anxiously to the queen. She was gasping for breath, her face bone white. She held her salt purse in her right hand, and her entire body was shaking, but he saw no wounds. A tremendous sense of relief swept through him, and he felt as though a stone had been lifted from his chest. With a swift little prayer of thanksgiving, Talmor found his voice.

"Majesty," he said. "Are you—"

"You attacked the dwarves," she said, still gasping for air.

She sagged a little, bracing herself on her mare's neck with her hands. "Not enemies. They tried to help me."

With a frown, Talmor looked over at the grubby band. The dwarves had edged away from the Thirst knights. At their feet lay the bodies of those Talmor and others had struck down. Aghast at his mistake, he shot the small, feral individuals a look of apology. "I thought they were abducting your majesty."

"I thought so, too, at first, but they were trying to get me to safety. I didn't want to get off my horse. I feel—" She broke off and clutched her belly, grimacing with pain.

Believing she might swoon, Talmor jumped down and sheathed his sword, running to her side to catch her as she began to sag from the saddle. His arms went around her, and he felt her body stiffen with pain. A different kind of fear gripped him, for he believed she was about to give birth.

"No," he whispered. "Majesty, 'tis too soon."

She opened her eyes as he carried her a short distance away from the uneasy horses and knelt with her still in his arms. Pears came running over and spread his cloak across the wet ground beneath her. Again she arched in pain, her hands gripping Talmor's hard.

"Talmor," she gasped, looking at him in panic. "You must help me."

He knew nothing of midwifery and found himself praying beneath his breath. Somehow he managed to smile reassurance at her. "Aye, majesty," he said, holding her icy hands in his. "I am here for you, as always."

"I'm afraid," she whispered. "Afraid. The hurlhounds—"

"The danger has passed. When you've rested a moment, we'll get you back to the hold."

She shook her head urgently. "No, I fear—they run in pairs. Pairs, Talmor!" Again, she choked off a cry.

Talmor held her shoulders, brushing her tangled hair back from her face. He shot Pears a glance of appeal.

His squire looked as worried as he. "If the babe's coming, there's naught we can do but let it."

"Damne, is that all you can say?" Talmor asked him. " 'Tis

too early, you fool! Can we not quieten her, ease her in some way?"

Pears shook his head. "I don't know of—"

Sir Bosquecel came running over to kneel beside Talmor. "What's amiss? Is she hurt? Did one of the Nonkind get to her?"

"Nay," Talmor replied grimly. "The babe's coming."

Sir Bosquecel turned pale. He scrambled upright, shouting to his men. In seconds, one of them was saying something to the dwarves, gesturing violently.

The tallest dwarf, clad in a ragged jerkin and wearing a cap pulled down nearly to his hostile eyes, shuffled up. Glaring at Talmor as though he expected to be attacked, he pulled out a small leather pouch and threw it on the ground, then retreated, shaking his fist.

Talmor picked up the pouch and sniffed the contents. The pungent smell of mingled herbs filled his nostrils, and he jerked back with a grimace. "What in Thod's name is this?"

The knight who spoke rudimentary dwarf came over. "They say it's hurtsickle, cowslip, and burdock, sir. Give her some in water, best if it's brewed, and that should ease her rightly."

Talmor hesitated, fearful that the dwarves intended to poison her.

The queen whimpered, clutching his hand even tighter. "Save my child, Talmor. Save my child!"

Her need of him, her fear, were almost more than he could bear. He nodded soothingly to her, determined that she, who had lost so much recently, would lose nothing else.

He handed the herb pouch to Pears. "Brew it. Quick, man!"

The squire's eyes were wide as they met Talmor's. He gulped, then nodded and ran to fetch water.

Sir Bosquecel was shaking his head grimly. "This is no place for her. Thod's mercy, how can we get her safely home?"

"I'll carry her, if necessary," Talmor said, never taking his gaze from her face.

It seemed to take an eternity for Pears to kindle a small fire. He warmed the water in a bark and sprinkled some of the herbs in it. The men watched in doubtful silence. The dwarves had retreated to the edge of the trees. When the brew was ready, Talmor took the cup from Pears's shaking hand and sipped it.

The taste was foul. It took all his willpower not to grimace. He waited a few moments, frowning, but it held no poison.

Propping her up gently in the crook of his arm, he put the cup to her lips and coaxed her to drink. She whimpered, tears running down her face, but he persevered until she sipped a little.

"Drink it all, majesty," he whispered as her head lolled against her shoulder. "Drink it for the baby."

She lifted her fearful eyes to his, then nodded and drank as obediently as a child. Her trust made him ache inside. Handing off the empty cup to Pears, Talmor longed to hold her close and murmur soft words into her blond hair. Silently he promised he would never lose his temper with her again, would never lower his vigilance again, would never let her flee into danger from a sense of despair again. He held her while she wept with pain and shuddered, and imagined a different life for them. If only she were a lady of the court instead of queen, he might have aspired to her hand. And if she'd never married Lervan, he, Talmor, would have taught her what it meant to be truly cherished by a man. He would have shared with her honest, simple love, and good friendship, and the kind of companionship that lasts a lifetime. This child would have been his, and they would not be lost refugees in these dangerous woods, but instead snug at home before a warm fire and its comforts.

The dream seemed so real in that moment as he held her. He could see it all, could hear the teasing laughter, could feel the joy of each day like sunlight warming the skin. He thought of her smiling in a garden, happy and contented. How she would blossom if only someone loved her for herself.

Her trembling eased, and the rigidity in her body slowly relaxed. Realizing he was holding her too tightly, Talmor drew back, forcing his dreams away into the black dungeon of no hope, and smiled at her.

"Better?"

She gave him a slight nod and turned pink as she grew aware of his arm around her.

"If she can stand, let's be on our way," Sir Bosquecel muttered.

At once she looked alarmed, and Talmor wanted to smite the man for frightening her anew. He wanted her to remain quietly where she was until he could be certain the birthing had been stopped, but already the queen was sitting up, awkwardly holding her stomach as she tried to regain her feet.

Helping her, Talmor made sure she was safely upright, then left Pears to steady her while he hurried over to the knight who spoke dwarf.

"Will you speak for me?" he asked the man.

"Aye?"

"Tell these men that I was wrong to slay their comrades unjustly. I ask their pardon for my mistake."

Missing his front teeth and already battered from too many battles, the young knight looked dubious. "Don't know that I can say all that."

"Try," Talmor urged him. "I owe them—the queen owes them—a great debt."

"Like as not they were trying to carry her grace off, when these Nonkind came at them," the young knight said, spitting in the bushes. "Don't get too friendly with their like."

"Just tell them what I said," Talmor ordered grimly.

The knight took a step in the dwarves' direction, held out his hands, and fumbled awkwardly through the apology.

The dwarf who seemed to be their leader, a wizened old fellow with a face like dried leather and a beard tangled with bits of twig and leaves, tugged at his jerkin and scowled. He said something curt and gruff, then he and his band melted away into the trees as though they'd never been there.

Talmor stared, but saw no glimpse of them and heard no footstep as they retreated. "What magic have they, to vanish so?" he asked.

"Little pagans," the young knight said, spitting for emphasis.

"What did their leader reply?"

"Well, sir, it weren't too complimentary." The knight grinned. "Best leave it at that."

"Sir Talmor!"

He turned at Sir Bosquecel's call and saw the queen walking unsteadily over to her horse. Swiftly rejoining her, Talmor said, "I'll mount, then the men will lift your majesty most gently up to me."

She looked at him, her mouth trembling a little. "I have caused such trouble," she whispered. "I shouldn't have ridden out alone."

"We'll talk of that later," he murmured to her, aware that she was not herself or she would never have apologized.

He jerked his head in silent command at Pears, who led Canae forward. The big horse was snorting and rolling his eyes. The other horses flung up their heads, ears flicking forward in alarm.

A baying sound from a nightmare filled the air, and with it came the awful stink of Nonkind. As Pheresa screamed, Talmor whirled around and saw the fourth hurlhound charging from the trees. It leaped on a knight and tore out his throat, then sprang after the next man, who stumbled back, slashing and cursing it.

Drawing his sword, Talmor shoved Pheresa toward her horse, but her mare squealed in fright and broke away, galloping off into the trees. The knights struggled to mount up, while their horses tried to bolt after the mare.

In the confusion, Canae reared, nearly knocking Pears off his feet, and Talmor knew he had no chance to get the queen safely mounted.

"Get back," he told her. "Stay behind me!"

A warning shout made him turn and brace his feet just as the hurlhound came his way. Gripping his sword with both hands, Talmor swung with all his might, and lopped off the creature's head. It dangled by a flap of tough hide, the jaws still snapping ferociously. Stumbling, the hurlhound hesitated, then blundered toward Talmor again.

Unable to believe it, Talmor stumbled back in horror.

Screaming something, Pheresa suddenly darted past him at the beast.

"No!" Talmor shouted.

She flung the contents of her salt purse on the hurlhound. It reared up and screamed, slinging its bloody head like something gone mad. Talmor pulled her back just in time to save her from being knocked down by the thrashing creature.

"Get back!" he shouted. "Pears, get her back!"

The hurlhound lunged crazily next at Sir Bosquecel. Mounted, the commander leaned low from his saddle and swung his sword in an effort to finish taking off the hurlhound's head, but the monster dived under his horse's belly and ripped it open.

Screaming, the horse reared and fell over, bringing Sir Bosquecel down with it before he had a chance to kick free of the stirrups and jump clear. Held pinned beneath his dying horse, Bosquecel cried out in pain, and the lurching hurlhound closed in on him.

Talmor ran at the creature from behind, knowing that he couldn't get there in time to save the commander. His sword seemed to be of no use anyway.

And suddenly, in his fear, urgency, and rage, the fire coiled within him. It filled the palms of his hands and flashed heat through his head and body. Long ago, he had sworn an oath that never again would he willingly unleash his curse on another. After that terrible day when he hurled fire at Etyne, determined to repay his older brother for taunting him; after he knelt screaming at his burned brother's side and inhaled the sickly stench of charred flesh and clothing; after he gazed into Etyne's eyes and saw their agony, Talmor swore to Thod that never again would he use this power by choice. It was too horrible a thing, something no mortal could properly control. And although Etyne had lived, the incident had cost Talmor his home . . . and his father's love. But now, he knew he had no stronger weapon than fire, no other way to save a life. Seeing the hurlhound pounce on Sir Bosquecel, Talmor broke his oath and let the fire go.

The hurlhound should have exploded in a huge puff of ash. It should have been torched, set on fire, and destroyed by the force Talmor unleashed. Instead, he saw the flames engulf the monster, blaze up with such intensity that everyone stumbled back, raising their hands to shield their faces. He saw the hurlhound crouch low as though it meant to topple over, then it jumped to its feet, restored and whole again. It absorbed the fire into itself until the flames vanished completely.

Red eyes blazing, it grew larger than before. Shaking itself like a wet dog, it threw back its head and howled an unworldly cry that sent shivers up Talmor's spine. Wondering what he had done, Talmor stared at it in horror.

The creature stared back, then came at Talmor impossibly fast, much faster than it had moved before. Realizing his attack had only strengthened it and endowed it with perhaps greater powers of destruction, Talmor swung his sword at it, determined to kill it or be killed. But it was too quick for him. Leaping above his swing, its huge paws hit his shoulders and knocked him back. Sprawling, Talmor hit the ground so hard all the air was driven from his lungs. In the impact, he dropped his sword, and with a desperate twist reached for his dagger. The hurlhound snapped at his throat, missed, and closed its jaws on his arm instead.

He felt a searing pain, so immense, so horrible, that he cried out. The creature shook him the way a dog shakes a rat, and he heard—and felt—the crunching snap of bone beneath the hurlhound's teeth. Agony poured through him, and he screamed again.

Then he slid deep into the darkness—where all was foul and terrible—and could not find his way out again.

PART III

Chapter Twenty-four

A fire was burning on the hearth while a cold winter's rain pelted the windows at Savroix. Snug in the privacy of Lady Hedrina's chambers, Lervan stretched his long legs with a sigh of contentment and held out his cup for a servant to fill with more wine. Drinking deep, he turned back to smile into Hedrina's sated blue eyes. She lay tangled in the bedclothes, one bare shoulder exposed where the sheet had slipped down. In front of the fire, a maidservant was filling a copper tub with fragrant heated water. The whole room smelled of steam, warmed wine, and Hedrina's perfume.

Sliding out of bed, Lervan wrapped himself in a velvet robe and stood drinking more wine. When Hedrina reached out to him, he clasped her hand happily.

"Come back to me, dearest," she murmured, her voice throaty with invitation. "I feel lonely."

Smiling, he leaned over to kiss her fingers. "Can't, my sweet. I've duties this afternoon."

Her full lips pouted. "Can't you dismiss your ministers for the day?"

"But we're planning my coronation," he said with a laugh, and released her hand.

She climbed out of bed, wrapping herself in a sheet, and came padding to him, all tumbled hair and dark blue eyes, her voluptuous lips parted in invitation.

He took a step back from her, refusing to let her kiss him. Annoyance flashed in her eyes, but he shook his head. "Nay, my sweet, no temper today. My coronation is of vital concern, and every detail must be right."

She frowned. "I care nothing for your majesty's coronation, since I cannot attend."

"Now, now, you must be patient. Are you not installed in the palace at last? Does that not make you happy?"

She lifted her gaze to his. "But I long to be with you at public functions, not hidden away as though you are ashamed of me!"

"You know the answer to that. You must be patient. While I remain wed, we must take certain precautions."

"You are king," she said, stamping her foot. "You can do what you like. And if I am your mistress, why can I not be part of the court?"

"You will be, very soon."

"You promised me."

"And I shall keep that promise," he said, kissing her below her ear. She arched closer, a wicked smile curving her lips.

He could not resist sliding his arms around her magnificent curves, and inhaled her perfume with a heady sigh. It was a shame to leave her, a shame not to give her all that she desired.

"Stop that," he said sharply, and pulled away. "You know that I permit you to bewitch me at times, but you will not keep me here when I wish to go."

"Forgive me. It's just that I adore you so."

He gestured, and a servant brought him his clothes.

Hedrina watched him pull them on. "There was a time when you could not resist me, Lervan."

He tugged the laces of his doublet impatiently. "When I am

crowned, my sweet, you will be allowed to rule this palace as you already rule my heart. Now I must go."

When he left the overheated rooms, still feeling a tug of regret for the duties that called him away, a delegation of guardsmen was waiting in the passageway to escort him to the privy chamber. Lervan strode along easily in their midst, and as they reached one of the public galleries, the smattering of courtiers present broke apart to bow to him as he walked by. He smiled at everyone, but his expression grew a little forced.

There was but a quarter of the court present. Some of the nobles were dead. Some had been hauled away as captives. The rest had fled to their private estates, ignoring his summons back to court on the pretext that bad weather prevented traveling. *The cowards,* he thought scornfully. He knew they feared another attack and preferred to keep their distance from the coast. Well, he'd dealt with the Vvordsmen quickly and decisively, and that was an end to the matter. He did not understand why his nobles remained shaken, nervous, and fearful. The attack had been a dreadful event, aye. But the barbarians were gone, and Mandria would recover from the insult.

As for the missing tapestries, the burned wing of the palace, and the gouges on some of the finest parquet floors, those were mere inconveniences, and they would be repaired.

He ceased to smile the moment he left public view in the gallery and entered his private passageway past the audience hall. Lackeys sprang to open the doors to the privy chamber.

With his thumbs hooked in his belt, Lervan swaggered inside and glanced around at the somber faces present. Dispatch cases and courier bags lay piled atop the desk. Chancellor Fillem was busy unlocking the documents chest to pull out unfinished business from their last meeting.

Lervan sighed, already bored with it all. Being king was supposed to be endless merriment, with banquets and tournaments and dancing and pretty maids all willing to enjoy the royal favor. He hadn't counted on endless meetings, boring talk, numbing details, or petty arguments among the ministers. Once he was crowned, and enjoyed complete power, he intended to eliminate much of this misery.

Cardinal Theloi, looking thinner than ever and very grave, advanced to meet him. "The king looks well," he said in greeting.

"The king *is* well," Lervan announced impatiently. "Well? Let's be at it. I suppose you intend to tell me that the price of silk velvet is now too dear for my coronation robes."

His little joke brought no smiles.

Chancellor Fillem, Lord Salba's successor but no improvement, was a plump individual with a greasy, pockmarked face and bushy brows. He bustled forward obsequiously. "Your majesty, we have received a communication from Thirst."

Lervan's patience dwindled yet more. "By that I suppose you mean another message from my wife, still threatening to bring upper Mandria down on us. She's all bluster, as I have told you before. The upland lords refused her, as was only right and proper, and she has no support."

"Your majesty, I fear this message is of graver importance."

"What?" Lervan said in mock dismay. "More trouble than my wife? Then let's hear it, man! At least 'twill be some variety from the usual dreary news of civil war and imminent disaster."

Fillem opened his mouth, but Theloi said, "If your majesty and I might have a private word."

They moved over to a distant corner of the room away from the others. The cardinal was frowning. "The queen has given birth. I regret to say that the child did not survive."

Lervan's momentary bewilderment gave way to consternation. "Damne! But it wasn't due until—"

"The queen suffered a mishap and came to her time early. The infant was born alive, but died within the hour."

Lervan frowned and looked away. He was not sure what to say about it. The child's prospective arrival had not meant much to him until now. "Girl or boy?"

"It was a son, your majesty."

"My son." He felt stunned at the thought that there could

have been a boy in his image, tagging at his heels, learning to ride and hunt at his side, growing up manly and tall. "What happened? Has she been ill?"

"We are informed that the queen was unwell when she reached Vurdal. She seemed to recover, but then suffered an accident at Thirst."

Lervan sent him a sharp look. "Of your planning?"

"No, your majesty," Theloi replied coldly. "I have informed you repeatedly that my influence does not extend to Thirst."

Lervan had not forgotten. It just pleased him to hear the old cardinal admit as much.

"I regret, sire," Theloi continued, "that details are so sketchy. This announcement was issued by Thirst, and my own informants do not—"

Lervan lifted his hand, and Theloi fell silent. "Will she die also?" Lervan asked.

"I do not know the state of the queen's health," the cardinal replied. "I believe there are concerns."

Half turning away, Lervan closed his eyes. *Please, Thod, let her die,* he prayed. It would be the answer to so many problems. War averted, no more contention for the crown, and Hedrina appeased, for she would be able to display herself publicly at his side.

Sudden emotion surged through him, rising in a tide that nearly choked him, then ebbed away. He had never hated Pheresa, although his initial interest had crumbled into indifference, then dislike long ago. Now he pitied her, aware that he might have kept his interest in her had she been able to relax and enjoy life the way he wanted to. But she couldn't share, couldn't unbend, couldn't let him rule at her side. She'd insisted on having control of everything, and now she'd lost everything. This news was a relief, in a way, such an easy conclusion to their union.

"Your majesty, may I express the council's deepest regrets at this terrible news," Fillem said.

Lervan opened his eyes and looked at the man, blinking back the brief moisture of tears. The ministers crowded around him, murmuring soberly, and Theloi stepped away, giving Lervan the tiniest nod of approval as he did so. Lervan held his gaze a moment, then slid his own away. And inside his heart sang a hopeful little chant: *Let her die. Let her die. Let her die.*

A knock on the door interrupted them. A clerk appeared, whispering to Fillem, who turned pale and faced Lervan. "Sire," he said, "a message has come from King Mux."

Instantly, the mood in the privy chamber darkened to resentment and fear. "What does that knave want now?" Lervan demanded.

"His representatives are at the gates, demanding more tribute."

Commotion broke out as everyone started talking at once. Scowling, Lervan said, "Turn them away! We have paid all the tribute we can afford."

Fillem shooed out his clerk. They waited, with Lervan pacing back and forth. Several of the men were muttering.

"This is an outrage," Fillem said. "Why can they not be satisfied? Will they ever agree to enough? How can we—"

The clerk returned, perspiring, and said, "They were very angry. They said they will come back in three days for the gold. If it is not given to them, there will be war."

Late that night, weary to his very bones and half-drunk, Lervan lay in his state bedchamber with Hedrina snuggled at his side. Only one lamp burned, at the far side of the vast chamber. The air felt very cold, and the bed hangings did not entirely keep out the drafts that whistled through the place. Sitting by the door, Sir Maltric snored softly, with his sword across his knees.

Lervan sighed fretfully. "These damned barbarians are ruining everything."

"Forget them, my dearest," Hedrina said. "Think only of us, here together at this moment."

He shrugged aside her comfort. "They will drive me mad with their demands. Do you know that my treasury is nearly depleted?"

"No," she said in surprise, lifting her head from his shoulder. "How can this be?"

"I am told I spend too much. Well, damne, a monarch cannot be a pinch-purse! Prices are outrageous, and everything imported costs triple this year." Lervan sighed angrily. "Or so I am informed by my minister of finance. What a worm Ulphonze is, always mewling about accounts. I'm sure that other fellow, Meaclan, had better sense. But where is he? Deserted the court, the craven scoundrel. He probably stole the treasury and sits on it now, counting dreits at night."

Hedrina kissed his cheek. "You worry too much. Have more wine."

"I don't want more wine. I'm drunk already," he said morosely. "I am told that if I pay tribute and thus avert war, I can afford only a pitiable ceremony for my coronation. Or I can spend my remaining funds on a state coronation in full pomp as I desire, but likely I'll be too busy fighting off Vvordsmen to care whether I'm crowned or not. Now, damne, Hedrina, what sort of choice is that?"

"Isn't there another way?"

He snorted in the gloom. "I don't see one. There was trouble enough when I paid Mux the first time. And the complaints that have rained down on my head ever since. Morde! He went away, did he not?"

"Indeed he did."

"Aye. And it's not my fault if he's threatening to come back again. What can I do about it?"

"Does the council advise war?"

"Aye, they want it. The old fools. They won't be riding against these barbarians, but I'll be expected to lead our forces in the thick of it."

She nibbled at his shoulder. "Your majesty will look splendid in armor."

"Well, I don't like the thought of it. I've seen these savages in action, my dear, and they're damned terrifying. Besides, there's the queen threatening civil war from the north. I can't fight her and the barbarians at the same time, you know."

"I am sure your majesty will think of the solution. You're so brave and clever."

"I don't feel brave and clever," he said wearily. "I feel underfinanced and cornered. There simply isn't enough money to do *everything*. If only Pheresa would die. She's ill, you know."

"I heard," Hedrina said quietly. "She did something foolish and caused your son to die."

He shrugged. "So 'tis rumored. But even if Thod takes her, that will not solve all the problem."

"What do you need?" Hedrina asked.

"More men. And more money. But, morde, I might as well ask for the Chalice of Eternal Life as get either."

"You can have exactly what you desire, my love," she murmured, nuzzling his ear.

"Nay," he said, shifting his head away from her caresses. " 'Tis not that simple. Even your magic kisses, my sweet, cannot comfort me tonight."

"Listen," she said, pressing her hand over his heart. "Why not form a new alliance?"

"If you think I'm going to appeal to Nether for help, nay! Theloi has warned me the Netherans can't be trusted, treaty or no treaty. They're lying in wait, ready to take advantage of our troubles. Turning to them would be like letting a cat into the birdcage."

Hedrina had begun to trace a complex pattern over his heart with her fingernail. "What about a treaty with Gant?" she whispered.

He flinched, but she was still tracing the pattern over his heart, repeating it endlessly. Frowning, he found himself saying, "What mean you by this?"

"Gant has wealth. Gant has an army."

He laughed softly. "Nay. Nether squashed Gant into the dust, and they haven't recovered yet."

"Gant can supply the men you need. Hear me, Lervan," she said persuasively, her nail tracing the pattern faster. He found his heartbeat thudding in time with it, and he felt breathless and strange. "Gant has special powers," she said, "which you need in this time of crisis. Why not use them?"

I have, he nearly said aloud, and clamped his lips shut in dismay. He would never confess aloud his part in Verence's untimely death. "You're dreaming," he managed to say, but his tongue felt thick and unruly. *How much wine have I drunk tonight?* he wondered. "The people," he said, struggling to speak, "would never accept such an alliance."

"Why need the people know? You don't really fear the Gantese, do you? What harm have they ever done to you?"

"They—they—" He stopped, unable to go on. His mind was spinning. He thought of another beauty long ago, with flashing eyes and unbound hair and their meeting in the woods. She, too, had clouded his mind and made his senses reel with forbidden thoughts. He could not recall her name, only that he'd killed her, and she'd laid a curse on him.

But the curse hadn't come true. He was king now, due to be crowned in a few months. Everything that he'd always desired was coming to him. He had only to be patient, had only to find his way through this difficulty, and then true power would lie in his hands.

Hedrina was still whispering, her voice like honey, fragrance, and smoke in his mind. He felt drugged by the persuasion in her voice. "Why fear Gant? Has their magic ever harmed you? Extend your hand in friendship, Lervan, granting trade routes between Mandria and Gant, and the Chief Believer will see that your enemies trouble you no more."

Acceptance filled his throat. He lay defenseless in her hands. For her, he would do anything. And yet, some lingering sense of caution came to him. "The queen," he said thickly.

Hedrina's caresses stopped abruptly, and he felt as though he'd been thrown over a cliff, plummeting headlong down into an abyss far from her. "Yes?" she said coldly.

"Let the Chief Believer prove his good intentions. Eliminate her, and I will agree to his terms."

Hedrina began to laugh. It was a cold, merciless sound. "Is

that all?" she asked. "My dearest, is that your only condition?"

He tried to think, telling himself to take care, but prudence had no chance. He was drunk or mad or bewitched, and if her little spells were an example of Gantese magic, he wanted more of them. Hedrina had become as necessary to him as the blood in his veins. He needed her too much to question what she said or did. After all, why should he care what befell Mandria if it allied itself to Gant? All he wanted was ease, luxury, and Hedrina's arms. The consequences could take care of themselves.

" 'Tis rumored she's protected by the Chalice, but, Lervan, is the queen's death all you require to seal this bargain?"

"That's all I want," he replied.

Her mouth was warm and soft, her skin like silk as she slid her body across his. "Then you shall have it," she murmured.

And Lervan lost himself in her fire once more.

Chapter Twenty-five

At Thirst, Aelintide came, the celebrations lasting for two days of feasting and merriment. After that, the snows fell, blanketing the hold and the land beyond it in a soft cloud of white. A bitter wind blew around the eaves, whistling through arrow slits in the defense turrets, rattling the shutters over the windows.

Pheresa lay in her bed, watching the shadows of a snowy dawn lighten to gray around her. That's what she felt, cold and gray and empty. So very empty. She had carried life, but it was gone now, extinguished and taken from her. Her son had never cried. His blue fists had been so tiny, so miraculously perfect. She glimpsed him once, wrapped in a cloth and rubbed by Oola before the fire, but then Oola's efforts had stilled and all was silent as the servant carried him away.

The door clicked open, and someone came inside, skirts rustling. A tray was set down beside her, and a lamp lit.

The light hurt Pheresa's eyes, and she turned her face away.

"Your majesty?" Oola said in concern. "I've brought you some good, hearty broth and bread. Have a little, won't you?"

Pheresa ignored her, and after a while Oola sniveled in her apron and left. Then the physician came. He asked questions in his calm, deep voice. Pheresa ignored him, too. What she wanted was gone, taken from her forever. She had never held her son, and she ached for him desperately, so desperately she wanted to scream aloud for Thod to give him back.

But her child could not come back, and she wanted nothing else. She could not cry out for him, and so she said nothing at all. She lay in this empty place, listening to her own breathing, and she did not want even that.

The physician's hand slid across her brow and rested there. "The fever is gone," he announced with satisfaction. "Your majesty will get better now. You will regain your strength, but only if you eat something. Will you not try?"

She frowned, staring at the wall. "Withdraw," she said coldly, and, finally, they went away.

Of course they came back. They always did, every few hours, to try to cajole her again. After a while she began to feel hungry, as though her body meant to betray her, too. She tried to ignore it, but the hunger only grew, and the next time Oola came with a tray, Pheresa nibbled a little of the pastries.

After that, she consented to sit up for a short time each afternoon, staring at the snow falling outside her window while the countess read aloud and Carolie embroidered. She did not want to grow stronger, but the physician's prediction proved correct. Her body, it seemed, wanted to live, even if her spirit was broken. This puzzled her, for she had read in her philosophy scrolls that a broken heart broke all else within the body, causing it to pine and wither. Yet in her case, this did not happen. She felt that her improving health was a betrayal of that small, sweet creature who had once lived inside her womb. They should have died together, and yet she'd been left behind.

Then it occurred to her that living with this empty ache in her heart and soul was Thod's punishment for having failed her child.

"Sir Thum is at the door this morning," Lady Carolie said to her one day. A wintry sun was trying to melt the icicles hanging outside the window. "He has come three times before. Will your majesty not consent to receive a visitor?"

"The queen sees no one," Pheresa replied.

With a curtsy, Carolie went to the door, and murmured to Sir Thum, "Nay, sir, she will not see you. I'm sorry."

"Is she ailing again?"

"She's much stronger, but she grieves as fiercely as ever."

"Have you told her about Talmor?"

"Nay, sir. She's not asked about him, and on the physician's orders we dare not mention his name."

"Pity. Well, thank you, my lady. I'll come again at a later time. There's much she should know."

Pheresa listened to this brief, soft-voiced exchange with a deepening frown. What did they mean about Sir Talmor? He was dead, surely. She had not wanted to think about it, had not wanted to face her part in bringing about his horrible fate. That was why she had not asked about him.

A feeling of restlessness seized her. Throwing back the bedcovers, she got weakly to her feet.

Lady Carolie jumped up to steady her balance. "Your majesty—"

"I will visit my baby's grave," Pheresa announced.

It caused a commotion, but the physician gave his approval. Pheresa was gowned and wrapped in numerous layers, with a heavy fur cloak pulled tightly about her. Then, carried in the arms of the gruff, taciturn Thirst knight who had been assigned as her protector, she was taken to the chapel. Inside the dim quiet place, she was set down, and she walked unsteadily past the altar and crypt and outside into a small graveyard, where a rowan tree spread gnarled branches above the headstones.

She gazed down at the stark inscription: *unnamed son of Queen Pheresa and Duc Lervan of Mandria.* The icy wind blew gusts that made her shiver. What a bleak, unhappy place, she thought. Her son should not be here, and yet what happiness had he known?

"He should have been named," she said.

Lady Carolie wept quietly into a handkerchief. The count-

ess looked cold and tired, her face haunted by memories of
her own.

The priest, unkempt as usual, shuffled forward with his
hands tucked deep in his wide sleeves. "'Tis impossible to
name him, your majesty. The church recognizes no premature
birth unless the baby lives. If—"

"Hush, Father," Sir Thum said, coming up. "She needs no
lecture on Writ at this time."

With the priest firmly dismissed, Thum joined Pheresa.
His hazel eyes were somber and kind. She was afraid he
would speak, but he did not, and after a few moments she relaxed and took comfort in his presence.

She wished she could cry. There would have been solace
and relief in tears. But her arrogance and stupidity had cost
the lives of her child and Talmor, and in her guilt she could
not weep for them.

Instead, her gaze swept across the other graves, searching
the names without finding Talmor's. At last she turned to Sir
Thum with puzzlement.

"Aye, majesty," he said quietly, watching her. "He lives
still."

She stared at him, unable to believe it, and found her eyes
suddenly awash with burning tears. Something that had lain
dead in her heart unfurled and began to lift.

"What say you?" she whispered, her voice thick and unsteady. "How can this be?"

"He's a strong man, stronger than most."

"But I saw him go down. I saw the hurlhound bite—" Her
voice failed her, and she could not say it. The images assailed
her mind, still too bright and nightmarish to endure. She shuddered and with great effort met Thum's gaze. "He cannot live
from such grievous wounds."

Sir Thum frowned, his mouth pursed in hesitation. Finally
he said, "Nay, majesty. He will not live much longer. I
thought, since he had been so long in your service and so loyal
to your majesty, that you might wish to see him."

Her head snapped up. Pride shut off the grief welling
painfully inside her. "Of course," she said. Her gaze swept her

attendants accusingly. They should have told her. How dare they let her think him dead, when all this time he'd lain suffering and dying alone?

With a grateful nod to Sir Thum, she said, "You are correct. I will see him now."

Lady Carolie hurried forward. "Perhaps your majesty should rest a while before—"

"Now," Pheresa said harshly.

As they left the graveyard, clouds closed the sky, and more snow began to fall. Trudging across the courtyard, Pheresa lifted her face to the swirling snowflakes and let them sting her face. Then she faltered, and her protector lifted her in his strong arms and carried her the rest of the way to a brick-and-stone storehouse. Its contents, apparently dried shocks of fodder, had been cleared away, leaving only a disordered trail of bits and leaves. Pheresa was carried downstairs through a stout trapdoor into what looked like a dungeon except for the lidded crocks standing along one wall and a faint scent of dried onions and apples.

Lowering her to her feet, the protector stepped back out of the way. She realized she did not know his name, but she asked no question. She did not want to know this grizzled, weather-beaten veteran of Thirst's constant dangers. She did not want to care about people anymore, and yet, when the guards opened a door and Talmor's squire popped out, looking startled, the harsh resolves and barriers inside her crumbled anew.

It took effort, but she made herself glance up at her new protector. "Your name, sir?" she whispered.

He blinked in surprise and turned red above his collar. "Kelchel, yer grace."

"Thank you, Sir Kelchel, for joining the queen's service."

He bowed, and she walked forward to where the squire and Thirst's physician were arguing in hushed voices.

The squire's round, boyish face held a mixture of recalcitrance, grief, and protectiveness. He looked at her as though she were the enemy, yet no matter what she felt about herself, 'twas Talmor's forgiveness she'd come for, not this man's.

The physician came forward to block her path. "Is this wise, Sir Thum? The danger—"

"He won't hurt the queen," Thum answered.

Startled, Pheresa looked up, but she realized at once what they were talking about. Until now, she'd shut the memory from her mind, along with so much else. Now there was no need to deny what she'd witnessed. During the battle against the Nonkind, Talmor had suddenly lifted his hand. Flames had surrounded him as though his clothing had ignited, yet he did not burn. He shouted something and hurled fire at the hurlhound just before it savaged him.

Disillusionment curled inside her. Talmor had lied to her about his magical powers. All this time she'd believed him to be a man quicker than most to sense trouble, when in reality he was a heretic who practiced sorcery. Worse, he'd lied in claiming to be half-Saelutian. No doubt Gantese blood ran in his veins, and that condemned him more than anything else. She marveled now that she had ever trusted him so close to her, and told herself she should not be here at all.

"Will your majesty approach the prisoner?" Sir Thum asked.

The gloomy place held the odors of illness. The air felt very hot. She noticed numerous pails of water standing about the room, and fear slid icy fingers along her spine.

The squire darted ahead of her, muttering to himself. He hastily smoothed the rumpled blankets across his master and gently lifted Talmor to slide another pillow beneath his shoulders, propping him a little higher. Then, with a fierce, protective glance, the squire retreated.

The physician and Sir Thum stood together, and Pheresa walked forward alone to Talmor's cot.

Unconscious, he looked diminished, as though all his robust vigor had been struck from him. His bronzed skin held a grayish cast, and a sheen of fever glistened on his brow beneath his tumbled locks of black hair. His left arm lay atop the blankets, and his hand moved restlessly, aimlessly across them. His right arm, his sword arm, was gone. She stared at the flatness of the blankets at his side, unable to get used to it.

His chest and right shoulder were heavily bandaged. Blood had seeped through the wrappings, and there was a sickly smell that she recognized all too well.

Shocked, she looked at Sir Thum, and he nodded without speaking. Sorrow tore at her heart. Why, she wondered, had they not done something to put Talmor from his misery? Why had they let him linger this way, suffering unspeakable torment while Nonkind poison worked its way through his body?

Her hand reached into her pocket to clutch her salt purse as Talmor's eyes dragged open and stared at her.

They were a stranger's eyes, wild and tormented. He opened his mouth, but made no sound. He seemed terrified of her, and his fingers tightened on his blankets.

Somehow she managed to find her voice. "Sir Talmor," she said softly and unsteadily. "The queen grieves to—to find you so unwell."

His panic faded. As he shifted his head restlessly, recognition slowly filled his eyes. "Majesty," he whispered.

She wanted to weep. Despite everything, he was still her dear protector, so faithful, so much a part of her life that she felt bereft without him. All her trust and belief in him came rushing back.

She sank onto the stool at his bedside and reached out to clasp his feverish hand. "Forgive me for taking so long to come see you."

His eyes drank in the sight of her, yet he seemed wary and unsure. "Come not so close. Not safe."

She did not release his hand. "I do not fear you, my friend," she said gently. Although she meant it as mere reassurance, the moment she uttered the words she knew them to be true.

The agony in his eyes lightened momentarily. He tried to smile, yet so pathetic was his gratitude, so vulnerable did he look, that she nearly lost command of herself. Tears filled her eyes, but she blinked them back and kept smiling at him.

"I thank you for my life," she said. "You have always been the one person I could rely on absolutely. This time, however, you have sacrificed too much."

He tried to answer, but his strength failed him. All the color left his face, and his eyes closed.

Alarmed, she rose to her feet. The physician came up, leaning over Talmor, while Sir Thum gently drew her back out of the way.

She realized tears were streaming down her cheeks, and she did not care. "Is he dead? Is this the end?"

The physician shook his head, and she pressed her fingers to her lips in relief. At that moment the room grew suddenly hotter.

Sir Thum escorted her out of there, but as she crossed the threshold she heard Talmor shout something incoherent. A metal basin went flying off a table to clatter on the floor. The squire, looking grim and heartsick, shut the door firmly.

Pheresa fought her emotions in an effort to keep her composure. "When he dies, he'll become Nonkind. What can be done?"

Thum frowned. "A lesser man, an entirely human man, would have been dead already, his body salted and purified, then staked in the river to freeze."

"Your majesty!" Lady Carolie cried out, hastening to her. "Pray come away and listen to no more. You are too ill to hear such—"

Pheresa turned on her angrily. "Silence! If you cannot compose yourself, leave me at once."

White-faced, Carolie retreated and stared at her with stunned, incredulous eyes.

Pheresa turned back to Sir Thum. "Is there no way to save his life? No way to purify the wound that he may live?"

"Aye, although as weak as he is now, the procedure might kill him." Thum frowned at her. "But considering what he is—"

"And what is that?" she asked in frustration. "I keep telling myself what I saw, and I cannot believe it."

"Only Believers wield fire as weapons, majesty," Thum said. "All the witnesses agree that he used his dark powers against you—"

"He used them to save Sir Bosquecel's life, as well as

mine," she said sharply. "And had the commander any gratitude he would be here, seeking some means of saving Sir Talmor, rather than condemning him."

"The commander lies abed with a broken leg," Thum told
her. "And the whole squadron saw the hurlhound take fresh
strength from the magic Talmor gave him. These wily Gantese agents are able to deceive anyone—"

"Can a Believer deceive *you*?" she asked. "Can you look
at someone with Gantese blood and not know the truth?"

Sir Thum frowned.

"You live in the service of a king with special gifts, and yet
you condemn this man," she said in growing anger, forgetting
that a few minutes before, she'd entertained similar suspicions. "Are you such a hypocrite?"

"Faldain is part eldin, not Gantese—"

"Is Talmor Gantese?" she demanded with a furious gesture. "Is he? Has he the look of that race?"

"No," Thum replied with obvious reluctance. "But with
arts and enchantments, many of them conceal their true visage."

"Could he do that while in such pain?"

Thum sighed. "I think not."

"Nay, sir. I think not as well."

"But your protector is *not* Mandrian—"

"He is half," she said quickly. "He told me in private that
his mother was Saelutian."

Thum's brows drew together, and he looked thoughtful.
"'Tis rumored sorcery can be found in the islands. Merchants
from afar often bring such stories. Sulein, the old physician
who served here when I was fostering, came from Saelutia.
He dabbled in the forbidden arts."

"Then—"

"But I have never heard of anyone save a Believer using
fire as a weapon," Sir Thum said firmly.

Despite her exasperation, Pheresa knew this argument was
futile. "If he lives—if he can be helped to live—we will determine the truth of this. I do not wish him to die, Sir Thum.
Order the physician to save him."

He hesitated, his frown deepening.

She wanted to shake him. "Did you not yourself escape Nonkind poisoning and the horrible fate beyond it? Would you not extend the mercy shown you to another?"

"But I am no *sorcerel*, majesty. I do not pose danger to others, as he will, if he survives."

"I have known the man these past two years and more," she said stubbornly. "Never has he offered me danger."

Wild laughter, followed by sobbing, came from within the sickroom. It grieved her to hear it. But Sir Thum stared at the door with an ever-deepening frown.

"You judge him unheard, sir," she said angrily. "You condemn him without trial and let him suffer torment that is indecent and cruel. I thought better of you, sir. I did indeed!"

Anger sparked in Thum's face. With snapping eyes, he said, "Your majesty is taking a risk—"

"If you did not intend for me to save him," she retorted, "why did you let me know he still lives?"

"I meant it kindly, that your majesty might have a chance to clear her conscience and bestow a blessing on a dying man."

"Bless this faithful retainer who has served me so well, but not seek treatment for him? Visit him, here in this squalor," she said contemptuously, "before I turn my back on him and leave him to rot condemned in unspeakable agony? This is a harsh sentence indeed."

"He is faithful to your majesty, but to the rest of us he poses danger."

"And why do you mention the queen's conscience?" she demanded, going back to what Thum had said. "Do you also dare judge me, sir?"

"You brought yourself here to be judged!" he said with a sharpness equal to her own. "Every monarch is judged, aye, and should be!"

"I—"

"Does the queen deny her part in this tragedy? Does the queen deny that she willfully put herself in mortal danger, costing the lives of four men, plus the injuries and—"

"Stop!" she shouted, awash in guilt. "You have said too much, sir."

"Nay, majesty, I have not said enough." His face was now as red as his hair, his wrath as fiery as hers. "Forget not that I rode to Nether with Dain and the others who sought to save you. I saw the courage of Dain and Alexeika as they fought their way back from Gant. I witnessed the valor shown at the Battle of Grov. I saw King Verence come in time, with the finest army in the world at his back. These, my lady, are sovereigns. These, my lady, are people that men gladly bend knee to. But you, in your quest to be queen, have felt sorry for yourself, have endangered yourself, have believed in the lies of fools, and have ignored the sage council of those wiser and more experienced than you."

She could not believe he was saying such things to her. Trembling with fury, she longed to order her guardsmen to silence him. But they were not with her, and this hold was not under her sovereignty, and this man owed her no allegiance. She was alone, save for a handful of attendants and servants, and the only warrior in all Mandria who was on her side now lay dying, accused of being a traitor and enemy agent.

"I did seek the advice of those who are wise and true," she defended herself angrily. "Faldain gave me nothing!"

Sir Thum nodded as though her comment had proven his point. "If your majesty expects the king of another land to do your work for you, then you deserve no throne."

"How dare you!"

"Aye, I dare. My father would call you liege, and my brothers, too, had you shown yourself worth a crown. You came here, cowardly, weak, and calling out to Nether for help. You turned to Nether first, before your own chevards. How could you insult them so deeply?"

Her lip curled. "Their insult to me—"

"Came after you insulted them first! If you would ask brave men to follow your banner, majesty, then you must lead them. You! Not Dain or your generals. And in Thod's name, show men your trust if you would have them give you theirs."

Silence fell between them. She was breathing in short, hard jerks, her fists clenched and trembling at her sides.

Abruptly he bowed. "With your majesty's permission, I will withdraw. 'Twas not my intention to say so much."

She was too angry to respond. He strode out of the cellar and up the steps, leaving her alone with her gawking attendants.

After a moment she felt the rage drain from her, and bowed her head.

"Majesty, you are too ill for this!" Lady Carolie cried.

Pheresa flung up her hand without turning around, and Carolie subsided. She kept her back to everyone, refusing to deal with whatever sympathy, pity, or condemnation she might possibly see in their faces.

Sir Thum's words continued to ring in her ears. Was this the way others saw her? she wondered. As a weak, spineless, uncertain creature? Was this why she could stir no followers? Was this what Faldain had tried to tell her the day he refused to lead his army behind her banner?

Her mind was spinning. She felt dazed by what she'd heard.

"Come away now, majesty," the countess said to her. "There's no more to be done here."

Pheresa's shoulders stiffened. Her head came up, and she stared at the door to Sir Talmor's sick room. "Oh, but there is," she said.

Stepping back inside the storeroom, she faced the physician's inquiring look and the squire's resentful one.

Now she understood why the squire was so defensive and uneasy. She met his eyes for a moment, then turned her gaze to Talmor.

They were in the process of changing the bandages, and she could not help but flinch at the gruesome sight of Talmor's wound. Beyond the ugly scarring and stitches, his flesh was inflamed and discolored. His blood looked dark and foul.

For a moment she feared she would lose mastery of herself, but with a hard swallow she walked forward.

"He can't talk to yer majesty now," the squire said. "Goin' Beyond, he is, bless 'im, and naught we can do about it."

"Something can be done," Pheresa said, staring at the physician. "You know how to save him."

The physician dropped his gaze and gave no answer.

"What's this?" the squire said suspiciously. "Is this true?"

Caught between them, the physician gave a delicate shrug. "Well, of course Nonkind wounds can be purified, to stop the spread of poison. But this man has lost too much blood. He cannot live in any case."

"You mean the knights of Thirst do not want him to live," Pheresa said harshly. "He's been condemned to die like this, untreated."

The squire's face turned red. He glared at the physician as though he meant to attack the man, then he knelt before Pheresa. "In Thod's name, majesty, if there's aught ye can do, order it before it's too late."

"What is your name?" she asked gently.

"Pears, majesty. I've served him all his life. He ain't what they're saying. I'll swear to that on the Circle! Calls the fire a curse, he does, and hates it. He spent his boyhood trying to drive it out of himself, only his mother's blood in him was too strong. He's put it away for years, he has, and it never gets away from him unless he's too angry or—or hurt to control it. He wouldn't never have used it if he hadn't been trying to save—"

She touched his shoulder briefly. "I know," she said.

Wringing his hands, Pears stared up at her. "Please, majesty! Ye know he's arrow true and would serve ye to his last breath. All he thought of was saving yer majesty's life!"

"Physician?" she said.

But the man, as soft of character as he was of form, shook his head. "I'm afraid I don't know what your majesty is asking me to do. I have treated this man to the best of my ability."

Anger scorched through her. "Get out," she said in contempt.

Reddening, he scuttled away.

She turned back to Talmor, who lay lost in the fever that consumed him. He was frowning, muttering beneath his breath, his left hand moving aimlessly back and forth across the blanket. Determination hardened inside her. She had lost everything else. She would not lose him, too.

"Pears," she said.

"Aye, majesty?"

"You love your master?"

The squire's face puckered. "Bless 'im, I do."

"Do you understand that his wound is tainted by Nonkind venom, and that this poison will turn him into a horrific creature if he dies?"

"He—that's why they lock us in, ain't it?"

She nodded.

He drew in a sharp breath. "Ah, damne, everywhere we go, it's always the same. Him doing his best to fit in, doing his best to be perfect for whoever he serves, even if it kills him and breaks him down, and then getting blamed for whatever goes wrong. I reckon this time, with yer majesty involved, they aim to make something profane of him so they can kill him sure."

"It is forbidden to kill the queen's protector without her permission," Pheresa said, feeling hollow and cold as she said the words.

"But if he turns Nonkind, they don't need to ask."

She nodded.

"Ain't right, majesty!" he cried, his eyes hot at the injustice. "Ain't right."

Pheresa thought of all the times Talmor had shown his valor. She would never forget the first time she saw him joust, when he had won the contest of lances with outstanding skill. She recalled how his handsome face had lit up when she chose him protector. So honest and forthright had been his admiration for her that she knew not then how to cope with it. She'd felt unworthy of such total devotion, shy of it, and too gruff with him in consequence. Never, from the moment he entered he service, had he failed her. And after they came here to Thirst, on that black day when a little band of dwarves tried to save her from harm despite her own stupidity, Talmor had once again come rushing to her rescue. She remembered the screams of battle around her, her own panic like something alive and clawing in her throat, the horrific baying of the hurlhounds, and Talmor—magnificent on his steed, his sword swinging, his face that of an avenger—plunging straight into battle against monsters he had never seen before, against monsters whose evil he did not fully comprehend. A lesser man would have hesitated, would have listened to fear. But Talmor had protected her to the end, despite his fateful mistake. He had revealed his deepest secret, had sacrificed everything, including his honor, to save her.

What price her life? This man's sword arm? This man's life? That the knights of Thirst should criticize him for his magic, should so misconstrue his intent and his powers, angered her past bearing. They had no right to do so, and if it meant putting aside her mourning and self-blame to defend Talmor and his tarnished honor, then she would do that. She owed him far more, but this, at least, she could do.

Meeting Pears's eyes, she studied the middle-aged squire and believed him to be as sound and true as his master. When she was a little girl, her nurse used to tell her that a man could be judged best by his servants. If they were honest and loved their master, then he was a worthy man. If they cringed, lied, stole, and feared him, then no matter how charming his manners and how fine his figure, he was a man to distrust.

Pheresa sighed. Why had she forgotten such excellent advice until now? She realized she had forgotten many things in recent years, had cast aside common sense and her own true feelings in favor of pride and ambition. She had much to answer for, she told herself. Much to reason through and rethink.

But now, there was Talmor to save if she could.

"His wound must be salted and cauterized with a magicked blade," she said.

Pears winced, and his gaze shifted to his master's face.

"I know," she said quietly. "That is why I asked if you love him."

"Aye, but—I don't know if he can withstand all that," Pears whispered fearfully. "We'll kill him sure."

She believed so, too, but she said, "Better he should die cleansed, with his soul intact, than otherwise."

The squire bowed his head, his shoulders shaking as he fought to command his emotions. "Aye," he said thickly at last. "Yer majesty knows what's best."

"Only I know not where a magicked blade can be found for the task."

"Couldn't his own blade serve? Or even my dagger?" Pears raised an angry fist. "I don't even know where his sword has got to, damn 'em. Got us confined down here like rats trapped in a bucket, and his mail and weapons rusting, most like, Thod knows where."

"Use this." She handed over her salt purse. "Liberally. I shall see that you are brought more. Use salt every time the bandages are changed."

She thought of how the physician obviously knew to do that, and how Talmor had been denied even such rudimentary care. Her anger burned even hotter, and she glared at Pears. "Can you do as I say?"

"Aye," he answered grimly. "That I can."

"You will not shirk from it? You will not falter from misguided feelings of mercy?"

"No, majesty. I'll do what he needs."

"Perhaps I should help—"

Pears flung her a look, and she fell silent. "I'll do it, majesty," he said. "I've done for him all his life. If anyone's to hurt him now, it had best be me."

She nodded, and gazed down at Talmor with her heart clutching anew. She saw death's hand on him, and fought a momentary surge of panic. *I shall not fail you,* she thought silently, making a vow of it, and gently traced a Circle on his fevered brow.

Chapter Twenty-six

All was dark, save for a candle burning low, guttering a little in the molten tallow around the wick. Intense heat consumed Talmor, bringing him from a troubled sleep with deep gasps for air. Wildly he looked around for a pail of water, but no fire blazed from him. He threw nothing, not even a spark. The blazing heat remained inside him, making his skin feel as though it would burst.

He thrashed in his blankets, trying to throw them off. If he did nothing else, he would cross the room and douse that candle. 'Twas the only fire in the room, for the hearth had crumbled to a pile of ashes and glowing embers. Water? He turned his head from side to side, seeking it to throw on the candle and the embers. There was too much heat. He could not breathe, could not think, because of so much heat.

But although he tried to get up, he could not. Something was wrong with his body, and it would not obey him. He rolled onto his right side, and pain shot through him with such intensity he could not even cry out. He flopped onto his back, shuddering and panting, while wave after wave of agony poured through him. At last it subsided, and he thought he would be sick. But he did not even have the strength to raise himself to vomit.

He lay there, spent and sweating, and after a time opened his eyes again. A hurlhound sat on the foot of his bunk, its black, scaled hide glistening in the candlelight, its hellish red eyes glowing intently. For an endless moment their gazes locked, then it parted its jaws so that saliva dripped off its deadly fangs, hissing as each small splatter landed on his blanket.

Transfixed with horror, Talmor stared at the beast, but it came no closer. It seemed to be waiting, and its evil gaze never left him for a moment. Another hurlhound crossed the room, seeming to materialize right from the shadows themselves, and leaped onto his bed. He could feel its weight pressing heavily on his foot, and fear choked his throat.

This one did not attack either. The loathsome pair simply waited, panting, their breath fouling the air as they watched him.

His heart raced and faltered. He had the sensation of drowning, and the huge beasts leaned closer, crouching as though poised to spring.

He struck at them weakly with his fist, but touched nothing save the air. They settled back, one of them licking its muzzle in disappointment.

They are waiting to eat my soul, he thought.

He realized then that he was dying, and they stood vigil over him. They would eat his soul, and he would be forever lost, unable to reach Beyond, damned in the most terrible way for all eternity.

Weeping, he cursed them, and reviled them, and denounced them in the name of Tomias. But they watched him patiently and did not go.

In desperation, he reached for the old ways that had been born in him, legacy of his mother, and with the force of his mind gathered the candlestick and hurled it at them.

The candlestick clattered against the wall beyond the foot

of his bed. The hurlhounds vanished, and Talmor felt a cool hand touch his face.

A worried voice said, "Sir! Oh, sir! Just have yerself a drink of this good water and lie still."

Talmor tried to swallow, but choked on it and instead let the mouthful dribble from his lips. "Tired," he said, moaning. "So . . . tired."

"Go back to sleep now. I'm with ye, lad, and all's well. Just sleep nice and quiet."

Talmor let his eyes fall shut, but sleep was no refuge. He dreamed of the queen, standing in an open place with sunlight glinting red sparks through her golden hair. Her brown eyes looked fierce and valiant, and she was shouting at a great crowd of people. He smiled, drinking in the vision she presented. How comely and straight she stood, her beautiful face stern and regal. She lifted her hands in supplication, her musical voice strong as she appealed to them on behalf of her cause.

The sight of her gave him strength, for she was so beautiful and fair. He loved her more than ever.

But a shadow fell across the sun, and the dream shifted. He felt himself seized by a powerful, outside force, one foreign to him. Although he struggled in an effort to throw it off, he could not withstand it. Dread and urgency filled him. He felt menace looming close by, ready to strike, but although he looked at the faces in the crowd, he saw nothing amiss. In the dream's strangeness numerous people suddenly stood between him and Pheresa, blocking his path. Swiftly he pushed them aside, trying to give her warning, but he could utter no sound. It was coming, this terrible danger. It was upon her.

Drawing his dagger, he spun around, elbowing an armed knight aside as the man tried to step between him and the queen. Then there was just he and Pheresa alone, deafened on all sides by a roaring crowd. Everyone was shouting at them, screaming words he could not understand.

Lifting his dagger, he rushed at her.

Her eyes widened, and her mouth fell open in disbelief.

"No!" he shouted, trying to stop himself, to resist the unseen force that drove him forward. "No!"

And she lay crumpled at his feet, blood staining her rich gown. Blood dripped from the dagger in his hand; blood splattered his arm and the front of his doublet. *Her blood.*

With a gasp, he jerked awake.

The heat was consuming him, driving him mad, and he could not shake off the horror of his dream. He would not kill her, he assured himself frantically. No force in the first, second, or third worlds could make him strike her down, and yet . . .

"No," he panted, struggling to get up. "I won't. *I won't!*"

He was pressed down, a voice soothing him, but he heard nothing save his own tormented fears. He would *not* kill her, he shouted in defiance. Yet the darkness and shadows edging closer seemed to mock him.

Frightened, he stared through the gloom at Pears's face. "Keep it back," he said desperately. "Light more candles and keep it back!"

"I will, sir," Pears promised, laying a cool cloth across his brow. "I'll keep the light shining for ye."

"I'll not obey you!" Talmor shouted, trying to lunge upright.

The pain washed over him, dropping him onto his pillows with a groan while the darkness crouched before him, lapping up his life force the way a cat laps cream.

Again he saw the terrible image in his mind, Pheresa lying at his feet bloody and still, and again he cried out his defiance. He would sooner stab the dagger through his own heart than harm her. What madness was this, he wondered in despair. What horrible creature was he becoming?

And the hurlhounds padded forth from the shadows, panting and slavering, to circle his bed.

Pheresa, gowned in velvet, her hair bound up in ropes of pearls, paced back and forth in the sitting room given to her use. Sir Thum, his freckled face looking wary and obstinate, stood before her. Sir Bosquecel, gaunt and worn, sat with her permission, his splinted leg propped on a stool.

Both men were shaking their heads. "Nothing like that is at hand," Sir Thum was saying.

"Then get it."

Sir Bosquecel looked shocked. "Majesty, that is quite—"

Her glare made him break off. "Do not say to me that it is impossible, for I'll believe no such lie," she told him. "Who makes such metal? Who forges it?"

"No one here!" Sir Bosquecel said quickly.

"No? Then how came Tanengard to be made here?"

He looked blank. "Tanengard?"

"Er," Sir Thum said, clearing his throat, "the sword that Thirst's smith made for the king years ago. Remember how he and Dain went forth to buy the metal, angering Lord Odfrey, who thought Dain had run away?"

A strange expression crossed Sir Bosquecel's face. He glanced at Pheresa, then let his gaze fall. "Forgive me, majesty," he said in a much-chastened voice. "I'd forgotten."

She was not inclined to forgive him. "Perhaps your memory had better improve swiftly, sir," she said in a cold voice.

"That smith ran off, years ago," Bosquecel said. "No one knows what became of the infidel. He was Netheran and not to be trusted."

She turned to Sir Thum. "Dwarves are said to make the best swords. Do they forge magicked weapons?"

"Sometimes, majesty," he replied reluctantly. "But such are dangerous things and not to be—"

"They withstand Nonkind, do they not?"

The men exchanged glances. "Yes, majesty," Sir Thum replied.

"I want such a weapon purchased on my behalf. Immediately."

"Your majesty is well protected inside these walls and has no need of such articles."

"Have I asked for your advice, sir?" she demanded in an

icy voice. "I wish a magicked weapon, preferably a dagger. I want it immediately, this day, if possible."

Sir Bosquecel sat straighter with a wince. "Majesty, even the dwarves do not make a common practice of forging such weapons. They are—"

A month ago, perhaps their obstruction would have stymied her and frustrated her. She would have given way to these fools, who were as hard to budge as boulders. But she was tired, worried nearly out of her mind, and determined to save Talmor at all costs.

"I command it," she said in a voice of steel.

Again, Thum and Bosquecel exchanged glances.

"Very well, your majesty," Thum said. "But please understand that in winter the dwarves go into their burrows and sometimes cannot be found until thaw. The master armorers are scattered throughout Nold and—"

"I want no excuses," she broke in. "Do as I require without delay."

But as they left, Sir Bosquecel supported on the shoulders of two stalwart men, Pheresa knew her command would come to naught. She had to find another way. But how?

Then an idea came to her. Hadn't Thum said that Faldain's old tutor used to dabble with magic? There must be something among Sulein's possessions that she could use to help Talmor.

When the steward answered her summons, she demanded access to Sulein's quarters.

"Sulein? But, your grace!" he said in dismay.

"Yes, Sulein. The physician who served here under Chevard Odfrey."

"Aye, of course, but—but all that's been shut up and closed away for years. It'll be dirty, and I've no doubt the mice have been at everything."

"I am not interested in matters of housekeeping," she said impatiently. "Conduct me there at once."

Reluctantly, he led her outside across the courtyard to a turret. Producing an enormous ring of keys, he unlocked the door and opened it, revealing a dim, dusty spiral of steps illu-

minated only by occasional arrow slits. Pheresa did not hesitate, but stepped across the threshold.

Sir Kelchel hurried to catch up. "Wait now. Let me go up
afore . . ."

Impatiently, she checked herself, allowing the protector to
ascend the steps first. On the small landing, the steward wrestled with the lock before he succeeded in opening the door.

A musty smell of mold and herbs wafted forth from the
chamber beyond. Repelled, she hesitated, and the steward
shouldered inside, pushing the door wide open.

"Filthy, just as I said," he announced. "Bide a moment
while I light a lamp."

It seemed to take him forever to find one, but at last she
heard the unmistakable rasping scrape of a strikebox. Illumination flickered forth, revealing a daunting amount of clutter.
A long table was strewn with scrolls, polished animal
bones, ancient tomes, fragile old maps, candle stubs, inkpots, and astrology charts. The shelves lining the walls held
countless bottles and jars, filled with liquids turned murky.
The labels, inscribed with arcane symbols, had faded until
they were almost illegible. Everything was caked with dust
and cobwebs.

Dismay spread through her. If she had hoped to find magicked metal here, 'twould take a long search indeed.

Putting aside her fastidious dislike of dirt and grime, she
picked up scrolls, opened wooden boxes, peered inside cabi-
nets until a sneezing fit drove her to try a different tactic.

"Had Sulein a strongbox?" she asked.

The two men began to search. After a while, Sir Kelchel
emerged from an alcove with a medium-sized box under his
arm. It was reinforced with iron straps, and its lock looked
difficult.

"The smith can break that," he said, hefting it. "Got somethin' in it, all right."

There was nothing else to find. She opened a scroll case of
moldy leather and felt something strange and unseen pass by
her face. Wondering if a moth had flown at her, she blinked a

moment, then reached into the case. When she touched a scroll, her fingers tingled.

Excited, she yanked it out but dropped it so that it went rolling beneath a chair. The steward dived after it, but when he picked it up he yelped and dropped it again.

Eyes bulging, both men backed away from it.

"What is it?" Pheresa asked.

"Best keep away, majesty," the steward said, making a hasty sign of the Circle. "That's evil, that is."

Kelchel put down the strongbox and drew his sword. He advanced on the scroll as though he meant to destroy it, but Pheresa darted ahead of him to grab it and stuff it in her pocket. Her fingers tingled and hurt from the brief contact, as though she'd touched prickly thorns.

"Come," she said.

"Majesty, ain't safe fer ye to keep that."

Well aware that she'd kept the scroll more from defiance than from any sense of true curiosity, she met Sir Kelchel's gaze steadily. "So I understand. Now let's seek out the smith."

The smithy was a circular building constructed around a forge. The roaring fire was fed by a sweating assistant manning the bellows. The smith, clad in a leather apron and an old tunic of linsey much spotted with cinder holes, tapped his hammer skillfully at the anvil as he formed a nail from a glowing red splinter of metal.

Hailed by Sir Kelchel, he gave a final rat-tat with his hammer before plunging the nail into a pail of water with a hiss. Tossing the nail onto a small pile, he put down his tools and wiped his large hands on his apron as he came over to the open window.

The protector told him what was wanted, and with a shy bob of his head to Pheresa, the smith fetched a chisel and his hammer. With one fierce stroke, he broke the lock, and Sir Kelchel opened the lid as though he feared a demon might leap out of the box.

The smith prodded a lump of gray stone with a grimy forefinger. "That's alchemy stone there," he announced.

Peering inside the box, Pheresa saw a strange collection of

objects. A purse of money containing foreign coins. A faded ink drawing of a girl's oval face and sad dark eyes. A woman's locket on a chain. Five little jars of liquid that sloshed when the steward shook them. He started to unstopper one, then flinched back with a curl of his nostrils and hastily replaced the jar.

Pheresa frowned in disappointment. "There is nothing here of use." Sighing, she lifted her gaze to the smith. "Have you any knowledge of—"

"Morde!" Sir Kelchel breathed out in an awed tone of voice that made her turn.

He was unrolling a piece of velvet between his hands, the shimmering cloth falling away to reveal a sheathed dagger. Even on this gray, snowy day, it shone and glittered. The sheath was made of hammered gold studded with an intricate pattern of large, faceted jewels. Admiringly, Sir Kelchel hefted it in his hand. " 'Tis a weapon fer a prince."

"Aye," the smith breathed, his own gaze avid.

As Pheresa admired its beauty, a wild, desperate hope began to dance inside her. Was it possible that this was the very weapon she sought? Hardly daring to believe it, she reached out and gently picked it up.

It was surprisingly heavy. She turned it this way and that before pulling the dagger from its sheath. The hilt was an intricate twist of writhing serpents, the pommel jewel an emerald cabochon as big as her thumb. The blade, slightly curved with a wicked, jagged point in no style favored in Mandria, was not steel but instead some golden-hued metal.

Excitedly she handed it to the smith. "Is this magicked metal?"

He looked instantly uneasy. Reluctantly turning it over and over in his large hands, he checked the balance and heft before wetting his finger and running it along the side of the blade. He lifted it and squinted down the edge, and finally he sniffed it from one end to another like a dog. He did everything but taste it, and she barely kept herself from urging him to hurry.

"Saelutian bronze," he said at last. "Very old, but still good. Not like steel, of course. Pretty, ain't it?"

Her hopes collapsed. She took the dagger, tempted to hurl it away into the snow. "Then it isn't magicked?"

"Nay, yer grace. Not so's I can tell. Not dwarf-forged, nor eldin made. There's where yer grace ought to look for spell-cast steel. In the mountains of Nold, deep in the Dark Forest, see? That's the best place to find it. Course there's no going there now with the deep cold on us."

Her disappointment hurt so much she wanted to weep. Instead, she quietly slid the foreign dagger into its magnificent sheath and handed it to Sir Kelchel. Her feet were numb from standing so long in the snow, and she was shivering under her cloak. Realizing her efforts today had been in vain, she suddenly felt very tired.

"Thank you, smith," she said, and trudged away.

The steward and her protector trailed after her. At the storehouse, she paused, but she felt so discouraged she did not have the heart to visit Sir Talmor.

"Forgive me, majesty," the steward said, "but what do you wish done with this box?"

She glanced at the strongbox under his arm. "Take it back where it was found, and lock up the turret."

With a bow he hurried off, his feet making tracks in the deepening snow. Although it was but midafternoon, lights were burning at some of the windows, and smoke from the cookfires curled dark on the dense, cold air.

"And this, yer grace?" Sir Kelchel asked, holding up the dagger. "Want it put back, as well?"

"Of course. It's King Faldain's property, I suppose."

Sir Kelchel started after the steward, but on impulse Pheresa called him back. "Wait. Perhaps the sight of it will cheer Talmor."

The protector frowned. "He don't need no weapon to hand."

"Say nothing against him!" she said sharply, taking the dagger from his hands. "He's not what you think."

"Yer majesty believes in him, an' that's a sign of a good heart in ye."

Pressing her lips together, she hurried down into the cellar so fast Sir Kelchel had to trot to catch up with her. But at Talmor's door, she bade the protector remain outside with the sentries. Kelchel frowned, but her gaze was so fierce he obeyed her.

The sick room smelled oppressive and foul, far worse than before. In fresh fear, she forced herself to smile and nod graciously in response to Pears's weary greeting.

"How does he?" she asked.

"Worse," the squire answered, exhaustion dragging through his voice. "The salt's kept him living, but I can't help but think it might be a mercy to let him go."

His voice cracked as he spoke, and he turned away, swallowing hard. She touched his shoulder a moment in silent comfort. "I won't stay long. Is he awake?"

"Aye, but not much in his right mind, bless 'im."

She steeled herself, then donned a cheerful expression and sat down at Talmor's bedside. "Hello, my friend," she said. "How fare you today?"

When he opened his eyes, such suffering lay revealed in their depths that it took all her resolve not to retreat.

After a few dreadful seconds he recognized her and dragged his lips into a brief smile. "Maj . . ."

Even the effort to speak clearly exhausted him. She put her fingers on his lips to silence him.

"Look at what I found today. Is it not pretty?"

As she spoke, she held up the dagger, making its jewels glitter and shine in the lamplight.

Pears hurried over. "Blessed mercy of Tomias! Is that—"

"No," she said with a swift headshake. "I'm sorry. I've failed."

Sorrow crumpled the squire's face. Turning away, he went over to the table, where he picked up a towel, then wadded it and threw it down. Lutel spoke to him timidly, and he swore in answer.

Tears pricked Pheresa's eyes, but she blinked them back.

She held the beautiful weapon before Talmor like a dazzling toy, then unsheathed it.

His face lit up, and he tried to reach for it. "Aldana!"

She did not understand what he said, and for a moment Sir Kelchel's warning filled her mind. But Talmor's smile made her stifle her qualms, and she put the dagger in his hand, curling his hot fingers around the hilt.

"Aldana's knife," he whispered, his golden eyes shining in wonder.

"The smith said it was Saelutian made," she remarked.

"Very old and . . . holy," he said. "Sanude had one."

At a loss, she glanced at Pears, who said, "Sanude was some old Saelutian tutor he had."

"I'm glad I found this. It pleases him," she said, watching Talmor shift the blade slightly to catch the light. He made it glow, doing that, and then with a blink she realized the blade was casting a light of its own, shining ever stronger until its radiance cast a nimbus about Talmor's bed.

Pears cried out, and Pheresa moved back with such haste she knocked over the stool.

"Merciful Thod!" she said, drawing a Circle. And then realization filled her. She leaned over Talmor in haste. "Is it magicked?" she demanded. "Has this knife special powers?"

His brows knotted together, and a dreadful expression crossed his face as he suddenly tried to plunge the dagger into his chest. Pheresa grabbed his wrist, and he was so weak she was able to take the weapon away from him.

He stared up at her piteously, the glow off the dagger shining across his tormented face. "Please . . ." he gasped, and fell unconscious.

Shaken by his plea, she backed away from him. The dagger's glow faded with distance. Frowning, she walked toward him, and the dagger shone brighter than ever.

"Put that pagan thing down, majesty, and come away," Pears said.

Feeling afraid, she laid the dagger on the table as he bade her. "The smith said it wasn't magicked."

"Well, if it ain't, I'd like to know what he thinks it is,"

Pears said scornfully. "Aldana's some kind of goddess in Sae-lutia. I don't know much about them pagan things, and Tal-mor's as much a member of the Circle as yer majesty. But maybe . . ."

His voice trailed off, and as Pheresa met his gaze, she knew they were thinking the same thing.

"We must try," she said. "There's nothing else."

He spun away from her, ordering Lutel to build up the fire in a hurry. While the boy set to work, Pears gingerly picked up the dagger with a cloth and squinted at it as though he feared it might cast some spell over him.

"Queer," he muttered. "Don't feel even a tingle in holding it. But look at it shine, like it's got a life of its own."

Pheresa frowned. She'd felt nothing when she'd held it either. Faldain and Gavril had both communed in some myste-rious way with their magicked weapons, but she apparently could not. A part of her felt humiliation; the rest of her re-joiced at the strength of her inner piety.

While Pears heated the dagger, Pheresa pulled back Tal-mor's blanket. Unwrapping his bandages stirred up the rot festering in his wound. She thought she would be sick from the stink of it, and wept as she exposed the horrible gash. It was not healing, and the venom in the wound was spreading red, swollen lines of infection across his chest. His flesh looked puffy and discolored, and a murky discharge was seep-ing through the stitches.

Pressing the back of her wrist against her mouth, Pheresa staggered away from him and opened the door. "Sir Kelchel, I need your help. You and these two guards."

They crowded in, then halted at the sight of Talmor lying exposed on his bed. One man swiftly drew the Circle, and the other cupped his hand over his mouth and nose.

"Is it over?" Sir Kelchel asked.

She shook her head. "I hope—I pray to Thod—that at last his salvation is at hand."

"It's ready, majesty," Pears called out.

"Hold him down," she commanded the men.

They stood as though rooted, while Pears held aloft the

heated knife. Its blade glowed brighter than ever, shining as brightly as lamplight, and the knights stared with mouths agape.

Sir Kelchel was the first to recover. Swiftly drawing a Circle, he blocked Pears's path. "What did ye to that?"

"Heated it, ye great lout," Pears said, trying to step past him. "Stand aside!"

But Sir Kelchel held his ground, and when Pears pushed him, the knight seized his wrist. The men struggled briefly, and Sir Kelchel twisted the dagger from Pears's grasp.

"Give it back, damn ye!" Pears yelled.

Holding him off, Sir Kelchel called, "Here, Alto, take it!" He tossed the dagger to one of the sentries, who caught it awkwardly in a fold of his cloak.

Furious, Pheresa headed for him. "Give that back, knave! How dare you interfere—"

But the man whirled around and ran. She started after him, but the remaining sentry swiftly blocked her path.

"Stand aside!" she ordered, but he did not move.

Wrathful disbelief swelled inside her. She wasted no more breath giving him commands he would not obey and instead rounded on Sir Kelchel. "You—"

"Majesty, forgive me. Whatever spell this Believer's minion is working, 'tis best ye come away now."

The man's ignorance was appalling, Pheresa thought. Even worse, it was probably going to cost Talmor his life. "You fool! Just when I have found the means of saving him, you dare stop me. You'll answer for this. I despise you! I dismiss you from my service!"

Although his face turned red, he spoke in a calm, measured voice, as though dealing with a fractious child, "Now, yer grace, come away from this den of evil. I'll see ye safe to yer chambers, and—"

"No!" she shouted. "I know what infamy is intended here, and I—"

"Yer grace, I am sworn to protect ye, and that I'll do, even if—"

A commotion sounded outside the door. Several knights, including Sir Thum, rushed into the sick room.

Sir Thum went straight to Pheresa. "Your majesty, how came you by that dagger?"

Contemptuously, she gestured at Sir Kelchel. "Let this craven fool tell you. He witnessed all."

Kelchel snapped to attention. "She found it in the old physician's turret, sir. In a strongbox that we had the smith break open. The smith did look the dagger over, and said 'twas no magic in it. Yet just now, when I came in, there that bewitched devil stood"—he pointed at Pears as he spoke—"holding up the dagger, and it glowing bright with whatever spell he cast on it. I tried to get the queen away, sir, but she won't come."

"Indeed I shan't," Pheresa said furiously.

Sir Thum frowned. "Your majesty—"

"You were a man of honor once," she said scornfully. "Now I have nothing to say to you."

Anger flashed in his eyes. "Majesty, I am trying to help you. What spell has been worked on the dagger to make it—"

"Nothing has been done to it save bring it here where Nonkind venom makes it shine. Does any magicked blade shine at all times?"

"No, of course not." Thum's brows lifted in dawning respect. "I beg your majesty's pardon. Sir Alto rushed in with such a babble of—"

She held out her hand. "Return the dagger to me, sir. I must use it to save my protector's life."

"I'm sorry, majesty."

All the blood seemed to drain from her, leaving her cold and light-headed. *Is there no end to the disobedience and obstructions in this Thodforsaken place,* she wondered wearily. "So you disobey me, too, Sir Thum. And I believed there was honor and justice to be found at Thirst. How wrong I was."

The men shifted their feet and muttered. Thum's gaze never faltered. "Your majesty has given us the means by which to try this man." Glancing at his knights, he gestured. "Take him forth swiftly. By the look of him, there's little time."

They surrounded Talmor, one man tossing a blanket across him. Pears rushed forward to intervene, but they shoved him back. Together they lifted Talmor, bed and all, and carried him out.

Pheresa watched them in horrified disbelief. "What are you doing?" she cried. "What mean you by this?"

"He's being taken to the Hall, where the magicked blade will be pressed to his wound," Sir Thum informed her. Outside, the faint sound of the hold's bell could be heard, already tolling a summons. "Before all assembled in witness, he will be tried by spell-fire. If he dies, he will do so as a condemned Believer. His soul will be damned, his remains cut apart, and his flesh salted without burial. But if he lives, he will then have the chance to give an accounting of his innocence before all."

Pheresa stared at him in disbelief. "You wait until now, at his final moments, to do what I asked of you from the first?"

"Until your majesty miraculously found this dagger, we had no means to obey."

Pears came up, his eyes wild with worry. "Majesty," he whispered, "if he should be too weak—"

"He's in Thod's hands now," Sir Thum broke in sternly. "If your majesty will accompany me to the Hall?"

Compressing her lips, she nodded.

Pears was wringing his hands. "Majesty, he won't intend any harm, but if he should—if he should lash out, like, will they—"

"I don't know," she said worriedly. She no longer knew what to think. This was what she'd been praying for, but now she feared what the result might be. And what if the dagger were somehow tainted and evil, as Tanengard had been evil? What harm might it do to Talmor? As for these powers he had, would he transform himself into some dreadful monster before their eyes and unleash destruction on everyone present? Pears seemed to think he might.

She looked at the squire, the worry in his eyes mirroring her own, and felt her courage falter.

"Thod have mercy on us all," she whispered, and allowed Thum to escort her outside.

Chapter Twenty-seven

The ordeal was over. The Hall had been tidied and fresh torches lit. A servant was raking up dirt, while others spread fresh rushes across the floor. The door stood open to allow fresh air to clear out the stench of corruption and burned flesh. In hushed voices, the knights talked in small groups. Cleaned of its grisly task, the Saelutian dagger glittered on a long trestle table next to a basin of salt.

And in the center of the room, Sir Talmor lay motionless, white-faced, but still alive.

Pheresa sat in a tall-backed chair, her hands white-knuckled where they clasped the carved arms. Her feet were propped up on a tiny footstool to keep them off the cold floor. Her ladies stood behind her, with Sir Kelchel close by. Her court physician, wearing long brown robes, eyed Talmor with fascination even as he offered Pheresa a restorative cordial in case she felt faint.

She feared she might collapse at any moment. Drained of emotion, she felt too spent by what she'd witnessed even to wave her physician away.

Talmor had survived the trial of spell-fire, as they called it. In front of the assembled knights, all standing armed as though they expected to do battle with a shapeshifter or worse, the flat of the glowing dagger blade had been pressed to Talmor's wound. There had not been, Pheresa discovered, any need to heat the blade. The magic within it provided fire enough.

Now, Pheresa gazed at Talmor's face. How drawn and gray it was. Even his lips looked bloodless. He lay as though already dead, his breathing so light it barely lifted his freshly bandaged chest.

The vigil had begun. Whether he would live or recover sufficiently to stand the second part of his trial was as yet unknown, but the purification ritual was finished.

Talmor's screams of mortal agony had been so horrific she felt as though she would hear them echoing forever in the depths of her soul.

The quiet now was a blessing. Pheresa shifted her gaze to her lap, where she held her jeweled Circle clutched tightly in her hands. She was still trembling. *My fault,* she thought in fresh guilt. *If I hadn't defied all orders and common sense and ridden out that day. If I hadn't ventured across the river into Nold. If only I had stayed where I belonged. If only I had never listened to Lervan and my council but had instead stayed at Savroix, none of this would have happened. I would have my son alive and Talmor whole. If only . . . if only . . .*

"Your majesty, come away," Lady Carolie said softly. "Whether he lives or dies, there is nothing now to be done. Your majesty needs to rest and sup. Come away now, please."

"I must know," Pheresa said.

The priest walked over to where Pears knelt beside Talmor's bed and touched his shoulder with compassion.

"Majesty, please."

Fighting a surge of exhaustion, Pheresa frowned. "I must stay here until I know," she said grimly.

"Word will be sent to your majesty of any change—"

"'Tis too cold here. He will perish of these drafts."

"They're bringing braziers to keep him warm," Lady Carolie said. "See, majesty? They're caring for him. You need not worry."

Servants filed in, carrying heavy iron braziers and hods filled with hot coals. While the fires were being prepared, Sir Bosquecel limped up, struggling awkwardly on his wooden crutch. He looked tired and in pain, for he had stood throughout the procedure.

"I owe your majesty an apology," the commander said with a bow. "It seems I may have misjudged your man, although what I saw him do troubles me. I do not understand it."

"Nor do any of us," she replied wearily. "But what he did was save your life, sir, and mine."

"Aye."

Relief sagged through her as she realized the general air of fear and condemnation against Talmor had faded. He might still be regarded as a creature of strange powers, but he was no longer considered a monster.

"Your majesty," her physician said officiously, "I really believe there will be no change in him for several hours. Please allow your ladies to persuade your majesty to retire. For the sake of your health—"

"Very well."

She rose to her feet and let herself be ushered upstairs to her chambers. There, in the snug privacy of well-heated rooms, she ate the food set before her and allowed herself to be bathed before the fire. Swathed in a warm bedgown, she lay down to sleep, while the countess and Lady Carolie curtsied good night to her, and Oola drew the bed hangings closed.

"Dear Thod," Pheresa prayed, "have mercy on us. Let us begin anew, with our hearts honest and clean before thee. Have pity, gracious Thod, and let thy hand rest on us with compassion."

She closed her eyes, but sleep did not come. The truth had to be faced. It had been looming at her now for quite some time, but she could deny it no longer.

She was in love with Talmor. She thought that perhaps she

always had been, from the day he rescued her from the Sebein and carried her indoors to safety.

From the hour he joined her service it had seemed natural that he should be with her almost every moment. The pleasant sense of ease and reliance that she felt in his presence had been with her from the start. He'd become a part of her, somehow woven into the fabric of her existence, and now she felt lost and unnatural without him. She needed him.

Sitting up, she stared wide-eyed into the night. *Needed him?* Aye, she thought, needed him as she needed her heart to beat or her lungs to draw breath. Needed him as a plant required the sunshine to live.

But was that love? Where was the giddiness and the urge to giggle? Where was the silly rush of infatuation so dizzy and fast that it left confusion in its wake?

She felt no such emotions, only a terrible, aching, empty sense of loss at the thought of losing him forever. If he died, she did not know how she would be able to continue. Today, she had felt his suffering so intensely it might have been her own. She had wept for him inside, her nails digging into her palms as she fought not to scream with him.

I love him, she thought. *I always have, and did not know it.*

But this should not be, she told herself with alarm. No lady of honor let herself fall in love with her protector. At least not respectably.

After all, he was a bastard son, born of a chevard and a foreign woman of mystery. This was no man worthy of a monarch's love.

But such snobbery shamed her. *I am not a queen tonight,* she thought. *I am a woman afraid for the man I love.*

A deep flush rose up her throat into her cheeks, and she gathered the bedclothes close, telling herself that she'd let the upsets of a very long and trying day confuse her. After all, what did she know about love except that it brought pain and unhappiness?

She had fallen for Faldain years ago, or had she? Was it love she had felt after the Battle of Grov, or an overwhelming sense of gratitude for his having saved her life? *Did I per-*

suade myself that I should love him, she wondered, feeling suddenly disconcerted. *Was I that young and foolish?*

Faldain had seen right through her, had seen the lie in her heart as clearly as though it were written in her face, but she had refused to believe him. What a fool she'd been for clinging to fantasies like a child.

As for Lervan . . . her emotions remained deeply tangled. She had married him, lived with him, borne his child. Such experiences had created some kind of connection between them. But love him? Nay, she never had. And she realized that in his case, as with Faldain and even Gavril, she had persuaded herself to feel the way she believed she should—dutiful, obligated, bound by ties ordained in the sight of Thod.

But it was not gratitude she felt toward Talmor, although Thod knew he had saved her life often enough. It was not duty or obligation she felt, but something stronger—a heated rush through her blood—something that made her heart suddenly race and her skin tingle. She rolled onto her side and hugged her pillow, wishing it was his body her arms encircled.

What would it be like to love a man like him, and know he loved her equally in return? What would it be like to come to him eagerly, from a sense of joy rather than duty? To be cherished in full measure, for herself rather than for her position?

Was it possible, despite all that had happened recently, to feel happiness and hope and delight again?

Faithful Talmor, she thought, so quiet and self-controlled, so dependable. Dear Talmor, with his handsome eyes that saw so much and judged so little. How she longed to feel his muscular embrace, how she wondered what the taste of his lips would be like.

Please live, she prayed, knowing she could not bear to lose him now. *Please, please live.*

Before dawn she awoke with a start and lay there listening, certain someone had called her name. All was still and peaceful inside her chamber. From their adjoining room, her attendants were not yet stirring. Yet she felt a sense of unease, a sense of something having changed.

Abruptly she sat up and scooted out of bed, throwing on a

heavy robe over her bedgown and thrusting her feet into slippers. Wrapped in her cloak, she slipped out of her chambers, with a sleepy-eyed Sir Kelchel—not yet forgiven but accepted back into her service—tagging at her heels.

It seemed a long way downstairs to the Hall, with a yawning page lighting the way before her with a candle, and the rooms and passageways dim, empty, and quiet.

Inside the Hall, gloom and shadows lay everywhere. Burned-out torches hung in their sconces. Icy drafts stirred the long tapestries, and the hearth lay cold. No fires burned in the braziers. The place was empty. Sir Talmor was gone.

Pheresa stared through the gloom like one demented. Grief clawed its way into her throat, and had she been a simple peasant woman without a lifetime's rigorous training in self-control, she would have wailed aloud. Instead, all she could do was stand frozen and horrified.

"Majesty," Sir Kelchel said quietly, "let me—"

"Is he dead?" she asked, her voice hoarse and strained. "Is he?"

"I know not. But it appears—"

"Find out. At once!"

He bent and spoke to the page, who went running out of the Hall. Shivering, she paced about, clasping and unclasping her cold hands together. She knew she should not have left him. What evil had been done in her absence?

The steward, one side of his face creased red from his pillow, his livery pulled on awry, his hair tousled, hurried in and bowed deeply to her. "He lives, your grace. He was taken to the infirmary, where he can be tended properly."

She closed her eyes against a sharp rush of feeling. "Take me there."

More gloom-shrouded passageways. More stairs. More icy drafts pouring in through arrow slits in ancient walls. She paid no notice to where she went or how she got there.

Eventually she was ushered through a rectangular room filled with cots, two of which held sleeping occupants, and into a tiny chamber closed off from the rest with a curtain of linsey. A small fire burned in a brazier to keep the air warm.

By the ruddy light of the fire, she saw Pears propped up awkwardly in one corner, swathed in a blanket, his age showing as he slept. The boy Lutel lay curled on the floor like an overgrown puppy.

And Talmor lay on a cot, propped carefully with pillows, his bandages clean and white. A bowl of fragrant liquid rested on the stool, with a cloth folded neatly over the edge. Setting the bowl aside, she sank onto the stool and dismissed Sir Kelchel with a wave.

In this rare moment of privacy, she smiled at Talmor as though she had never seen him before. His face was manly, with well-molded cheekbones and a straight nose. Asleep like this, he might be any Mandrian knight, wellborn of noble lineage. It was when he was awake, and his golden-hued eyes were alert with a directness and fire uncommon, that he seemed exotic and different from most men. His dark hair curled and waved across his brow, as unruly as ever, and in the strong line of his throat she could see his pulse throbbing steadily.

A tremor passed through her, and she longed to touch that place with her lips. Yet she dared not wake him.

He slept quietly, with no fever to toss his sleep. After a while she grew bold enough to grasp his slack hand, and his skin felt cool to the touch.

A slow sense of relief spread through her. Pressing her cheek against his knuckles, she let her tears fall freely. She had not lost him, she thought, giving thanks in her heart. He was going to live. He would recover, and they could forge a new life together.

"Pears says you heal quickly," she whispered to him, gently pushing his black curls away from his brow. "I am so glad of it, for you must get well as fast as you can. There is so much ahead of us." Her throat choked with fresh tears. "When you are awake I shall sit here and beg your forgiveness as I beg it now. Oh, Talmor, I have made so many mistakes. I have been blind to the things that truly matter. I refused to see the truth that lay before me all the time."

Behind her, Pears stopped snoring. She glanced over her

shoulder, but he shifted in his sleep and in a moment a low rumble issued from his lips once more.

"I am so sorry," she whispered to Talmor, who breathed quietly and steadily. She studied the rim of his dark lashes on his cheeks. "My folly has cost us both so much, but if we can start again, perhaps I'll be able to do better. I don't really know how to be a queen. I came to the throne with good intentions, but they mean little compared to what we actually do. I thought ruling was a matter of dignity, hard work, and taking up responsibilities, but it involves more than that, something I lack. Perhaps Lervan has it, and that is why the people have turned to him instead of me. I don't know. It hurts to be rejected by my nobles. It hurts to know I have lost my people's respect, if I ever had it. I think when I came here and everything was going so terribly wrong that I went a little mad. I was such a fool. I—I thought only of my misery and never considered the harm I would do, both to my sweet baby and to you, my dear friend. Please forgive me. I do not think I can ever forgive myself."

Emotions choked her throat, and she paused a moment, swallowing hard. "I remember what you said about the islands, how lovely and gentle they are, with soft days and fragrant nights. Let us go there, away from all that has gone so wrong for us. Let us go far away."

Talmor turned his head slightly on his pillow but did not awaken. She let her fingers slide across his, and sighed.

The confession did not relieve her troubled heart as she'd expected. Although she'd decided to run away to exile with him, saying it aloud gave her no comfort.

She watched him a moment, studying his face, then bent her head and gently kissed his hand. Rising, she turned around to find Pears standing behind her, watching her.

Their eyes met in silence. Embarrassment swept her like flames, and her chin lifted haughtily for a few seconds before she mastered herself.

"He loves ye," Pears said softly. "Know ye that?"

Her throat closed on a lump as she nodded. "We shall go to Saelutia."

Pears scowled. "Ah, not there, I beg of ye!"

"Why not?"

"Because it ain't no good for him there, bless 'im."

"'Twas his suggestion."

"Aye, I'm sure he offered it, but his father took him there when he was just a scrap of a boy, thinking to get rid of him and all the bother he was."

Her brows knotted in sympathy. "Was his childhood so very difficult?"

"Aye, 'twas rotten," Pears said frankly. "His half brothers hating and tormenting him night and day, and him with a temper that his father couldn't beat out of him. Well, he learned to control it finally, after he nearly burned one of his brothers to death, but he was provoked, majesty. He didn't do it out of meanness or by intention. Scared him so much he swore he'd never do it again."

"And his brother?"

"Got well and is married now, with a passel of children just like him."

"I do not understand this fire in Talmor," she said warily. "What power does he possess?"

Pears looked uneasy. "That's for him to tell yer majesty. But I'll swear to ye that he's never used it against a living soul except his brother, and only because he was provoked harsher than a boy can take. He's no monster, but he can't live in Sae-lutia, no matter what he said to ye. I seen that myself."

She felt her tender new dreams crumbling around her. "I don't understand."

"Well, there's odd ways in them islands. Things unseen that the natives understand and we don't. All I know is that from the day Talmor stepped ashore he heard voices in his head and all kinds of things that nearly drove him out of his wits, bless 'im. For three days we put up with it, him tortured and unable to sleep and crying his heart out that he couldn't stand no more of it. His pa meant to leave Talmor with them, but one of the elders said it were sinful to mix Mandrian blood with the holy blood of the goddess, and that Talmor was cursed."

"How?"

"He said Talmor had fire he couldn't master and was hearing voices of the gods that he'd never understand. He said that Talmor would go mad and die if he lived there. That he had to stay off the islands and far away from his mother's people."

"Did he ever meet her?"

"No. She'd been sacrificed to appease the goddess Aldana after she sinned."

Pheresa gasped. "That's horrible!"

"Aye, pagan ways get right bloody at times. At least the fellow was honest. Talmor's pa brought him home and even got a Saelutian tutor to make him learn how to handle them curses. But he can't go back to—"

"No," she said quickly, her cheeks very hot. At that moment she would have given her crown if Pears had never overheard what she'd said. "I—I wasn't serious about it. I was just saying things to cheer him."

"Yer majesty's right kind," Pears said with a fleeting smile. "But he's got some potion in him that's making him sleep heavy. It's been the first he's had to deaden the pain, bless 'im."

Astonishment mingled with fresh anger swept her. "And Mandrians call everyone else barbarians," she said with heat. "Such cruelty is inexcusable."

"But that's changed now, thanks to yer majesty not giving up on him."

"I owe him much more than that." Gazing down at Talmor, she began to cry. "His arm—"

"He'll never blame yer majesty," Pears said. "Ye needn't fear it."

"The fault was mine."

"Nay!" Pears said gruffly. "He won't see it that way, unless ye make him. Why every knight knows he could be crippled in battle. And a protector is prepared to take any risk for the one he serves. Talmor won't brood over it."

"But I must repay him. I must find a way to—"

"Don't be a fool!" Pears said sharply, then gulped as

though he realized what he'd said. "I—I beg yer pardon, majesty. I didn't ought to say that."

She said nothing.

"It's just that Talmor's a steady man with a good head on his shoulders. But if ye get to pitying him and weeping over him and saying how sorry ye are for ruining his life, why ye'll cripple him certain."

She fought back her tears, tormented by the temptation to ask this plain-spoken squire if there was any hope for her and Talmor now that he'd been so terribly injured. Would Talmor, with all his pride, believe her love was honest and not simply born of pity?

The silence between them stretched out uneasily. Clearing his throat, Pears brought forth her replenished salt purse and the dagger.

She took both in surprise. "How did you get this?" she asked, holding up the jeweled dagger. "I thought Sir Thum kept it."

"Ain't his to keep, is it?" Pears said, evading her question. "Ye found it. 'Tis yers now."

"Thank you."

"He'll mend quick," Pears said, nodding at his master. "As soon as he's able to ride, we'll go forth and trouble ye no more."

"How can you say that!" she cried, forgetting the need to be quiet. "Nay! I'll not turn him out like a dog to fend for himself."

"He can't serve as yer protector. Ye know that."

"There are other positions."

"He's proud-hearted. He won't accept pity."

"What, then, will he accept?"

"Why, a good pension and a word of kindness, thanking him for his service—"

"I'll do nothing so cold-hearted and cruel," she said angrily. "I'll not turn him away as though I do not care, as though I—"

Something made her glance over her shoulder. She saw Talmor awake and watching her. Everything inside her froze.

How much had he heard, she wondered. From the bleak look in his eyes, everything.

Her heart sank. Any ploy she might use now would be hopeless. Any assurance she gave him would not be believed.

She told herself that everything vital and important to their future depended on what she said next. He looked so fragile lying there, so hurt and weak, so close to the veil between worlds. If she erred now, he could yet slip away from her.

All her training in court life, training in masking her feelings and holding her regal composure, came to her aid now. In an instant she knew that if she gave way to her desire to rush to his side, weeping and casting assurances at him, all would be lost, just as Pears had warned her. Feeling a fresh surge of tenderness, she wanted more than anything to take his hand and share everything in her heart. That was the only way to make him understand, but his face was set hard with suspicion.

Seeing him look at her in that way, as though she'd become an enemy, cut her to the quick. Firming her lips, she ignored her tumultuous emotions and swept him with her most imperious look.

"I am told you heal quickly," she said briskly. "The queen is pleased to learn it."

He frowned, looking disconcerted, and she hurried on, not giving him a chance to speak.

"The queen depends on you, sir, to return to her service as soon as possible."

In an instant his suspicion formed anew. Bitterness worked his mouth. In a weak, thready voice, he whispered, "I regret I cannot serve your majesty again."

"That's right," Pears said with more boldness than was permissible. "I was just telling the queen that ye'll want to ride out as soon as—"

"Have done," she snapped at the squire, and, red-faced, he retreated.

She turned back to Talmor. "You will continue to serve," she said. "You will remain with me."

"Impossible."

"Why?" she demanded, although inside she quailed at her own deliberate cruelty. "You pledged your allegiance to me, sir. I do not release you from service."

Anger flashed in his eyes, but again Pears could not keep quiet. "Yer majesty is forgetting his arm."

Devastation flashed through Talmor's face. She watched him struggle through the realization, the memories of what had happened, the awful future that stretched before him. This man had prided himself, indeed had built his life, on his prowess as a warrior and man of arms. Now his foundation was swept away. She understood all that, and ached for him.

Yet she dared not show the pity he so obviously feared. *Stay strong,* she told herself desperately, forcing herself to say, "You have another arm, do you not? There are one-armed knights who serve in the army. You are not released from duty for an excuse as feeble as that."

"How . . . *kind*," Talmor said bitterly.

"Nay, sir. I am not kind at all. For all you've suffered and will continue to suffer, I—I am sorry." She swallowed hard but did not allow herself to falter again. "But we each carry our scars from this ordeal, sir. I cannot afford to lose even one man who supports me if I am to remain queen of this land."

The fierce anger in his eyes faded. He let his head sag on the pillow and sighed, as though very tired.

Watching him, she felt herself quaking inwardly at the barrier she was building between them with every word. This was not what she wanted. She yearned to take his hand in hers and admit her love, an emotion that was aching for release now inside her. She wanted to tell him everything, make him understand that she would run away with him anywhere if only they could be together. Her throne no longer mattered the way it once had. Oh, why must he look at her so bitterly, like a stranger, while his squire urged him to leave her?

Men and their confounded pride, she thought.

"I regret . . . I must insist on dismissal from . . . service," Talmor said tiredly.

"Refused."

"Majesty—"

"Refused!" she said.

Anger flashed in his face. "Your majesty is . . . desperate indeed."

"As soon as you quit this bed," she said ruthlessly, "you will train to use weapons with your left arm."

"I would be as useless as an untrained novice. Starting over . . . 'twould take years to—"

"You have until early spring."

His eyes narrowed at the challenge she flung him, but he said nothing.

"You are the best warrior in this realm," she said. "Even with your left arm, you should be able to prove yourself at least the equal of other knights."

"The queen has an exaggerated opinion of my abilities," he whispered. His face had lost its faint color, and looked gray and strained again.

She knew she had stayed too long, and this argument was doing him no good. But she intended to make her point. "You talk as though my cause is lost, sir. Well, I have not given up, nor will I permit you to."

"I think I have no choice but to retire from the action, majesty."

This new cynicism in his voice frightened her. He sounded so cold, so remote, as though everything but anger and bitterness had died in him. This Talmor was not the man she knew and loved. And she did not know how to reach him.

"You speak nonsense, sir, and when you are a little stronger you will feel differently."

"The queen refuses to face facts."

"Say nothing to me about what the queen does or does not do!" she said furiously, and both men looked sharply at her. "You heard me talking to your squire about the best way to cajole you, but the queen is tired of using feminine ways to achieve her ends. You have your orders. I expect you to obey them."

He scowled. "I'm half a man—"

"There's no gain in lying abed and feeling sorry for yourself," she said sharply. "I tried that, and"—her throat suddenly choked with tears as she thought of her baby—"it avails nothing save to beget more misery."

No sympathy softened his expression. "Your majesty's anxiety about her throne is—"

Pears hurried to him and bent low, murmuring rapidly in his ear. Talmor's frown deepened, then he shot her a look that held both startlement and compassion.

"Majesty," he said in an altered voice, and suddenly the man she knew was back, "I regret what I just said. I did not know about the child."

Pretending her eyes were not ablur with tears, or that her arms did not ache with emptiness, or that her thoughts did not turn to that tiny grave where it was so hard to believe that Thod's will was always for the good, she lifted her chin with a pretense of pride. "I need you, Talmor, whole or half. You must stay until my cause is won."

They stared at her, Pears and Talmor both, as though they could not believe their ears. Glaring at Pears, she longed to say, *What did you expect from me if I am not allowed to weep and be gentle with him?*

The compassion in Talmor's eyes faded, replaced by anger of a different kind.

In an instant she realized her mistake, but there was no undoing her rebuff of his apology. In her effort to hearten him, she realized she'd acted too arrogant and cruel. And now she'd made him hate her. Despairing, she did not know how to correct her blunder, and so she gave him a curt nod, her eyes awash with tears, and fled.

Chapter Twenty-eight

Reaching her rooms, she waited impatiently while Kelchel went in first to check that all was well. Her bedchamber lay in shadow, and when he would have lit a lamp, she bade him go. Her ladies still slumbered in the adjoining room, and she did not want to awaken them. Dealing so harshly with Talmor had swept her emotions in every direction, and all she wanted at this moment was solitude and privacy.

Stifling a yawn, Sir Kelchel departed for his small quarters just steps away. There were sentry knights posted outside her door as usual.

Sighing, she threw off her cloak. It would be dawn soon, and at this moment the night lay still and cold and somehow at its bleakest. She started for her bed, only to turn away for she knew she could not go back to sleep. Yet if she sat down and waited for day, she would only worry about Talmor. She might even weaken and go back to him.

Both her instincts and intelligence told her she must not do that. Talmor must be allowed to find his own way through what had happened, without her clinging pity. She dared not state her love for him until he was ready to hear it. All her life she had turned to any mentor or friend she could find to solve her problems for her. But now, because she loved this man, she found herself caring more about his welfare than her own. She understood that he needed time to heal. He could neither protect nor advise her right now. Already she regretted her urge to flee with him into exile. It had been an impulse born of sheer emotion and most ill-considered. Not because he could not abide in Saelutia. There were, naturally, other places of exile. But because she would know herself to be a coward, a failure, and an abdicator, and he would always fear that she'd gone with him because she could find no other alternative. How, she asked herself, could love exist on such a crumbling foundation? They would end up resenting and hating each other, and she did not want that.

She decided that the best way to distract and calm herself was to take action of some kind. She would issue an official warrant requesting the royal treasury safeguarded at Clemenx. If Lervan had not spent that as well as Savroix's treasury, she could use the gold to pay hire-lances. And she would pen orders to her father, directing him to bring her the Mandrian army under his command. Although the Duc du Lindier had always seemed extremely fond of Lervan, Pheresa told herself that a father's loyalty was surely stronger toward a daughter than toward a son-in-law.

With new purpose, she placed her salt purse and dagger on one side of the desk and fumbled in the gloom with a strike-box until she succeeded in lighting the lamp. Someone had filled it too full with oil, and the wick gave her trouble before it finally caught.

A warm yellow glow of light filled her room, driving back the oppressive shadows. Smoking a little, the lamp gave off a pungent oily scent. Here at Thirst, lamp oil was pressed from greasy colberries harvested in bogs. Poorly strained and stored in wooden barrels, it was much inferior to the fish oil imported into Savroix. If the light stealing under their door did not awaken her ladies, Pheresa told herself, the smell of the lamp oil probably would.

Determined to hurry about her tasks before she was interrupted, Pheresa pushed aside the basket of scrolls the priest had sent her earlier. She opened her writing box, took out sheets of parchment and her inkpot, and placed a length of sealing wax alongside the royal seal. With all arranged to her satisfaction, she was drawing up her chair when the sound of a soft plop from the direction of her bed made her turn around.

Something gray and slick, like a gigantic slug, rolled over on the floor and righted itself. Headless, monstrous, no longer than her forearm and twice as big around, it quivered and pulsated, one end of it lifting as though questing for prey before it began squirming right toward her.

Disbelieving, she stared at the soultaker in dawning horror. In an instant, her memories flashed back to that horrible day in Grov, when she had watched a monster similar to this one cut its way into Gavril, rendering him a soulless husk. And now, it was coming right at her, squirming and pulsating its way across the floor with more speed than she believed possible. She stood rooted, unable to move, trapped with a sick sense of fascination and fear.

The thoughts running through her mind were frantic. How came it to be here? How had it found its way past Thirst's walls? In Thod's mercy, how came it to be inside her bedchamber, hiding on her bed, lying in wait for her?

Her mouth opened, and she gasped for air, but could not scream. It was like being in a nightmare, yet she knew she was not dreaming. The presence of evil filled her room, so tangible it seemed to suffocate her. A part of her mind screamed at her to run, cry out for help, get away from it, yet she remained frozen, as though held by an invisible force.

Her heart was hammering wildly, and she feared she might swoon. Yet she knew that if she fainted, she was lost forever.

Not until the creature bumped against the toe of her slipper and began nudging obscenely along the hem of her gown did she succeed in breaking free of her trance. Screaming, she kicked it with all her might.

It went flying through the air and bounced off the wall, landing with a wet plop that released a noxious stench of rot and filth. Pheresa screamed again, and tried to run for the door. In her terror, she stumbled into the chair, knocking it over and nearly falling with it. By the time she righted herself, the soultaker was on her, climbing her skirts. Reeling back against the desk, she screamed again, and tried to beat off the creature.

"Sir Kelchel!" she shouted just as Lady Carolie flung open the door. "Sir Kelchel!"

The soultaker latched onto her fingers. She felt its slimy surface, the clammy, half-rotted texture of its hide. The evil of it seemed to flow straight into the marrow of her bones as it started up her arm. She shuddered in panic, knowing it would be at her throat in seconds. The countess was screaming. Lady Carolie had fainted on the floor. The sentries rushed into the room with drawn swords, only to stop in horror. Sir Kelchel arrived, his clothes awry, and halted with an oath. None of the men moved to help her.

Pheresa backed into the desk, beating at the creature on her, uttering little moaning screams with every breath, furious that no one came to her aid. Then from the corner of her eye, she glimpsed the salt purse lying on her desk.

By then the soultaker had nearly reached her shoulder. If she stopped beating at it, it would leap to her throat.

"Too late," she heard Sir Kelchel say. "It's got her."

Furious, she wrenched herself around and seized the purse. Her fingers fumbled desperately with the strings, but there was no time to get it open. The soultaker was sucking at her throat. Using the heavy purse like a leaded weight, she knocked the monster off. The soultaker landed on the desk, rolled, and sprang at her waist. This time she succeeded in yanking open the purse and with an oath dumped the entire contents on the monster.

A shrill cry rent the air, a cry no human throat could make. Writhing madly, the soultaker fell onto the floor. Its gray skin shriveled and puckered from contact with the salt. While it was convulsing and flopping about, Sir Kelchel stumbled forward.

But Pheresa was quicker. She grabbed her Saelutian dagger—now glowing with a golden light so intense it made her squint—and stabbed the creature again and again.

The last time she struck, yellow fire blazed through the monster, and it exploded in a cloud of ash.

Kelchel recoiled, shielding his face. "Blazing mercy of Thod!"

Coughing, Pheresa straightened upright and tried to convince herself it was over.

"Is yer grace hurt?" Kelchel asked.

Shuddering, she tossed the dagger on the desk and slapped the ashes of the destroyed monster from her wrist and hand. She was trembling all over, filled with disgust and horror and anger.

Stepping over the unconscious Lady Carolie, the countess hurried to Pheresa. "Your majesty," she cried. "What *was* that thing?"

"A soultaker," Pheresa said.

The countess uttered a little scream, but although she turned as white as her bedgown, she did not faint. "Quick," she said to the men. "Send for the physician. Send for the priest."

"I'm unharmed," Pheresa said. As she spoke, her gaze went to Sir Kelchel, her sworn protector. He had hesitated. Her safety was at stake, and he had hesitated. As had the sentries. Thinking that this was twice he'd failed her, she glared angrily at Sir Kelchel, who reddened and looked away. To the sentries, she said, "Tell me how Nonkind came to be lying in wait in my chamber."

Looking disconcerted, the men shook their heads.

"Find out," she snapped.

Saluting, one hurried off to sound the alarm, while the other searched the room systematically. By now Lady Carolie had revived, but as soon as she gained her feet, she climbed atop a chair, sobbing and calling on Tomias for mercy. The countess, still pale and shaken, her gray hair hanging down her back in a braid, remained close to Pheresa.

"Will your majesty not sit down?" she asked.

Pheresa shook her head. This was not yet over.

Kneeling, Sir Kelchel bowed his head. "Yer grace, forgive me. I could not strike it for fear of taking off yer head."

She thought fiercely, *Talmor would have pulled it away and then cut it to pieces.* She thought, *I saved myself. With three armed men in the room, I saved myself.* Beneath her anger, she felt a surge of new self-reliance and confidence.

"Majesty," Sir Kelchel said, pleading as she remained silent. "What else could I do? Forgive me, for having failed ye."

"We shall discuss this later. Help the man search."

His eyes clouded, and he rose to his feet like a whipped dog. "Aye."

"What may I do, your majesty?" the countess asked softly.

"I must bathe," Pheresa replied, shuddering. "And the room needs airing." Glancing down at herself, she saw specks of the creature's ashes scattered across her skirts. Fresh repugnance filled her. "This gown," she said in a choked voice. "Take it away and burn it."

The countess curtsied, then turned to Lady Carolie and clapped her hands sharply. "Climb down from there and stop your hysterics," she said. "Make yourself useful to her majesty and attend her, as is your duty."

"But the room!" Carolie answered fearfully, holding her skirts close. " 'Tis unsafe!"

"There's nothing here, m'lady," the sentry announced, his hair ruffled from his search beneath the bed.

Lady Carolie jumped off the chair and ran to order water heated. By now, the entire hold was in an uproar. Pheresa could hear shouts and slammed doors everywhere. Outside in the courtyard below her windows, the cadenced sound of marching feet told her the entire fighting force was being assembled.

Sir Thum arrived, clad only in tunic and leggings, his eyes wide with alarm. In his wake came Sir Bosquecel, limping on his crutch and looking like a thundercloud.

Kelchel went to the commander at once. "A soultaker was in her grace's room, sir. 'Tis my fault it got to her. I was tired and thinking only of the human kind of assassins. Never thought Nonkind could be lurking about. I've asked her grace's pardon, but she'd be right not to give it."

Sir Bosquecel growled something to the wretched protector, while Sir Thum studied Pheresa with a frown. "There's a mark on your majesty's throat."

Reaching up to touch the place, she could not conceal a shudder at how close she'd come to death. "It was hiding in my bed, lying in wait there." In the darkness, she thought, she had nearly lain down, unaware of its presence in the bed-clothes. It could have been at her throat in seconds, and she would have had no defense. She swallowed hard, well aware that even in a lighted room, with a weapon at hand, she'd barely survived. "I was going to write letters at my desk, and it came at me there instead." She touched her throat again, trying to push the memories away, and lifted her gaze to Thum's. "All these years, since Nether, I have carried salt everywhere with me. The courtiers at Savroix always teased me for it. Had I listened to them, had I ceased to carry it—"

The horror of the attack swept over her anew, and she suddenly had to sit down. They surrounded her in concern, asking questions like quacking ducks, until the commotion made her head pound. She was trembling all over now, unable to stop herself, and furious about it.

The physician arrived and, knowing others would require proof that she was untainted from this Nonkind attack, Pheresa submitted to the man's examination. The priest prayed over her, giving her unction. Had she been tainted, the holy oil would have burned her. Kneeling before him with a scroll of Writ in her hands, Pheresa waited until he finished his blessing before she rose to her feet.

"I want new quarters," she announced.

"Majesty, we have searched every inch of this—"

"It got in somehow. I cannot use these rooms with peace of mind." She glanced at the bed as she spoke, and shuddered. She could never sleep in it again.

With much bustle and commotion the move was achieved. Meanwhile, the entire hold was searched from cellar to turret roof and every servant was questioned. Sir Bosquecel gave the sentries on duty at Pheresa's door a blistering reprimand and ordered them locked up for further interrogation. In the afternoon he reported to Pheresa to apologize officially on Thirst's behalf for having failed to safeguard her.

At the end of the week, an assembly was mustered in the Hall. No other Nonkind had been discovered in the hold, but everyone remained uneasy. Lord Renald had ridden over from Lunt to inquire about the queen's health, and this small chink in the hostility of the upland chevards toward her was encouraging. Mindful of what Thum had said to her about insulting the chevards when she first came, she received Lord Renald graciously as though he had not previously joined with the others in defying her. But she was distracted this day, and gave him little time, for Talmor was to be tried.

The latest claim against Talmor was that as a Believer, he had summoned the soultaker into the hold and commanded it to attack the queen.

Such a preposterous accusation infuriated her. She argued hard in his defense, saying that Talmor had proven his innocence by surviving cauterization with a magicked blade. But Sir Thum pointed out that as long as Talmor eluded an accounting he would only continue to look guilty. Besides, no other explanation for the soultaker's presence in the hold could be found.

Pheresa's popularity among the Thirst knights had soared since the attack. Tales of her courage had circled the barracks. The fact that she'd fought off a soultaker, one of the most loathsome and dangerous of all Nonkind, and destroyed it without assistance had rendered her a heroine in the men's eyes. She was once again the Lady of the Chalice, and each time she appeared the knights and peasants cheered her lustily.

She wished her popularity was strong enough for her to establish Talmor's innocence on her word alone. She told herself that she must show complete confidence in his innocence. Accordingly, she was attired in her best gown and sat in a tall chair with carved arms, the Saelutian dagger lying in her lap beneath her hand. Her hair was dressed in the most elaborate court fashion, and she wore her diadem. Her ladies in waiting were also attired in their best, and the costly exquisiteness of formal court raiment provided a dazzling contrast to the plain, old-fashioned Hall and the knights garbed in serviceable hauberks. Beneath torchlight shining to dispel the gloom of yet another snowy day, Pheresa's jewels glittered and flashed fire at her slightest movement. She sat erect, stony-faced, and regal, and every person who entered the Hall was made forcibly aware of her majesty.

Watching the knights gawk at her, then hastily assume their places, Pheresa thought how easy it was to impress simple folk with a bit of panoply. Sir Kelchel, still on duty as her protector for the lack of anyone better, plus five other knights, stood behind her with grim alertness.

Lord Renald entered, clad in a red velvet tunic, his long hair brushing his fine shoulders. A look of appreciation showed on his face as he bowed deeply to her. She favored him with a regal gesture of acknowledgment and permitted him to sit next to her. On her other side stood another tall chair, its back embroidered with Thirst's coat of arms surmounted by a small crown. A bare sword lay across the seat in representation of Faldain's authority. Sir Thum took the chair next to it. And beside him, his leg propped up on a stool, sat Sir Bosquecel.

Off to the side stood the priest, holding a bowl of holy water and a Circle. Behind him waited a cluster of guards, alert in case anything should go wrong. An air of anticipation filled the Hall. The hubbub grew louder until the herald pounded on the floor with his staff and called out for order.

A hush fell across the crowd, and the doors opened to admit Talmor and his guards. He walked in unaided, and Pheresa's heart leapt at the sight of him. He was terribly thin, and the strain of his injury had worn his face, but he carried himself erect, walking with a trace of that old lithe stride. He wore a plain tunic of gray wool, a color that did not suit him at all, and his empty sleeve was tucked inside his belt.

Slowly but steadily, he advanced until he stood before her. His honey-colored gaze met hers, but slid away as though they were strangers. Although she wanted to cry out in dismay, she held herself silent, aware of the watching faces, and permitted no expression to cross her face either.

Talmor bowed, slightly and carefully. An involuntary pull of his mouth revealed that the movement gave him pain.

The herald stepped in front of him. "Sir Talmor of the queen's service," he cried in a voice loud enough to be heard to the back of the room, "you are brought forth to answer charges of sorcery, treason, and endangerment of the queen's life. Will you hear those charges and answer them truthfully?"

"I will."

"Will you swear your honesty on a scroll of holy Writ?"

"I will swear."

A page stepped forward, holding a wooden tray where lay a scroll. Pheresa's dagger began to glow faintly inside its sheath. With a start she recognized the scroll as the one she'd taken from Sulein's quarters. In all the confusion since, she'd forgotten about it, had forgotten her intention to see it returned to the turret as something better left alone. She glanced at Sir Thum, and saw both him and Sir Bosquecel watching Talmor intently. Realizing they had laid a trap for her man, she tightened her lips angrily.

There was no way to warn him. She braced herself for whatever might come, and vowed silently that whatever these tricksters of Thirst did today, she would somehow see real justice done.

With his left hand Talmor reached out to pick up the scroll. Pheresa could hardly bear to watch. She believed his powers would either allow him to handle it without harm, or else he would sense it was dangerous ahead of time. Either reaction would prove him to be a *sorcerel*.

"Take it and swear," the herald said sternly.

Talmor's hand closed around the scroll. Shock flashed in his face and with an oath, he flung the scroll at the hearth. It missed the fire and went rolling beneath the benches where some of the pages were seated. Jumping up, they went after it. Shaking his hand in obvious pain, Talmor glared angrily at Sir Thum.

Meanwhile, Lord Renald sprang to his feet with his hand on his sword. "So Writ proves you to be—"

"Hold yourself, my lord!" Pheresa commanded, raising her hand to stop him from cutting Talmor down. Her furious glare swept the others. "This is supposed to an accounting, sirs. Put an end to such trickery."

A cry of pain from one of the pages made her glance his way. Murmuring swept through the Hall, and Pheresa said, "Let no one save the priest pick up the scroll and bring it forth."

The priest, his tonsure freshly shaved, and his robes new for the occasion, looked startled. "Majesty," he said, looking disconcerted. "I—I fear I—"

"Do as the queen commands!" Lord Renald said sharply.

Putting down the ewer of holy water, the priest cautiously approached the scroll. Using a fold of his wide sleeve, he picked it up off the floor and brought it back.

"This is not Writ!" he announced. "Who has substituted this evil thing in the place of truth?"

"Who indeed?" Pheresa asked. She glared at Sir Thum as she spoke, but he seemed unmoved as he gestured to Talmor.

"Come forth, sir," Thum said, "and show us your hand."

Angrily Talmor obeyed him. His palm was red from where he'd touched the scroll.

Sir Thum nodded. "Let it be noted," he announced, "that this scroll is spell-locked and does no doubt contain evil writings."

The priest dropped it on the floor and stepped back hastily, making the sign of the Circle.

"It was taken from the old turret where Sulein, a known dabbler in the dark arts, did keep his possessions," Sir Thum went on.

"Sulein!" Sir Bosquecel said, coming suddenly to life. "That foreign dog was an evil man, a betrayer, and a charlatan. Thirst is well rid of him!"

Several knights drew the sign of the Circle. Pheresa wished now that she had never taken the scroll, but had she not gone to Sulein's quarters, she would not have found this magicked dagger that had saved Talmor's life, and her own. Her fingers tightened on it possessively before she suddenly remembered how Gavril had fallen under the spell of Tanengard until it drove him mad. She forced her hand off the dagger entirely.

"Aye," Thum agreed. "Thirst is well rid of Sulein, a bad man, who came to a bad end. As many of you know, King Faldain commanded Sulein's possessions to be left undisturbed, lest harm come to any servant attempting to destroy these artifacts. No, good priest, do not kick the scroll onto the fire. Leave it lie where it is for now."

Uneasily the priest retreated. Again, murmuring swept the Hall, and Talmor glanced briefly at Pheresa before he faced Sir Thum. "How many other tricks am I to endure?" he demanded.

Sir Thum sent him a cool look indeed. "Let us instead say that you have passed one test, proving to every man in this room that you are no caster of spells. If you were, the scroll would not have burned you."

Talmor frowned, and Pheresa sent Sir Thum a look of grudging respect.

Thum gestured at the priest, who brought forth a scroll of genuine Writ and handed it warily to Talmor.

Holding it in his hand, Talmor turned about to face the assembly. "I have agreed to answer the charges against me truthfully. This do I swear." He handed the Writ back to the priest.

Lord Renald resumed his seat beside Pheresa, but he was frowning. "Get on with it," he said to the herald. "I promised my family I'd be home in time for Selwinmas feast."

With a little bow, the herald cleared his throat and faced Talmor once more. "Hear the first charge! You are accused of casting fire."

"He's a fire-knight!" someone shouted from the back of the room. "I saw him feed that hurlhound with fire. Saw him as plain as plain! He's a Gantese devil, and he's got no right to live!"

Commotion broke out. The herald pounded his staff on the

floor, but no one heeded him. Talmor whirled around, his eyes darting as though he sought the one who'd spoken.

"Come forth!" he shouted, clenching his fist. "Say that to my face, sir, and I'll give you challenge for answer."

More shouting rose up. "Let 'em fight! Trial by combat!"

Fear swept Pheresa at what these crazy fools might do. As for Talmor, why could he not keep his temper? He was making things worse.

Unable to remain a bystander any longer, she rose to her feet. With flashing eyes, and a set face, she stared them down until a restless muttering quiet filled the Hall once more. "The queen has been told that Thirst is the most backward corner of the uplands," Pheresa said in a ringing voice. "The queen did not believe it until she came here and saw for herself what bigotry and idle superstition plagues the hearts of men otherwise valiant and true. For shame, men of Thirst. For shame!"

"He casts fire, majesty!" the man at the back of the room shouted. "He's a fire-knight, the worst kind!"

"The enchanters of Saelutia wield fire. So also do the *sorcerels* of Nether. In battle, they create huge pillars of flames to confound the enemy." Her gaze swept their angry, fearful faces, then settled on her physician. "You, learned sir, use fire to clean your instruments of surgery. Fire is a cleansing force as well as a destructive one."

"That foreign demon fed the hurlhound fire, yer grace!" shouted another knight. "I fought there that day for ye. I saw it!"

"And I saw it, too!" she retorted. "I saw a man who had never fought Nonkind before unleash a weapon wrongly and mistakenly."

Sir Thum rose to his feet and bowed. "Forgive my presumption, majesty, but perhaps 'twould be better to let the man answer for himself."

Anger scorched her, but she resumed her seat. Glancing at Talmor, she saw him looking at her quizzically, his dark head tilted to one side. She felt a wave of heat rise into her cheeks, and dropped her gaze from his like a shy maiden. Her heart suddenly pounded.

"Well, Sir Talmor?" Thum asked. "Witnesses, including the queen, have seen you wield fire. How do you answer this charge?"

" 'Tis true," Talmor said. "In an effort to save the queen's life, and that of Sir Bosquecel, I did unleash fire against the hurlhound to destroy it."

"But the monster was not destroyed."

Muscles bunched in Talmor's jaw. "No, it was not. The fire made it stronger. I had never seen a hurlhound before. I did not realize my mistake until it was too late."

"How come you to possess such magical powers? Are you Gantese?"

"No. My mother was a priestess of the Saelutian cult that worships Aldana, goddess of fire."

Fresh shouting broke out, but Talmor waited until it was quelled before he continued. "She rebelled against the rules of her order, fled to Mandria, and did bewitch my father for a time. When I was born, she acknowledged that she had sinned against her vows to Aldana. She left me in Mandria and went back to the islands, where she was punished by being sacrificed to the goddess."

"Then you acknowledge that you are a *sorcerel*."

"No. I am cursed with fire that brings harm to others. After many years and harsh training, I learned to control it."

The herald frowned, and Sir Thum leaned forward. "You control it by using it as a weapon?"

"No. I control it only by not using it. Otherwise, it brings disaster."

"Explain."

Talmor's frown deepened, and Pheresa held her breath in certainty that he would be too prideful to obey.

"Explain, Sir Talmor."

Thum's sharp tone seemed to get through to Talmor. "When I was a boy," he said slowly, his eyes clouded with memories, "I was hot-tempered and full of arrogance, as boys often are. One day in a quarrel with my older half brother I unleashed the fire. I nearly killed him, and my father banished me forever from his hold."

He paused a moment while the Hall remained silent. "On the day I hurt my brother, I vowed before Thod that I would never let the fire escape me willingly again. I kept that vow until the queen was attacked. Once again the fire caused only disaster. Believe me, sir knights, it is indeed a curse I would thankfully relinquish."

Pheresa stared at him while the quiet lengthened, and felt tears of pride sting her eyes. *Well said,* she longed to tell him.

Sir Thum nodded. "I have fought fire-knights," he announced. "As you all know, I was once their captive and lived for a time imprisoned in Gant. To become a fire-knight, a Believer must eat the fire of Ashnod. In doing so, through a series of horrible rituals, he becomes so burned and mutilated that he is too horrific-looking for mortal eyes to bear. Whatever Sir Talmor is, he is no fire-eater."

Noise swelled through the Hall, and beneath the din Talmor and Sir Thum exchanged a long, level look. Watching them, Pheresa realized anew how immensely clever Sir Thum was.

The herald rapped on the floor with his staff. "Hear the second charge! Did you, Sir Talmor, plot treason to abduct the queen, thus forcing her to abdicate her throne and permit the usurper Lervan to take her place?"

A furious roar filled the Hall, with everyone shouting at once. Pheresa found herself on her feet without realizing it. She glared at Thum, but he and Sir Bosquecel were scowling angrily, looking equally surprised.

Talmor was white around the lips with fury. "Who laid that charge?" he demanded. "Let the man come forth!"

For a moment no one responded, but then the priest defiantly shoved his way forward. "I did!" he cried shrilly. "On written orders of my bishop. I have them here."

Pulling out a document, he handed it to the herald, who in turn handed it to Sir Thum. While he read, Pheresa seethed. "Another plot of the church," she muttered angrily, and flung up her hand for quiet.

As the noise died down, she said, "My council persuaded me to leave Savroix while it was under attack. Sir Talmor protected me from the abduction of a church knight named Sir Brillon, who meant to see me imprisoned." She paused a moment to draw breath. "And I have *not* abdicated my throne!"

A new cheer went up. Sir Thum tore the letter in half and nodded to the herald.

"By testimony of her majesty, Queen of Mandria," the herald called out, "the accused stands cleared of the second charge. If any doth protest the clearance of this charge, let that man speak now or forever hold his tongue."

Quiet fell over the Hall, and after a moment the herald banged his staff once more. "Hear the third charge! The accused has endangered the life of the queen in her very quarters and—"

"How so?" Talmor asked hotly.

"Through sorcery—"

"I have answered that charge."

"Ye set a foul, filthy soultaker on her!" a voice cried out. "Ye dirty agent of Gant, ye were hired to do it!"

Talmor whirled around, reaching for the weapon at his belt that wasn't there. "A lie!" he shouted. Before anyone could stop him, he strode onto the dais and knelt at Pheresa's feet. Pale of face, his eyes narrowed and dangerous, he asked, "Is this fact? Was your majesty hurt?"

Before she could answer, the guards dragged him back. She saw him flinch in pain from their roughness.

"Stand there," Sir Thum ordered him sternly, "and answer as you are questioned. Can you command Nonkind?"

"No!"

"Can you shapeshift?"

"No!"

"Can you, with the force of your mind, compel others to do your bidding?"

Talmor glared at him. "If I could, I'd be a free man at this moment."

The sharp, hostile questions continued to fly at him. Glancing down, Pheresa noticed that her dagger was glowing even more brightly than before. With a frown, she pulled it partway from its sheath and its intense yellow radiance spilled forth. Something, she realized, was wrong. Everyone was staring at Thum and Talmor, everyone except one individual . . . who was staring at her.

The priest, his face knotted in a grimace of hatred. As her astonished gaze met his, he snarled a silent curse and rushed at her, pulling something from inside his sleeve as he did so.

Something black and slender came hurtling through the air right at her. Unfurling a set of leathery black wings, its scaled hide glistening in the torchlight, it screeched a hideous cry of danger that shot Pheresa to her feet. A putrid stench filled the air, and suddenly everything was confusion as it flew right at her face. Screaming, Pheresa ducked. Its talons raked the air, barely missing her. Dropping to her knees, she drew the dagger but had no chance to use it. Screeching, the thing wheeled about beneath the ceiling beams, then dived at her again.

Shouting a prayer, Lord Renald flung himself between the monster and Pheresa. He swung his sword, but too late. Nonkind talons sliced across his shoulder, sending him reeling away.

Then Talmor was there, running to put himself in danger. He had no weapon, nothing with which to fight.

"Talmor!" she cried out, and tossed him the golden dagger.

He caught it by the hilt, and as the creature flew at her yet again, Talmor plunged the dagger into its belly. The beast screamed, and black blood splattered across Talmor's face as it buffeted him with its wings. Then it exploded in a noxious cloud of ash and smoke, and Talmor sank to his knees with a little groan.

Everyone rushed forward, but it was Pheresa who reached him first. "Talmor—"

He was winded and spent, but he managed to point at the priest, who was now trying to slip away. The guards pounced on him, and after a brief scuffle, dragged the man out.

Sir Bosquecel steadied himself on his crutch, looking grim indeed. "I think we now know where the soultaker came from. With your permission, majesty, I'll question this assassin."

Pheresa nodded, and Sir Bosquecel limped out like a man set on vengeance. A yell from Lord Renald told her his wound was already being salted. She looked at Talmor, who still knelt, breathing hard. His face was scratched, and a trace of blood was seeping through his tunic at the right shoulder.

"Your hurts must be tended without delay," she said in concern, no longer caring who saw what she felt. "Dearest Talmor, once more you have come to my aid."

He grimaced as he tried to pull himself upright. Someone helped him to his feet, and he swayed a moment before he sent her a glimmer of a smile. "The habit of protecting your majesty is difficult to break."

"I think," Sir Thum said, "that this entire matter has been settled. Sir Talmor has proven himself on all counts to be innocent and honorable. Let no more be said against him."

A roar of acclamation went up, while Pheresa beckoned swiftly to the countess.

"There remains one final matter," Pheresa announced as the countess placed a document in her hand. "The queen owes Sir Talmor her life many times over. He has proven himself to be a superior protector, able and loyal beyond all thought of his own safety. Even today, once more, he has proven it before you all."

Clapping broke out, and she smiled at Talmor who was staring at her very seriously indeed. "In anticipation of today's accounting finding Sir Talmor innocent of all charges—and now, in gratitude for his actions just moments past—the queen hereby rewards this man by naming him Baron of Edriel, and granting to him those lands and their income, and such vassals and serfs as are bound to the estates, with full right of title for himself and his heirs to come."

Talmor looked stunned.

Laughing with satisfaction, she handed him the document of deed and investiture with her signature written boldly above the royal seal.

He held the parchment as though it might break in his hand. All the color had left his face, and he seemed stunned. "Majesty," he said at last. "I—I don't know what to say."

"No words are necessary," she told him.

"Edriel guards one of the richest trade routes along the

eastern border," Sir Thum said, looking impressed. "You are amply rewarded indeed, my lord."

Talmor stared at him as though dazed. "I always wanted something like this," he said quietly, returning his gaze to Pheresa. "'Twas always my plan, but I—I don't know how your majesty knew—"

"The reward is only a fraction of what you deserve," she said warmly, wishing they were alone now so that she could say all that she felt.

But he'd begun to frown. Almost angrily, he thrust the document back at her. "No, your majesty. I—I am overwhelmed by such generosity, but I cannot accept it."

Her own annoyance rose. "Why not?"

"Come, sir!" Thum said in amazement. "Your modesty does you credit, but do not overplay it. Only a fool would refuse such a grant."

"I have my reasons," Talmor said tightly, "and they are sound ones."

Pheresa saw the way he looked at the document, however. She knew his desire to accept the title was battling whatever troubled him. She knew also how stubborn he could be when he felt himself in the right.

She swept the others with a glance. "Withdraw from us, that we may speak privately."

Looking curious, they obeyed, and she and Talmor walked over to stand by the hearth. She spread out her hands to the warmth a moment before turning her gaze on him.

"Tell me the truth of this," she said, her voice low and furious. "Is our quarrel to stand forever? I would forget it. Why can't you?"

"There is no quarrel," he said. "Your majesty mistakes the matter."

"Then explain it at once! You concern me greatly, Talmor. I know not what to make of you."

He sighed, and she feared he would remain close-mouthed, but then, with a grimace, he said, "I have another power that was not discussed today."

Her eyes widened. "Go on."

"I have premonitions. Not often, but they come true."

"You mean you see the future?"

"Nothing as grand as that. But from time to time I know about a future event. Mostly it comes to me as a feeling, a sense of imminent danger perhaps, but sometimes I . . . dream."

She began to have an ominous feeling of her own. "And you have dreamed?"

"Aye."

"What about?"

He hesitated so long she thought he did not intend to answer, but at last he whispered, "Your death."

A chill ran up her spine. She stared at him hard, so many questions racing through her mind she could not decide which to ask first.

"It will be my fault," he said hoarsely, "and I—I cannot bear to think of it."

As her bewilderment faded, she felt a rush of compassion for his obvious distress. "How could it be your fault?" she asked, touching his arm. "Even today, you protected me. I know I was cruel at our last meeting when I said terrible things, but 'twas only to keep you from despair. I'm sorry I was so harsh. Since then I have longed to take back every unkind word—"

"Majesty, stop," he said, emotions swimming in his eyes. "I bear no grudge for what was said in my sick room. Were it not for you, I would be dead and my soul damned with me. You said what I needed to hear, and stopped me from pitying myself. Were the choice mine, I would never leave you."

"Talmor!"

"But I know that I will bring you harm someday. How or when, I do not understand. Rather than see you lie dead at my feet, I must quit your service now."

"No!"

"I must go from you," he said firmly. "Nor can I accept a reward when someday I might strike you down."

"You could not do it!" she cried.

"But I have foreseen—"

"No, Talmor! No matter what you think you know, only Thod is witness to our future. Take the title, for I bestow it on you whether you are willing or not. 'Tis done and signed. Besides," she said with a wry little laugh, "until I am crowned it isn't worth the parchment it's written on."

His lips curved in reply, and for a moment their gazes looked deep. Then someone in the Hall coughed, and with a start Pheresa recalled that while she and Talmor might be out of earshot, they were hardly alone.

"Enough," she said sternly. "You are a baron now, and I need you with me."

Whatever he might have replied was interrupted as he suddenly turned pale and swayed on his feet. Alarmed, she beckoned for assistance.

"We have taxed your strength too much this day," she said. "Withdraw, my lord, and let your injury be tended."

"Better see to that scratch," Sir Thum warned him. "Here, you men, help him."

"Majesty," Talmor said, his eyes filled with such a mixture of emotions she could not read them all, "I—"

"We will speak more of this later," she said softly, "but I warn you my mind will not be changed. Go and rest now."

As he walked out slowly with the support of two knights, Pheresa watched him with concern.

"What was all that about?" Sir Thum asked.

Believing enough of Talmor's secrets had been shared for one day, Pheresa shrugged. "These events have overwhelmed him. With a few days' rest, he will be more sensible."

Sir Thum frowned as though he intended to ask more questions, but at that moment a courier came striding in. His cloak was white with snow, and tiny icicles hung from his beard. Looking half-frozen, he peeled off his gloves and swept Pheresa a bow.

It had been many weeks since she'd received any dispatches. She stared at the man now in surprise, especially when he flung back his cloak and revealed the royal crest on his tunic.

"I bring a letter from the king," he announced, and handed it to her on bended knee.

A low muttering swelled through the men still standing in the Hall.

Shocked that Lervan now openly dared to call himself king, Pheresa stood rigid and stone-faced while the countess stepped forward to take the letter. She held it up, and at Pheresa's curt nod, broke the seal and unfolded it before she handed it to Pheresa.

Taking the letter without glancing at it, Pheresa said, "Someone give this courier warm drink and food."

The man was shown out swiftly. Sir Thum and Lord Renald, pale and hastily bandaged, stood beside each other, frankly watching as Pheresa turned her back to read the letter.

It was short and to the point, with none of Lervan's usual style of preamble. In fact it was no letter at all, but instead an announcement of his petition to the church to dissolve their marriage prior to his coronation. She read it three times before its meaning took hold in her mind.

Feeling as though she'd been stabbed with ice, she crumpled the letter, walked somehow to her chair, and sank down. Her ears were roaring, and the room seemed to have grown misty and distant.

After a few moments she grew conscious of buzzing voices and someone bending very close to her, asking over and over, "Majesty, are you ill? Majesty, can you hear me?"

With a slow blink she perceived that it was Sir Thum, his freckled face creased with concern. She shivered, then somehow marshaled her strength and looked up.

"What has happened, your grace?" Lord Renald asked her, looking equally concerned. "What can we do?"

In a toneless voice, she told them the news. Lord Renald's expression grew cautious, but Sir Thum swore openly.

"Legally, Duc Lervan has no right to pursue this action," he said to her. "Your majesty understands this, of course."

"He says that I deserted our union," she replied, feeling both shame and humiliation at having to air such matters publicly. "He says that I—I fatally endangered our child. These are his grounds for the suit of divorce."

She tried to go on, tried to remain calm and composed, but her mouth began to tremble. Never before had she hated Lervan so much. *He* had been the one who betrayed their union. He had dallied with numerous other women from the beginning of their marriage. He had usurped her rights of sovereignty, committing treason by naming himself ruler in her stead. And now, he punished her for losing the child. Nothing could have wounded her more cruelly.

"May I?" Sir Thum asked, and pulled the letter from her unresisting hand. He read it swiftly, then wadded it into a ball. "Morde! That cur!"

She forced her gaze up to his. "An unnecessary blow, is it not?" she asked with a smile as false as her husband's heart. "He has already won everything."

"Ten to one he's got another woman he wants to marry," Renald said, then turned red as Thum glared at him. "Uh, forgive me, your grace. I have no right to speak so bluntly."

"You do but say the truth," Pheresa said wearily. "Her name is Lady Hedrina. She has been his secret mistress for some time. No doubt he now flaunts her openly."

"A fine fellow who would be our king," Renald said in disgust. "I heard how he pays tribute to those Vvord dogs. 'Tis said he's too cowardly to fight them."

"A petition of divorce takes time," Sir Thum said thoughtfully.

She shrugged. "I doubt it. He is in league with Cardinal Theloi. I am sure his eminence will see the matter accomplished swiftly."

"It will still take time. They cannot break all the rules without exposing their hand too openly."

"The coronation will occur three months hence," she said bleakly. "Even if I contest the petition, it will avail little."

"What does your majesty intend to do?" Thum asked.

She met his hazel eyes with a look of implacable determination. Gone were her feelings of resignation, gone her intention to go quietly into exile. Lervan had insulted her in every way possible as a monarch; he had insulted her as a woman, and now he insulted her as a wife and mother.

"I shall face him," she said with a voice of steel. "I shall stand before him and force him to steal my crown before the people as witness."

Thum and Renald exchanged glances.

"Forgive me, your grace," Renald said in a kind voice, "but that's folly. If you go back, you play right into his hands. He'll have you arrested and silenced forever."

"Let him try!" But she was nodding as she spoke. "Aye, my lord, you are right in what you say. But if he arrests me, he'll have to do it before the people and on the very steps of the cathedral."

"You can't go south without an army. That's madness," Renald said. Then his gaze faltered from hers, and he turned a bit red. "The upland chevards have met again. We've decided not to proclaim ourselves Edonia but to remain a part of Mandria."

For a moment she knew a ray of hope, but as she gazed into Renald's eyes it died within her. "I see," she said coldly. "You will give Lervan your allegiance."

"We shall give the *sovereign* of Mandria our allegiance," Renald said firmly. "Whether, and until, the throne is won by either you or Duc Lervan, we'll take no sides."

She wondered why he thought this news would comfort her, but then rallied herself and gave him a nod. "Thank you, my lord. 'Tis a proper decision. The queen should never have demanded such infamy of you. You are right to avoid civil war."

"Your majesty—"

"The queen came to her upland lords angrily seeking revenge on the man who had wronged her. She did not consider the cost of such revenge, and she deserved the answer you gave her. She deserves it still."

Renald stared at her with both surprise and dawning respect.

"If your majesty has no army," Sir Thum interjected

calmly, but with a tiny nod of approval, "you cannot ride to Savroix. 'Tis a noble intention, but a futile gesture."

She frowned. "Savroix was given into my care by King Verence. I surrendered that responsibility temporarily to Lervan, and he has created disaster. Futile or not, I shall go back."

"But—"

"I have sent word to my father, asking him to give me the forces under his command."

"Lindier support you?" Renald burst out in disbelief. "He'll never—"

"I believe he will," Pheresa said firmly. "Give way, sirs. Lervan has flung a gauntlet down, and I mean to pick it up. There's no other course I can live with."

Chapter Twenty-nine

Lervan entered the palace chapel with his customary swagger, his cloak swinging from his shoulders, and flung up his hand to stop his retinue. "Leave me! The king's prayers are private ones."

Bowing, his courtiers and attendants backed out. Lervan listened to them gossiping in the passageway as the thick wooden door was closed. Leaving Sir Maltric to guard it, Lervan walked alone up the aisle, went past the altar, with its snowy cloth and burning votives, and ducked into the shadows beyond. A private door opened for him, and he found himself inside a small robing room, stuffy with the smells of incense and ecclesiastical wool.

Cardinal Theloi, as thin and cold-eyed as ever, rose to his feet. "I thank your majesty for agreeing to this meeting."

"Well, 'tis damned inconvenient," Lervan said, tugging off his gloves. "I'm in the midst of a thousand details—"

"Preparing for a coronation is no easy task, but surely the end result is sufficient reward?"

Lervan threw back his head and laughed. "Your eminence

grows more pompous every day. Come, excellency! Let's get to the matter at hand, for I've little time."

"It concerns the queen—"

"Damn the infernal queen!" Lervan said. "If that's all you want to talk about—"

"She is precisely what we must discuss," Theloi said sternly. His green eyes bored into Lervan. "She is en route—"

"So I have been informed. It matters not a jot. I've given orders for her arrest the moment she shows herself at the palace. Or in the town, for that matter."

"I do not believe that would be wise."

Lervan snorted. "She's a traitor!"

"She's the legal Heir to the Realm," Theloi insisted. "I have warned your majesty repeatedly that the greatest caution must be exercised in dealing with her."

"She's a traitor and an abdicator," Lervan insisted.

"Even accused of both crimes, she still has a legal claim to the throne. It is hers by right of—"

Lervan scowled. "Have your sympathies swung to her?"

"Not at all," Theloi replied smoothly. "But I am a pragmatist, your majesty. I do not expect problems to vanish simply because I want them to."

"Take care, excellency," Lervan said. "I did not come here to be criticized."

"Then know this: the petition of divorce is not yet finalized. Nor will it be before tomorrow."

Fury swept Lervan. He was exhausted, and of late more and more obstructions seemed to block his path. "You promised me that the church council would comply—"

"It takes seven months for a petition of divorce to work its way through channels. Both parties must perform certain acts of penance, and carry out—"

"I don't want a lecture about church policy!" Lervan shouted, turning away from the old man. "I am to be crowned tomorrow, and I don't want to ascend my throne shackled to Pheresa!"

"Are these *your* sentiments, sire? Or the Lady Hedrina's?"

Theloi spoke softly, but his barbed questions stung Lervan's conscience.

"You've disapproved of the divorce from the start," Lervan said. "Even though you know it's best if I am rid of Pheresa forever, you still cling to your religious prejudices."

"Royal marriages should not be dissolved," Theloi said firmly. "Your union with Queen Pheresa is your only legal validation for assuming the throne."

Lervan clamped his hand on the jeweled hilt of his dagger. "Never say that to me again!"

"I merely state the truth."

"Well, damn the truth! It's exactly this sort of nitpicking legal trickery that constantly undermines me, and I'm tired of it. Pheresa ran away, while I stayed behind to hold this kingdom together. I deserve the crown, and by Thod, I shall have it!"

"No one is saying you should not be crowned tomorrow. No one has worked harder than I, your majesty, to see that come to pass. I merely suggest that you abandon the petition of divorce. Welcome the queen's return. Treat her gently before the people."

"Bah!"

Theloi frowned. "Her popularity rises anew. Since your majesty levied these new taxes—"

"I'll hear nothing against the taxes," Lervan said sharply. "How else am I to pay for both the coronation *and* the rebuilding of the palace?"

"Were tribute not still being paid to the barbarians, the royal treasury would not be drained dry."

"How many times will that be thrown at me?" Lervan asked in exasperation. "The army failed to repudiate the Vvordsmen. I was against a campaign, but you, and my council, all insisted on it. And what happened? Disaster! Now we pay double tribute, thanks to you. Had the matter been handled *my* way, there would be no need for such heavy taxes. Your eminence wastes my time."

"I beg your majesty's pardon," Theloi said quietly. "I simply want to make it clear that your popularity has been dam-

aged by this unfortunate combination of events. The queen,
on the other hand, is the chosen Heir, and the people know she
is returning. If your majesty's rule is to be a long and successful one, I strongly advise you to make some sort of public reconciliation with her."

Of course she was popular, Lervan thought bitterly. She'd
remained conveniently absent while he was forced to do all
the hard work and make all the unpopular decisions, such as
the levying of harsh taxes. He intended to levy more before he
was through. As for Pheresa, he knew that if she returned, she
would undermine his authority and render him a powerless
figurehead. He clenched his teeth together, vowing that he
would never be a capering consort again.

"I know it is not what your majesty wants," Theloi was
saying, "but sometimes compromises are necessary for the
best interests of the realm."

"If she returned, bringing my heir," Lervan said with
forced calm, "I would follow your grace's suggestion. But her
part in the death of my son is unforgivable. I will never take
her back."

"Tomias teaches that forgiveness is the—"

"A pox on Tomias!" Lervan said, and his blasphemy made
even the cynical cardinal's eyes widen. "Pheresa will not dare
enter the city without her father's support, and Lindier will
not give her the army. I've seen to that. The people will neither see her nor know she's been arrested. Officially, I intend
to say that the queen is ill and has retired to the cloister."

Theloi's green eyes had gone frosty. "And if the people do
not believe what they are told?"

"They'd better." Adjusting the folds of his cloak across his
shoulders, Lervan flicked the cardinal a contemptuous glance.
"Thank you for your advice."

"I wish your majesty would follow it."

Glaring, Lervan strode out of the chapel without another
word. The cardinal's disapproval seemed to ride on his shoulders, but angrily he shook it off. He was king, and he would
make Lady Hedrina his queen, and that was all there was to it.
Already scout patrols were searching the roads, with orders to

seize Pheresa and her retinue. Come tomorrow, he would possess everything.

With a gasp, Talmor sat bolt upright, forcing himself awake. The night pressed dark and quiet around him, while the camp slept peacefully in the woods. Breathing hard, Talmor tried to shake off the terrible dream: Pheresa splattered with blood, lying crumpled at his feet, the stained weapon in his hand. With a grimace, he wiped the perspiration from his face. Thod's bones, he thought in despair, it was still going to happen.

He hadn't dreamed this for several weeks, not since the Nonkind venom was purged from him. Consequently, he'd convinced himself that it had been only a nightmare born of the fever, not a real premonition. Besides, she'd survived two, possibly three, assassination attempts at Thirst Hold during the winter, especially if he counted his suspicion that she'd been somehow enspelled or lured into riding into the Nold forest on that fateful day. He even suspected that there'd been an attempt to poison her, but a greedy page sneaking treats off the tray intended for the queen had fallen ill instead. And now that they were traveling southward, they had faced countless dangers, including muddy, almost impassable roads, a river too swollen and swift for barge travel, and throngs of people heading for Savroix to see the coronation, attracting bandits and cutthroats at every bend. All these dangers she had survived, and he'd let himself believe they might yet have a chance to prevail.

Tonight Pheresa's little party camped close to its destination, just under three leagues from Savroix. If they rode out at dawn, and evaded whatever traps surely lay ahead, they should reach the city just barely in time to stop Lervan.

And then I will kill her, Talmor thought.

Anguish choked him, and he flung aside his blanket to stride out of the camp. The sentry standing guard let him pass without question. Ducking beneath low-hanging branches, Talmor pushed his way through the brush and out to the edge of the woods in sight of the road. A fat, white moon blazed in the dark heavens. Insects were singing in the wet grass. It had rained in the night, and the air felt fresh and pure.

But he felt tainted and hot and desperate. What was this evil inside him that planned to do so horrible a deed? What lingering contamination from his Nonkind wound still festered in his heart?

For weeks now, his sleep had gone untroubled. Every day he'd driven his body to the limits of its strength and endurance, training himself to fight with his left arm, and every night he'd tumbled into his bunk to sleep the dreamless sleep of total exhaustion. Each dawn, when he awoke, he felt relief, but now he knew he'd been deluding himself.

The dream had returned tonight, on the eve of Pheresa's greatest challenge. Talmor told himself he would not harm her. No force, however dark and magical, could ever prevail on him to strike her down and yet . . . the dream remained as vivid in his mind as though it had been branded there.

It made him afraid, so afraid his entrails knotted, and he wanted to run far from here, as far as a man could travel, and go even farther beyond that.

A soft rustle through the grass startled him. Gripping his knife hilt, he turned swiftly to face the shadow approaching him from behind.

Despite the darkness, he recognized her. The tight line of his shoulders relaxed, but although he dropped his hand from his weapon, inside he felt tenser than ever.

"Is something wrong?" Pheresa asked, her voice a soft whisper.

He stiffened. *Yes!* he longed to shout. Instead, he backed himself against the trunk of a tree and tried desperately to remain calm.

She came closer. "Talmor, what is it? Do you hear something—bandits?"

"No."

She sighed, halting next to him beneath the tree canopy. He found the intimacy unbearable, for he both longed to put his arm around her and take possession of her lips even as his mind screamed at him to get as far away from her as possible.

"I could not sleep either," she said in her low, musical voice. He could listen to her speaking forever, and yet . . . and yet . . .

"I must leave you," he burst out, unable to contain himself. "Forgive me, but I—I cannot complete this."

"Talmor!" she said in surprise. "Not this again!"

He could not continue for fear he would blurt out the truth. Wildly he strode away, moving blindly, thinking only of getting free of her.

She followed, running out into the open next to the road. At once, he whirled around and grabbed her arm, pushing her back to safe cover.

"Are you witless?" he whispered furiously. "You will give away the whole camp if anyone is lurking nearby and sees you."

She wrenched free of his grip. "If I am witless, then you have run mad. What is wrong? Speak plainly, and no more evasion."

He groaned to himself and struggled to find a reply that would satisfy her. They had grown close during their time at Thirst, no longer queen and protector, but friends finding tentative, common ground. He had taught her how to fight, although many disapproved of the queen running about the practice field in leggings like a man, learning to wield both dagger and thinsword. She'd worked very hard to acquire competent skill, although not mastery, of these weapons. In private, they'd dropped all pretense of formality, and if at times their eyes met and held too long, or if he sometimes forgot what he was trying to say simply because he was thinking of how the sunlight spun gold in her hair, well, what of it? She'd given him wealth and a lordly title. She'd given him purpose again as her teacher. She'd kept him from wallowing in despair during the first bleak days following his injury, and he knew her heart was his for the taking. For a few weeks, they'd enjoyed a special time, where it was possible to forget what lay ahead. Every day, he'd yearned to declare his feelings openly, yet caution had stopped him. She was not yet free; once she returned to Savroix she might never be; and baron or not, his rank would never approximate her own. Oh, Thod help him, right now he longed to pull her into his embrace and kiss her until she was soft and pliant against him, until they were both lost in a kind of sweet madness, whispering soft words that meant nothing and everything to each other.

And if he gave way at last to his desires, if he took not only her friendship and trust but her love as well, what kind of monster was he? For come tomorrow, if he did not leave her, whatever mysterious force had plagued him since the hurlhound's attack would surely force his knife into her sweet body and rend the life from her.

He had warned her once, and she refused to listen. Now, he loved her ten times more, and his tongue felt frozen in his mouth. All he could utter was a mute sound of anguish.

"Talmor," she insisted, "you must talk to me. I cannot bear to see you suffer like this. Are you"—she paused—"afraid?"

"Aye." He hated admitting it. "I am."

"We've talked this over many times. I will not be dissuaded from confronting Lervan."

Talmor closed his eyes and said nothing.

She came even closer, a fragrant shadow standing beside him, her skirts brushing against his legs. "The dream you had, the warning you gave me long ago," she said quietly. "You still believe it will come to pass."

Despair swept him. "I know it will."

She was silent a moment, then she said, "According to the informants, Lervan has set many traps. He's certain to try to keep me from entering the city. We've discussed all that and laid our plans. I think Lady Carolie will be able to impersonate me splendidly."

"Do you think I can just stand by and watch you die on the cathedral steps?" he said savagely. "I cannot bear it. I—"

"Say no more," she pleaded, pressing her fingers to his lips. "You frighten me when you talk about it. You almost make me believe your vision will come true."

"It will!"

"You cannot be sure," she replied. "No one save Thod knows our future, and many things can happen."

"Don't you understand?" he cried. "I—"

"I understand that you love me, and I love you!" she said, clinging to him. "Do we abandon Mandria and run away together? If so, say it, and I will obey your desires. I would follow you to the ends of the known world."

For an instant he let himself believe it, but his common sense put a swift end to what she offered. "If I am to be the agent who destroys you," he said, his voice raw, "then where we go does not matter. When the time comes, I will still hurt you."

"You could never do it." Her voice was so tender it nearly unmanned him. "I trust you. Why can you not trust yourself?"

"The Nonkind poison must still be inside me," he whispered, confessing his worst fear. "I think it will force me to do this heinous crime."

"No!" she cried. "You are *not* poisoned. You do *not* belong to the darkness. Talmor, you've had countless opportunities to kill me, and you've taken none of them. The Saelutian dagger does not shine in your presence. You are not evil. I know this idea has taken possession of your senses, but put it aside and believe in yourself as I believe in you."

He wanted so desperately to accept what she said. In silence, he kissed her hand.

She stroked his cheek. "If I were not a queen," she whispered hesitantly, "would you let yourself . . . love me?"

Unable to endure more, he caught her close and kissed her long and hard, until both of them were panting for air and lost in a tangle of shared emotions. At last, he forced himself to stop. "I have wanted to do that since I first met you."

She sighed. "And I have been waiting for you to do that for months."

Happiness filled him, momentary, brilliant, bittersweet. He forced himself to say what he'd longed to tell her for years. "I love you with all my heart and soul, Pheresa. Queen or not, I adore you and reverence you. I always have and always will."

She sighed happily and rested her head on his chest. "Then I have more than any kingdom could give me."

He touched her silky hair gently, his hand trembling from the emotions inside him. "I cannot stay with you. Don't refuse my request. Please, for your own sake, let me go."

Her fingers clutched his tunic. "Talmor, oh, Talmor, will nothing I say persuade you?"

He held her tight, his heart thudding against hers. "We cannot build on false dreams, Pheresa. You know that."

"You say these things because of Lervan. Because a divorced woman cannot remarry."

He realized her feminine mind had leaped over all the difficulties to what she considered essential. A part of him delighted in how freely she offered her heart and future to him, yet the rest of him knew better. Whether she believed in his vision or not hardly mattered. He knew it would come to pass, and he knew also that he must find the strength to withstand her.

"We will find a way past Lervan," she whispered. "My dearest, I know we will."

Anger rekindled in Talmor, and for a moment he allowed himself to be distracted. "That knave has insulted and slandered you long enough. He deserves a sword in his—"

"And if I begged you to attack him, would you do it?" she asked. "Oh, do not answer that! There is no honor in such a question. I am so tired, Talmor. At times I feel certain that what I'm doing, however futile, is right, but then my courage fails me, and I'm afraid of what is to come."

He kissed her again, holding her close while she sighed and molded herself against him. Then, regretfully, he forced himself to let her go.

"I shall ask again," he said heavily. "Let me leave you."

"Never!"

"I remember when I lay on my sickbed and you browbeat me, claiming you needed every man you could coerce into supporting you. How fierce you were."

"I was cruel, hateful! I loathed every word I uttered."

"But you did exactly right," he assured her. "You kept me

from harming myself in my despair. Your sharp words hurt for a little while, but the good they did more than made up for the rest."

"Talmor—"

"Let me finish. For your sake, I must be harsh and unkind to you now. I must leave you here, not knowing whether you will reach Savroix safely. I must do what I think is right, in order to keep you from harm. Lervan may accept you back."

"That cur—"

"Or he may order your arrest. But you'll still be alive, and that's all that matters."

"Nothing matters without you!"

"You do not mean that. Sometimes duty must outweigh what we want."

As he spoke, he stepped away from her, but she clutched his sleeve desperately.

"No!" she cried. "No! 'Tis not the same. I'll not release you. I love you. I need you."

A terrible force rose inside him, and he pulled free of her grasp. "Then I must defy your majesty," he said.

He turned to walk away from her, but she caught him again and held on. Scowling into the darkness, he said, "You are just making this harder."

"I need you," she said, weeping. "I *need* you! If you go, you take my heart, and how then shall I live?"

"You cannot live if I am near you."

"Please! My courage is false without you. We all know I have no chance of prevailing against Lervan, that my final grand gesture is doomed, yet I must try. Oh, please, my friend, my love, *please* stay with me now. Without you at my side I lack the strength or the character to go through with what honor and conscience compel me to do."

"You are stronger than you know, Pheresa," he said gruffly.

"You know our plan, how desperate it is. Without you, I shall be alone. How can I get to the cathedral without your help? You know I cannot do it on my own."

"Please—"

Her fingers tightened on his wrist. "I must face Lervan. I must! And without you, I have no hope of it."

Her pleas, her tears were weakening him. Feeling a surge of resignation and futility, he kept his gaze turned from her, for he could refuse her nothing, not even this.

"You don't know what you ask of me," he whispered.

"I *do* know," she said fiercely. "I ask you to stay with me to the end. Once I am arrested, I shall never see you again. Is that not enough pain for us? Must you make it harder now? Oh, Talmor, please, I—"

"All right," he said softly, giving in. He kissed her, tasting the salty tears on her cheeks. "Don't cry now. I won't leave you."

She clutched him, sobbing against his chest, and he held her tight, with his chin resting on the top of her head. He could feel her relief, but he knew his terrible dream was going to come true, after all.

Great Thod, he prayed, *have mercy and let me stab myself, when the time comes, rather than her. Let me die in her stead, and give me unto the darkness that she may live.*

Chapter Thirty

The following day, disguised in a hauberk and leggings, her cloak hood pulled up to conceal her face, Pheresa tightened her reins to steady her prancing horse as she and Talmor jostled with the rest of the throng squeezing through the city gates. The harassed guards had long since given up trying to maintain a checkpoint and were simply letting the tide of people flow into the city. Military force—both the army and church knights—was in strong evidence along the crowded streets, obviously searching the faces of the crowd. The men looked alert and dangerous, and Pheresa rode past them with her heart thumping hard.

She sent up a quick prayer for the safety of Lady Carolie, the countess, and the rest of her faithful servants. This morning the little retinue had set forth along the muddy road in the wagons, with Lady Carolie dressed resplendently in one of Pheresa's queenly gowns, and Pheresa's banner flying. Whatever trap had been set on the main road would catch an impostor, not the true queen. Pheresa and Talmor had taken a different route, galloping cross-country through the broad river valley that widened into a delta surrounding Savroix-en-Charva.

Everywhere, she had seen the scars on her land left by the Vvordsmen raids. Burned out villages, abandoned farmsteads . . . and here in the city, so much was changed since the great fire of last autumn. So many buildings were gone. The streets looked wide and open. New construction had sprouted up everywhere, but it was all different.

A fanfare of trumpets in the distance made her look up sharply. She stared at the spires of the huge cathedral, rising tall above the other buildings. With its bells pealing out a triumphant cascade of sound, it at least seemed untouched by the swath of destruction that had ruined so much of the city.

For a moment she could not breathe. "We're too late," she said. "The procession has begun."

The crowd was streaming toward the cathedral, some people running, others calling out to friends. Everyone wore their finery, and children skipped here and there, playing with long streamers of festive ribbons tied to sticks.

In despair, she thought of the beautiful gown and jewels crammed inside her saddlebag. She had intended to be splendidly attired and beautiful, waiting on the steps when Lervan arrived. And now, after the long days of hard riding and danger, she was too late.

"The procession must be just entering the city," Talmor said. "There is still time."

She met his golden eyes and saw his pride in her, his love, and his worry. Her own courage surged back, and she gave him a fleeting smile. "Let's haste, then," she said, and spurred her horse forward.

They pressed through the crowd as fast as they could, and finally turned off the main avenue into a winding series of narrow streets that led them to the rear of the cathedral. She stared up at its massive walls, feeling uncertain and nervous, wondering if she could yet be in time.

"No time to dress now," she said with a moan.

"Thod's bones!" Talmor replied urgently. "Leave off your vanity and ride ahead of me."

She sighed. Being a man, he didn't understand that a woman's appearance was sometimes her greatest asset and most powerful weapon. Pheresa knew all too well the effect her beauty had on others and had intended to use it against Lervan today. He, of course, would be dressed in finery like a strutting cock, and now she must face him in this ugly man's garb, mud-splattered, and her hair wild about her face.

"Morde," she whispered, and reached into her saddlebag to pull out her diadem. She slid it on and swiftly readjusted the hood of her cloak.

Talmor was gesturing to her. "We'd better leave the horses and make our way on foot."

She dismounted at once, but untied the strings holding her saddlebags. They contained the royal seal and all her documents of authority. "Not without this."

He slung it across his shoulder, then set his hand grimly on his sword hilt. Gathering her muddy cloak close, Pheresa hurried beside him down a long narrow street. The cathedral wall loomed over them, reminding her of how foolhardy and ridiculous her plan was.

Honor requires it, she told herself firmly. Verence had entrusted her with the kingdom, and before she completely broke that trust by losing the realm to Lervan, she must go through with this final confrontation.

When they reached the square, it was already filled with people, all craning their necks to see the approaching procession. She could hear the drums and the trumpets. People were cheering, and the throng swayed and chattered with excitement.

Talmor elbowed a way through for her, and she hurried in his wake, feeling tense and suffocated beneath her hood. She was shaking with nerves, and she could not remember what she intended to say. A stalwart line of palace guards in bright green cloaks, standing shoulder to shoulder with pikes in their hands, brought them up short. Talmor tried to shove past them, but a snarling guardsman slammed him back into the crowd. He fell sprawling, and people laughed and jeered.

"This is as close as the likes of you get," someone said.

"What's the matter?" another shouted. "Lost yer fancy invitation?"

Ignoring the laughter, Talmor scrambled to his feet and glanced at her with a shake of his head. She frowned, staring at the sunlit steps. Dignitaries had already assembled there. She recognized most of them, and yet held here with the rabble she might as well be leagues away.

"We'll not get through now," Talmor whispered to her. A worried frown creased his brow. "I'm sorry. If we could have gotten here ahead of the guards—"

"No," she said, refusing what he was saying to her.

"It's no use. We'll try to get inside another way."

Angrily she stamped her foot. "No, I say! Once he enters the cathedral, 'twill be too late."

A mighty drumroll crashed and reverberated off the buildings. Talmor looked past her. "It's too late now."

Turning, she saw the front of the procession coming up the avenue already. Bold pennons waved in the breeze. The sunlight glittered off polished armor and silver-studded bridles.

Fierce determination welled up in her. She kicked the nearest guardsman in the back of his knee. As he staggered, she ducked under his arm and darted past the barricade, running into the sunshine and partway up the steps.

There was instant commotion. Two of the guards ran after her, while the rest struggled to re-form ranks and hold back the surging crowd. Talmor was left behind, and she glimpsed his frantic face just as one of the guards caught her roughly by the arm.

"Release me, varlet!" she shouted, and flung back her hood. "Who dares seize the queen without her permission?"

His eyes bulged in recognition, and his hand dropped from her arm. "Majesty!" he said in confusion. "I—"

More guards came running up, one of them wearing the insignia of an officer. "Get this knave back—"

As Pheresa turned to glare at him, the officer broke off his sentence. Tossing her head so that the sunlight glinted off her diadem, she swept back her cloak and stood there with her golden hair hanging over her shoulder in a long braid, and her hand resting lightly on the hilt of her thinsword.

Had she dropped from the sky, the men could not have looked more astonished. "Well, sirs," she said boldly, "will you say I have no right to be here?"

Shame filled some of their faces, but the officer scowled. "We have orders for your majesty's arrest."

She drew her thinsword partway. "Will you fight a woman on these hallowed steps?"

They looked disconcerted, and she seized the opportunity to hurry higher up the steps before the guardsmen blocked her path once more. She did not mind now, for she was high enough to be seen by the crowd.

It was murmuring, still thrusting itself against the barricade of guards. "Look!" one man shouted. "That's the queen herself!"

In moments, his shout was echoed across the square. "The queen! The queen is here!"

In the excitement, people streamed into the official procession and caused great confusion on all sides. While the guards dealt with the chaos, some of the dignitaries hastened down the steps to Pheresa, holding their long robes in their hands, their astonished faces red and distraught.

"Your majesty, please—"

Pheresa glared at them imperiously. "Bow when you address me! Are you all dogs, forgetful of your manners?"

As they obeyed, one pockmarked man wearing a chancellor's chain stepped forward. "Your majesty, please withdraw. This is a great day, a happy day. Do not ruin it for his—"

"Duc Lervan cannot be crowned without my presence and my authority," Pheresa said loudly for all to hear. "I am the chosen Heir. 'Tis *my* coronation day, not the consort's."

The officials exchanged looks of dismay. "But, your majesty," Lord Fillem said in a placating manner she found despicable, "this matter must be settled at another time and place. Not now."

"Why not?"

"Your majesty, have the grace, the ineffable courtesy to

step aside. I beg you. 'Tis most unseemly to quarrel here at Thod's house. Take yourself away before the king's wrath descends on you."

She did not budge. "I am told by these men that my arrest has been ordered. Well, then, am I to be clapped in irons and led away before the people? Or will you not allow me to stand and confront my husband, this man who would usurp my throne and my crown?"

Lord Fillem edged closer to her and bent down to her ear. "Your majesty, consider some modesty as befits a lady of noble birth. You have been divorced—"

She slapped him. "You lie! Lervan's petition has not been granted, and if you think to shame me, my lord, you are mistaken. Let Lervan remove his mistress from the royal bed before he casts slander at me! He seeks divorce only because his harlot wants to be queen in my stead. If you think I will retire meekly and modestly, you are a fool. 'Tis Lervan, coward and betrayer that he is, who should depart in shame."

Looking aghast, Lord Fillem gestured frantically in an effort to shush her, but Pheresa made sure she could be heard by all those close by. A roar went up from the crowd nearest the steps, and the chancellor glanced that way. The royal carriage had arrived.

Turning pale, the chancellor bowed to her. "Perhaps this matter is best left for you and the king to sort out," he murmured, and retreated.

She glared after the coward before she swept a look of defiance at the guardsmen. They, too, glanced at the carriage, then at a nod from the officer, moved aside.

Pheresa stood in the center of the steps, aware that every eye watched her, and held herself erect and proud while she waited for Lervan to come.

Lervan was waving to the crowd from his carriage, the breeze ruffling the magnificent plumes of his cap, the springtime sun beating a bit too warmly on his ermine-clad shoulders. Beneath his cloak, he wore a doublet fashioned from heavy cloth of gold, and over it a splendid chain studded with emeralds. A monstrous tailor's bill lay on his desk at the palace, but he was not thinking of his staggering debts now. Instead, he smiled at the cheering crowds and waved with satisfaction.

As his procession wound its way past the final turn of the street and entered the spacious cathedral square, however, some sort of commotion took place. His carriage lurched to a halt, and Lervan raised his brows as he saw some of the crowd streaming unchecked across the path of his pennon-bearers. Marechal du Lindier, riding horseback beside the carriage, stood in his stirrups and squinted ahead.

"What is it?" Lervan called out. "What lies ahead?"

The duc dropped back into his saddle. "Nothing, your majesty. The guards are dealing with it. The crowd is simply too excitable."

Drawing in a deep breath, Lervan sat back. Restless with anticipation and impatience, he drummed his fingers on his knee. "Tell the guards to hurry. I am not to be kept waiting," he ordered.

An equerry hastened away, while Lindier continued to stare ahead. Lervan saw Lindier suddenly turn pale; then the marechal frowned.

"Well?" Lervan demanded. "What do you see?"

"The queen awaits your majesty on the steps."

Lervan froze. For a moment he did not hear the trumpets, cheering, or shouts. Although he'd laid plans against her return, he'd convinced himself that she would go meekly into exile rather than risk coming back. And how in Thod's name had she managed to avoid every snare and assassin cast her way? Hedrina's friends had failed to get rid of Pheresa, and he vowed he'd see Hedrina on her knees, begging forgiveness for this. The very last thing he'd wanted was a public confrontation with his wife, yet here she was, obviously determined to make his coronation day a misery. Thod's mercy, he thought, why did women cause so many problems?

"Sire—"

Jerking from his thoughts, Lervan glared at Lindier. "What

are those fools doing? I gave orders for the guards to arrest her on sight!"

Lindier leaned down from his saddle. "Sire, that might excite the crowd too much," he said quietly. "Look yon. They are cheering her name."

Hearing the shouts, Lervan stood up in his carriage and glared at Pheresa. Clad in male garments, she waved regally to the crowd, and it cheered even louder.

Qualms swept Lervan, and he sank down like a stone. "Is she mad?" he asked. "How dare she appear like this, wearing such ridiculous garb? What's to be done?"

"Get her inside out of sight, then arrest her," Lindier said.

Lervan stared at him with a mingling of panic and anger. "But if we go inside together, it means I accept her as my— No! I won't do it. Have her cleared away now."

"Sire," Lindier said with a touch of impatience, "she has no army, no support save this cheering rabble. She cannot prevail against you. Remember that, and meet her with confidence."

Lervan grew calmer at his words. "You are right. Yes, of course."

His carriage rolled forward into the square, but it was hardly the flourishing arrival Lervan had intended to make. The trumpets that were supposed to sound a fanfare for him failed to blow. He could feel everything going wrong. But as he climbed down from the carriage a tremendous roar of acclaim rose from the crowd.

Lervan's courage returned immediately. The people loved him, he assured himself, and the coins that had been distributed in the town last night ensured the people's continued devotion. Pheresa was a fool who'd walked into his trap. Smiling, he waved to the crowd, and, with Sir Maltric at his heels, swaggered forward to meet her.

Pheresa had lost sight of Talmor in the crowd. Feeling very much alone, she stood waiting as Lervan came to her. He looked as handsome as ever, and his raiment was magnificent indeed. She noticed immediately that he wore none of the regalia stored in the treasury chamber and wondered with a prick of anger if King Mux of the barbarians now possessed those items. Replacing the coronation robes must have cost Lervan a fortune, paid for no doubt with the new taxes, and she despised him for his robbery, vanity, and weakness of character.

As their eyes met, revulsion filled his face. "Surely you are a bit—er—underdressed for the occasion, my dear," he said.

After all that had happened between them, was this all he could say? Enraged, she somehow kept her temper. "Well, your grace," she replied, using the title deliberately and seeing his face flush when she said it, "no doubt your attire cost enough to clothe us both." She glanced aside at those listening to their every word, and said even louder, "Or perhaps enough to have rebuilt part of the city."

Flushing, Lervan glared at her with such ire she expected him to order her arrest, but instead he visibly checked himself and turned to the crowd.

"My people!" he called out, "see this woman who should have been your queen! See how low she has fallen. She stands before you today, unrepentant. She refuses to display shame for her perfidy and cowardice. This adulteress, having corrupted her own protector, having fought my petition of divorce, which would have given her the chance to retire and live quietly while atoning for her sins, instead comes here today to cause what trouble she can."

Noise rose from the crowd, while Pheresa struggled to control her rage. *Say nothing too hasty,* she told herself. *Let him puff his slander before one and all. His actions have already condemned him.*

Lervan pointed at Lindier, who stood nearby. "See our brave marechal!" he shouted. "Father of this woman. Even he, despite a father's natural tenderness toward his own daughter, has turned from her. Can any of you doubt her guilt?"

Jeers and boos rose up, echoing raggedly across the square.

While Lervan spoke, Pheresa glared at her father, but he

refused to meet her gaze. Disappointment welled up in her throat, bringing with it the old hurt. He had never been fond of her until she became queen. And even then, he had proven himself a disloyal intriguer, with ambition and caprice his strongest qualities.

As for Lervan, she wondered how he could lie and charm his way through life so easily. Why did people believe what he said, when his actions spoke so plainly of selfishness and greed?

"Enough!" she cried out, interrupting what Lervan was saying now. "Put an end to your lies, Lervan, and let these people hear the truth for a change." Staring across the sea of faces, she stretched out her hands in appeal. "Have you forgotten the night Savroix-en-Charva burned? Have you forgotten that the palace was *saved* only because Lervan paid the barbarians to depart?"

Anger swelled through the crowd. A few men began to shake their fists, crying out.

She said even louder, "Do you not know that the royal treasury of both Savroix and Clemenx lies empty because so much tribute has been paid? Do you not care about the taxes that take food from your children's mouths, taxes spent not to rebuild this fair city, but to clothe Lervan in gold and hang jewels on his mistress?"

A shout rose up at her words, and she continued, "What glory does Mandria know now? We might as well be a conquered people, for Lervan has allowed the barbarians to put their feet on our necks."

More shouting made it impossible to be heard. Pheresa waited for the crowd to finally quiet down. When Lervan tried to speak, she swiftly pulled a document from her pocket and held it aloft.

"Here, good people, is my nuptial contract! Come and read its terms as decreed by King Verence, stipulating that Lervan was to be consort only—never king!"

"Silence! Silence!" Lervan said savagely, rounding on her. "You ran away. I had to save them. And I did!"

"You saved your own hide," she said in contempt, "but

what else have you done? Your greed has emptied Mandria's treasury. Your cowardice has brought Mandria shame. Your duplicity has divided Mandria back into two halves, weakening the entire realm and putting all of us at the mercy of our enemies. This is what you have done." She turned back to the crowd, and shouted, "Is this scheming coward the king you want?"

Yelling, the people surged against the guards trying to hold them. Everyone was shouting at once, and in the terrible racket and commotion Pheresa saw the line of guards break. People streamed through despite the knights on horseback struggling to head them off.

Sir Maltric reached for his weapon while a shaken Lervan retreated up the steps to stand beside Pheresa. She moved away from him, and glanced at the guardsmen on her other side. They were watching Lervan, too, and she saw their officer frown before he abruptly strode toward her. With qualms, Pheresa believed herself finished. Well, she thought, trying to keep her courage, she'd had her say. Let Lervan do as he pleased now. She'd denounced him publicly, and if the people still wanted him despite hearing the truth, then they deserved him.

"Your majesty," the officer said hoarsely.

Both she and Lervan turned to him.

"Arrest her now!" Lervan ordered.

Pheresa stiffened, bracing herself, but instead the officer knelt before her, as did the other men with him. "I give the queen my allegiance," the officer said, and his men repeated the oath.

Down in the square, the beleaguered guardsmen stopped fighting the crowd and let them draw near. Lord Nejel and other commanders of the guards came running up the steps to her. Ignoring Lervan's sputtering protests, they knelt at her feet, too. "Majesty, we serve you alone," Lord Nejel said.

Pheresa could hardly believe it. The palace guard was hers again.

"Thank you," she said in gladness. "The queen accepts your loyalty, knowing you all to be men both good and true."

The crowd began to jump up and down, cheering anew. Frowning, Lervan retreated up another step.

Meanwhile, Cardinal Theloi emerged from the cluster of dignitaries and bowed to her. "Your majesty, welcome back," he said. His voice was as cold and dry as ever, but his actions were clear for all to see. "On behalf of the church, may I say that Thod has blessed the queen in bringing her safely back to her people."

She stared at him, amazed by how quickly he had deserted Lervan after years of plotting on his behalf. Out in the square, the church knights drew their swords in salute. "The queen!" they shouted. "Long live the queen!"

Lervan glanced around him as support continued to shift to her. He was sweating and a tide of red color surged into his face. "Theloi!" he cried in outrage. The cardinal's cold green eyes met his without mercy.

"I am sure your grace welcomes the queen's return most of all," Theloi said.

Lervan's face drained of color. His mouth trembled a moment before he visibly pulled himself together. Turning to her, he even managed a semblance of a smile, and then as though magic had been done, his charm was back, his smile broadening, his eyes alight.

He reached for her hand, his fingers tugging at her ring of state before she freed herself from his grasp. "Ah, Pheresa," he said in a rallying tone that did not fool her for a moment. "My dear, of course you know we are all delighted to have you home once more. I have been preserving the throne for you. I saved your palace just as I promised. You may be unhappy with my methods, but Savroix still stands, as you will soon see."

"I am glad to hear it," she said.

He cocked his head to one side, and his mouth quirked in the little smile that had once charmed her. "Oh, you're angry with me. I can see that. Well, what if I lost my head for a while? I know I shouldn't have tried to be crowned without you, but it was all so tempting. I just could not bear to let the day of coronation go by without taking action. Mandria needs a crowned head of state, after all. I know I was wrong. Will you forgive me?"

She stared at him, saying nothing.

"I think, yes, I think we had better discuss everything," he said, glancing around for support. "Start anew, find the best solution. You are a lady both intelligent and reasonable. Will you not agree that I deserve some reward for my efforts to hold the realm together in your absence?" He smiled at her, so cocky, self-assured, and charming. "Come, my dear, let us make amends. We were meant to rule together, and that we shall."

She saw what he was up to, and a part of her had to admire his audacity. Like the others around her, he had seen an opportunity to patch up this business to his advantage, and he had seized it. She realized that if she refused him, she would appear churlish and vindictive. Although support had moved to her side, she was by no means certain that she really had it. Perhaps negotiation was the best course. She would have to learn to stifle her hatred and resentment in order to deal with Lervan, but the damage to the realm could be repaired.

But even as these thoughts ran through her mind, she found her gaze shifting past Lervan to where a tall, lean figure suddenly pushed his way free of the crowd and came up the steps toward her. The sight of Talmor, his bronzed face set and angry, his black curls atumble on his brow, filled her with a surge of love. How she adored this man, who was so noble and honorable, so courageous and truthful.

She knew then that she could never again be the weak, uncertain Pheresa of old. She could not negotiate with Lervan, could not come to terms with his treason, could not forget all he had done against her. If she gave way now, she would despise herself forever.

"Well, my dear?" Lervan asked, reaching out his hand in friendship. "Shall we go inside?"

Lifting her chin high, she stepped back from him with her eyes suddenly blazing. "No, Lervan," she said in a voice loud and firm. "You are a traitor. I trust you not, not will I bargain with you."

"But—"

"No! I go alone to be crowned," she said. Turning her back

on him, she gestured at the guards. "You men, see that the duc's way is barred."

Swiftly she headed for the door of the cathedral, going up the steps with her heart thudding at the sudden courage she'd found. She knew she'd done the right thing, even if her new supporters turned back to Lervan now.

"Pheresa!"

It was Talmor's voice that shouted the warning.

At the same time, she heard a faint sound right behind her. Whirling around, Pheresa saw Lervan rushing at her, drawn dagger in hand. Cursing her name, he lunged.

There was no time to panic, no time to do anything but react exactly as Talmor had taught her. The long afternoons of drills on Thirst's wintry practice field came to her aid now. She dodged Lervan's strike instinctively and reached for the Saelutian dagger on her belt. Caught off balance when he missed her, Lervan stumbled on the steps and could not recover in time. She plunged her dagger deep into his side.

They froze there, glaring into each other's eyes. Lervan's gaze burned with hatred mingled with astonishment. Then the color drained from his face, and he sagged against her. She saw him try to lift his weapon, but it dropped from his fingers. He fell onto her, dragging her down. Pinned by his weight on the steps, she struggled to shove him off.

Lervan's body was yanked away, and Maltric stood over her with an upraised sword. Crying out, he swung at her, but Talmor came at him from behind and plunged his blade into Sir Maltric's back. The old protector fell, and Talmor stood there, grim and furious, his bloody weapon in his hand.

Then knights and officials surrounded her.

"Pheresa!" Calling her name, heedless of protocol, Talmor pulled her up against him. She was shaken, winded, with Lervan's blood smeared across her hauberk. Wild-eyed, Talmor stared at her as though he saw a ghost.

She smiled at him, a little tremulously, and handed him her dagger to clean.

Like a man dazed by something he cannot believe, he took the weapon and wiped it on his leg. "It came true, almost exactly as I foresaw it," he murmured. "But I was wrong about everything." Sudden light filled his eyes, and he looked at her like a man reborn. "Wrong!"

She realized the premonition that had worried him so dreadfully had indeed come to pass, despite her refusal to believe in it. "You must learn to interpret your dreams better," she murmured, and forced herself to look down at Lervan.

His body lay sprawled at her feet, blood staining his gaudy robes.

The smell of blood reached her nostrils, and she suddenly felt sick. With her head spinning a little, she wanted to sit down. Never had she killed a man before, and she was stunned by her own capacity for violence. She had laughed and danced with Lervan. She had lain in his arms. She had borne his child and mourned it alone. Yet the deed was done, and although she longed to throw herself into Talmor's embrace and weep, she knew that if she fainted or showed any weakness now, she would lose the respect of the warriors around her.

With all her will and determination, she held herself together and turned her gaze firmly away from Lervan's corpse.

Silence lay around her. Defiantly, she faced her subjects, and as Talmor handed her cleaned dagger back to her, she slid it into its sheath with a set expression.

Her father was the only man who dared approach her. Angrily, he said, "I think the queen has gone mad. What has prevailed against her mind during her long absence from us? How dare she strike down our king—"

"Lervan was not your king!" Pheresa said harshly. "His attack on the queen's person was treason. You know it, as do all these men!"

Lindier glared back at her. "You have forgotten how to be a woman. You are barbaric—"

"I am queen!" she shouted. "And I have given him mercy by sparing him a public execution."

Her father lifted a fist and shook it at her. "You had no right—"

"Nay, I have every right to defend myself against those who turn against me." She stared into her father's angry eyes and knew that he would never change. And now, driven by anger or grief, he had gone too far.

"Including you," she continued more quietly. "You chose the wrong side in this contest. I am sorry."

He stared at her, a corrupt old man, and his defiance collapsed. He opened his mouth without a sound.

She glanced at the guardsmen standing alert nearby. "Arrest the marechal on charges of treason. He has plotted to rob me of my throne."

"No!" Lindier shouted, but the guardsmen surrounded him and swiftly led him away.

She watched through narrowed eyes, letting none of her emotions show. The dignitaries behind her were murmuring and exchanging glances. Lord Fillem began to edge away. She glimpsed his flight from the corner of her eye and knew that more arrests would follow. Lervan's supporters, she vowed, would be cleaned out with a ruthless hand.

"The queen!" a voice shouted, and around her the cheers went up, louder than ever. "The queen! The queen!"

She faced her people with her head held high, her visage stern and regal, and knew at last what it meant to rule. This, she thought, was Verence's legacy. The people's trust resided in her hands once more, and she knew that she would not fail them again.

She started up the steps toward the cathedral, where her crown and scepter awaited her. As she passed Talmor, she saw his face shining with pride, and her own heart lifted in answer.

He followed in his old place at her heels, but she paused and reached out to him with a smile.

"Nay, my lord," she said quietly. "Walk at my side from now on."

Silently, a little wide-eyed, he stepped up beside her. Pheresa let her gaze linger on his a moment. Whatever the future might hold for them, she told herself, and whether their love remained private or became public, they would face it united, with mutual honor and respect.

Together they walked into the church to see her crowned at last.